MIND

MEDICI PROTECTORATE BOOK TWO

CONTROL

PURITY. CLARITY. **BEGINNINGS.**

ALSO BY

STACI TROILO

THE **MEDICI PROTECTORATE** SERIES
BLEEDING HEART
MIND CONTROL
BODY ARMOR
TORTURED SOUL

THE **CATHEDRAL LAKE** TRILOGY
TYPE AND CROSS
OUT AND ABOUT
PRIDE AND FALL

MYSTERY, INK: MYSTERY HEIR
LOVE SET IN STONE
PASSWORD

MIND

MEDICI PROTECTORATE BOOK TWO

CONTROL

PURITY. CLARITY. **BEGINNINGS.**

STACI TROILO

L A G A N

OGHMA CREATIVE MEDIA

www.oghmacreative.com

Library of Congress Control Number: 2018944159

ISBN: 978-1-63373-331-2

Interior Design by Casey W. Cowan
Editing by Gordon Bonnet

Lagan Press
Oghma Creative Media
Bentonville, Arkansas
www.oghmacreative.com

ACKNOWLEDGEMENTS

TO THE FOLKS at Oghma Creative Media for bringing this book to fruition, especially Casey Cowan for the designs and Gordon Bonnet for the editing… a sincere thank you.

To my beta readers for helping me make this the best book it could be, you have my heartfelt appreciation.

To my grandparents, John and Mary Naccarato, without whom this novel—this series—would never have come to be. I'm so proud of our heritage and so proud to be part of your family.

To my parents, Robert and Carmella Smith. Your constant support and encouragement never cease to amaze me. Many thanks.

To my children, Seth and Samantha, for all you are and all you do. My life would be incomplete without you.

And, as always, to Corey, the love of my life. Your love and support mean more to me than you will ever know. Thank you.

To the world's best grandmother,
Mary Naccarato

For the lessons you taught through your words, but more importantly,
through your actions. And for your unwavering support and love.
Words can't express my gratitude.

In the twilight hours, starshine glows
as merely tiny embers in the black
Its magnificence to only grow brighter
while the midnight hour forces daylight back

And though the starlight twinkles on in ink
Its purpose not to shine but just to guide
The branches of the tree will bloom new buds
Growing evermore o'er the divide

As long as just one leaf in bud or bloom
On the boughs continues not to fade
Starlight will shine in watch over the branch
And guard the new green, always at its aid

The light divines the stones to always shield
And not until the end their duty yield.

1

VINNIE CLAIMED A corner table in the shadows and watched the gorgeous redhead toss back shots like she competed in a contest. He didn't see anything happy about the hour, and his workday was far from over. While the ginger with the pixie cut grew far too relaxed, his muscles tensed. His work got harder by the minute.

Because of *her*.

A waitress slinked up to his table. Even in the dim lighting he could see she wore way too much makeup, probably put on with the same paint sprayer she'd used to put on her jeans. Her tight, low-cut top left little to his imagination, but he wasn't in a creative mood. She smiled and leaned over to take his order.

"Club soda with lime."

She lingered, finding reasons to touch his hand and even his thigh before turning away. Then she dropped her pen and made a show of bending to retrieve it before finally leaving to place his order.

Vinnie shook his head and tried not to roll his eyes. Weariness settled on him from his day job. Well, both his day jobs, but he couldn't rest. He needed to stay on high alert. The redhead wasn't just fascinating—she was his job, and he'd be damned if he'd screw it up just to slake his thirst or ease his tension.

It had been days since he'd had a good night's sleep, and exhaustion threatened to overwhelm him. He thought about changing his order to something with caffeine, but he didn't want to wave at the waitress, much less talk to her. Even with his focus compromised, he couldn't miss the less-than-subtle invitation she kept throwing his way. The less he dealt with her, the better.

So he'd stick to club soda and fight the exhaustion on his own. Skip the booze and the flirting. His interests lay elsewhere.

Like on the now-drunk titian he'd followed in.

And would take home.

Soon, if he had anything to say about it.

There had been a steady stream of traffic since he had taken his seat. Some gathered around the bar or at tables, but most headed toward the dartboard or the poolroom in the back. He tracked all of them. Someone stopped at the jukebox, and soon "Ah! Leah!" blasted through the bar. The younger members of the crowd cheered and started singing along. They did love Donnie Iris around here. Western Pennsylvania was nothing if not loyal to their local sports teams and artists.

The older guys, likely fixtures who kept the bartender company most days, started grumbling about "that loud rock and roll garbage." Vinnie stifled a smile.

And then she spoke. A little too loud. A lot too slurred. "Just leave the bottle, Peppi."

"You only call me that when you're drunk."

"Not drunk. Leave. Bottle."

"I don't think so," the bartender said.

"Joe. Better? Now, bottle."

He patted her hand.

Vinnie could tell the guy was fond of her. He had a certain rapport with the regulars… some he told jokes to, some he traded insults with. But with her, he smiled. Spoke with patience. Used endearments.

Joe reached behind him. "I think you're done. Maybe some coffee, honey."

She pounded on the bar. "I'm done when I say I'm done. Either leave the bottle or keep on pouring."

Her voice carried, words garbled and run together like one long word. Vinnie would have had no trouble hearing her over the jukebox if he had been back in the poolroom, though understanding her may have been difficult. He made his way to the empty stool beside her and gestured to the waitress to serve him there—like she had missed him changing seats. Her pout and glare toward his new bar-mate would have made him laugh if he wasn't so preoccupied. And so damn tired.

Vinnie propped his elbow on the worn wooden bar and rested his boot on the brass foot rail. Then he turned to face the fiery drunk. "Trying to drown your sorrows?"

He thought she tried to glare at him, but it looked more like a squint. Hell, maybe she simply couldn't focus.

"Who said I had any sorrows? And who asked you, anyway? Don't you have a bar wench to flirt with? Leave me alone." She downed another shot.

Had to give her credit. She hadn't made eye contact with him when he entered the bar, nor had she turned around once since he'd been there. But drunk though she was, she still managed to know where he'd been sitting and who'd been propositioning him. He looked away from her and across the bar. She must have been watching him through the mirror, though for the life of him he didn't know when she would have found the time. Her head had been buried in one shot glass after another since he crossed the threshold.

Joe refilled her glass. Vinnie narrowed his eyes and the bartender hurried to the other side of the bar to wait on other patrons.

"Obviously you don't want my company tonight, but I'm not leaving you alone in your current condition."

"Damn right I don't want company. What gives you the right, coming into our lives?" She picked up her drink but continued to talk before downing the contents, gesturing widely with her arms. A few drops of whiskey sloshed over the side of the glass and onto the floor.

"Jo," Vinnie tried to grab the glass before she doused him in the amber liquid, but she lifted it out of his reach. The remaining whiskey landed in his lap. Seriously?

She kept flailing her arms, keeping the now empty-glass out of his reach. Her voice grew louder. "There you go again, telling me what to do, taking charge. 'Your father's death wasn't an accident, Jo,' and 'You're descended from the Medici, Jo,' and my favorite, 'The prophecy sent us to protect you, Jo, so you have to live with us.' I've had enough of your daggers and powers and plots. I want out of all of it. Leave me alone."

The jukebox was loud, but Vinnie worried her drunken ramblings were louder. Most of the people in the bar had stopped their own conversations and stared at the two of them. His fears were realized when the waitress came over.

"What's this about daggers and powers?"

"Do drunks ever make any sense, sweetheart?" He flashed her the smile he reserved for pub crawls and old ladies and forced his gaze to drift to her cleavage. He hoped she got flustered and bought his excuse, maybe moved on altogether. Jo's rant wasn't exactly believable under the best of circumstances.

The waitress blushed and leaned over, affording him a closer view he didn't want. Before he had to figure out how to dig his way out of that one, the bartender summoned her to the other end of the bar. She pouted but sashayed away using way too much wiggle in her steps.

But he had more pressing concerns. Averting his attention from the waitress to Jo, he panicked. She looked ready to launch into a tirade, and he feared she would reveal too much in her impending rant.

He gripped her thigh so hard she yelped, stopping her from saying whatever she'd been planning.

Instead, she yelled, "Hey! Let go of my leg!"

His jaw clenched, and he managed two words between clenched teeth. "Let's. Go."

"No." She whistled to get Joe's attention. "Come on, Pep." With clumsy fingers, she gestured for a refill, and he approached.

Vinnie covered her glass with his own fingers. "The lady's had enough."

The bartender looked from Vinnie to Jo and back. "I need to get something from the back." He threw his towel over his shoulder and hurried off, making sure to stash the bottle of whiskey out of her reach.

"Coward!" Jo called after him.

Vinnie took a hundred-dollar bill out of his wallet and held it up between two fingers so the waitress could see it. Jo leaned over the bar and yelled after Joe, who had retreated through a door marked "Private." Vinnie ignored her and spoke to his new biggest fan, who had hurried over when he held up the money. "Cash us out. Change is yours."

The smile returned to the waitress's face. "All of it? Thanks, sugar."

Vinnie stood and grabbed Jo's elbow. "Let's go."

She tried to shake his grip, but he had her firmly in hand and wouldn't let go.

"Get your meathook off me. I'm not done here yet."

"You're done. Bill's paid. No one here is going to serve you."

"You think Gi-you-sep-py's gonna send me out with a big lunk of a man like you if I don't wanna go?"

"You think he's going to let you stay? You're disrupting his customers." Vinnie dragged her toward the door.

"Dino, Paulie... you just gonna sit there?"

She aimed her question toward two of the regulars at the end of the bar. They didn't look comfortable with confrontation. Vinnie gave them a closer examination. Late fifties, maybe early sixties, both graying. One short and rotund, the other slight of build and average height. Difficult to tell anything more while they sat huddled together discussing Jo's—or their—predicament. Before they had to answer, Joe returned and saved them.

"I called your sisters. Franki said if the big guy was with you, I should send you home with him. So..." He looked at Vinnie. "You Vinnie Falco?"

"Yep." Vinnie showed him his ID.

"See our girl gets home safe."

"Yes, sir." He tightened his grip on Jo's arm and dragged the still-arguing woman out of the bar.

"YOU HAD NO right!" Jo stormed around the den in the brotherhood's compound. Well, she tried to storm around. The floor kept tilting and furniture kept moving, so she found herself bouncing onto couches and ottomans a lot. Finally she slumped onto the tipping floor and prayed the room would stop revolving. It was too difficult to focus on her sisters and their protectors when they kept spinning past her so fast. Or maybe it was she who spun. She felt like she was on a merry-go-round, an evil one that rocked side-to-side while she went up-and-down and all around.

"Vinnie," Franki said, "can you tell us what brought this on?"

"Yeah, V," Gianni said. "What happened today?"

Jo tried to focus on them, tried to listen to Vinnie's explanation, but couldn't. They were shadow people, fusing together into a fuzzy smear as her carousel spun out of control and into darkness.

When she woke, she knew five things, in no particular order and in various degrees of importance. One, she had somehow made it to bed. Two, it was not her own bed. Three, she was not in the clothes she had worn the day before. Four, she was profoundly embarrassed and angry, or would be if she could muster the energy for such emotions. And five, she had a hangover the size of an Irish distillery.

She groaned and tried to sit up, but the noise hurt her ears and the mere act of moving caused her pain. So she settled on reclining with her eyes closed and praying for relief.

The door opened with a soft click, and she recognized Vinnie by his woodsy scent. Her humiliation was complete. If she could just pretend to still be unconscious, maybe he'd leave her to die in peace.

When he perched on the bed and put a damp cloth on her head, she groaned at the soothing coolness. So much for pretending to be sleeping.

One of her father's saying popped into her throbbing head.

God answers all prayers. He just doesn't always give you the answer you want.

She tried to sit up again, but he pushed her back down.

"Easy there, Red. You had quite a night."

"What happened?" she managed to croak. Her throat felt like she'd choked down a roll of fiberglass insulation. Her tongue wasn't much better. She wanted a drink, but as soon as she thought the words, her stomach gave an uncomfortable roll and she thought better of it.

"I'll make you a deal. I'll tell you about how the night ended if you tell me why it began the way it did."

She fluttered her eyelids until her vision adjusted. It wasn't light in his room—his shades were drawn—but the sun filtered in around the edges and a lamp glowed softly on the nightstand. Despite the darkness, his mood was bright. He was too damn chipper for her state of mind. She wanted him out of her room. But he wasn't in her room, was he? It appeared from the black linens and the clothes strewn haphazardly, well, everywhere, that she had spent the night in his room.

"You know, Vincenzo," she said, her voice so quiet he had to lean in to hear her, "I've made all the compromises I care to make. Tell me, don't tell me—I don't really give a damn. But make no mistake. The next time I end up in a bed that isn't mine in clothes that aren't mine, the choice had better *be* mine, or I'm going to make sure I take possession of something else that isn't mine." She had met his gaze, but then purposefully let her stare trail down his torso and linger between his legs.

He cleared his throat and shifted his position on the bed so she had to look at some other part of his body.

"Your sisters are worried about you. The guys are worried." He cleared his throat again. "So am I. You're my responsibility."

How could she forget? Since her father's murder, the lives of the whole Notaro family had been turned upside down. "The Brothers" had infiltrated every aspect of their lives in order to keep them safe. She couldn't deny that her sister and mother had indeed been victims of a nefarious plot that saw them both kidnapped and injured. Her mother was still in a coma and safely hidden away, presumed dead by their enemies. Franki, her oldest sister, had survived her attack. And fallen in love with her personal bodyguard.

Unfortunately, Jo wasn't so lucky. She was currently arguing with hers.

"Yes, yes, I know. Brotherhood, prophecy, blah, blah. I still have work to do, Vinnie."

"I'm well aware. That's why, in addition to my responsibilities for MDH, I am watching you twenty-four-seven by working as a lackey on your precious construction site. Do you think I enjoy hauling shingle bundles up ladders and carrying drywall room to room?"

"It keeps you fit."

"I don't need the exercise, thanks. I get enough training here when I'm putting you through your paces and then working out with the guys. And I have enough on my plate without you going all Amy Winehouse after work. I was up with you most of the night. At the very least, I think I'm entitled to an explanation."

"You think you're entitled to an explanation?" She pushed off the pillows, forced her spine rigid, and threw the washcloth on the bed. "I wake up undressed in your bed and you want an explanation?"

"You aren't undressed, Jo. You're in one of my shirts."

She fingered the soft cotton of the too-big tee. It was comfortable against her skin. The last time she'd seen him in it was the day Gianni had hurt himself in the clearing. Jo suppressed a shudder and focused on their discussion. "And why is that? Exactly how did that happen?"

He raked his hand through already-disheveled hair. Tufts of sable settled back into disarray after his fingers' invasion, untouched waves licking at the collar of his own t-shirt. It had been too long since he'd had a trim, and the ends of his hair had begun to curl around his ears and at his neckline.

Despite her frustration, her fingers trembled, itching to reach out and smooth the tousled mess. Jo ran her hand through her own pixie cut. She probably looked frightening. It felt like her hair was doing its best impression of a porcupine. "I want answers. And a mirror."

He raised an eyebrow. "Since when are you vain?"

"Since when do you care what my morning routine is? Just get me a mirror and some clothes." When he didn't budge, she realized she would have to answer questions or parade across the room in front of him wearing nothing but his shirt. Weighing her options, she decided her emotional privacy was worth more than her physical privacy by about a hair's breadth, so she threw the covers back and swung her legs to the floor. When she leapt to her feet, she left her stomach behind. All she could do was clamp her hand to her mouth as her knees buckled and the floor rushed up to meet her head.

Thank God Vinnie was quicker.

He grabbed her under the arms with one hand and had a waste bin at her face with the other. As it turned out, it didn't matter. She retched violently, but only managed dry heaves. He leaned her against the bed so she could support her own weight, and while she gagged into the trashcan, he rubbed her back and put the washcloth on her neck again. It wasn't that cold anymore, but it helped soothe the sting of embarrassment that crept up on her as the sickness died down.

When she was done, he helped her back into his bed and fluffed the pillows behind her head. She refused to open her eyes, dreading what she would see in his—pity, anger, humor, condescension. His emotions didn't matter. Her humiliation trumped anything else, and she needed to regain some semblance of control.

"Please get me a mirror and a change of clothes," she whispered, keeping her eyes closed.

Her only answer was the soft click of the door closing behind him. Only then did she open her eyes. She was alone. Alone and mortified. Not only had he undressed her last night, apparently he'd stayed up with her while she did God knew what, and she had capped the whole miserable experience off by nearly vomiting in his lap. Her gaze went to the light scars on her arms. It seemed some mistakes couldn't be outgrown.

The quiet snick of the door opening made her jolt out of her memories and back into reality. Franki walked in carrying a large tray. On it sat dry toast, ginger ale, a change of clothes, a brush, and a hand mirror. "Special delivery."

"Hey." Jo scooted over so her sister would have room to sit on the edge of Vinnie's massive king-sized bed rather than walking around and crawling on top of the other side. "Thanks for bringing this stuff."

"Vinnie said you needed it. And he said you wouldn't want him bringing it back to you. What happened?"

Jo sighed and again ran her hand through her disastrous hair. "Oh, you know. The usual. I got drunk after making him miserable at work. I passed out in his den in front of my family and his. He apparently carried me to his bedroom and undressed me, then cared for me all night, only to have me wake up, yell at him, and then dry heave while he held me in his arms. I'm not sure if I should be ashamed or angry, but I'm certainly not feeling sociable at the moment."

Franki squeezed the bridge of her nose and got up to pace the floor. She turned to Jo, who nibbled at her toast. "I'm not sure what Vinnie told you, but he didn't undress you last night. The twins and I did."

Jo put her toast down and coughed on some crumbs. Franki whacked her on the back and handed her the glass of ginger ale. Jo downed a few gulps and caught her breath. Her eyes watered, and she swiped the tears off her cheeks. Then she set the tray aside. "What do you mean you and the girls did? I thought Vinnie did. Why am I in his room if he wasn't the one who changed my clothes?"

"It's kind of a complicated story."

"Simplify it."

"Well, after you passed out, we knew you were going to be in for an ugly night, so we didn't want to leave you alone. Gianni and I had planned on—"

"Spare me those details. Skip ahead."

Franki blushed and smiled, but continued on with her story. "Well, um, I was going to be busy, so the twins were going to stay with you. But Donni had an early meeting and Toni was going to be onsite all day, and we didn't think it was a good idea for them to be up all night when they had full and early days today. So Gianni and I said we'd cancel our anniversary plans."

"Anniversary? It hasn't been a year."

"No, but it's the three month anniversary of our first—"

"No." Jo held up her hand. "Keep it to yourself. I don't care. What happened next?"

"Vinnie didn't want us to cancel. Gianni's been in such a good place since we talked after... he got shot."

The night their mother had almost died. Jo wouldn't have been able to say it, either.

"But I know Vinnie worries about him. So he said he'd stay up with you. He just wanted to be in a room where he was most familiar with the environment, so he didn't have to turn on lights and wake you up while he was running back and forth to the bathroom when you were sick. Everyone agreed that was the best solution, so he carried you here. I was going to get your nightclothes, but he gave us an old shirt of his to dress you in. He said if it got ruined it didn't matter, so not to worry about it. And here you are. As to what happened overnight, I didn't ask. And you know what you did this morning, so... well, now you're caught up."

"Mmm hmm."

"How about a little quid pro quo?"

"What?"

"Catch me up. What brought on the booze-fest in the first place?"

Jo sniffed and stifled a gag. "Ugh. I smell like vomit. Do you think Vinnie will care if I take a shower?"

"Don't change the subject on me, little sister. I can still pull rank on you."

Jo shoved a whole piece of toast in her mouth. "Srry. Cnt tlk wf mm mw fl." Crumbs flew out of her mouth and down her throat again, making her cough through the wad of bread. She grabbed the clothes Franki brought her and scrambled to the other side of the bed, onto the floor, and toward the bathroom. It offered sanctuary. Running inside, she slammed the door behind her to drown out Franki's protests.

And immediately regretted making so much noise.

Once her head settled, she got to work. First she took a bunch of toilet paper off the roll and spat the toast in it, then tossed the bundled wad in the trash. A quick drink of water helped her recover from choking on the toast crumbs. It didn't do much for the taste in her mouth, but not having her toothbrush didn't deter her—her fingertip worked fine in a pinch. Then she gargled with mouthwash and felt marginally better when her mouth tingled with a fresh burst of mint, a far cry from the toast crumbs, ginger ale, vomit, and stale whiskey she had been tasting. After scrubbing the night off, she might feel ready to face the day.

She crossed the bathroom to the exquisite black marble shower and turned on all the jets. Franki continued to knock intermittently, but Jo kept ignoring her. She wasn't ready to face anyone, and there was no way she was skipping one of her favorite things to deal with something she wanted to avoid.

Jo grabbed a washcloth, stepped into Vinnie's shower and moaned. There were times, many times, she missed her own house, but when she showered was never one of them. The rainfall showerhead cascaded water down over her, and instead of the droplets pelting her and intensifying her headache, they massaged her scalp and relaxed her. Several body sprays set into the black marble tile inundated her body, the jets' liquid fingers kneading the tension out of her muscles, seeking the stress that went not just bone deep, but to her very soul, and relieving it. She sat on the tile bench in the gorgeous shower and allowed the water to soothe her.

Losing track of time was easy in such a luxurious haven. Jo didn't know how long she sat there, but the bathroom had filled with steam, and Franki had finally stopped knocking. It was probably time to stop basking in the water massage and actually wash off the embarrassment from the previous night.

Taking Vinnie's soap off the shelf, she lathered the washcloth and began rubbing slow and soft circles on her neck and shoulders. There was lingering soreness there that the pressure of the washing helped to erase, and the scent of pine from Vinnie's body wash invaded her senses, enveloping her in a surprising sense of safety.

She continued, gently cleansing her chest, her stomach, and her shoulders before she clutched the cloth tightly in her hand. Despite the froth of the lather and the cover of the steam, the whiteness of the scars on her arms seemed to stand out like beacons against her heat-reddened skin. Unbearable shame and rage consumed her, bringing all her expunged tension with it. Jo clenched her fist around the cloth and scrubbed at the scars, wailed at their refusal to wash away and at the physical pain she inflicted on herself.

The shower no longer held any appeal. She finished washing quickly and turned off the sprays.

Fluffy black bath towels sat on a nearby rack, and she snatched the top one off the pile. A quick buff and she was dry, then she tossed the towel toward the hamper. She grabbed another towel and wrapped herself in it, seeking warmth from the plush cotton, but not expecting to find any.

She wasn't disappointed.

Despite having taken a scalding shower, she was chilled. The bathroom was too steamy to use the mirror, and she didn't feel much like primping at the moment, so she pulled the towel more tightly around her, grabbed her things off the counter, and returned to Vinnie's bedroom.

As expected, Franki had gotten tired of pounding on the bathroom door. She had gone but had left the food tray behind. Not that Jo had any desire to eat or drink anything. Still queasy from the night before, even now-flat ginger ale wouldn't settle the churning she felt. Spinning head, salivating, roiling stomach… where had Vinnie left that trash can? Stumbling back into that steam was out of the question, and the toast was about to make a return appearance.

She made a valiant effort to hold down the toast, primarily because locating the trash can was going to require too much effort. Instead, she tossed the towel aside and climbed onto Vinnie's bed. Maybe it was the hangover, maybe it was the turmoil, but she felt nothing but relief as darkness claimed her again.

VINNIE SAT AT the kitchen table, his head supported by his work-raw hands. He had Jo to thank for that. She had him dragging boards all over the site yesterday after lunch, and the blisters he'd gotten carrying shingles that morning had burst open somewhere around who-gives-a-shit in the afternoon. Well, he supposed it wasn't all her fault. She'd told him to wear gloves. But who had the time to buy them?

He was up before her everyday dealing with the legal team at MDH headquarters in Italy. When she was ready to head to the site, he put in a full day of construction work with her crew so he could secretly act as her guardian. And once they returned to the compound, there was usually training or a debriefing to deal with.

Buy gloves. When the hell was he supposed to do that? He shook his head, and the slight friction of his stubble against his palms caused his blisters to burn. He hissed.

Gianni entered the kitchen and took a San Pellegrino out of the refrigerator. "What's wrong with you?" He popped the top of the can and downed the whole thing while Vinnie glared at him. Gianni tossed the can in the recycling bin. "What?"

"Why the hell are you so happy?"

Gianni grinned.

"Never mind."

"Come on, V. I've never known you to be so down. What gives?"

"I'm not down. I'm tired. Some of us work, oh, I don't know, all the fucking time."

"Chill. I just asked. If you need some time off, just say so. We'll move some things around, make it work."

Vinnie looked at him. He hated to show weakness, but he felt like he was going to fall on his face.

"Really, V. Just say so. Anytime. Well, almost anytime. Just not now."

Vinnie's balloon of hope deflated before it even took flight. "What now? The anniversary of the first time you had an anniversary?"

"Shut up. We aren't that bad."

"Yeah, you are."

Gianni flipped him off. It was a testament to Vinnie's exhaustion that he didn't even react. "Go clean up, V. We need to go into town."

"What the fuck for?"

"McGuire wants to see us."

Merda.

He hated Dave McGuire. The cop was in charge of the girls' father's murder investigation, and he'd taken an instant disliking to the men. He tried to link them to John's murder, but had been unable to do so, much to his disappointment. Because he couldn't arrest them, he harassed them on a regular basis.

"And again I ask, what the fuck for?"

"Didn't say. Just said he needed the four of us. And that we might want legal counsel."

Vinnie cursed. "He knows I'm our legal counsel."

"He just says that to piss you off."

"It worked."

"You going to be able to handle this?"

"McGuire?" Vinnie scoffed. "You seriously just ask me that?"

"You don't look like you're really bringing your A-game today."

"I don't need it with him. The guy's an asshat."

"An asshat with a badge who is itching to arrest us. He's not an idiot."

"There's nothing to arrest us for."

Gianni stared at him.

"I'm fine." He pushed away from the table. "I'm going to go shower. I'll meet you guys in the garage in twenty."

Vinnie stalked upstairs and opened his bedroom door. He didn't knock—why would a man knock on his own door? True, he'd left Jo in there earlier, but he'd already sent Franki in with the stuff she'd asked for, and Franki had come back down half an hour ago and hadn't mentioned any problems. Surely that meant his sanctuary had been returned to him.

Wrong.

Jo lay naked on his bed, luminous ivory skin juxtaposed against his black sheets. Dampened hair capped her head, a bonnet of cinnamon locks darkened by shower water, glistening in the glow of the lamplight. She whimpered. Restless, she reached for something, someone. He knew she sought comfort, but he stepped out of her reach. She wouldn't want it from him—from anyone—and he didn't have time to offer it.

He stepped to the foot of the bed, took hold of the covers, and pulled them over her, letting them fall softly over her sleeping form so as not to wake her. She snuggled down into the bed. Seemed to settle into a more restful sleep. Vinnie reached toward her and brushed a stray lock of hair from her face. She sighed and grabbed his hand.

Che cazzo?

The response he felt was primal, visceral—started low in his abdomen and surged through his body.

He'd felt nothing but concern for her when he'd seen her undressed, and she'd practically been on display like a diamond in a velvet box. So why did a mere touch of her hand create such a reaction? He shook his head, tried to clear it, and yanked his hand away from her.

After grabbing a change of clothes from his closet, he stormed out of his room, shutting Jo and his arousal behind him. A quick shower in the gym would wake him up and wash away any confusion.

Or so he told himself.

2

VINNIE LED HIS brothers into the police station. They'd spent so much time there in the past few months, it felt as familiar to him as a friend's home. It just wasn't as welcoming.

Industrial desks lined the left and right walls, covered with the usual detritus of active police work—folders, notes, computers, phones, pens, and papers. A door to the chief's office on the right wall and a door to an interrogation room on the left wall created an imaginary barrier between those desks and the lone desk in the back which had become a depository for coffee, pastries, and casework overspill. Behind it was the ongoing cases board. The last time Vinnie had seen it, the Notaro murder was the only case on it, and the only active leads were the four of them. Since then, the disappearance of John's wife, Mary, had been added to it, along with two other unrelated cases being handled by different officers.

Vinnie's favorite officer, Horace Daugherty, stood at what seemed to be his favorite place—the pastry table. Easily three hundred pounds, mostly height and gut, Horace was a wealth of information. When they could get him alone. He had slipped them information twice over the last few months that eventually led them to save Franki's life. Vinnie didn't think they'd be that lucky this time. McGuire was already waiting for them in the doorway of the interrogation room. Horace waved to them with a cup of coffee, chocolate glaze staining his full white mustache that lifted in a grin as they walked by. Vinnie nodded his greeting and crossed the threshold into the interrogation room, pausing briefly when he passed the surly cop to look down at him.

McGuire cut an imposing figure in uniform—around six foot or more, athletic build, dark coloring. Probably intimidated a lot of people in that doorway. But Vinnie was taller, bigger, darker. And he usually did the intimidating. McGuire didn't flinch as Vinnie loomed over him, but he didn't smirk, either, so Vinnie took it as a win and entered the room, followed by Gianni, Nico, and Coz.

McGuire shut the door. "Sit down, gentlemen."

They all remained standing. Vinnie didn't trust his polite demeanor. The guy hadn't said a cordial word to them since they'd first met. Not really even then. His civility only made Vinnie more suspicious of him. He crossed his arms and waited for McGuire to continue.

"Very well. Stand if you'd like. You could be here for a while. I've got some questions about the night Mary Notaro disappeared."

"We've already answered all of your questions," Vinnie said.

"No. You came in and filed a missing persons report."

"Actually, her daughters did that."

"And you, as their legal counsel, were with them, Mr. Falco. Since then we've conducted an investigation, and that's led to more questions. Like, for starters, why would they need legal counsel to file a missing persons report?"

Gianni took a seat, and Nico and Coz followed suit. Only Vinnie remained on his feet. If he sat, he ran the risk of exhaustion catching up to him, and he figured he needed to hear McGuire out.

"Now, I want to cross all my T's and dot all my I's on this one. If John's murder is tied to her abduction, I'm going to find out. So we'll start at the beginning, even if it takes all day."

"Abduction?" Vinnie asked. "Who said Mary was abducted? To my knowledge, she's just missing."

Hell, she wasn't even that. The Brotherhood knew where she was. At least, Mike did. She hadn't been abducted.

She'd been *saved*.

Too bad he couldn't tell this asshole that.

Dave ignored him. Instead of answering, he opened a folder and leafed through some notes. "Here's a good place to start. Why would the Notaro girls need you as their counsel if you had just come to town to do business with them a few months ago? NBD has an attorney on staff if they need representation, which, in this instance, they didn't. So, why were you involved in this matter, Mr. Falco?"

Well, that certainly wasn't a question Vinnie had prepared for. He stared at McGuire for a moment, completely at a loss as to what he was fishing for.

Gianni came to his rescue. "Why is that relevant? And why are you asking him? Shouldn't you be asking one of the sisters why they asked Vinnie to accompany them to fill out the report?"

McGuire tapped his pen on his folder and looked back and forth between Gianni and Vinnie. "You know, you two've been a problem for me since I met you, ever since you came in here with that bogus story about your stolen rental car."

"That wasn't—" Gianni said.

"Save it. I know you had the—" he held up his fingers and used air quotes "—proper paperwork." He closed his folder and leaned his elbows on the table. "Here's the thing. I'm not stupid. I'm just bound by the law. I know you weren't here to report a stolen car. You were just here fishing for information. Just like I know you," he looked at Vinnie, "weren't here to support the girls when they reported their mother missing. You were here to make sure they didn't say or do the wrong thing. I just can't do anything because I don't have any proof. Yet. Now, what I don't understand is why the girls would hide their mother's abduction." Again he shot a pointed stare at Vinnie. "And why you four would want to hurt this family. So—" He leaned back in his seat and crossed his legs. "You can make it easy on yourselves and tell me what you did. I might be able to get you a reduced sentence for your cooperation. Or you can make it difficult, and I'll see you all get the maximum sentence."

"Maximum sentence?" Vinnie said. "For what?"

"Anything and everything I can pin on you. Starting with Mary's murder."

"Mary's not dead. Or abducted," Vinnie said. "She's just missing."

"Tell that to the body we fished out of the river this morning. Coroner's working on getting an ID as we speak. And I'm going to make sure you go down for it."

JO WOKE WARM and hangover-free. And with twice the shame she had when she passed out. She was still in Vinnie's bed, but this time she was naked as an unshingled roof, completely exposed except for the covers that someone had thoughtfully pulled over her. She didn't remember doing it herself, so she prayed to whatever saint was in charge of hangovers and stupidity that it had been Franki or one of the twins. Then, trying to put the ordeal out of her mind, she set about getting ready for the day.

The tray of food Franki had brought earlier was completely unappealing, so Jo decided she'd grab something on the way to the site. That would give her more time at work, anyway. The last blow her ego could suffer was calling in sick after yesterday's fiasco, so every second mattered. She looked at the clothes Franki had grabbed for her—cotton pajama pants and an old but favorite tee. No matter. If a potato sack was the only option to get back to her room, then that's what she'd wear. She needed to get dressed for work.

She hurriedly donned the clothes Franki left for her and grabbed the hand mirror. Leaving something behind meant having to return or having Vinnie come to her room later, and the less she saw of him privately in the next, oh, decade, the better she'd feel. Just thinking about the last twenty-four hours and what he had witnessed brought a blush to her cheeks. She raised the mirror to her face to see how badly flushed she was. The glass rippled, fogged...

She saw herself on top of a building under construction. Nothing new there, but she was scared—terrified—and that was new for her. Someone stood with his thumb on a device, maniacal desperation gleaming on his face. He looked toward the makeshift elevator shaft and she followed his gaze, knowing the wires and blinking lights didn't belong. Vinnie hefted himself onto the platform from the floor below, took his gun from his holster, and unsheathed his dagger, but the stranger only laughed. His glee hadn't abated when the explosion rocked the building. She expected to be engulfed in flames, but instead, somehow, she was drowning...

The mirror surface fogged, rippled, and soon she saw only her reflection—not the flushed features of shame she had initially expected but the bloodless white of shock. Jo turned the mirror over and traced the flower intricately etched into the back of the antique metal. Her trembling legs gave out and she collapsed onto Vinnie's bed. Should have recognized it sooner. Would have, had she been paying attention.

This wasn't just any mirror. Franki had brought her the family heirloom. The occult mirror of Catherine de' Medici.

The very mirror Catherine had used to read her future, that had then been passed down through the generations, finally ending up in their possession. Others in the Medici line had used it, intentionally or not, to view their futures. Jo never would have believed in such nonsense if Franki hadn't predicted her own hostage situation from it only months earlier. Maybe even that wouldn't have been enough to convince her. But her own mother had foreseen her father's murder in that same mirror. It was enough to make her give serious thought to the validity and possibility of what she had just seen.

It was enough to make her furious that Franki had given her that mirror.

She stormed out of the room to confront her sister and found her eating lunch with the twins in the kitchen.

"Jo," Toni said, "you look better. We were worried."

"I made a frittata." Donni gestured to the pan. "There's plenty here. Do you feel up to eating?"

"How could you?" Jo ignored the twins and marched straight up to Franki.

"How could I what?" She took a bite of eggs, seemingly unfazed by Jo's latest tantrum.

"This!" While she waved the mirror in front of her sister's face, she thought about smacking her over the head with it. Instead, she put it on the table and crossed her arms in front of her chest. "Well?"

"Well, what? You asked for food, clothes, and a mirror. So I brought you food, clothes, and a mirror. I'd think you'd be a bit more grateful."

"Grateful? I needed work clothes and you have me in pajamas."

"You can't go to the site. Vinnie's not here right now, and all the guys are gone. You can't go alone."

"I don't care. I have to go."

"Gianni gave me strict orders, Jo. No one leaves the compound until they're back. End of discussion."

"Ooooh!" Jo stamped her foot. "What about this?" She picked up the mirror and thrust it in her sister's face.

Franki pushed it aside and took a sip of water. "Again, you asked for a mirror, I brought you a mirror."

"But why this one?"

Franki smiled and shrugged.

Toni covered Jo's hand with her own. "Something happened, didn't it?"

Donni rushed over. "You saw something, didn't you?"

Jo shook off Toni's hand and put the mirror back on the table. "Shouldn't you both be at work?"

"The guys got called to a meeting somewhere," she said. "We're grounded until they come back."

"And you listened? Whatever. You can stay here if you want. But I have to get to work. It's bad enough I'm late."

"Gianni said—"

"I don't care what he said. I have work to do. I'll be fine without my baby-sitter for a few hours."

"You don't know that," Donni said. "Look at what happened to Papa."

"Papa walked into danger knowingly. I'm going to a construction site where my foreman and about a gazillion other guys will have my back if I need help. I'm sure Vinnie won't be far behind me, and if he doesn't show, I promise I won't close the site. I'll let Chuck do it so I'm not there alone."

"Chuck's already handling things for the day," Franki said. "I called him and asked him to take care of it."

Jo glared at her. "You had no right. I'm in charge of construction, not you. I'm going."

"I don't like it," Toni said. "Maybe one of us should come with you."

"And what are you going to do if there's trouble? Scream for me?"

"We've all been training really hard," Donni said.

"Well, here's hoping you don't have to use what you've learned."

"You're going to get me in trouble," Franki said.

"Is Gianni your boss or your lover?"

"Depends."

"What you do behind closed doors is your own business."

Franki put her fork down. "That's not what I meant, and you know it."

"I need to change for work. Put this," she gestured to the mirror but didn't touch it again, "back where you got it, and don't show it to me again." She headed out of the kitchen.

"Aren't you even going to tell us what you saw?" Franki called after her.

Jo kept walking and ignored her sister. In the hall, she remembered she'd been too drunk to drive home the night before. She called back over her shoulder, "I'm taking your truck, Toni," and headed up the stairs.

VINNIE'S THOUGHTS GREW sluggish. Processing McGuire's latest bombshell was proving difficult. Tired. That was it. He was tired and hallucinating. Surely he didn't hear correctly.

Keeping his face emotionless, he glanced around the room. McGuire might see four bored and expressionless men in his interrogation room, but Vinnie knew his brothers, knew the signs. Nico's eyes moved the slightest bit, but very fast, like he was scanning a document. He did that when he thought through a problem. Gianni tilted his head to the side like he was examining McGuire, but Vinnie knew he was really trying to relieve the tension in his neck. A glance at Coz's feet showed he was wiggling his toes in his boots—a barely-controlled flight response. He itched to get out of there. No, Vinnie hadn't misheard. McGuire had a body. It wasn't Mary's, but the cop didn't know that. And he wanted to pin the death on them.

"You said you had some questions for us," Vinnie said.

"I did, didn't I? Let's start with everything you did the day Mary disappeared. I want to know every move you made from the moment you woke up to the second the Notaro girls noticed she was gone."

"Well, maybe you should have asked us that then, because I didn't log brushing my teeth on my calendar."

"You're pretty defensive for a corporate attorney."

"And you're fishing. Again. We'll be leaving now, unless you have a reason to hold us?"

McGuire didn't reply, but the smirk on his face had Vinnie clenching his fists. He wanted nothing more than to knock him off his chair. They left the cop making notes in his file. Vinnie shut the door just harder than he had to, the metal echoing off the jamb and through the nearly-empty station.

Horace hadn't moved since they walked into the interrogation room. Still with his back to the open cases board, he poked through pastry boxes with one beefy hand, a steaming mug of police sludge in the other. He looked up and raised his coffee in salute.

"Hey, Horace," Gianni said.

"Gentlemen." He took a bite of some glazed confection. "How'd it go?"

"Oh, the way things usually go with McGuire," he continued. Vinnie elbowed him in the ribs. "What can you tell us about the body you found?"

"Tell you? Not much. Don't have the coroner's report back yet."

Vinnie considered him for a minute. There was always more where Horace was concerned. The information was helpful. Getting it sometimes proved tricky, though.

"Okay. If you can't tell us anything, is there someone who can tell us more?"

"Nope." Horace took another bite, the crackled glaze falling onto the desk.

It was like playing "Hot" and "Cold" with a child, and he had gotten colder. Clearly Horace wouldn't say anything more on the matter. "What evidence is here? Is there something you can show us?"

Before he got his answer, McGuire came out of the interrogation room and nearly ran into Nico. "What are you guys still doing here?"

"They were just leaving. I offered them a croissant, and we got to talking."

"Does it look like they want a croissant?" He turned from Horace to face the men. "If you want to chat, come back in the room. We've got plenty to discuss."

Vinnie and McGuire didn't move, their gazes fixed on each other in silent battle. Gianni finally pulled his brother away, and they headed toward the door. Vinnie couldn't help but turn and give McGuire one last look. The cop had wasted no time on him, though, already headed toward his desk, head buried in a file. A quick glance at Horace proved marginally more productive. He looked at a series of pictures in a folder and winked. The coroner might not be done with the body, but there was obviously something worth seeing in the preliminary photos. What did the cop want them to see?

Outside, the guys headed to the car. Vinnie stopped them. "We need to get back in the precinct. Or the coroner's office."

"And how do you plan on doing either of those things without McGuire knowing?" Nico asked.

"And more importantly, why do we need to bother?" Coz said. "We know it's not Mary."

"Horace had a file of photos. He tried to turn them so I could see them as we were leaving. I think there's something he wants us to know."

"All of us aren't getting back in there," Gianni said. "I don't know if even one of us could."

"So we split up. You and I can go back for the photos, and Nico and Coz can go to the morgue."

"Again, I think we'll be spotted."

"You can run interference for me with McGuire while I look at the photos. Nico, maybe you can hack into the fire alarm system at the morgue and set it off. When everyone's out of there, Coz can break you two in to look at the body."

"What the hell are we looking for?" Coz asked.

"I guess we'll know it when we see it. Horace seemed to think we'd want to see the photos. McGuire obviously didn't want us to know something."

"I don't like it, but I'm game," Coz said.

"Gimme the keys," Nico said. "We'll be back for you as soon as we're done."

"Meet us at Flo's Diner. Don't screw around." He ignored the dirty look Nico sent his way and the finger Coz shot in the air.

"So, do you have any idea how to get past McGuire?" Gianni asked.

"Yeah, I have a plan. But you aren't going to like it."

Gianni's phone went off and he checked the screen. "Hold on guys!" he called. Nico and Coz stopped halfway to the car.

"What's going on, G?"

He tucked his phone in his pocket. "Nothing good."

JO PULLED UP to the construction site while most of the men were away at lunch. The only work vehicles there were the ones from the very subcontractor she wanted to avoid. Picking up her phone, she called Chuck Tyson, her lead foreman.

"Hey. Franki said she talked to you this morning. Thanks for handling things."

"No problem. Everything okay?"

"Yeah, I'm actually at the site now."

"Something wrong? I just left five minutes ago. Things looked good."

"No. Nothing's wrong." She hesitated for a moment. "The only subs here right now are from Palmeri."

"I'm coming back."

"No, that won't be necess—" but he'd already severed the connection.

It was bad enough she had missed the morning. She couldn't let Enzo Palmeri see her sitting in her truck waiting for backup. The banished effects of her drunken binge made a sudden reappearance, making her stomach seize in a pre-retching cramp. She swallowed the saliva pooling in her mouth and willed her body to relax.

Once she was certain she wouldn't puke or pass out, she squared her shoulders and climbed out of the truck.

The house under frame was for a long-time client. It was the first of many set in a gorgeous forested area, this one for the client's daughter. Others would soon be going up around it as her client screened his daughter's new neighbors. He was essentially building a housing development for his family and friends. Jo wasn't sure his discrimination was entirely ethical, but she was just the builder, so it wasn't her problem.

At the moment, she just wanted to focus on the vista. When she took the time to enjoy her surroundings, she felt utterly at peace there. The area was up on a hill with a spectacular view of the valley below. Franki had made certain the house design blended into the scenery rather than detracted from it, and as the structure went up, Jo found herself again amazed with her sister's talent. As Jo built it, she could see it would be a sanctuary for her client's daughter.

What she wouldn't give for a sliver of that safety and solitude.

She stepped into the house and listened for sounds. Most of the activity seemed to be in the basement, but she could hear someone puttering around in what would be the master bath. Torn on where to go, she decided if Enzo was there, he'd be supervising the basement work, so she headed for the master.

She chose wrong.

As she picked her way over tools and supplies, the plumber finished whatever he had been doing and turned toward the doorway. Her gaze locked onto Enzo Palmeri. She stood, immoveable, like she had epoxied her boots to the subflooring.

"Jo! I'm so glad to see you. When you weren't here this morning, I was afraid I wouldn't have a chance to talk to you. I've wanted a chance to be alone with you for some time now."

She tried to back away, but still felt glued in place. Instead, to stop his advance, she held up a hand. "I was busy this morning. I'm still busy now. I just needed to check on the site before I went to my next appointment."

He took another step closer, tucking his tools into his belt, freeing his hands. Then he reached for her.

She trembled, but all she could do was shake her head 'no.' Her feet still betrayed her, forcing her to stay, allowing Enzo to indulge in whatever activity he wanted to force on her this time.

"Relax, Jo. It's okay."

But it wasn't okay. Sweat trickled down her spine, chilling her to her core. He could assure her all he wanted. She knew better than to trust him.

Loud stomping footsteps heading toward them diverted both their gazes. Chuck appeared in the doorway of the master bedroom and narrowed his eyes. "Problem here, boss?"

Jo couldn't find her voice, but Enzo supplied the answer. "No. No problem. Jo and I were just catching up."

"Old friends 'catch up,' Palmeri. You and Miss Notaro were never friends."

Jo watched the two men size each other up, and, just like years before, Enzo cowered under Chuck's sizable frame. It came as no surprise to her. Most people would acquiesce to a man who towered over almost everyone he met. Chuck had great genes. He had been muscular the day she'd met him in junior high. And he'd only grown bulkier from years of construction work. His penetrating stare from icy eyes stood out in fearsome contrast against his dark skin, made even more noticeable by the lack of hair on his smoothly-shaved head. He had intimidated greater men than Enzo Palmeri. He was massive, intense... the black, frightening version of Mr. Clean.

And he was on her side—again. Thank God.

Enzo babbled a few nonsensical syllables, but never found actual words.

"I think it's time you leave," Chuck's voice was low, just above a whisper. The threat was palpable nonetheless.

Enzo scooped up a toolbox and left without even a backward glance.

Jo's feet finally broke free of their self-imposed bonds. She stepped toward Chuck and collapsed into his arms, allowing him to bear the full brunt of her weight. He guided her to a stack of sheetrock, lowered them onto it, and held her. She snuggled into his embrace and allowed herself the luxury of a good cry into his broad shoulders—an indulgence she had denied herself for a long time. He rocked her and hummed softly until she had cried herself out.

She pulled away and mopped at her face and then his shirt. "I'm sorry."

"Don't be ridiculous."

"I seem to be making a habit of this."

"Yeah, once in high school and once now. Call me again when another decade passes."

She laughed and slapped him on the arm. Running her hand through her hair, she sighed. "God, I've had a rough day. First I made a total ass of myself last night and this morning at home—"

"What happened?"

"Never mind. Moving on. Now you have to see me like this."

"Like what?"

"I just blubbered like a fool for what felt like forever. I must be all red and blotchy. And redheads don't wear the color red well. This one doesn't, anyway."

"Nah, you look fine. Well," he squinted at her, "your eyes are a bit red."

"That could just as easily be from my hangover."

"You got wasted last night? Good party?"

"No. Enzo."

"Jo, we really don't need him here. We can wait a week for one of the other plumbers."

"I don't want to get that far behind schedule. Besides, he's almost done."

"But look what it's doing to you."

"I'm fine."

"Bullshit. You're drinking at night, missing mornings. He had you cornered in here this afternoon. You were shaking like my mama's Jell-O salad. And I haven't seen you cry like that since your daddy died. And before that? Since the first time we dealt with Palmeri. What would you have done if I hadn't come back?"

"They should be done tomorrow. It's just one more day. Surely I can do that. I just need to get through tomorrow with no other issues or distractions, and I'll be fine. You'll help me, right?"

"Yeah, I'll help you. Always. Come here, you foolish woman." He took her in his arms again.

Screeching tires and slamming doors made them both jump. Chuck went to the rough-in for the window facing the front of the house. "Guess I'm starting now. I don't think the drama is done for the day."

3

FOOTSTEPS THUNDERED ON the wooden subflooring toward them. Jo hid behind Chuck, afraid of the latest unknown headed toward her.

"Who the hell's this?" She recognized Gianni's voice and stepped out from behind her human shield.

"I'm the foreman. Who the hell are you?"

Gianni started toward him, but Vinnie stopped him.

"He's okay," Vinnie said. "He's—were you crying?" He crossed to Jo in two steps and grabbed her arm, pulling her closer to him and tipping her face up with his free hand so he could better examine it in the light.

She saw panic and fear flash over his features before he settled on fury. She just wasn't fast enough to stop the explosion.

He spun toward Chuck and tucked Jo behind him. "What'd you do?"

Gianni, Nico, and Coz advanced on Chuck.

"Hey!" Jo said, pulling on Vinnie's arm. "I'm fine!"

He didn't face her when he answered. "You don't look fine."

"Thanks a lot."

He half turned toward her, seemingly unwilling to take his eyes off the foreman. "That's not what I meant."

"Leave Chuck alone. He was here to help me."

Vinnie turned and gave Jo his full attention. "I'm listening."

"No. Not here. Not like this. Chuck, go downstairs and check on the progress in the basement. Apparently I'm leaving for the day. Can you close the site for me this afternoon?"

"Sure thing." It didn't escape her attention that he didn't meet her gaze either, choosing instead to keep staring at Gianni, Nico, and Coz.

She sighed. "Chuck?"

He turned toward her and walked around the men, toward the doorway.

"Hey," she said. "Get Jerry and the boys on the roof this afternoon. And call me tonight, let me know how everything goes. The heating and electric subs seem ahead of schedule. If it looks like they're going to be finished, get the inspectors scheduled for late tomorrow. Palmeri should be done plumbing by then."

"Got it." He left with a slow, deliberate swagger she recognized as a 'you-don't-want-to-fuck-with-me' to the guys. Chuck was the only man she knew who would stand toe-to-toe against the brothers. Four against one? He'd lose, but he wouldn't go down easy. When he called later, she'd owe him another thank you for the afternoon and a huge apology for this mess.

Vinnie rounded on her the second Chuck's footsteps were out of earshot. "Okay, he's gone. Spill it."

"He wasn't the reason I didn't want to talk. And I'm not airing dirty laundry at work." She held up her hand before he could butt in. "I don't care that no one's in this room. I'm not talking here."

"We left important business to protect you," Vinnie said.

"And like I told Franki, I didn't need protecting at the site. You have nothing to worry about. I have work handled."

"Didn't look like it to us," Nico said.

"Do you always bawl at work?" Gianni asked.

"You!" She jabbed her finger in his chest. "This is your fault. Giving us ultimatums. If I want to go to work, I'm damn well going to go. You might boss my sister around, but you don't boss me. Got it?"

"I don't boss your sister around, and with respect to the Protectorate, I do have to make decisions. I'm the only one with full powers right now. I have to consider everyone's safety—even hard-heads like you."

"Hard-heads! Why—"

"Shut up!"

Vinnie's outburst stunned Jo into silence. Everyone turned to look at him.

"I've had enough. I don't know when I last slept. I've lost track of the number of jobs I'm doing and the lies I'm telling. If I'm going to protect you, the last thing I need is you fighting me and my brothers on it. So here's what's going to happen. Jo, you're with me and G. We'll take your truck. You're going to help us get a look at photos at the police station. Coz and Nico will take our ride and see if they can get into the morgue. We'll all meet at the compound to find out what everyone learned. Then you're giving us some answers. No arguments. Let's go."

He headed out before Jo could argue. She looked at Gianni.

"He's the strategist of the group. No point in questioning him. He'll just pull rank."

She was pissed, but she was also outnumbered. Throwing a tantrum would be futile, so she filed out with the others.

"SO WHAT DID you learn?" Sal asked his protégé.

"I think we're going to have an opening soon. Jo's cracking under the constant surveillance. She went to a bar herself last night, and she took off on her guardian today."

"Is there a reason you didn't do something about that?"

"She went off alone, but before I could make a move, she was with people again. Workers at the site, her foreman, and the Brotherhood came by."

"All of them?" Sal asked.

"Yeah. All four."

"That means the others were vulnerable. You should have called it in."

"For what reason?" he asked his boss. "We still can't find where they are."

"You need to keep me in the loop. Real time updates. We need to accelerate our timetable. The Organization won't wait for us much longer."

"I'm on Jo. She's going to be our way in."

"Take help if you need it. And keep me informed."

He left his boss, ideas churning in his head. Jo would give them what they needed. He just needed one small break.

VINNIE GRIPPED THE leather-wrapped wheel until his fingers ached. The three of them squeezed together on the bench seat of an old beat up Chevy pickup Toni used to haul landscaping materials. Why Jo had taken that vehicle when so many better ones had been available to her, he hadn't a clue. But there they were, smashed together like a panini.

He slammed on the brakes in the lot a block from the police station and almost fell out of the cab in his haste to distance himself from her. Exhausted. Too wiped out to think straight. He banged the back of his head against the driver's side window. Let it rest there. Closed his eyes. Took a couple of deep breaths.

Time to get his shit together. And he'd start by doing his job.

Gianni and Franki had gotten out the passenger side and quietly strategized on the other side of the truck. Deciding not to wait for them, he headed toward the station. They rushed to catch up with him, but he strode paces ahead of them, so desperate to get on with the task at hand that he didn't even ask what they had discussed.

He was the damn strategist of the group, anyway. If they used a plan, it would be his. Or none at all.

An idea struck him and he stopped mid-stride, turned and looked Jo over. She wore boots, jeans, a low-cut tight tank, and an open button-down over it with the sleeves rolled up. "I don't suppose you'd consider losing the work shirt?"

"What?" She pulled the shirt closed over her tank.

Like that made a difference. He knew what was going on under that shirt. He knew what was under all of it, but he didn't want to dwell on that. His own clothes began to grow tight in the crotch, but he put those thoughts aside and continued pursuing his plan. "Look, Jo. McGuire seems to have a thing for you."

"Don't be ridiculous."

"It's always you he gravitates to. You he tries to protect. I need you to exploit that."

"What?"

"If you can distract him for a few minutes, we can get a look at the photos Horace has."

"You're whoring me out?"

"I'm not asking you to sleep with the man. I'm asking you to tantalize him. Flirt. Show a little more skin than your neck and forearms. Divert his attention long enough for us to get some information."

"Do you know how long I've tried to avoid his attention?"

"So you do know he likes you."

She crossed her arms and glared. "Of course I do. I'm not blind. But I don't reciprocate the feeling. And now you're sending me into the lion's den. Alone?"

"Actually, I don't know that she should go in alone," Gianni said.

"What? We need to look at the photos."

"I can look at them myself. You should be there to make sure McGuire doesn't grill her, get her to say something she shouldn't."

"He'll be more likely to take his time with her if they're alone."

"But we don't *need* a lot of time. We don't want him with her for very long."

Vinnie thought for a moment. He should have seen that angle. Gianni was right. "I'll go in with her. You check out the photos. Cough when we're clear to leave."

"Don't I get a say in this?" Jo asked.

"No," Vinnie and Gianni said together.

Vinnie thought she stomped her foot slightly. She huffed a little and didn't say anything else.

"Let's fix you up," Vinnie said.

She raised an eyebrow but stayed silent.

He started to slide the shirt off her arms, but she pulled on it, keeping it tight against her body. As his hands grazed her bare shoulders, he met her gaze. Her skin was warm, soft. The smell of his soap reached him, but on her it wasn't just a fresh pine, but something else. Something more. On him it was masculine and woodsy, but on her? Musky, mysterious.

Jo shrugged one shoulder at a time, hiking the shirt back onto her slender frame. He lifted her arms out to her sides, and she stood there, compliant, soundless. Waiting for his instruction or ministrations, the only sign of her nervousness her shallow breathing.

Grasping the collar of the garment, he ran his hands down along the opening until he reached the low waist of her jeans. His fingers trailed the top of her waistband and he unbuttoned them, then he grasped the ribbed cotton of her tank and tugged it free. He rolled it up, higher, higher… exposing first her navel, then the subtle contours of her toned abs, then, as she sucked in a breath when his knuckles grazed her sensitive flesh, part of her ribcage.

His gaze never wavered. She never dropped her arms, allowing him to make whatever adjustments he felt necessary.

Next he tucked the back tail of the work shirt up under the tank so it wouldn't fall. His fingers paused briefly as he ran them over her bra. He wondered what color it was, what the front looked like. Knew it would only take him seconds to have her out of it. Before losing himself to his fantasies—or acting in reality—he took the front ends of the shirt in his hands. Finally averting his attention, he looked down to tie the tails in a knot under her breasts.

And wished he hadn't.

The effect was spectacular. The tight, rolled-up tank created the illusion of a tiny sports bra. The work shirt he knotted under her breasts lifted them up and put them on display. And if anyone could manage to tear their stare away from that, the tails of the knot formed an arrow straight toward her navel and the unbuttoned waistband of the low-rising denim. He tried to swallow, but his mouth was too dry.

Too much. There was no way she was going in there like that, giving Dave an open invitation to wonder, to dream.

To fantasize.

Hell, no.

His fingers fumbled to close the button of her jeans.

He met her gaze again, and she bit her lower lip. He didn't know if she was uncertain or if she was trying to torture him, but she was definitely having the latter effect.

Gianni cleared his throat, and Jo dropped her arms.

"Ready?" Gianni asked.

"I'm rethinking this plan," Vinnie said.

"Why? She looks great."

"That's the problem," he said through clenched teeth.

"I look like a *puttana.*"

"You look wonderful," Gianni said.

"Are you— Are you sure this is the way to do it?" She looked down, and her cheeks flushed.

"Positive. Vinnie's the strategist. He never leads us down the wrong path. This will work. McGuire won't be able to take his eyes off you."

Vinnie struggled not to punch his brother in the face. It was bad enough thinking about McGuire ogling her. He didn't need G doing it, too. He definitely didn't need her asking him for encouragement.

"Maybe this wasn't such a good idea," he said.

"Look, I wasn't crazy about this plan either, but I'm even less crazy about standing in public like this while we debate it," she said. "Let's just go in and get it over with."

Vinnie sighed. "Let me do most of the talking."

But she was already walking in the door.

It was probably a good thing. Vinnie had completely forgotten they were standing on a sidewalk in broad daylight until Jo had mentioned it. It was probably better someone else took the lead for the moment.

SHE FELT LIKE one of those magazine girls who pose with wet soapy sponges by hot rods. Sure, those pictures hang in garages and teenage boys' bedrooms across America, but no one believed they were about the vehicles. Even Mario Andretti couldn't tell you what kinds of cars were in those photos. And if he was there right now, he probably wouldn't know she had red hair, either.

What the hell was she thinking? She was fairly certain she had said no when they asked her to do it. Told her she was doing it. Then Vinnie had his hands on her and she didn't think at all. At least, she didn't think about the job she had been asked to do. Idiot.

And what did that get her? In deeper with another guy she wanted—needed—to cut out of her life. If she thought Dave was clingy before, she hated to think what he would be like after he saw her in this get up. He'd be like sawdust in shellac. At least furniture could be saved with power tools, chemicals, and elbow grease. She didn't know how she would save her sanity if Dave got more smitten than he already was.

Leaving the brightness of the neighborhood behind, she crossed the threshold and entered the drab, depressing interior of the police station. Relief washed over her as she took in her surroundings and realized very few people would stand witness to her humiliation. Horace Daugherty sat at his desk eating a huge triple cheeseburger.

Jo closed her eyes and inhaled. The unmistakable aroma of grill smoke, beef, and Mildred's special seasonings wafted to her, tantalizing her until her mouth watered and her stomach grumbled. No one made a burger like Millie, and she was starving. Even the obscene amount of grease and Horace's aversion to vegetable toppings couldn't stop Jo's hunger. She eyed the burger with desire, momentarily forgetting why she was there.

"Jo! What a nice surprise!"

Dave's voice cut through her hunger and sat in her stomach like acid. Why was she doing this? A quick glance at Vinnie buoyed her resolve. Under the strain of gnashing teeth, his jaw muscles bulged. Not unlike the corded muscles in his forearms while he clenched his fists.

But what steeled her most were his eyes. The shadows under them portrayed his fatigue even as the heat in the dark brown depths revealed more than a thousand words ever could—barely-contained fury, embarrassment, sorrow, and torment.

And when he met her gaze, she saw something else there. Something more primal, passionate. Something a little dangerous and a hell of a lot more decadent smoldering just beneath the surface. For just a moment, fires sparked in the depths of the windows to his soul.

She read desire in his eyes.

That probably explained the embarrassment.

And God help her, if she was reading him right, she knew just how he felt.

She squared her shoulders, forgetting until it was too late that doing so would thrust her already scantily-clad breasts forward, and she turned to face Dave. His gaze fell about a foot too low to meet hers directly. No matter. She had a job to do. Maybe it would work to her favor.

"Dave. I came as soon as I heard you had the guys in today. Is there somewhere we can talk?"

"Sure, sure. This way." He led her toward a door marked "Interrogation Room" with a guiding hand on the small of her back. It didn't escape her notice that Vinnie inhaled sharply as Dave's hand touched her skin.

When they got to the room, Dave opened the door from beside her and, rather than moving out of her way, stayed stretched in the doorway holding the knob so she had to squeeze past him to enter the room. Despite his efforts to close the door quickly, Vinnie followed behind. Jo took a seat, expecting this to take a while.

"What are you doing here, Falco?"

"The lady asked me to bring her here. Moral support."

"I'm the only friend she'll need."

"I'm here at her request. Let her be the judge of that."

They both looked at her. As if wearing her pay-attention-to-my-breasts top wasn't bad enough, having two men argue about her was just too much. "Dave, please. Let's not make this more difficult than it needs to be. You shouldn't have hauled the guys in here today if you had questions for us. You should have just come to me."

He crossed to her and took her hand in his. "Honey, I didn't want you to worry. These—" he stared pointedly at Vinnie before returning his gaze to her, "—guys can handle a few tough questions. Especially if they don't have anything to hide."

She wasn't sure if it was the implications against Vinnie's character or the way Dave's thumb stroked her knuckles, but she could tell by Vinnie's breathing he was close to losing it. She pulled her hand away from Dave's and ran it through her hair. "It's not about them. It's about Mama. Did you find her?"

Okay, she went off script, but she didn't know how to keep talking about Dave being unfair to the brothers without angering him or Vinnie—or both of them—and honestly, she didn't know if she'd be able to rein them in if they lost it. Lying seemed like a better choice, even if it risked blowing Gianni's chance at talking to Horace.

"I don't think now's the time to discuss this." Dave sat back in his seat, assuming a more professional role.

Jo forced tears to her eyes. Truth be told, it wasn't that difficult to manage. "I need to know. If you found her, if Mama's gone…" Given the last two days she'd had, crying came easily. Enzo's reappearance in her life was enough to summon gallons of tears, and that was before everyone she lived with witnessed her humiliation. She let a few drops spill over her eyelashes and down her cheeks before she reached for Dave and grabbed his hand. "Please, Dave. Tell me what you know."

He rubbed his face with his free hand then covered her hand with his. "Jo, honey, nothing is concrete yet. We've got to do tests to ID the body."

"Body," she managed to say, sounding something like a hiccup or sniffle.

"It's a small town. If we get positive confirmation, we'll release her to the mortician and have her fixed up before we ask you to formally ID her. It's not standard protocol, but I'll make an exception for you. They'll pretty her up as best they can for you."

"I want to see her now." She heard Vinnie sigh, but ignored him. "*Please.*"

"No."

"Yes."

"You don't even know if it's her."

"Then show me photos."

He just looked at her. "They won't do you any good."

"I need to know, Dave. The waiting is torture. Please. As a favor."

He stared at her. He took so long she thought for sure he would deny her. Then he shook his head. "I think it's a bad idea. But I just can't deny you anything. Wait here. I'll go get the photos for you to look at."

She sprung to her feet. "Don't bother. I'll come with you." She rushed to the door before he could change his mind.

This wasn't ideal. No one wanted McGuire hovering over their shoulders while they looked at the pictures, but at least this way all three of them would have a chance to see the photos and maybe find whatever clue the guys were looking for.

WHEN VINNIE HEARD Jo stop talking about the brothers and start talking about her mother, he didn't know what she was thinking. And now, as they headed out to look at the photos—the one place they should absolutely avoid—he knew she either had misunderstood her role or had lost her fucking mind.

He slid his chair back from the table, taking care to scrape the feet along the linoleum. The grinding echoed loud enough that he trusted Gianni could hear it and take precautions. That was the only warning he'd be able to send him. It wasn't much, but he hoped it would be enough.

Dave opened the door and gently pushed Jo out of the room before him. Then he looked down his nose at Vinnie. "Didn't your mother ever teach you any manners? Oh, right. Your mother didn't raise you, did she, orphan-boy?"

Vinnie curled his hands into fists and started to lunge at the guy, but the heat of his dagger against his back stopped him. He needed to start thinking clearly. Cold-cocking a cop, especially in a police station while carrying a weapon, was about the dumbest thing he could do.

McGuire was just trying to bait him. Bastard was good at it, too. But Vinnie wouldn't give him the satisfaction. Besides, there were more important things to do—like looking at the coroner's photos.

"Go ahead," McGuire said quietly. "Give me a reason to lock you up. I've got a cell down this hallway with your name on it, and I'm just itching to toss you in it. Get your buddy involved. There's room for him, too."

Vinnie quelled his anger and gestured to the door.

"No? Nothing. You're not so tough, Falco. I've got your number. It's only a matter of time." McGuire walked out after Jo. Vinnie took a deep breath, reminded himself the prick was just doing his job, and followed them out of the interrogation room.

In the main area, Gianni and Horace Daugherty stood by the coffee maker, each holding a steaming mug. Horace tapped his finger against his. McGuire led Jo over toward the open cases board.

"Horace, where's the coroner's photos of the Jane Doe?"

"Should be on your desk." Horace gestured with his cup.

McGuire grabbed the folder, and they gathered around the catch-all table. Vinnie looked at Gianni, but he couldn't catch his attention. McGuire held the folder tight to his chest and grabbed Jo's hand again. Jackass.

"Jo. You sure you want to do this? These aren't pretty. You might not even see anything you can recognize."

"I'm sure. Spread them out."

McGuire moved some folders and old doughnut boxes and spread out the photos on the corner of the table. Jo covered her mouth and studied them. Vinnie wasn't sure if the pictures bothered her or not, but they bugged the hell out of him.

Of course it wasn't Mary. But he knew who the woman was.

EVERYONE IN THE room fell silent as McGuire arranged the photos on the table. The only sound was Jo's ragged breathing and the soft ting-ting of Horace's wedding band from his tapping his fingers against his coffee mug. Jo tried to cover as much of her face as she could. She tried to see if Vinnie and Gianni had seen enough of the photos without Dave noticing where she was looking. She had certainly seen enough of the images. Unable to gauge their reactions, she finally put her hands down and turned away.

"Those are awful. And completely unrecognizable." Thank God that wasn't anyone she knew. The body in the photos had suffered a horrific fate.

The little amount of skin left on the corpse was a sickly greenish-blue, clustered in the crevasses of the body like the neck, the crooks of the arms, and the fingers. The rest appeared to have been ripped off in strips or eaten away, leaving most of the skull and ribs exposed. Muscle on the limbs looked like badly-butchered meat. Leaves tangled with twigs and other flotsam in the last few snatches of the matted hair. Only rags remained of her clothing, filthy and nondescript. What the fish hadn't eaten of her tissue, the river had bloated to an exaggerated size. The ring the woman wore looked more like a band around a pale cigar than jewelry on a finger. She doubted the woman's own mother would recognize her in that condition and thanked the Lord there was no way it was Mama.

"I'm sorry I made you show them to me."

"I'm sorry I let you look." Dave scooped the photos together and shoved them back in the folder. "As soon as preliminary testing comes back, I'll let you know what we find out. In the meantime, why don't you let me take you out for a drink? Try to put this all behind you?"

"No, thank you. I'm going to have the guys take me home. I've had a long day, and I just want to rest." She started toward the door.

"Speaking of home, Jo, it's been difficult reaching you there lately."

"If you need any of us, call our mobile numbers. That's the best way to reach us. We all work crazy hours. Thanks, Dave." She left before he could continue the conversation. He had begun to fish for information, and she wasn't about to give him any.

Outside, she headed straight for the parking lot. Determined footsteps behind her told her Vinnie and Gianni were right on her heels, but she didn't know when it would be safe to talk, so she didn't say anything. When they reached the truck, she turned to face them. They all began talking at once.

"Did you have to be so friendly with him?" Vinnie asked.

"Why did you have to antagonize him?" Jo asked.

"Thought you were going to give me more time," Gianni said.

"Abbastanza!" Jo flung her hands in the air. She put them to her temples and closed her eyes. "Enough," she repeated softer in English.

Vinnie stepped to her and, taking her hands in his, lowered them in front of her, rubbing them with his thumbs. His fingers heated her skin. She hadn't even realized she was chilled. She started shaking.

"Breathe, *bella.*"

She took a deep breath, felt it shudder through her lungs. Looking up, she found herself mesmerized by the flecks of amber and cognac in the deep brown of his eyes.

"Again, *bella.* Breathe."

His voice seemed farther away, but all she wanted to do was obey him. She took another deep breath. It was smoother, softer. Filled her lungs easier. Her hands stilled, and she felt warmer.

He squeezed her hands gently and let them go.

His withdrawal released her from the strange thrall she was in, brought her back to the grim reality of the moment. She had just viewed horrible atrocities forced upon an unknown woman, and as bad as she felt for the poor victim, she had a perverse sense of relief that it hadn't been her mother. All of this while lying to a police officer.

She was probably going to hell.

"I'm sorry, Gianni," she said. "I had to improvise."

"It doesn't matter," he said, voice low, hollow. "I got what I needed to."

"I thought it was her," Vinnie said. "Shit."

"What am I missing?" she asked.

"The ring," Vinnie said. "That's not just some trendy jewelry store purchase."

"That's Sal's signet ring. It's been in his family for generations. Maybe hundreds of years." Gianni's voice grew softer. "When I was younger, he said since he had no kids, he'd give it to me when I was old enough."

"What happened?" Jo asked.

"He met Carla."

The pain in Gianni's eyes would have been evident to Jo even if she didn't know him. She had learned over the last few months that his power left him susceptible to emotional triggers more than other people. He turned and started walking away from them, and she started after him.

Vinnie held her back and shook his head. "Yo, G."

Gianni yelled to them over his shoulder, never breaking stride or making eye contact. "Go ahead without me. I'll meet you back at the compound."

"But—" The compound was miles away. And she had so many questions.

"Let him be, Jo." Vinnie's eyes were slightly unfocused, and he had a luminosity about him that wasn't there a moment ago.

"Are you using your strategy power?"

He shook his head slightly and his eyes cleared, focused. His glow diffused, and he looked himself again. "Just for a second. I needed to know what was best for him. Let him walk it off, he'll be fine. The bar isn't that far away, and he needs some time alone to process this."

"The bar?"

"We brought your keys with us. He's going to get your truck."

Oh, right. She hadn't driven home last night. She'd been too busy making an ass of herself. Instead of revisiting the miseries of her drunken excursion, she changed the subject.

"I hate it when you use your power and don't tell anyone."

"Get in the truck, Jo."

He leered at her, giving her a slow once over. She was suddenly aware of her state of undress and hurried to the passenger side of truck, scrambling into it. Vinnie climbed in on the driver's side. Now that she didn't need to be sandwiched against him, he felt too far away.

"Tell me about Carla."

"Fix your clothes. You're distracting me."

Their gazes locked in a silent battle of wills. When Vinnie let his stare drift down, Jo quickly undid his earlier fashion adjustments. His lips quirked and he started the engine.

"Tell me."

"There isn't much to tell." He headed toward the compound at a speed that caused the battered old truck to shimmy. "Carla was Sal's girlfriend. Now she's dead."

"You mean he *murdered* her. And the cops are looking to blame it on you."

"We have no proof of that yet, but yeah, probably."

"But why? And what do we do about it? And—"

"Stop. There is no 'we' in this. The Brothers will handle it."

"But the cops think it's Mama."

"It's not."

"They involved us."

"I involved you to get a look at the photos," he said. "Which I've done. Now you're uninvolved."

"But—"

"No. Your part is done. You have your own job to do, which I am also a part of. And, if I'm not mistaken, you owe everyone an explanation for last night."

"I don't think I ever agreed to that."

"Damn it, Jo. I'm about at the end of my limit with you."

"What are you going to do about it?"

He didn't answer. But she noticed a faint luminescence about him as he continued driving.

4

VINNIE FINALLY HAD time to rest. Gianni wasn't back yet, which of course had Franki freaking out, but he took two minutes to calm her nerves and then asked the sisters to make dinner.

It would keep them busy and give him time to catch a quick nap.

He had trouble relaxing, though, impatient for dinner's end when he'd finally learn what had sent Jo on a bender.

The events of the night before had put them all in danger. He was all for letting off a little steam at a bar, but Jo had nearly blown their cover, blathering on about the Medici and prophecies, powers and daggers. If Little Miss Spray-on Clothes hadn't been so easy to distract, the situation may not have been so easily contained. Jo's scene there, combined with whatever the hell that was at the construction site that afternoon... well, she could be damn sure she'd be coughing up some answers.

And he supposed everyone needed to be brought up to speed on Carla and McGuire. Of course, Jo would try to lead with that. Not going to happen.

Damn, he was beat.

He removed his boots and just left them where they fell. His preference was to sleep naked, but he was too damned tired to undress. Instead, he yanked the covers down and crawled onto his bed, falling face down on the soft black sheets. Eyes closed, he took a deep, relaxing breath and burrowed his head into the pillow.

And immediately snapped his eyes open.

His sheets smelled like her.

Che cazzo? He just wanted to rest, but even in his sanctuary he couldn't find peace. Hints of Jo assaulted his senses. The organic scent of the soap tingled his nose. As he tossed and turned, his hands scraped across the sheets, bringing to mind the feel of her clothing under his fingers when he adjusted her outfit. The black linens on his bed reminded him of how she looked when he found her just that morning, skin glowing, a gorgeous contrast against the dark décor in his room.

Again his body betrayed him, growing aroused merely from the memories whirling through his mind.

Merda, he was losing it. He needed to get some sleep before he did something he regretted. He was her protector, not her lover, and he needed to remember that.

Time to check on the guys. A short text to Nico and he got a quick reply. They were five minutes out. No point in staying in his room if he couldn't sleep. At least he could bring the boys up to speed. He sent them a text telling them to meet him in the gym.

Vinnie took the long way around to the basement door, steering clear of the kitchen. Told himself the detour wasn't to avoid Jo specifically, but rather so he didn't have to talk to any of the women. At least not until he had spoken to his brothers.

Getting some space where Jo was concerned was merely an added bonus.

In the gym, he grabbed three waters and bypassed the sparring room, opting instead to go to the equipment room. He straddled the seat of a padded incline bench and leaned back against it. Because he had a few minutes to kill before Nico and Coz arrived, he called Gianni. He was relieved when he finally got an answer.

"Yeah."

"Just checking in, G."

"It's all good."

"Yeah?"

"I said I'm tight, V."

Vinnie could hear the fight was out of him. His voice was soft, steady. "Franki was worried. I settled things for the time being, but if you don't show soon, she's going to freak again."

"I'm on my way back now. I'll be there in about ten."

He heard his brothers walking down the stairs. "All right. Listen, the boys just got here. We're meeting in the gym, but we'll wait for you."

"Go ahead and catch them up. Traffic's light. I can probably make it in five."

Vinnie heard the truck accelerating before Gianni disconnected the call. There was no point in telling him not to rush. Gianni was as much a speed freak as Vinnie was, so slow was never an option. In general, he was an excellent driver, but he was used to high-end sports cars that cornered like they were on rails, not mammoth trucks with loose construction supplies in the bed. Vinnie tried not to think about it, tried to focus on his brother's abilities behind the wheel.

Didn't matter. Vinnie resigned himself to worrying until Gianni arrived safely. It was a sign of his exhaustion that he couldn't trust Gianni and shrug the anxiety off. He wondered vaguely if he was going to crack a molar from clenching his jaw so damn tight and forced it open to drink some water.

Nico and Coz chose seats on other equipment benches and Vinnie threw them each a bottle.

"I see you took the most comfortable bench." Coz gestured to Vinnie on the incline bench.

"I was here first."

"Where's Gianni?"

"On his way. Told me to fill you in on our part while we waited for him."

Coz snorted.

"What?"

"At least you have a part."

"That place was like Fort fucking Knox," Nico said. "Who knew a morgue would have so damn many people around in the middle of the day? We kicked around a few ideas but finally decided not to risk it. We'll just go back tonight when the graveyard shift is on duty. It'll be easier to breach when there's a skeleton crew there."

"No need," Vinnie said. "We know who it is. We saw the photos. It's Carla."

"Carla?" Coz said. "Carla who?"

"Carla Raffaelli?" Nico said. "Sal's Carla?"

"You know it. We saw it with our own eyes. Shook G up."

"He spent a lot of time with her," Nico said.

"I think it was more than that. He needed to take off for a while."

"Then what?" Coz asked.

"And where'd he go?" Nico asked.

Someone cleared his throat in the doorway, and Vinnie looked up to see Gianni standing there. "You made good time. Any trouble?"

"Not really. After I cleared my head, I needed to retrieve the information Carla left me."

Vinnie assessed him. His brother seemed calm, more in control than when they separated earlier that day. He held in his sigh of relief. Then Nico and Coz exchanged a glance. Not wanting to discuss his edginess, he changed the subject.

"So, what did Carla leave you?"

Gianni grabbed his own water bottle, cocked a brow at Vinnie's choice seat, and looked around for the remaining places to sit. He chose to stretch out on the floor mats, resting his arm over his eyes.

"G?"

He sighed, then spoke in a hollow voice, leaving his face covered. "Remember a few years back when I spent the summer here in Pennsylvania with Sal?"

"Remember it?" Vinnie said. "Shit. I hated that summer. Every time we did partner drills, I was stuck with Dante Tosto."

"Man, I forgot all about that prick," Coz said.

"Wish I could."

"Anyway," Gianni went on, "that summer, I got to know Carla pretty well. She was really nice. They were both into each other, but I got the sense she was more invested than Sal was."

"He had to have been pretty taken with her if he gave her his family ring," Vinnie said. "She had to mean something to him. Especially since he promised it to you."

"What are you talking about?" Nico asked. "What ring?"

"His signet," Vinnie said. "That's how we recognized Carla in the photographs. The body is in pretty bad shape, but the ring sealed it. Sal had promised it to Gianni since he didn't have kids, but then he gave it to Carla."

"For all I know, he still has it promised to me in his will. Or he had more than one ring. Maybe it's a replica. Hell, I don't know. Maybe it did mean something to him that he gave it to her. Or maybe it was just his way of putting her off. He gave her his signet ring when what she really wanted was an engagement ring."

"That's not unreasonable," Nico said. "I'm sure she expected to marry him. They were inseparable for years. He brought her everywhere."

"Except to the altar," Vinnie said. "That had to sting."

Gianni snorted. Vinnie sensed there was more to his reaction than just this surface conversation. He'd pick at that scab later.

"What's this have to do with where you were today?" Nico asked.

"That summer, Sal was kind of off. God." He tensed for a minute, then relaxed again. "I wish I'd seen it, done more. We might have prevented all this."

"What are you talking about?" Coz leaned forward, resting his elbows on his knees.

"He used to let me go with him on jobs, but that summer he kept me distant. I didn't even spend much time with Rico, Marcus, or Paolo when they were around. Sal isolated me. A lot. That's why I spent so much time with Carla. She was the only person he let me see regularly. I think she knew something wasn't right, too."

Gianni had stopped talking, and Vinnie was getting anxious. "Why?"

After a long pause, he continued. "One evening, we were sitting in Carla's backyard after dinner. We'd had several bottles of wine, and she was playing some Rat Pack music. Sal was spinning her around the patio, dipping and weaving all over the place. We were all laughing and enjoying ourselves. Then his phone rang, and he sobered up real quick. He passed Carla to me to dance with and went inside to take the call. While Carla and I stumbled around, she pulled close to me and said something I found really weird at the time. She said she loved me like a son, and if something happened to her, she wanted me to dig up her fig tree and transplant it at my home. Said it was her most treasured possession and she wanted me to have it, but I had to do the work myself. I asked her why. If it was so special, wouldn't she want to give it to Sal? But she was adamant it go to me. She said, 'Dig it up, Giovanni.' I mean, it was a fucking tree. Like I cared, right? Then Sal came out. She put her finger to my lips and said, 'Shh,' and immediately changed the subject."

"She must have been really wasted," Coz said.

"That's kind of what I figured at the time. I'm surprised I even remembered that conversation. But today, after I saw what happened to her, the memory just kind of hit me. I thought maybe there was more to it than a drunken request. So I went to her house and dug up the fig tree."

"What?" Nico asked. "Are you fucking crazy?"

"In broad daylight?" Coz said. "With Sal MIA?"

"What'd you find?"

Everyone looked at Vinnie. Even Gianni moved his arms from his eyes and sat up for the first time since he crashed on the mat.

"How did you know I found something?"

"Well, there really wouldn't be any point to this story if you hadn't."

"You aren't going to fucking believe it."

JO CHOPPED PEPPERS like they had personally wronged her. The *thwack, thwack* of the knife on the cutting board echoed through the kitchen, slicing through the conversations her sisters were having. Finally, they stopped talking, stopped working, and stared at her. When she noticed all activity had ground to a halt around her, she paused, knife poised to strike the offending vegetable. "What?"

"That's what we'd like to know," Toni said.

"Why are you mutilating our dinner?" Donni asked.

"Yeah," Franki said. "If we mess it up, we're going to have to pay to have food delivered and clean up."

"The guys are on cleanup," Jo said. "Vinnie promised."

"Not if we don't follow through on our end," Toni said. "Remember when Coz and Nico were deep frying wings and burnt them? They both bought dinner and cleaned up. The precedent's been set."

"Fine. I'll be more careful."

"Why don't you just tell us what's wrong so you aren't mad anymore?"

She really hated how Franki cut right to the core of the problem all the time. Sometimes a problem needed to be approached from the side. Or the back. Or avoided all together.

"I almost forgot! I'm supposed to call Chuck and get tomorrow's schedule worked out." She put down the knife and left the room.

"You can run, but you can't hide!" Franki called after her. "We have all night!"

The den afforded her the most privacy at the moment. "Chuck," she said into the phone. "How are things at the site?"

"None of the subs will be done today. Assuming everyone hits their targets tomorrow, we should be ready for inspections day after. If things look good by lunchtime, I'll make the calls and get the inspectors set. Just make my life easier and stay home. There's no reason for you to come in for a few days. I'll stay on top of everything. Boss."

She smiled a little at him adding her title like it was an insult or an afterthought. She knew it was neither. He cared for her. But she couldn't let him deal with Enzo Palmeri on his own, even though for Chuck it wouldn't be a hardship. That was a problem she had to face on her own. "We'll see what tomorrow brings. Thanks for handling all the details. Call me if anything comes up, okay?"

"So does that mean you won't be in?"

"It means you're opening the site. Talk to you tomorrow." She disconnected before she had to listen to more than a syllable of his swearing.

The smell of peppers and onions wafting out of the kitchen assured her dinner was well in hand. She ran her hand through her hair. The thought of facing the Italian Inquisition was more than she could bear at the moment, so the kitchen was out. They guys were probably hunkered down in the office, going over surveillance or something. She wasn't tired, so she didn't want to hide in her room—particularly if that was where Franki had stashed Catherine de' Medici's mirror. What she really needed was to burn off some steam. She took the long way around, bypassing the kitchen, and headed down the basement stairs toward the gym.

At the bottom of the steps, she rounded the corner and smacked into Nico.

"Sorry, didn't see you there," he said.

"No worries."

"Hey, Jo," Coz said.

"Jo," Gianni said.

She hadn't realized they were down there. If they hadn't been heading out, she'd have turned and gone back up the way she came. She and Nico began the ridiculous dance of moving the same direction as each other a few times before he grabbed her by the forearms and moved her aside. "'Cuse us," he said, and they all filed up the steps past her.

She grabbed a bottle of water out of the refrigerator and headed for the sparring room. Time alone with the kicking bag sounded like just what she needed. When she stopped outside the door, she found it unusually dark in there. Normally, at least the low wattage lights were kept on so people could see where they were going, but someone had turned all the lights off. No matter. She'd been training there for so long, she knew where the controls were on the wall. Stepping into the room, she flipped all the switches.

"*Che cazzo!* Didn't I tell you I wanted to be left alone?"

Vinnie sat up quickly, but she hadn't missed the huge bulge in his pants between his legs. He didn't seem to be doing anything about it when she walked in, but maybe he just hadn't gotten to it yet.

"Oh. Jo. Jo? What are you doing here? You're supposed to be—I'm sorry. Of course you can…" He let his thoughts trail off, and he cleared his throat. He rubbed his eyes with one hand, the other he hurriedly put in his lap to shield it from her view. After he yawned, he continued. "Let me start over. I'm sorry I yelled. I thought you were the guys. They knew I was trying to get some sleep down here, and I was irritated they interrupted. I realize you weren't aware of that, though."

She stood and stared at him, unable to get that initial image out of her mind.

"Do you need me?" he asked.

Well, wasn't *that* an interesting question?

Her mouth was suddenly quite dry. She wasn't sure she could speak without her voice cracking. When she did, she sounded much huskier than she usually did. "Bed."

His eyebrows shot up as much as his voice. "Excuse me?"

It was her turn to clear her throat. "I mean, your bed… what's wrong with it? Why aren't you in it? It's not because of me, is it?"

He looked at her in a way that she couldn't really read. Although she was fully covered, she felt like he was seeing her half-dressed like she was earlier that day, or maybe even more exposed.

She fought the urge to fidget.

"No. It's not you. It's me." He stifled a yawn. "We were meeting down here, and I was just too tired to go upstairs. But if you want to use the room, I'll get out of your hair."

Watching him twist to stand while trying to keep himself covered amused her. Distracted her for a moment. Then she snapped to her senses, planned on telling him she'd just go. Before she found the words, he pushed to his feet.

Vinnie was so tired, he weaved and kind of lunged. She rushed toward him, reached out to catch him, and they interlocked in a tangle of limbs and compressed torsos. She felt his arousal brush against her abdomen.

He hissed.

Instantly, her body charged to life. Pinpricks of energy danced everywhere his body touched hers, pooled low in her core. Desire betrayed reason, tightening every cell of her flesh, right down to the tips of her breasts as they brushed against his chest.

She looked up at him, he down at her, and their gazes locked. The fires she saw in his eyes earlier smoldered, merely burning embers, his eyes darkening. Their breaths mingled, and she grew lightheaded.

"I've been thinking about this all day." He nuzzled her nose with his own. She gripped his arms tighter, not sure if she held him up or he her. Breaking eye contact, he dipped his head and murmured in her ear. "Once, just to get it out of my system."

His breath was hot, his teeth scraped her earlobe, and the sensations sent electricity racing through her.

Her nails dug into his arms, and she tipped her head back to give him better access. He tormented her with nothing but feather-light kisses, the teasing pummeled her into submission.

His lips skimmed her jaw line, breath warming her flesh and heating her blood. She lifted her head slowly back toward him, guiding his path. He nipped her lower lip.

No one had ever done that to her before. The sensation shot through her and stoked the fires he'd already ignited. She gasped at the feeling, and as she took in air, she took in his tongue. He let go of her arms and dropped his hands to her waist, pulling her even tighter against him.

His body molded to hers, fused them together. Jo threaded her hands in his hair.

Wrapped those soft sable strands between her fingers and pulled him deeper into the kiss. Someone groaned. Him? Her? It didn't matter.

One of his hands reached up to cradle her back while the other slid down to caress her backside. Another jolt of electricity surged through her, and her eyes snapped open.

My God! What was she doing, acting like the *puttana* she dressed as earlier that day? Blood running cold, she dropped her hands and pushed herself back from Vinnie, severing the kiss before it evolved to its natural conclusion.

"Do you care to explain that?" he asked.

"Do you?" She knew he meant her changing her mind, but she preferred to focus on him starting the kiss to begin with.

He stood there, still aroused, and not bothering to hide it. Before either spoke again, Franki yelled down the stairs, "Dinner!"

"I didn't eat much today. I'm ravenous." Jo bolted up the stairs, knowing full well he'd catch her in her lie. Her appetite was completely gone. She couldn't fathom how she'd take a single bite.

But by the look that had been on Vinnie's face, she knew he was hungry. And she didn't think it was for food.

THEY HAD HOT sausage sandwiches for dinner. Vinnie managed to seat himself directly across from Jo. She couldn't look more miserable if she was getting a root canal.

What was he thinking, just one kiss? Who gets over any obsession with one kiss? Everyone knows if you can't swim, you stay out of the water or you drown. He should have stayed the fuck out of the water. Because now he was pretty damn sure he was in over his head. And sinking fast.

He watched her pick tiny pieces of bread off her roll and nibble at them. Ravenous, his ass. She hadn't taken an actual bite of anything since they'd sat down. And God help him if she did. If he had to look at her while she put a link of sausage in her mouth, he might blow a load at the table.

Maybe he should take G up on his offer and bug out for a few days. Blow off some steam somewhere. If he did, maybe he could get her out of his system before it was too late.

She looked up then and caught him staring at her. Keeping her gaze locked on his, she picked up her sandwich. As though reading his thoughts, she opened her mouth and took a slow, languorous bite, licking her lips as the juices ran down her chin.

Witch.

She smiled and chewed. With vigor.

He shifted in his seat, his pants uncomfortably tight.

No, he wasn't going anywhere. But he was getting to the bottom of her behavior at the bar the night before.

"While we're all here and because this isn't official Brotherhood business," he said, "I thought we should discuss what happened last night."

Jo almost choked on her sandwich. "I thought we were going to talk about that after dinner."

"That time is reserved for Brotherhood business. Last night wasn't Brotherhood business. So I figured we should get it out of the way. We have a lot of actual business to discuss tonight, so we might as well put this behind us."

"But we have a no-business-over-dinner rule," she said.

"Again, that's not business."

"But it's my business."

"You're not getting out of it. You owe us an explanation. Especially me, since I have to cover your ass every damn day." His mind immediately went to how he covered her ass earlier that night. Hers must have too, because she turned a violent shade of red and couldn't look at him.

"I don't see why I have to share personal business for you to do your job."

"You don't have personal business until this is over. Don't you get that?"

"I can't live in a bubble for the rest of my life!"

"Where is this coming from? How is this any different from last week? Or last month?"

"Just because it's not different doesn't mean it's not insufferable."

"Do you all feel this way?" Vinnie glanced at all the girls sitting around the table.

"I know you're protecting us, so I can wait this out," Donni said.

"It'll be worth it in the long run," Toni said.

"It doesn't bother me." Franki smiled at Gianni and grabbed his hand.

"Of course it doesn't bother you," Jo said. "The two of you are about a cell away from fusing together into one organism. Tell you what. Since it's so important that my dirty laundry be aired, you do it. You tell Gianni my deepest, darkest secret, and he can share it with the group. Then the two of you will have another anniversary to celebrate—the day you broke my heart." She stood and dashed away from the table.

"Jo, wait." Franki hurried after her.

"We're not that bad," Gianni said. "We don't celebrate everything."

"Yeah," Coz said, "you do."

Vinnie got up and followed Franki and Jo.

Jo flung open her bedroom door, and Franki and Vinnie followed her in.

"You might pull that shit on a room full of people," Franki said, "but you aren't pulling it on me. Spill."

Jo looked at Vinnie, but didn't say anything. Tears welled in her eyes.

Franki turned to him. "I'll get it out of her faster if you just go."

"No." His heart broke for her. He wanted to kick someone's ass and pull her into his arms. He didn't know who to go after, and he knew she didn't want his comfort, so he stood there, impotent to help. "It's time she learned to open up to me, too. We need to know this. You're her sister. I'm her guardian."

He turned to Jo. "It's just us, Jo. You're safe here. What's going on?"

She looked back and forth between the two of them, then she threw herself into his arms and sobbed. He held her tightly and rocked with her, crooning softly in her ear and stroking her hair. Over her head, he met Franki's gaze. She looked as puzzled as he felt.

He guided Jo over to the bed and sat with her. The room used to be Mike's. When the sisters had first moved in, Jo and Franki had shared Gianni's room, and Gianni had shared with Vinnie. Once Gianni and Franki hooked up, it became obvious to everyone that they wanted to bunk together. They kept sneaking off to be alone, and people—unfortunately for all parties involved—kept finding them together in the oddest and most uncomfortable of places.

In light of those awkward meetings, Mike gave up his room to Jo, and Franki and Gianni moved back into Gianni's room. Mike didn't really need a room. He'd finally revealed his astral projection and teleportation powers, so the ruse of staying there had become unnecessary.

Jo hadn't really had a chance to personalize the room yet. It still only had a bed, dresser, and chair in it. Donni yearned to customize it, but Jo wouldn't even let her in the door, so the room remained sparsely furnished and undeco-rated. The midnight blue linens matched the chair and the roman shades. Hell, they obviously matched Jo's mood at the moment. But it was way too dull a room for such a usually vibrant woman.

Vinnie cradled her against his chest until she was cried out, then he tipped her chin up and looked into her eyes. "What's the problem, *bella*?"

"Not what. Who." She looked at Franki then buried her head in Vinnie's chest. "Enzo Palmeri."

5

JO COULDN'T BELIEVE she had basically crawled into Vinnie's lap, but at the moment, she sought strength and couldn't think of anyone better to offer it than him. He gave it to her in calming whispers, soothing caresses. Strong arms enveloping her, protecting her from her demons. A solid, steady heartbeat telling her all would be okay.

She gained enough support from him to utter the two words that haunted her for nearly a decade of her life. Enzo Palmeri. Her sister would have to tell Vinnie the rest—after the obligatory tirade. There was nothing more she could say. She buried her head back into his chest, prepared to ride out the wave of Franki's wrath.

Vinnie's fingers found the underside of her chin and tipped her head up. The overhead light shone too brightly for her tender vision, and she squinted at him. He was backlit—his face fully shadowed, dark like her mood but infinitely more dangerous. "Where do I find him?"

"Vinnie," Franki said.

Jo collapsed back onto him, relieved at not having to speak.

"You don't understand. This goes all the way back to high school. She's just reliving history."

"No. You don't understand, Franki. If it's a problem for her now, then it's a problem for us. I'll deal with it."

"It's nothing you can deal with."

"I guess I won't know that until someone tells me."

"It's not my story to tell."

Jo stayed quiet.

"Well, if she's not talking and you're not talking, I guess I'm off to find Palmeri. I'm sure one way or another I can get him to talk."

He stood, lifted Jo in his arms, and placed her gently on the bed. She curled into a fetal position. Her attention never left their conversation, but she wasn't sure if she should intervene. Wasn't sure if she wanted to. Maybe she was about to get justice for how she was wronged all those years ago.

"Vinnie," Franki said. "Please. We don't even know what set her off this time. Sometimes she just has these episodes. She'll get over it."

"I know what set her off. There's a Palmeri Plumbing working at the site. She's obviously been in touch with the guy. Does that change your mind about telling me anything?"

Jo moaned as she tried to decide what to do.

"I'm leaving." He headed for the door.

"Jo." Franki's anguish was palpable.

"Wait," Jo said.

Vinnie turned around.

"She can tell you."

"No," he said. "It's your story. You tell me."

"I can't," she whispered. "It's humiliating."

"Vinnie, listen," Franki said, "when Jo—"

"Stop. Would you mind leaving us alone please? Jo and I need to talk."

Jo met his gaze for the first time since she was in his arms. Then she quickly looked away. She knew she couldn't deny him anything he asked if she looked into those dark, penetrating eyes, and she wasn't ready to make a full confession.

"If you need me, I'll be right outside." Franki squeezed her hand and left the room, closing the door behind her.

He sat on the edge of the bed and remained silent for a long while.

When she couldn't stand it any longer, she asked, "What are you waiting for?"

"You."

She turned to look at him.

"There. That's better." She started to roll away again, but he stopped her. "Josephina." His tone was firm, and she looked at him again.

"You sound like my father."

"Believe me, I don't have any fatherly intentions toward you."

She felt the heat flush her face, felt it intensify when he smirked.

"None of that now. You have a story to tell me."

All the blood that had just rushed to her face drained away just as quickly. Her hands felt cold, and she rubbed them together before they began shaking.

He drew the blanket up and tucked it around her. "You're giving this memory power over you. Tell me what happened, and then let it go."

She closed her eyes and snuggled into the pillow and the covers, content to let it all melt away. But Vinnie wouldn't let it go. Maybe he was right and it was time she did.

"I was sixteen." Her voice sounded weak and far away, even to her own ears, but if she stopped to analyze it, she'd never finish the story. "Franki was going to Louie Sardone's start-of-summer party. His parents were away, so it was supposed to be the biggest bash of the year. I begged her to let me go with her. She finally agreed.

"They collected keys at the door. He didn't want anyone being irresponsible." She let out a mirthless laugh. "Irresponsible," she said under her breath. "They also collected cell phones. Louie's dad was a cop, and any photos of the party made public could ruin his dad's reputation. I didn't have a problem with it at the time. Seemed logical. Who knew I'd need my phone to…." Her voice trailed off while she relived some memory.

Vinnie rubbed her arm, brought her attention back to him.

"Anyway," she continued, "Franki and I got separated, and I got loaded. I mean, really trashed. I went room to room looking for her, and I ended up in a guest bedroom. Louie's mom was a photographer, and she had a collection of old cameras in there. She had one of those real old ones that you stuck your head under the cover to use, and she had some of the kind our grandparents had with the lens caps that you didn't know you left on. She even had a few Polaroid cameras sitting around. Enzo walked in, and I grabbed a Polaroid and took his picture. I had a huge crush on him then."

She got quiet for a minute.

"Then what?" he prompted.

"I asked him if he'd seen Franki, but he hadn't. I told him I didn't feel well and I needed her. God, if only I'd had my phone to call her." She closed her eyes and took a deep breath.

"And?"

"And that was the last thing I remembered. Until school that Monday."

She was quiet again. This time he waited for her. The memories almost silenced her completely, but she battled past them, knowing Vinnie was right and she had to face her fears.

"I passed out." Her voice grew quieter. "While I was out of it, Enzo undressed me and used the Polaroid to take photos of me. Shared them with everyone. By the time Monday rolled around, the whole school had seen them. Franki, being a graduating senior, wasn't in school anymore, so I didn't even have her to help me deal with the fallout. It was me against Enzo and the photos, the rumors, and the whole school."

"When you were passed out, did he..."

"No. There was no evidence to suggest that. I don't know how much groping there was, but he didn't—he didn't do that. It didn't matter, though. Everyone believed he did."

She heard him cracking his knuckles and felt his weight leave the bed. Opening her eyes to take a peek, she saw him pacing and running a hand through his hair, his jaw muscle ticking a staccato beat. She decided telling him the rest of the story at that minute probably wouldn't be the best of ideas, so she skipped ahead to present day.

"Anyway, he keeps wanting to talk to me. I really don't want to have anything to do with him. He had me cornered earlier, but Chuck had run him off before you got there. He helped me through high school, too. He's a good friend."

"I'll have to give him my apologies for any misunderstandings, then. Apparently he was doing my job."

"I thought your job was to protect me from death threats from Italy."

"My job is to protect you. Period."

She sat up. He crossed to her, sat, and drew her into his arms. God, he smelled like the forest after a spring rain—fresh, alive with promise. She took a deep breath and allowed him to just hold her for a minute, feeling protected and safe.

He pushed her back and looked down into her eyes. "I'll go deal with him and this will be over."

"Vinnie, no. The damage was done a long time ago. And he'll only be working for us one more day."

"Let me do this for you."

Her family had wanted to help. Chuck had wanted to help. No one had ever asked like that before. Or was he telling her?

"Stay here. When I get back, we'll have the Brotherhood meeting."

"At least let me come with you. You know, for closure."

He looked at her for a minute, then extended his hand.

VINNIE THOUGHT THE easiest way to reach the bastard was for Jo to text him to meet at the job site. The pervert would probably cream himself on the way, but there was no way he'd turn down an invitation from her if he was still harassing her all these years after high school.

He couldn't imagine the embarrassment she had endured in school. Or all the years since, every time she bumped into someone who had seen the photos. The fact that she occasionally worked with the asshole really steamed him. He didn't know how she tolerated it.

They arrived at the site before Palmeri. Vinnie let go of the wheel and cracked his knuckles. He'd been gripping the wheel so tightly, his hands hurt.

Flexing his fingers to get blood flowing in them again, he turned to look at Jo. Her eyes were wide, and her skin was even paler than usual. "Hey. You okay?"

"I thought I wanted this, but now I think I just want to go."

"You need this."

"I don't need you in jail for assault. Or worse."

Could she see the murder he felt coursing through his blood? She deserved to be avenged. No woman deserved to be treated the way she'd been treated. But he knew not to cross the line. He would restrain himself. For her sake.

"Let's just go, Vinnie. I changed my mind."

"I didn't. Besides, he's here."

The Palmeri Plumbing van pulled up beside their truck, and Enzo jumped out. He was at their driver's side door when he stopped, hand in the air to knock on the window, and realized Jo wasn't alone—Vinnie sat behind the wheel.

Vinnie flung the door open and hit Enzo with it, knocking him backward into the dirt.

"What the h—"

"Wait!" Jo jumped out of the truck. She rushed around to where Vinnie loomed over Enzo.

Vinnie bent down and grabbed Enzo by the shirtfront, other hand cocked back ready to punch.

"What's going on?" Enzo held his hands in front of his face, making no move to go on the offensive.

"Vinnie! No!"

Vinnie paused, unsure what to do. Every cell in his body screamed to exact justice for the young girl that piece of shit had wronged, but in some deep recess of his mind he knew physical violence would only hurt her more. He shook the man but didn't strike.

She began to cry. "Why, Enzo?"

"Why, what?"

"Why did you do that to me? I had such a crush on you, and I was so drunk. I needed help. And instead of helping, you took advantage of me."

"No, Jo. I didn't."

Vinnie lifted him higher, ready to strike him for the lie.

She stepped closer. "How can you say that? The pictures, my clothes…"

"Don't you remember any of it?"

She shook her head, and tears streamed down her face.

He put his hands down to support his weight and looked at Vinnie for permission. Vinnie lowered him slightly to make him a little more comfortable, and he continued his story. "I found you in that room, and you asked about your sister. I told you I'd help you find her, but you got sick. You threw up everywhere. I took you into the bathroom to clean you up, but I didn't know what to do. Remo Linza came in, and I sent him to find your sister. That's when it all went to hell.

"I hosed you off in the shower, but I just made a bigger mess. Then I saw a robe on the back of the door. So I asked you if you cared if we got you out of those wet things and into the robe, and you agreed.

"I stripped you down in the tub—I looked as little as possible, I swear—and then I got you into the robe. I helped you into the bedroom so you could rest while I scrubbed out your clothes. I looked for a blow dryer to dry them, but couldn't find one, so I just spread them out to air dry.

"When I came back in the room, Remo had you naked on the bed and had already taken the photos. He passed them around and told everyone I was with you. People rushed up to see.

"I covered you back up and guarded the door, but everyone thought I was being greedy with you, and it just made things worse. I had a hell of a time keeping other guys out of there. It scared me to think of what they would do to you. I told them they had it wrong, but none of them listened. Everyone was so drunk.

"I didn't know what to do. I figured you'd straighten things out at school Monday morning, but you never did. I thought you must have liked that people thought we were together, so I didn't correct anyone. I had no idea it had actually bothered you until years later."

"People thought I was a common whore! A *puttana*! Why would I like that?"

"I don't know. I thought you liked me."

"I did. Until then."

"After all this time has passed and you were still mad at me, I figured something else had to be wrong. I've been trying to talk to you about it on and off for the last few years, but I can never get you alone."

Vinnie dropped him and looked at Jo. He didn't recognize her expression, but she no longer looked angry or devastated. Did she really believe that load of shit? The story seemed awfully convenient. Too convenient. But she seemed to accept it, no questions.

Maybe that's what she needed to move on. Even if it ate him up on the inside, he'd let her decide how to process it and handle it. He looked at her.

She had stopped sobbing, but tears still pooled in her eyes.

"Enzo, I'm sorry. I've been blaming you for so long, and it wasn't even you."

Oh, hell no. She not only let him off the hook, she took responsibility for it? He stepped forward, but she glared at him.

"Well," Enzo said, "I'm partially to blame. I let it happen."

Partially? Vinnie thought his jaw would break under the strain of his clenched teeth. And still Jo didn't react.

Enzo took out his phone and showed them a picture of a beautiful baby girl. "This is my Serafina. If anyone ever treated her the way you were treated, I'd kill the bastard." He stood in front of Vinnie. "I get why you're so pissed. I've said my peace, cleared the air, so if you still want to…" His voice trailed off, and he closed his eyes.

"Oh, Enzo, no," Jo said. "Don't be ridiculous."

"Are you fucking kidding me?" Vinnie exploded. Rage and disbelief roiled through him in red waves of fury. No way was the guy on the up and up. The slime and the smarm practically oozed out of him. He wanted so badly to bash Enzo's face in, but he needed Jo to want it, too. That wasn't going to happen, though. She'd bought into his lies. Hell, she took the blame on herself. He clenched his fists.

She jumped in front of Vinnie, put her hands on his chest and pushed him back. A human shield. For that piece of garbage. He ran his hands through his hair and stepped back to keep from pushing her aside and killing the guy.

"Go home to your little angel, Enzo," she said over her shoulder, still looking at Vinnie, pleading with her eyes. "We're good."

Enzo ran to her and threw his arms around her. "I'm so sorry, Jo."

Vinnie growled and stepped forward, but she waved him off. Then she returned the hug gingerly. "Go home, Enzo."

"See you tomorrow?"

"Bright and early. I want all my subs done and out by the end of the day."

"Yes, boss."

He smiled and saluted, then ran off to his van.

"Jo," Vinnie said as they made their way more slowly to their truck.

"Let it go, Vinnie."

"But—"

"It's been a long day," she said. "I just want to put it all behind me. Let's go home."

He sighed. Back to avoidance. He'd at least give her that. For the time being, anyway. "Feels like about a week since I slept."

"Let's get back so you can go to bed."

"You sure you don't you want to talk about this?"

"Not now. I need to process it all first."

She held something back, something more than why she'd accepted Enzo's lies, but he had no idea what. She obviously had no intention of telling him. He'd get it out of her, though. And he could think of several methods of persuasion he'd like to try to use to coerce it out of her.

WHEN THEY ARRIVED at the compound, the kitchen was clean and everyone was in the den with various drinks. Jo wanted no part of it, so she headed straight for the stairs.

But Vinnie grabbed her hand and turned her around. "Meeting, remember?"

Of course she did. She'd wanted to forget about it, but clearly he wasn't going to let her. She followed him into the den.

Based on her behavior at dinner, Jo felt obligated to share what had happened, but she dreaded going into all that with everyone, particularly if Franki hadn't gotten the men up to speed. Thankfully, Vinnie spared her.

"Okay, Brotherhood business." Vinnie stretched out on the floor, leaning his back against the sofa and propping his elbow on the ottoman. He took a San Pellegrino off the tray and opened it, the effervescent hiss silencing the room as effectively as a judge's gavel. After a long swallow, he said, "Are the women up to speed about McGuire's latest brilliant idea?"

"You mean calling you in for questioning?" Donni asked. "Yeah."

"It's a good thing he did, though. Right?" Toni said. "Otherwise you wouldn't have learned about the body."

"True," Coz said.

"Our search at the morgue was a bust," Nico said. "We couldn't get in. But Gianni has something."

"With Jo's help, we learned that the body is Sal's girlfriend, Carla Raffaelli."

"How'd Jo help?" Franki asked.

"Never mind." Jo's cheeks burned at the memory. She glanced at Vinnie, who smiled and took a sip of his drink.

He didn't meet her gaze. "It's not germane to the story."

"Anyway," Gianni said, "I remembered something weird Carla had said to me once, so, on a hunch, I went to her place and dug under a fig tree. I found something she left for me."

"Back up," Franki said. "What hunch? What happened? When was this?"

"Again, none of that is important right now, *cara*. What I found is. She buried a box full of stuff and a note for me. Let me read you what this says."

Giovanni,

If you're reading this, then something's happened to me. That makes me sad, not because I'm gone, but because I didn't want to believe that my Salvatore is doing what I think he's doing. But I've seen too much lately to think otherwise. Hopefully you read this before it's too late for you, too, sweetie. For both of you.

Of all his friends, I don't know which ones to trust. Lately, there has been a whole new set of people around. I don't trust any of the new people. He's introduced some of his old friends to the new people, but some of them are completely in the dark about his social circle. I'm pretty sure you're in the dark. Consider this a warning.

I don't know if all the old friends like the new ones. I'm pretty sure the new ones don't like all the old ones.

Giovanni, I'm scared. I hope I didn't hear them correctly, but I'm pretty sure they're planning the death of at least one—if not more—of Sal's old friends. I pray to God I'm wrong. I pray even more it's not at Sal's hands. But the way he's been acting, I just can't be sure.

I've heard him mention Legatus once or twice. I think they have something to do with these new friends. Please get Sal out of that group. He loves you. He'll listen to you. I don't know what he's involved in or who he's involved with, but if anyone can save him, you can.

Please, help him. I beg of you. Because if I'm gone, I clearly wasn't enough. It's on you now.

Carla

They all sat in silence, going over the implications of Carla's final message.

Gianni finally spoke. "I know her letter is a jumbled mess. She drank a lot those last few years. Sounds like she was drunk when she wrote this. Knowing what I know now, I can't say I blame her."

"So how can you believe anything in it?" Franki asked. "How do you even know what the hell it means?"

"It sounds to me like his new friends were from Legatus, and some of his old friends were involved. If we can track down the rest of the Brotherhood from Sal's generation, we might get a lead on Sal and Legatus."

"A jumbled mess?" Vinnie said. "That's like saying my room is a 'tad' disorganized. That letter reads like a damn Dr. Seuss rhyme. Old friends, new friends, cold friends, blue friends. I'm not sure she's reliable."

"Yeah, man," Coz said. "If Vin can recognize that it doesn't make sense, then you know it's a garbled mess."

Vinnie whipped a peanut at his head. After it bounced off his temple, Coz laughed, picked it up, and ate it.

"Still," Nico said, "she's all we have to go on now. What do you guys think? Is she the death they were planning?"

"No," Jo said. "Papa. They were planning Papa's death. She heard too much. She knew too much. That's why he killed her, too."

Franki, already sitting beside Gianni, curled into his side. The twins hugged each other. Jo, sitting in an overstuffed chair by the unlit fireplace, looked across the room at Vinnie. She wanted nothing more than to cross to him and nestle into his arms, but that wasn't appropriate. She was alone, and as always, had to stay that way. Instead, she chewed on her lip and gripped the arm of the chair. Vinnie's leg twitched, as though he was going to stand up, but then he relaxed back against the sofa again.

"I'll double my efforts to find the rest of the old Brotherhood," Nico said. "I'm just not sure where else to look. Anyone have any ideas?"

"Maybe Mike will actually tell us," Coz said.

Vinnie snorted. "He's the one who hid their trails from us to begin with. Don't count on it."

"Maybe this'll help," Gianni said. He tossed a paisley address book to Nico. "We talked about it earlier, but I wanted the girls to see it before I gave it to you. It was in the box Carla buried."

"She's got all the Brothers in here," Nico said, leafing through the book. "Us, Sal's generation, even the generation before them."

"Anything on Legatus?" Vinnie asked.

"I don't know. I don't know who's in it. But there are names I don't know."

"We'll need to give this to Mike," Gianni said.

"After the girls look at it, and I scan it in," Nico said.

"Of course," Mike said.

Everyone turned to see Mike standing in the doorway. "Dominico, once again I seem to have surprised you."

"This time you didn't use the damn door. I don't think anyone else is just going to pop the hell into a room."

Mike chuckled. "Ladies. It is good to see you again, although I am sorry it is under these circumstances. Gentlemen, I think it best if we adjourn to chamber. Giovanni, please bring the box you found at Carla's residence."

"Excuse me, Mike?" Jo said.

"Yes, Josephina."

"We'd like to come too."

"Pardon me?"

"Well…" Jo glanced around the room.

Everyone but Vinnie looked at her—some had wide eyes, others had open mouths. Vinnie, however, stared at a fixed space on the wall, his hand behind his back where he'd tucked his dagger into his waistband. His skin had taken on the slight luminescent hue she'd come to recognize as his glow when using his power.

She squared her shoulders and continued her discussion with Mike. "We've been living here for a while now, and we never get to be a part of the chamber stuff. It impacts us, too. We've never even seen that room."

"Chamber is for Brotherhood business."

"We're Brotherhood business. And you said no more secrets."

"This is not a matter of secrets. It is a matter of tradition. They will tell you what you need to know."

Vinnie adjusted his shirt in a way that reminded Jo of their trip to the police station that day. She wasn't sure what she'd gain from revisiting that, but she trusted his power. Or his judgment. Or both.

"I've had a rough day. I had to see pictures of a dead woman today. That could have been my mother. Speaking of which—"

Mike held up his hand, silencing her. "Come, Josephina. Ladies. You may join us in chamber this evening."

She scrambled to her feet and met Vinnie's gaze. Before she could smile her thanks, his glow dissipated, and he headed out of the room.

AT THE BOTTOM of the basement stairs, Mike fiddled with five hooks on the wall until a panel slid open, revealing a secret room beyond. Jo tried to see what Mike did, but he blocked her view. It wasn't that she thought she'd need to get in the room without anyone granting her access. She was certain she could get someone to let her in if she really wanted to return.

No, her interest was in the mechanism that released the panel. Franki was designing MDH's new facility in Italy, and Jo was working closely with her sister because she had to figure out the mechanics behind making the secret access panel work. The technology fascinated her, but the room Franki designed hadn't made an impression on her. She thought of it as any other room.

But then she stepped inside the room Mike opened, and all concerns about the device's construction ceased. She could do nothing buy appreciate her surroundings.

The room stole her breath.

Despite being relatively new, it felt centuries old. Candles stood on ancient iron stands and had what looked like years of drips trailing down them. The room smelled of beeswax and old parchment, and Gianni lit the candles with a mere nod of his head, a gift he'd gleaned from the alchemical powers bestowed on him from his red marble dagger.

Candlelight flickered and bounced off a glass-encased parchment in the corner, lending a warm glow to everything in the room, softly illuminating shelves of ancient leather tomes and scrolls and a gorgeous pentagon-shaped walnut table centered in the room. Inlayed in the table was a star whose points were of five different colored marble slabs—red, white, green, black, and gold, each with a groove for a dagger chiseled out of it. The men each stood by the point of the star corresponding to the color dagger they wielded. The women filed into the room and stood near the glass case.

Mike turned around to face the shelves and pulled on a copy of Machiavelli's *Il Principe*. The door to the room slid closed without a sound. He took his dagger out of its sheath and looked around. All the brothers but Vinnie took theirs out, as well.

"Do we have to do the ritual?" Vinnie said. "We have guests."

"They wanted to see what chamber is like. This is what chamber is like. We will do the full ritual. It is through rituals, after all, that your powers came to be."

"Fine." He yanked his dagger free and gripped it so hard his knuckles turned white.

Between that and the scowl on his face, Jo realized he disagreed with Mike's decision.

"Brotherhood of the Stone, how say you?" Mike said.

Gianni placed his red marble dagger in the groove on the red marble inlay of the star. "Brother of the Red Marble. Here do I serve. Passion, blood, vengeance."

Mike said, "Welcome Brother of the Red Marble. Here you will serve. Passion, blood, vengeance."

Vinnie sighed and placed his white dagger in his groove on the table. "Brother of the White Marble. Here do I serve. Purity, clarity, beginnings."

Mike answered, "Welcome Brother of the White Marble. Here you will serve. Purity, clarity, beginnings."

Nico, at the green star point, placed his marble dagger in the groove. "Brother of the Green Marble. Here do I serve. Life, balance, transformation."

"Welcome Brother of the Green Marble. Here you will serve. Life, balance, transformation."

Coz, by the black point, fit his dagger into the groove on the table. "Brother of the Black Marble. Here do I serve. Resilience, protection, potential."

"Welcome Brother of the Black Marble. Here you will serve. Resilience, protection, potential."

Mike, last to go, placed his gold marble dagger in its groove on the gold point of the star. "Protector and Benefactor."

The men said together, "Welcome, Protector and Benefactor of the Order."

"Concentration, honesty, defense."

"Concentration, honesty, defense," they replied.

"As they need."

"So we will serve," the Brothers said in unison.

"Take your seats," Mike said.

While the guys argued with Mike about whether the men should sit or the women, Jo stood, riveted. Vinnie squirmed, obviously uncomfortable with the ritualistic aspect of chamber. But it fascinated her. She could, for the first time, see where the power came from in the marble daggers.

While the debate continued over who should sit—the men for ritual's sake or the women for manners—she turned her attention to the glass case.

"Is this the prophecy?"

The room fell silent.

"Yes, Josephina. That is what began your odyssey."

She had heard it before, but seeing the words made it somehow more real. She read it aloud.

> *In the twilight hours, starshine glows*
> *as merely tiny embers in the black*
> *Its magnificence to only grow brighter*
> *while the midnight hour forces daylight back*
>
> *And though the starlight twinkles on in ink*
> *Its purpose not to shine but just to guide*
> *The branches of the tree will bloom new buds*
> *Growing evermore o'er the divide*
>
> *As long as just one leaf in bud or bloom*
> *On the boughs continues not to fade*
> *Starlight will shine in watch over the branch*
> *And guard the new green, always at its aid*
>
> *The light divines the stones to always shield*
> *And not until the end their duty yield*

"Why's it in English?" Jo asked.

"Pardon me?" Mike said.

"Well, if Michelangelo wrote it, shouldn't it be in Italian?"

"Ah," he said. "I see your confusion. Just as we conduct our ritual in English here because we are in America, the prophecy was written in English because it was about Americans."

"Michelangelo knew English?"

"He is an alchemical master. He created the philosopher's stone to defy death. He created these daggers, imbued them with supernatural powers, and bestowed them upon the men who wield them. Do you not think him capable of learning a simple language?"

"How did he know all this was going to happen?"

"He knows much, my dear Josephina."

"Does he know what's going to happen to us? And to Mama? Did he know what was going to happen to Papa?"

Mike sighed, crossed to Jo, and took her hand. "He knows many things, dear one, but he does not know everything."

"I need to know what he does know. All of it."

6

VINNIE HAD TO hand it to her. For a woman, she sure had a pair.

Even they never pushed Mike like that. Well, almost never. And he certainly wouldn't react as politely as he did to Jo's insistence.

"You have been afforded the protection of Michelangelo's warriors. You live in our residence. You have been granted access to our private inner sanctum, something never before granted to another Medici descendant. I believe I have been more than generous, more than fair."

"I never said you weren't generous, but I'm not sure you have been fair."

Mike's dagger twitched on the table.

Surely Mike wouldn't do anything to harm the very people they were there to protect? Of course, he wasn't beyond teaching someone, anyone, a lesson. Vinnie wasn't sure if he should step in or let her continue. She flung off Mike's hand and stepped forward.

Vinnie looked around the room. Everyone seemed as surprised as he felt. His star point put Mike between him and Jo. He was in no position to help her if she needed it. Without breaking rank, he was helpless to come to her aid, and if he left his spot at the table, Mike's wrath could be incalculable. Any action Vinnie took could only make matters worse for her. Vinnie slowly inched his hand toward his dagger, hoping to get a flash from it—even a glimmer of a strategy toward diffusing the situation.

"You cannot possibly understand the gravity of the situation. As usual, no one has been following international news. You have no idea of the instability in Italy. You are no closer to determining Salvatore's whereabouts, yet you insist on going to your places of work every day, placing yourself in untold jeopardy. These men are not just warriors. They are assets to me, Miss Notaro. And they have value to my company apart from the Brotherhood."

"You talk about them like they're numbers on a spreadsheet. They're people, Mike. They have value to us as human beings."

"And you think I do not see their value? I, who have known them far longer than you?"

Vinnie saw Mike's dagger twitch again. He was getting no ideas from his own dagger, other than the desperate sense that he needed to do something to cool them off, and quickly. But he already knew that.

"I knew them since they were young. I brought them out of that orphanage, took them under my care, watched them grow." He stepped closer to her with each sentence. "I gave them purpose and a sense of belonging. It was *I* who—" He stopped and looked up, wiping his cheek with an irritated flick of his hand.

"What?" Jo asked.

He shook his head. "Not in chamber," he muttered. A fat drop of water plopped on his face, and he swiped it off with his knuckle.

Vinnie had to strain to hear him, but he didn't miss the slow but steady leak from the ceiling.

"Mike?" Jo said.

"Josephina, I am sorry for my outburst. It was uncalled for. Just because I am concerned for the well-being of my men and, consequently you and your sisters, does not give me the right to berate you for your curiosity or lack of understanding. I hope you can accept my fullest apologies. Right now, however, we must hurry. I fear we are having a plumbing problem and if these pipes burst, many of the treasures here will be ruined or lost to us. We must adjourn this meeting and clear out this room."

"End the meeting if you have to," Jo said, looking up at the coffered ceiling tiles, "but I can probably fix your leak."

"For that, I would be most appreciative."

"I'll need to turn the water off. Hope no one needs a shower." She left the room. The girls followed her out.

"I thought we came down here for a meeting," Vinnie said. "What was so important we had to do all this? And shouldn't we discuss whatever it was before we leave?"

"The discussion will have to wait," Mike said.

Vinnie scowled. "Well, let's go, then."

"No," Mike said. "We must end the meeting. Properly. It is critical that the rituals be followed. Perhaps now more than ever."

Rolling his eyes, Vinnie said, "Don't blame me when this place floods."

Instead of ignoring or berating the sarcastic retort, Mike stared at Vinnie, the corners of his mouth twitching like he was holding in a smile. "Indeed."

"What's that mean?" Vinnie asked.

Mike wiped another drop off his face and resumed his spot at his star point. Disregarding Vinnie's question, he grabbed his dagger with his right hand and held it to his heart. "Concentration, honesty, defense."

Coz stood and grabbed his dagger. Holding it to his heart, he said, "Resilience, protection, potential."

Nico stood, picked up his dagger, and held it to his heart. "Life, balance, transformation."

Vinnie mimicked his brothers' movements with his own dagger. "Purity, clarity, beginnings."

Gianni, last to go, picked up his dagger. "Passion, blood, vengeance."

"As we break this ring," Mike said.

"Ever shall we serve," they answered.

"Do you want us to grab boxes and clear the room?" Nico asked, his gaze clearly on the laptop in the corner.

"Do not worry. I have every faith Josephina will handle the problem."

"All right," Nico said, and they filed out, leaving Mike alone in the room.

Vinnie, the last Brother out the door, looked back to see Mike staring at him and wiping another drip from his face.

JO WANTED A chance to talk more with Mike—alone—but Vinnie wouldn't let her go down to chamber without him. For whatever reason, he seemed to be worried about her being alone with Mike. But she wasn't afraid. Mike had just been worked up about the situation. She knew he wouldn't hurt her. It didn't matter, though. By the time she had gathered her tools and turned off the water at the main valve, Mike was nowhere to be found, in chamber or anywhere else in the compound. That didn't stop Vinnie from accompanying her.

And she was much more nervous alone with Vinnie than she was alone with Mike.

He climbed on a chair and stood on the table to start taking down ceiling tiles without her asking. When he lifted his arms, his shirt rose, revealing olive skin pulled taut over sculpted muscles. She couldn't see the whole six pack, but given the two muscles she got a peek at, the others promised to be nothing short of spectacular. Besides, she'd seen him shirtless before. From a distance. She had a good idea of what was under that shirt.

Her toolbox slipped out of her hand and landed with a clatter, startling her out of her reverie. Vinnie nearly dropped the tile out of his hand. Unfortunately, or fortunately, she wasn't sure, he lowered his arms, and with them came his shirt.

"Everything all right?"

"Hmm?" She bent to straighten her tools. "Oh, this? Sorry. Slipped right out of my hands." Could she be more of an idiot?

He cocked an eyebrow. "Do you need more tiles taken down, or is this enough?" Water dripped on his neck and down onto the collar of his t-shirt, but he didn't move.

She envied those droplets for the moment. Then she wondered what he'd do if she licked them off.

What the hell was she thinking?

"Um, that's enough."

He jumped down off the table and stood, staring at her.

She spread a tarp over the table and chairs, then she put her toolbox on the table and climbed up where Vinnie had been. The massive iron chandelier centered above the table hung at eye-level, its flame-shaped bulbs casting a bright glow in her face. At five-foot-six, she guessed she was eight to ten inches shorter than Vinnie. She shone the flashlight on the pipe as she stretched to reach the opening he'd made, but even on her toes she couldn't quite reach. Shit. About an inch too short.

"This is the tallest damn basement I've ever been in. We'll need to move the table, and I'm going to need a ladder."

He vaulted up beside her, put one hand on her waist, and reached his other hand into the opening beside hers. His reached the pipe easily. "Just tell me what to do. I'll be your hands."

His body molded to hers, his front fitted intimately against her back, like two lovers dancing, alone and uninhibited. She didn't argue, didn't step away. His breath, hot and moist against her neck, would have had her succumb to almost anything. She nodded against him, her mouth too dry to manage any words.

He moved back a step, taking her with him. A drop of water landed on her collarbone, a cool reminder of where she was, and she pulled away from him. His hand stayed on her hip, and his fingers dug in, spinning her toward him. She looked up into eyes dark and hooded, the light flickering embers in their depths. Did he want it as badly as she did?

What exactly did she want?

She moved away, searching for perspective. "Sorry about the water. I turned it off, but there's still some standing water in the pipe." Leaning into her toolbox, she grabbed rags, sandpaper, denatured alcohol, and epoxy putty. She swallowed, calmed herself, then spoke. "First you want to scuff the area so the putty adheres better." Her voice was too high. She cleared her throat and handed him a rag and the sandpaper.

He dried the pipe and started sanding it while she held the flashlight for him. Her focus alternated between his re-exposed abs and his flexing arms. When his muscles stopped rippling, she looked up to see him holding onto the pipe and staring at her. She'd dropped the flashlight so the beam pointed at his navel.

She felt the heat in her face before he spoke.

"See anything interesting?"

"Um...."

"I do."

"Vinnie, I—"

"Take a good look at this pipe."

What? The *pipe*?

"What do you notice?"

She shone the flashlight into the opening again and looked at the pipe. He had sanded around the tiny hole where the leak was so the epoxy putty would bond to the surface of the pipe. Otherwise, there was nothing to look at. The pipe seemed clean as the day the plumber installed it.

"I don't see anything noteworthy." She moved the flashlight and looked at Vinnie. "So?"

"So, other than the hole, I don't see anything wrong at all. The pipe looks practically brand new. Almost like the water just bored a hole through the damn thing."

"You're right." She shone the flashlight in the opening again to look at the pipe. It was pristine.

"So how the hell did it spring a leak? Even one that small?"

"I don't know." She kept examining the pipe. "I don't see any spider cracks. Still..." She moved the beam of light all along the pipe. "It must be some kind of defect. I was going to replace the pipe, anyway. The putty's just a temporary fix. I'll handle it tomorrow."

Vinnie didn't look convinced, but Jo removed the light and proceeded to the next step. "Here." She handed him the denatured alcohol and another rag. "Clean off the area you just sanded. It has to be free of all debris so the putty sticks."

He took the items, and she refocused the light on the leak. Before he turned to begin work, their gazes locked. Light from the chandelier bathed one side of his face, turning his olive skin a radiant bronze in the glow. Shadows darkened the other side, his high cheekbones and strong jawline hidden from the only illumination in the room. He was light and dark, good and bad, angel and demon.

Which side would he choose to show her if she stepped closer?

Which side did she want to meet?

He wiped the area and handed the items back to her. His hands lingered a bit before releasing the bottle and rag to her. When their fingers touched, she knew the next part would be the hardest for her to get through.

Back at the collection of items she'd gotten out, she grabbed the epoxy putty. "This has to be kneaded until it's soft and malleable." She started squeezing it between her fingers.

"Soft wasn't exactly what I had in mind," he said.

He reached over and interlaced his fingers with hers, working the putty with her. The heat of his hands quickly warmed the putty, preparing it for application. Even when it was ready, he didn't stop.

"We only have a three-minute window," she managed to get out between shallow breaths.

"I'm going to need much longer than three minutes."

He began massaging her fingers, and she let the putty drop from her hands. Then he pulled her tight against him, claiming her mouth with his in a searing kiss. His dark side had won, and she reveled in it. No gentle lead-in this time, no seductive preamble. Just a primal seizing and taking of what he wanted—and she surrendered to it.

One hand at her back and the other threaded through her hair, he pulled her tightly to him, trapping her hands between their bodies. She needed him closer and squeezed her arms out and around his waist, molding to him, fusing their bodies together. A groan escaped him, and she captured it, swallowed it. His arousal rubbed against her belly, and she knew he was as lost to it all as she was.

He moved his hands to her backside and shifted his stance, his thigh pushing between her legs. It was her turn to groan as he ignited sensations she'd long ignored.

Jo tipped her head, tried to take the kiss even further, even deeper. He already invaded all her senses, but she wanted more. She'd never been kissed that way before, and she didn't want it to end.

He nibbled at her lips, her jawline, her neck, and she heard his ragged breathing over her own thundering pulse. Emotions surged through her, too powerful to contain, too fast to identify.

Something cold splattered on her cheek, a stark contrast to her flushed skin. What? Surely she wasn't going to humiliate herself by crying?

Once, then again. She pushed away, took a quivering breath. A third splash. Water. Not tears. She looked up and realized the leak dripped on them. Another drip hit her in the eye.

She stepped back further, turned away. Felt the heat of shame flushed her face. My God.

She didn't have a clue in the world what she was doing. Another thirty seconds and she'd have been splayed on the table like a virgin sacrifice. Never had she been more grateful for a plumbing leak.

"Let's finish our work so we can finish what else we've started," he said, voice raw and husky.

Jo bent down to pick up the putty, but it had already hardened. She broke off a new piece from the package and kneaded it, not allowing Vinnie to help. When it was ready, she handed it to him along with a rag. "Dry off the pipe again. Then spread the epoxy putty over the leak. Make sure the whole thing is covered and you get a tight seal."

He looked at her but didn't say anything.

She held the flashlight for him again. Once satisfied with his work, she began repacking her toolbox. "In about an hour, it should be completely dry. Leave the tiles out of the ceiling so it gets good ventilation. Besides, I want to do the full repair tomorrow, anyway."

Vinnie jumped off the table and helped her down. Together, they folded the tarp, then he took the bundle from her. He offered to carry her toolbox, but she sneered at him and carried it herself.

At the foot of the stairs, he grabbed her arm. "So, are we going to continue this where we left off?"

Jo considered pretending she didn't know what he meant but had no desire to extend their conversation. She needed distance, so she tried to end the discussion quickly and honestly. "I don't think that's a good idea."

"Are you trying to tell me you weren't as into that kiss as I was?"

"What I felt is immaterial. I've had a long and emotional day. You're exhausted. We let the situation get to us. I think tomorrow we'll be grateful that one of us was clear-headed tonight and… well, didn't act on whatever this is. Was. I need to turn the water back on."

When she returned, she saw he had waited for her. There was no point, though. Having nothing more to say, she climbed the stairs before he could debate with her.

Everyone was still in the kitchen. She had hoped for a quick and quiet retreat to her bedroom, but obviously that wasn't going to happen.

"You almost got away with it," Franki said. "Nice try."

"What'd I do now?" Jo asked. She could feel Vinnie's disapproving glare behind her without even turning around.

"The vision," Donni said. "You didn't tell anyone about it yet."

"Yeah," Toni said. "The meeting's far from over."

"Did you know about this, Vin?" Nico asked.

She was probably the only one who heard him sigh, he did it so quietly. "No. She didn't tell me."

"You've got to tell us these things, Jo," Gianni said. "We all need to know, but especially your warrior. How's he supposed to protect you if he doesn't know what's coming?"

"I'm going to bed." She turned toward the hall and ignored the protests of the throng of people in the kitchen. Vinnie's voice was surprisingly absent from the verbal onslaught, but she knew he was pissed, nonetheless. "We'll continue this discussion tomorrow, but I'm beat and I need to sleep."

"Jo—"

"No, Franki. Not tonight." She stomped up the stairs with her toolbox, not even bothering to store it in her truck for the night. As tightly as she was wound, she didn't think she'd get any sleep, but she definitely wasn't sticking around for any further family discussions.

No matter what her body wanted, her heart just wasn't ready for anything he could give her.

"VINNIE, WAIT," GIANNI said.

Vinnie just wanted to go to bed. When everyone else would be sleeping tomorrow morning, he'd be up on a conference call with the legal department of MDH. Then Jo would leave early and he'd have to rush to follow her to the job site. He'd been averaging three or four hours of sleep for the last two weeks. It wore him down. He didn't need anyone to pull him aside for a fucking lecture. He knew his job—all three of them, actually. He'd been working at them nonstop for months, thank you very much.

"How do you not know what her vision was?" Gianni asked.

"Are you fucking kidding me? How the hell would I know? The only reason you knew Franki's was because her house was under surveillance, and she talked about it. Well, the compound isn't monitored inside like their house was, and Jo's not talking to me about these things, so I didn't know. Apparently her sisters knew. Why don't you chew their asses out?"

"I told you earlier today if you were overextended we'd shuffle some things around. Mike said there's a problem in Legal—"

"You might be in charge here, but you aren't my boss at MDH."

"I didn't say I was, but Mike needs the deal with Gemmora to go through, and he said there have been problems with the contracts."

"I'm on it."

"Do you need help?"

"You know what, G? You can kiss my ass. The problem with Gemmora is that the Vice President of Mergers and Acquisitions hasn't been available to meet in person, so they're getting cold feet. I've been restructuring the contracts to take M&A's role out of it as much as possible, assuring them that it's a non-issue anyway. They want to be dealing with R&D so they know their product will be in good hands when they sign over. Anything else you have to say, Mr. Vice Fucking President of Mergers and Acquisitions who's not available for meetings?"

"Mike didn't tell me that."

"Mike doesn't know, because Mike didn't ask, and I didn't bother him with it. It's my job to worry about. Not yours, not his."

"Can't Pasquale handle some of that?"

"You'd think, but apparently not. He calls me about fifty times a day with questions and problems. Between holding his hand and holding Gemmora's CEO's, I'm surprised I have a hand free to wipe my own ass."

"Well, you need some down time."

"What I need is to go to bed instead of standing here getting a lecture for no damn reason."

"Go to bed. But we need to get Jo talking."

"She said she'd talk tomorrow."

"And if she doesn't?"

"She will."

"And if she doesn't?"

"She will. One way or another, she will."

"If things aren't back on track tomorrow, I'm intervening and you're taking some time off."

Vinnie clicked his heels together and stood at attention. "Yes sir, captain sir."

Gianni flipped him off.

"I'm going to bed now."

"Good. You look like you need it."

Vinnie returned the middle finger salute.

Gianni just laughed and walked away.

Vinnie started for the stairs but then backtracked and went into the kitchen. "Hey Franki? What do you know about Remo Linza?"

"Why?"

"It's not—just tell me what you know about him." He sighed when she didn't answer right away. "Please?"

"He's one of the sweetest guys I ever met. Is he involved in this somehow? Do we need Nico to run a check on him or something? I think he became a priest and has a parish down in Virginia. I can't believe he'd have anything to do with—"

"No. No worries. Thanks. 'Night."

He knew that bastard Palmeri lied about that night. Telling Jo would open all those old wounds again, which no one needed at the moment. Still, didn't she have a right to know? Maybe he'd tell her when everything else blew over. If he decided to stop at her room, it wouldn't be for that conversation. Or any conversation at all.

Vinnie trudged up the stairs and paused at Jo's door. He raised his hand to knock, changed his mind and reached for the doorknob, then rejected both ideas and continued down the hall. It was probably best he waited. There was no way he'd bring his A-game when he could barely keep his eyes open.

Still, he couldn't help but glance back one more time before entering his room. He wondered what she was wearing, or if she wore anything at all. Was she thinking of him? Dreaming of him?

He entered his room and closed the door. Damn, he had enough to deal with. He didn't need to torture himself, too.

A glance at his rumpled black sheets brought the image of her naked body rushing to his mind. A body that earlier was pliant under his fingers, a body that his mouth had just begun to explore.

Yeah, definitely torture. And definitely needed to stop.

He went into his bathroom and tried to put her out of his mind. He grabbed a quick shower, brushed his teeth, and returned to his room, dry, naked, and exhausted. Then, turning out the lights, he flung himself onto his bed and inhaled. His last thought was of Jo before he plunged into sleep.

THE MAN WATCHED Sal light a cigar and lean back in his chair.

"I'm sure I'm right. Jo's the ticket. The guys and I know she's losing it, and—"

"That's all you have?" Sal interrupted. "Tell me something new. Something more than your hunches."

"She went off alone with her guardian today."

Sal just looked at him.

"Give me a few days. She's ready to crack."

Sal chewed on the end of his cigar. "A few days. *If* the boss agrees."

He fought the urge to pace while Sal put the line on speaker and dialed. He'd hoped Sal would give him the green light without making that call. Maybe, just maybe, the news would be good enough to keep the wolves at bay. Those wolves didn't just chew and swallow. They savored their meal for days.

The call was answered without a greeting. Sal began speaking. No preamble, no introduction.

When Sal finished, there was just silence on the other end, then the line went dead. He took the silence on the other end of the line as acceptance and assumed Sal did the same. Considering the alternative never even crossed his mind. With a terse nod at his boss, he left the room, hoping the next time they met, he'd have better news.

WHEN JO AWAKENED the next day, it was still dark outside. There was no reason to get anyone else up. Vinnie needed his sleep, and she felt safe at the site. Besides, she didn't want to have to explain anything to anyone, at least not for a while.

Leaving her room, she saw a light coming from under Vinnie's door. Figured. Didn't he ever sleep? She'd have to be extra cautious so he didn't hear her.

Even though they had been staying there for a few months, she still wasn't accustomed to every nuance of the house. She crept down the stairs, groping at the handrail for guidance. Once on the ground floor, she didn't turn on lights but rather kept her hands in front of her as a buffer against bumping into anything. She reached the garage safely but didn't see her truck in its regular spot. Then she remembered she found it in the driveway when she was looking for her toolbox the night before. Gianni had driven it home for her and hadn't pulled it in. That just made her job easier.

Instead of needing to raise the bay door, she let herself out the side entrance. Getting in her truck, she put it in neutral and coasted down the driveway. No one, not even the perpetually awake Vinnie, would know she was gone.

When she got to the road, she fired up the engine and hit the gas. Cold air blasted her face and classic rock nearly shattered her eardrums. Holy Mother of— Startled by the noise, she jerked on the wheel and swerved on the road. Quickly righting the truck, she turned the volume down and put the blower on a much more comfortable temperature. Men.

Jo pulled into a drive-thru for a cup of coffee then headed to the job site. It was the first time in months that she was free to do her job without a shadow behind her. It was liberating knowing that she didn't have to check her mirrors to see if Vinnie was still behind her. Like she could lose the speed demon if she tried. This time it wasn't necessary to keep tabs on her tail. He was still at home.

When she reached a desolate stretch of wooded road about a mile from the job site, someone plowed into her tailgate and sent her into a spin. The last thought she had before wrecking was that she probably should have checked her mirror once in a while. Or she shouldn't have left the compound without Vinnie.

VINNIE HUNG UP the phone in disgust. Pasquale got more useless every day. If the useless asshole wasn't the most knowledgeable person in Italy right now about the Gemmora deal, he'd fire his sorry ass. But he didn't have time to train anyone else, especially long distance. As soon as they got back to regular day-to-day operations, if they ever got back to regular operations, that guy was toast.

He looked out his window, expecting to see the sun rising over the treetops. Nope. Still too early for daybreak. *Merda*. His four-hour nap wasn't enough to get him through the day, especially one starting on such a shitty note. Wondering if he had time to catch a quick snooze before Jo got up and headed for the job site, he started to turn back to his bed. Movement on the driveway caught his eye and drew his attention back outside. The last thing he expected to see was Jo sneaking down the driveway.

"Fuck. Me."

No time to wake the others. She wasn't their responsibility, anyway. He dressed quickly, grabbed his gear, and headed out the door. Hopefully she wasn't too far gone that he couldn't catch up quickly. He hopped in his Maserati and gunned it. If she headed somewhere other than the job site, he was screwed.

What if she was heading to meet another man?

Ridiculous.

Still… He gripped the wheel tighter and pressed harder on the already-floored pedal.

His eyes briefly scanned the gullies he passed, looking for signs of wreckage. This was just the kind of opening Sal was waiting for—finding one of the sisters alone and vulnerable. Mike and Gianni would rain holy hell down on him if something happened to her.

But it wouldn't compare to what he'd do to himself if she was hurt. Or worse.

About a mile from the job site, he spotted two vehicles on the side of the road—a Hummer he didn't recognize and her truck. The backend of hers was smashed to shit, and the front end of the Hummer was crumpled and steaming. He didn't see Jo or the other driver, and the driver's side doors of both vehicles were open. He grabbed his phone and snapped a picture of the license plate, forwarded it, then hit speed dial.

"G. We've got a problem. One mile short of the construction site. Jo's missing. Looks like someone ran her off the road. I'm in pursuit. I sent you the plates. Have Nico trace them so we know who we're up against." He hung up before he had to answer any questions or listen to any lectures. They could bitch at him later. He flipped his phone to vibrate, grabbed his flashlight, checked his weapons, then dashed into the woods.

7

VINNIE DARTED AROUND trees and brush as dawn broke dull and dreary along the horizon. Five minutes earlier there had been a promising glow in the early morning gloaming, but with the shifting weather and the canopy of leaves above him, the flashlight had become his only hope of tracking her. Inky clouds roiled across the sky, churning over each other in their haste to envelope the heavens, obscuring the sun and what little light would have been available to him through the trees.

He pumped his legs faster, trying not to lose Jo's trail before the inevitable rains washed them away.

About half a mile into the forest, he skidded to a halt. Standing perfectly still, not even daring to breathe, he focused, tuned out his thundering heartbeat. Tuned in to sounds not native to the woods.

Thrashing—to his right, heavier than most fauna.

A feminine shriek followed by a man yelling, "Shut up, bitch!" confirmed his suspicions.

They were close.

Jo screamed again, and fear seized him. Rain started falling. He wouldn't be able to track them much longer.

Gripping his dagger, he took just a second to debate whether to use stealth or force as he pursued them, and he assessed the risks. If her captor wanted her harmed, he'd likely have done so already. If he continued with a careful pursuit, he risked losing them in the storm. Vinnie decided force would pose less threat to her, and he charged through the trees toward the sound.

Crashing through the brush, he burst into a small clearing. A man in a dark hoodie had Jo pinned against a tree, one thigh between her legs, left hand gripping her wrists above her head. In his right hand he held a long-handled switchblade against her neck.

"Didn't expect to see you this morning, Vin."

Vinnie didn't have time to fear for Jo's safety. His training kicked in, all senses primed and attuned. The first thing he realized was, although her attacker didn't turn around to face him, he knew who the vile motherfucker was.

"I should have fucking known Sal would recruit you, Dante."

"Recruit me? Shit. I looked him up when I heard what was going on."

The rain began to fall harder, easily breaking through the forest canopy and soaking Vinnie. Jo and her captor, against a tree, fared just a bit better, giving Dante a slight edge.

"You want to explain to me how you put those pieces of the puzzle together?"

"You always did run in the wrong circles, man. I go where the power is. That's why you're out of touch. And in this case, out of time."

"Wrong again, asshole. I'm not letting you leave with her, and if you even try to hurt her, you're dead. Your only hope of getting out of here alive is to release her. Now."

Dante slowly turned his head to face Vinnie. An evil smile played over his face. "I don't plan on leaving with her or hurting her, Vin. I think I'm going with option three."

Vinnie's blood pumped colder than the rain dripping over him. Because Dante had taken her alive, he thought she was safe. It never occurred to him that Dante might actually kill her. Jo's eyes widened with fear, but she was still pinned to the tree and unable to fight for herself. To give her any chance at all, he had to get Dante to move before hurting her. Or worse.

"We aren't alone out here, Tosta." The skies opened and pelted them with stinging sheets of rain. Vinnie had to yell to be heard above the noise. "Do you honestly think I'd be out here without backup?"

"You each have one charge. Yours is her. And you're about to be out of a job."

Vinnie's mind raced. If he threw the dagger and missed, he was without his most valuable weapon. Unlike Gianni, he'd never been successful at calling it back to him before. If he fired his gun and missed, he could hit Jo. If he charged and hoped for the best, it could take too long and Dante could just kill her. But he was out of time. He had to decide.

Dante turned back to Jo. She moved her mouth, but Vinnie couldn't read the words through the rain.

If only it wasn't raining.

He pointed his Sig Sauer, and the rain stopped. Thank God.

Vinnie heard thrashing behind him.

"Besides, Falco. Do you honestly think I'd be out here alone?"

Vinnie fired his weapon.

Jo collapsed, and Dante screamed.

The noise in the brush behind Vinnie grew louder, but he couldn't check to see if it was Dante's men or his own. Dante ran off into the woods, and Vinnie ran to Jo. Her shirt was saturated with blood. Good Lord! Had he shot her?

He scooped her up. Her tear-filled gaze met his before her eyes rolled and her lids fluttered closed. Blood spurted from the gash across her throat. Vinnie dropped to the ground and put pressure on her wound. Scanned her body for other injuries. Couldn't muster an iota of relief when he saw no evidence of a gunshot.

He was losing her.

"V!"

"Vinnie!"

He could hear his brothers, but he couldn't go find them. Jo was dying, her blood flowing over his fingers and into the earth below them.

"Here!" he yelled. "G, hurry! She needs healing! Now!"

The Brothers crashed through the brush.

With weak fingers, she grabbed his free hand. The gurgling stopped.

Good sign or bad?

He squeezed her hand and cradled her in his lap. "Now, G! Fix her!"

Gianni's closed his eyes, his brows drew down as he concentrated. When nothing happened, he knelt beside her and put his hands on her forehead and chest, but still she didn't revive.

Vinnie felt tears roll down his face, saw them land on Jo's wound, but he couldn't stop them from falling. "Jo, damn it! Don't you die on me!"

Gianni got out his dagger and placed it across her throat. Nico and Coz stood behind him, each with one hand on his shoulder and a dagger in the other hand to share their strength and power with their brother. Gianni crossed his hands over his dagger and started chanting under his breath. Soon his body shook with tremors, and Coz and Nico wove on their feet. Vinnie hardly noticed his brothers' efforts, keeping his focus on Jo. He rocked her, begged her to come back. More tears fell and landed on Gianni's dagger, hissing like ice on hot stone.

Jo's eyes snapped open and she gasped.

Gianni, Nico, and Coz fell back onto the wet ground.

She inhaled a deep breath. And another.

The brothers released collective sighs of relief. Vinnie clutched Jo tightly to him and just breathed with her. He took in the scent of pine and earth, blood and sweat, and something inherently her, and he clung to it. Looking up, he planned on thanking Gianni, but all his brothers still lay sprawled on their asses. Vinnie hadn't seen them so wrecked since they had worked on Franki's life-threatening injuries in the woods behind her house several months before. He hoped scenes like this didn't become habit. For the moment, he held his thanks to himself. All he wanted to do was check Jo head to toe and make sure she was all right.

"Are you okay?" He looked into her eyes. Her neck and clothes were covered in blood, her skin streaked in places where his tears had begun to wash her clean.

She nodded, her head cradled in his lap. "I'm fine." She turned to where

Gianni was still sitting on the ground. He'd finally started moving again. "I owe you one. Thanks."

"It wasn't just me. It was all four of us. But you're welcome."

"Four?" Vinnie said. "I didn't help."

"I think it was you who sealed it, V."

"Me? What'd I do?"

"Your tears, man. The healing didn't work till your tears hit my dagger."

"You cried for me?" Jo looked into Vinnie's eyes.

As much as he had craved an intimate moment with her, he didn't want it on the damp blood-soaked earth in front of all his brothers. He definitely didn't want it to be a discussion about him sobbing like a baby. He helped her sit on her own and clambered to his feet.

"We need to get out of here. Dante said he wasn't alone."

"He's probably not lying," Nico said. "There was another vehicle there when we pulled up."

"Get Jo back to the compound. I'm going to go to the construction site and check on things there." When Jo started to complain, he held up his hand. "Don't even bother. You've been through hell. You aren't going anywhere but home. You're lucky I don't send you to the hospital for a thorough check-up."

"But—"

"No. I've got it covered. I'm the only one familiar with the site, and I'm the only one up for it. I'll see all of you at home once things are taken care of. I need to be sure they didn't go there and set up a booby-trap or something." Vinnie headed down the path by himself before the rest of them even made it to their feet.

He wasn't looking forward to rehashing that story in front of his brothers. Or Jo's sisters. Or Mike. Or hell, even Jo. He couldn't believe he fucking cried like that. If Gianni was right, it was a good thing he did, but… *Che cazzo?* Maybe he really was losing it.

Or the exhaustion had finally gotten to him. That had to be it.

He got in his car and texted Gianni. Hopefully Nico could find Dante from some camera feed. Vinnie was pretty sure he had shot him, but he had no proof. He turned his phone off to avoid a whole text conversation with his brother, then he drove to the job site. There was only one truck parked there, and Vinnie knew it belonged to Jo's trusted foreman. Obviously he was there to get things running for her. The alternative would mean he was involved with Sal and Dante, and Vinnie just didn't think the guy rolled that way. Still, he'd have to have Nico check him out.

He peered between studs to the interior beyond but didn't see the man, so he headed for the basement and found him squatting by the furnace, reading a tag. "Tyson."

"Falco." He didn't bother getting up or turning around. "You here to try and settle a score with me about the boss lady?"

"No. Actually, she told me her story, and we called Palmeri out here to confront him last night."

"You took her to see that bastard?" This time he did stand up and turn around.

"Not only did we meet him, we heard his side of the story. Says it wasn't even him who spread the pictures."

"Bullshit."

"That's his story, and Jo believed it."

"You let that punk-ass weasel get away with talking circles around the truth?"

"I wasn't there when it happened, so I don't know what went down."

"But you believe him?"

"I didn't say that. I just know Jo's calm now, so I'm content with the resolution."

"I'm not."

"That's on you. Talk to Palmeri and hear his side for yourself."

"You can be damn sure I will."

"Won't mean anything one way or another, but it doesn't matter. That's not why I'm here, anyway. Jo had an accident this morning."

"What? She okay?" Chuck took a step toward him.

Vinnie held up a hand. "She's fine, but she's not coming in. She needs you to handle everything. Managing the work today, the schedule for tomorrow, the inspections. All of it."

"Not a problem. Tell her I'll call her with an update later today."

Vinnie stood there, assessing the man. He was cool and capable, definitely the type Sal would go after, but he was far too loyal to Jo for Sal to use. He just didn't see him as the enemy.

"Something else?"

"I'm sorry about when we burst in here on you. I saw her crying, and I jumped to conclusions. I didn't know... Well, now I realize... I mean, I know you wouldn't hurt her, and I know how you helped her before. I just... Thanks."

Chuck looked at him for a moment then took out a bandana and tied it around his head. Without the light reflecting off his bald pate, he blended into the darkness. Vinnie could see why Enzo was scared of him. Thank God this was the man who stood up for Jo. "So you're the one, huh?"

"The one, what?"

He shook his head. "Do I have to give you the 'If you hurt her' speech, or are we tight?"

"Excuse me?"

Chuck bent back down and resumed examining the tag on the furnace. "Yeah. Whatever. Listen, I don't know what shit you guys have going on, and I'm not going to pry. Your business is your business. But Jo has been my business for years. If you need something to help her out, you let me know."

"You have a thing for her?"

"Nah. We gave it a shot once, but it was awkward. We're friends. Nothing more. She would've been best man at my wedding if she was actually a man."

"How long you been married?" Vinnie watched the man's back stiffen. "Sorry. I didn't mean to cross a line."

"No. You didn't. Jen died two years ago. Jo was there for me. So like I said, if she needs something, you let me know. Now get out of here. I've got work to do."

"See ya, Tyson."

Chuck grunted something Vinnie couldn't make out as he climbed the stairs. The sun was out and the clouds were mostly gone. The only signs of the storm at dawn were the puddles dotting the rutted ground. He picked his way to his car and headed home. Despite his love of speeding on the highway, he drove under the speed limit. He wasn't looking forward to his part of the pending discussion.

JO PACED AROUND the kitchen island while the twins hovered. They had each hugged her, yelled at her, and hugged her again. They currently invaded her personal space to make certain she didn't disappear and somehow spontaneously die without giving them proper notice.

When she couldn't take it any longer, she went to see Gianni. She found him hunkered down on a recliner in the den, a glass of something on the rocks in one hand and a bag of ice in the other. She assumed it had been on his head, but he got to his feet when she entered the room and put the items down on the table. Even Franki walked away when she knocked at the door. Something about her approaching the man responsible—or according to him, partially responsible—for saving her life seemed to warrant a bit of privacy.

"I need to go out."

"You're joking, right?"

"No. I need to run an errand."

"Jo." Gianni tipped his head right and left, cracking his neck.

She could only imagine the tension he must be feeling. It was way too early for liquor or injuries, and he had both. But she felt the walls pressing in on her, and they were named Franki, Donni, Toni, and Brotherhood, so she had to get permission to leave. "Look, my sisters are driving me nuts." She left his oppressive instances out of it. "And I won't be long."

"You know I can't send you out alone."

"Send Nico with me."

"He's busy."

"Doing what?"

He sighed. "Not that it's really your business, but he's trying to tap into satellite coverage of the area you and Dante were. We're hoping we can see where he escaped, who he was with, and whether Vinnie shot him or not."

Jo bit her lip. After a moment passed in uncomfortable silence, she said, "Then Coz can drive. My truck's busted up, anyway. Guess I should call for a tow." Her thoughts trailed off.

"We've got it covered."

Of course they did. "Thanks. But regardless, I need to get out of here and away for a while."

"Vinnie will be back soon, and we have a lot to go over."

"He's going to the site. He won't be back that soon. And I promise you I won't be long."

"What's so important that you need to leave? Can't you just go down to the gym or something?"

"Please, Gianni?"

"I need to know where."

"Why?"

"It's non-negotiable."

She bit her lip but knew he wasn't going to cave unless she answered. "I want to visit my grandmother."

"You can't call her?"

"I need to see her. And I need to get out of this house. It's stifling in here. My sisters…" Again she let the thought hang, unfinished.

He didn't answer for a long time. He just stood there, staring at her. Finally, when she was certain she'd lost the argument, he said, "Coz drives. You go only to her house. Straight there, straight back. No detours. I'll text you when V's back, and I'll expect you within an hour of his arrival."

She threw her arms around him. "Thank you." A quick peck on his cheek, and she darted out of the room and called for Coz.

THEY PARALLEL-PARKED in front of a tiny house on a nondescript street in her hometown. Each house on that block was well-tended and tidy, but one just screamed 'welcome' to her. It might have been the geraniums in the urns or the impatiens lining the plant beds. It could have been the crisp white siding or the bold burgundy awnings flapping in the breeze. Maybe it was the wicker furniture on the porch with the overstuffed cushions. But most likely it was the fact that it was Nonna's house, and she knew inside waited one of her favorite people on the planet.

She bounded up the steps and rushed inside. "Don't you lock your doors?"

"Don't you wipe your feet?" Carmina climbed down a stepladder and wiped her hands on her apron. She walked over to Jo and embraced her. "Let me look at you." She held her at arm's length. "You aren't eating enough. And you. Come here, Roberto." Coz stepped around Jo and bent down to receive a hug. Jo had never even heard him enter.

"You really should have your doors locked, ma'am."

"Don't you 'ma'am' me. You know me too well for such formalities by now."

"Sorry, Carmina. Nonna. Just a habit, I guess."

She patted his cheek. "It's all right. Shows you were raised proper."

"Speaking of formalities, when are you going to start calling me Coz?"

"When you get your name legally changed from Roberto. Now, are you here with news of my baby girl?"

Jo instantly regretted not calling first. She saw her grandmother's eyes cloud with worry and grabbed her hands. "No. No, Nonna. I just wanted to talk. It's been a while."

"Come to the kitchen."

Jo protested, but to no avail. Her grandmother was already through the dining room. She looked at Coz who shrugged his shoulders and gestured toward the back of the house. The two of them trailed after her.

"Nonna, we aren't hungry."

"Nonsense." She already had an antipasto plate started. "Wash up, both of you." She pointed to the sink and waited until they started washing their hands. "Jo, you can help me. Get cookies out of the freezer. I've got tarelli, biscotti, pizzelle, and chocolate chip."

Jo shook her head and handed Coz a hand towel. "What kind do you want?"

"They all sound good. You pick your favorite."

"He likes them all," Nonna said, "take them. I'll make more tomorrow."

"It's just the two of us."

"Josephina, are you sassing me?"

"No, ma'am." Jo ignored her grandmother's stare and took the cookies out of the freezer. She put them on a tray while Nonna turned back to her work, completing the antipasto and cutting homemade bread. She put a coffeepot and cups on the table, and little plates and napkins.

"Why are you still standing there?" Nonna asked.

Jo turned around to see Coz standing in the archway, visibly struggling for an appropriate response. Before he got her grandmother riled up, Jo thrust a plate in his hand and guided him to the kitchen table. "He's eating. See?"

She whispered to him, "Sit down and load up."

"No one told me to sit."

"It's not the military. Just sit and help yourself."

She watched him sit and dig in while she put the cookie tins away. The blissful look on his face told her he enjoyed himself as much as she usually did when she ate her grandmother's food. Too bad she didn't have an appetite. "Nonna? While Coz is eating, do you think we could take our coffee out to the porch? The flowers are so pretty right now and the weather is just lovely."

Coz raised an eyebrow, but he didn't say anything.

Her grandmother poured two cups of coffee and handed one to Jo. "If you want anything else, Roberto, you let me know."

They didn't wait for him to answer, but headed through the house and out the front door. A light breeze caused the awnings to bump against the columns and brought the scent of lilacs to Jo's nose. The wind must have come from the back of the house, because that's where her grandfather had planted lilacs when she was a little girl. The bushes were huge now, and positively lovely this time of year.

"I'm always delighted to see you, *cara*, but I don't think you came to talk about the weather and look at my plant beds."

Jo sighed. "No. No, I didn't." She still didn't speak, though.

"I'm not getting any younger, Jo."

"How did you know Nonno was the one?"

"So it's about a man. And not the man sitting in my kitchen."

"How do you know? What's wrong with him?"

She laughed. *"Madonna mia,* honey. Nothing's wrong with that one. But he's not for you. The two of you care for each other, but not that way. No, you're here about someone else."

"You see too much."

"I just see what's right in front of me. Maybe you should try it sometime."

Jo sighed. "I don't know if I'm ready."

"If you wait until everything is perfect, you'll be waiting forever. What are you really worried about?"

"I talked to Enzo Palmeri."

Carmina let out a string of curses that made Jo blush.

"Nonna! Please! You don't understand. It wasn't him. He tried to help that night. A different boy was responsible. Enzo shouldered the blame all these years."

"You believe that?"

"Why wouldn't I?"

"Maybe it's easier to believe that than to face the truth."

"Maybe it is the truth."

"Eh. Six of one, half a dozen of the other. You're obviously ready to move on. And you found someone to move on with. What's the problem?"

Jo traced a finger up her arm and followed the path with her gaze. "I haven't told him everything. I don't know if he'll still want me." She dropped her voice lower. "I'm damaged. Broken."

"Josephina, you look at me."

Jo looked toward her grandmother but only managed to stare at her feet.

"Now."

She finally did as she was asked and looked into her grandmother's eyes.

"As we age, we get battle wounds and scars. No one gets through unscathed. That's part of life. But it's what's inside that counts. And inside, you are strong and fierce. And Jo, you are whole."

"I don't feel whole. I feel… shattered," she whispered.

Carmina got up and took Jo in her arms. "I've never seen someone so unbreakable. You tell him everything. If he's worth anything, if he's worthy of you, he won't run."

"And if he does run?"

"What if he does?"

"I think I might physically break."

"You won't."

She squeezed her grandmother back, then pulled away in a panic.

"Oh, God, Nonna! What if he doesn't run?"

She chuckled. "Count your blessings, *cara*. Count your blessings."

Jo's phone vibrated in her pocket, and she took it out to read the message. It was from Gianni. She rubbed her finger across Vinnie's name before closing the message and returning the phone to her pocket. Coz came to the door with his phone in his hand. "Gianni texted. Vinnie's back. We need to go."

"Okay."

"I'll wait in the car." He stepped outside. "Thanks for the food. I don't eat like that often. Everything was wonderful."

"My pleasure, Roberto. Come back soon." She hugged him goodbye, and he walked to the car. Then she turned back to Jo. "Vinnie, huh?"

"What?"

"He's the one."

"The one, what?"

"I suppose you can't see your reaction when his name is mentioned."

"What reaction?"

Nonna smiled. "If you need me, you know where to find me. Face your fears, Josephina, and you can have everything you've been dreaming of." She kissed her. "Now run along. You shouldn't keep your man waiting."

"I don't have a man."

"Are you sure about that?" She took their coffee cups into the house before Jo could muster an answer.

Jo muttered to herself the whole way to the car. When she slammed the door, Coz looked at her. "What?" She glared back.

"I thought we came here so you'd be in a better mood."

"Yeah, I thought so, too."

"You should have eaten something. Her bread is awesome."

"Thanks. I've tried it before."

"The tarelli were excellent."

"I'm aware."

"Do you think she'd give Gianni the recipe?"

"Donni has it."

"And the—"

"Coz? Shut up."

"Okay."

They drove in silence for about thirty seconds, then Jo said, "We're making good time. Can we make one more stop?"

"Gianni said there and back, no detours."

"Just one."

"I gave my word, Jo."

"Please, Coz. I won't tell, and they'll never know. I need to see my dad."

He tapped his fingers on the wheel but didn't answer right away. Finally, he said, "You know it'll be dangerous, right? They'll probably have a lookout at the cemetery."

"One minute. I just need to see his grave."

"You women give me *agita.*"

So what if she aggravated him? She got her way. With a smile of satisfaction, she sat back in her seat.

When they got to the cemetery, someone was already at the grave. Coz wanted to keep driving, but she convinced him to stop. She recognized the truck and the man kneeling at the tombstone.

Chuck.

Coz insisted on getting out of the car first, and he held his gun in one hand and his dagger in the other instead of leaving them hidden under his jacket. When he nodded the all clear, she hopped out of the car and jogged over to the grave.

She stood on her toes and wrapped her arms around her foreman. He returned the hug with a quick pat before stepping away.

"What are you doing here?" she asked.

"I drop by sometimes, just to pay my respects. Things went well this morning, so I thought I'd let the old man know we had a good day. And I wanted to tell him I was keeping an eye on you. I don't think he's happy you had an accident."

"You're not happy I had an accident."

"You should have called me."

She batted him on the arm. "I'm fine."

Coz, standing sentinel, squinted toward the tree line. "Wrap it up, Jo."

"One minute. I didn't even talk to Papa, yet."

"Jo," Coz said.

She turned back to Chuck. "I'm in a rush, but I want a full report. You'll have to call me later with the details."

"Sure. No problem." He stood there while she knelt at her father's tombstone.

The grass and flowers were in full bloom, such a cheery contrast to the snowy, dreary day they buried him. She bowed her head and said a quick prayer, hoping he and God heard everything in her heart.

"Come on, Jo," Coz said. "We need to go."

She stood up. "One more minute."

A shot ricocheted off her father's headstone and Coz and Chuck each grabbed one of her hands, pulling her low to the ground.

"Can you get her to the car?" Coz asked Chuck. "I'll lay down cover."

"Yeah. I got her."

"On my mark," Coz said. They exchanged the looks of warriors, and then Coz made the slightest gesture and Chuck yanked her arm, keeping his hand on her head and their bodies bent low.

He dragged her down the slope and threw her into the car while Coz traded gunfire over his shoulder and made his way down a different path.

"Are you okay?" Chuck asked.

"Yeah."

"Move to the passenger side. Lock your door and stay down," he said.

"Where are you going?"

"He needs a distraction to get to you safely."

"Are you crazy?"

She lunged for him, but he was already out of the car. While she scrambled to the passenger side, she watched him. He ran in the opposite direction that Coz had gone, yelling and waving his arms, weaving through the trees. There was more gunfire, and she turned to see Chuck fall. Then Coz dove into the car, and they took off at speeds never before seen in a cemetery.

She looked out the back window to see where Chuck was. He lay in a heap on the ground, and gunmen approached him.

"Keep your damn head down!"

"We need to go back for him!"

"It's too late, Jo. They have him."

"But maybe—"

"It's too late!"

She had bruised her thigh on the emergency brake when Chuck tossed her into the car and began rubbing it to alleviate the soreness. Who the hell put a brake handle on the left side of the driver's seat? Even as she grumbled, tears fell silently down her cheeks. Nothing, not even the pain in her leg, took her thoughts away from Chuck. "I'm sorry. I just thought—oh my God! You're shot!" A bloodstain covered his side and grew wetter and larger as she stared at it.

"Call Gianni. Tell him what happened. I don't think we're coming in hot, but I'm not sure."

He spun the car out of the cemetery and onto the road. On a regular day, she figured it would take her about fifteen minutes to get back to the compound. Coz would probably make it in ten. But at the speed he currently drove, assuming they didn't die in a fiery crash, she estimated they'd make it back in about seven.

She prayed he could make it that long.

"Okay." The tears stopped as she recognized their dire predicament. No time for wallowing or weakness.

She fumbled in her pocket for her phone.

"Are you all right?" he asked.

"Yeah. I'm fine." Her fingers trembled as she pressed send.

"Good. I think you should drive the rest of the way." He pointed the car toward the side of the road and passed out.

8

JO GRABBED THE wheel and pulled to the right. Coz must have had his foot on the brake before he passed out because the car's speed decreased, but not fast enough. The passenger doors scraped along the guard rails, and she feared the car would flip before slowing to a stop. Her only hope was the emergency brake. Icy panic flooded her veins when she glanced down and didn't see one.

In a heartbeat, a painful heartbeat where her muscle threatened to burst right through her sternum and out her chest cavity, she remembered bruising herself earlier in his vintage Ferrari. The handbrake was on the driver's side. Unlatching her seatbelt, she flung herself over his lap, grabbed the emergencey brake, and yanked up on it.

She didn't even want to think about the damage that caused. All she worried about was getting the damned car stopped and getting Coz the help he needed. The car skidded to a stop amid the racket of squealing brakes and screeching side panels.

Jo smelled the acrid burning chemical odor first, then she saw the smoke and wondered how she'd get Coz out of the car and to safety before they were truly in danger. Only then did she hear Gianni screaming at her through the phone. She'd totally forgotten she'd called him.

Coz still hadn't regained consciousness, so she searched the floorboards for where the phone had fallen. Before she put the receiver to her ear, she heard Gianni yelling.

"What the hell is going on over there?"

She screamed right back at him. "Gianni! Help! Gianni! Are you listening? Heal him! Send your powers out and heal him! He's been shot!"

There was a brief rustling and then Donni was on the phone. *"Jo. Listen. Gianni needs you to put pressure on the wound."*

"I already am." While Donni was getting on the phone, Jo had stripped off her button-down and Coz's seatbelt and had pressed her shirt against the wound. "Why are you on the phone? What's going on? I need to move him. I smell smoke."

"Gianni is sending his power out long distance, but he's still beat from earlier. Nico's trying to lend him some energy. Vinnie left about five minutes ago when you weren't here. He should be to you soon." Her voice got softer. *"If there's a chance of fire, you should get out of there."*

"I'm not leaving him. It's my fault he's hurt. Besides, he wouldn't leave me."

"Still..."

"Would *you* leave him?"

"No, probably not."

"Hey, his eyes are fluttering. Tell Gianni I think it's working. And by the looks of the car flying down the road, I think Vinnie has found us."

"Oh, thank God."

Jo heard Donni talking to Gianni in the background while she checked on Coz's wound. It seemed to have sealed on the outside, but she had no idea what was going on with him internally. His coloring was still off, and he hadn't done more than moan once since Donni switched places with Gianni on the phone.

She feared there wasn't anything else Gianni could do for him until they got him home and took the bullet out. The screeching tires signifying Vinnie's arrival should have relieved her, but even the tires sliding on the asphalt sounded angry. She hated to see what the man behind the wheel looked like.

Vinnie ran toward them, fear and anger etched on the planes of his face. He yanked open the driver's side door, reached in, and grabbed her face with his index finger and thumb, tipping it up so he could assess her. "Are you all right?"

"I'm fine. It's Coz. He's been shot. I think Gianni has the bleeding stopped, at least on the outside, but I can't get him to come to. And I smelled smoke. We've got to go—"

"That's just the brakes." He'd already dropped her face and put his arms under Coz to lift him out of the car. "Can't you smell it? You used the emergency brake to stop the car, didn't you?"

"Well, yeah, that was the only way to get it to—"

"Good. That was—" he hefted Coz out of the car and started to walk toward his vehicle, grunting the last word out "—smart."

She scrambled after them. "What about the car? Should I try to drive it?"

"You can't drive that. Nico'll deal with it later." He settled Coz into his vehicle and strapped him in. "Just make sure you have any personal items. We have to get out of here. I'm surprised no one's been by yet. This is a back road, but it's not that private. We've been lucky to not have been spotted."

"Vinnie, I'm—"

"Don't even say it. Get in the back beside him and keep him from moving as much as you can."

She reached into the mangled car for her purse and the phone. "But—"

"Damn it, Jo, not now. Don't you get it? You didn't listen. You never listen. And because you had to do whatever the hell you wanted, your life was in jeopardy, and my brother may have given his for yours. Something, by the way, that I'm supposed to do. And I'm going to have to live with the outcome of this misadventure. So save the apologies. Just sit there, keep an eye on him, and shut the fuck up."

Vinnie climbed into the driver's seat of his car and slammed the door. Jo hurried in behind him. He peeled out before she had the door closed.

She didn't utter a sound the entire way to the compound.

VINNIE DIDN'T REMEMBER the drive home. Didn't remember the turns on the road, the songs on the radio—or even if it was on. If Jo had spoken, he didn't notice, although he was pretty damn sure she was quiet. Every muscle, every joint, ached from the constant tension. He'd probably been gripping the steering wheel and gearshift like they were lifelines, because his fingers were actually numb.

He knew Gianni had done all he could because Coz had stopped bleeding. Externally, anyway. What was going inside him was another matter. When Gianni had been shot, he still managed to stay conscious. At least until they operated on him. Coz's injuries looked like they were probably a hell of a lot more serious. Coz was the one brother whose dagger's power helped him control death, even if he hadn't quite mastered it yet. And he was the one out cold with a bullet in his gut.

Vinnie burst out of the car before he even had the keys out of the ignition. Gianni and Nico waited for him holding the top of a collapsible table they obviously planned to use as a makeshift stretcher. They headed toward the car as quickly as they could with the PVC slab between them.

Jo's sisters stood behind them, out of the way, but close enough to assist as soon as they were needed. They all had red-rimmed eyes, but none cried at the moment. Jo got out of the car and moved out of the way. Her sisters surrounded her, and the physical and visual assessments began immediately.

Vinnie leaned into the car and lifted Coz's unresponsive form out in much the same way he had put him in. When Gianni and Nico held the tabletop between them, Vinnie gave them a quick scrutiny. He had a feeling that if he lay Coz down on the slab, all three of the men would end up on the ground. "Just go. I've got him."

"This would be better for him," Nico said.

"Not when you collapse under the strain." Vinnie shifted Coz in his arms. "You look like shit, and I'll need you inside."

Gianni started to protest.

"Fuck, G. He's not light. Get the hell out of my way." He stepped around his brothers and led a parade of protestors into the house and down to the gym.

The gym took up nearly the entire expanse of the basement and was segmented into different partitions. They all used the equipment room and the sparring room on a regular basis, but Vinnie headed for a third section, an all-tile room with a medical table in the center, a sink in the corner, and all sorts of medical equipment in the cupboards along the walls.

The room had been outfitted for the guys to deal with minor and major injuries—that was before Gianni and Nico had learned to heal most of their injuries with just a thought. There was a drain in the floor, and that's what disturbed Vinnie the most. He didn't even want to think about the last time they were in there and what they had to rinse down that drain.

Couldn't even consider what might be rinsed down it later that day.

Coz's weight would have been a burden had he been alert and the distance been short. Instead, his brother had been deadweight and Vinnie had carried him a long way, around corners and down stairs. By the time he laid Coz on the table, his legs trembled, his arms shook, his clothes were soaked, and he huffed like he had emphysema. He felt the way he thought Gianni and Nico looked, and that scared him. Where would they get the power to heal him?

"Someone better call Mike." Even Vinnie's voice sounded weakened. "We're going to need the extra juice."

The girls gathered equipment from the cabinets and spread everything out on a paper-covered cart. They all stopped their work, turned to the men, and began firing questions in rapid succession.

"Why do you need the extra juice?" Franki asked. "You've been doing too much. It's taken too much out of you. Can you even do another healing?"

"Why do you have to call Mike?" Donni asked. "Doesn't he keep tabs on you? Shouldn't he know what's going on? Shouldn't he be on his way? Why isn't he here? What if he can't come? Can you do this without him?"

"What does Coz need?" Toni said. "What can we do? Maybe we should just take him to the hospital. We can come up with a story of how he got shot to keep you out of it."

"Yeah," Jo said. "With Chuck shot, there's bound to be a report being filed. We're going to want to put a spin on this."

"Chuck's been *shot*?" Donni said.

"Stop. Just stop," Vinnie said. He sank to the floor in the middle of the room near the table, and for the first time noticed Gianni and Nico, flat on their asses, each leaning against the doorframe. They'd been uncharacteristically quiet, so he hadn't even looked to see where they were or what they were doing.

If the situation wasn't dire, they'd probably be asleep in another minute.

He took his cue from them and tried to grab a moment's rest. With nothing to lean against, he tented his knees and rested his arms on them. Then he let his head hang forward onto his arms and took some deep breaths.

"But Chuck—" Donni said.

"We have more pressing matters," Vinnie said. "We need a plan. Now." He looked up and gestured to Gianni. "Look at him. I'm not convinced he's going to make it through this surgery, and I can't do it without him. Franki, you're going to have to link with him. Maybe we'll get lucky and tap into more of that power-of-love mojo that saved him during his surgery.

"Nico, call Mike now. I'm not waiting for him. We're going in, with or without him. Coz doesn't have the time to wait. Then you're helping me with the surgery.

"Donni, Toni, I hope you aren't squeamish, because you're going to have to assist. Everybody, scrub up."

"What about me?" Jo asked.

The last thing he wanted was for her to witness him fail. She'd already blamed herself—hell, he'd flat out accused her of it in the car—she didn't need to see his brother die.

His breath hitched on that word. No, he couldn't let her witness that.

"You've done enough. Go wait in another room. It's too crowded in here as it is." He wanted to bite back the words as soon as he said them, or at least his curt tone, but he didn't have the time. It ripped at him to see tears well in her eyes, but she didn't let them fall, at least not in front of him. He almost called her back when she turned away and walked to the door, but what could he say in five seconds to make up for being a total ass? Nothing. Probably nothing in five months of groveling.

"I'll be right in the hall. Just yell if you need something." She walked out and pulled the door closed behind her.

He wanted to tell her that he wanted to spare her further hurt if something went wrong, that he needed to focus on Coz and couldn't do that with her in there, but he had no time to convince her of any of that, so he turned back to the task at hand. His brothers didn't look at him, choosing instead to struggle to their feet, scrub their hands, and get into position.

The girls, however, took a different approach.

"How could you do that to her?" Franki said, whisper-yelling at him so Jo wouldn't hear.

"Don't you think she feels bad enough?" Donni said in the same tone.

Toni wiped Coz's head with a cool cloth. She shook her head, but didn't add to the haranguing he was tolerating.

"Look," he said, "I was mad and scared, and I took it out on her. I'll make it up to her later. But if something goes wrong, she really doesn't need to see it, does she? She's in a bad place as it is. She doesn't need to witness—" He sighed. "The best place for her is anywhere but here."

"I don't know if that's noble or the stupidest thing I ever heard," Franki said.

"I'm voting noble," Donni said.

"I'm voting stupid," Gianni said. "She's right outside the door. If this goes south—when this goes south—she's going to know, and she's going to come in. And she's going to be pissed because she wasn't in here. She's going to feel like she could have done something."

"You want her in here? Ask her back. I can't deal with this right now."

"I think we should just start," Nico said. "His coloring is getting worse, and we don't know what we're getting into."

"I want to make one more plea for the hospital," Toni said.

"No," the three men answered together.

"He wouldn't want it," Nico said.

"We don't have a cover story, anyway," Gianni said.

"And we're out of time," Vinnie said. "Nico, you reach Mike?"

Nico shook his head.

Vinnie sighed. "Ladies, step out of the way. It's time. Toni, you're going to have to monitor his vitals. Can you get that equipment on him?"

"Equipment?"

"There." He gestured to monitoring equipment Nico had brought over on a cart. Nico helped her set it up.

"Where'd you get that? Why do you have this?"

"We have equipment like this in all our facilities. We used to need it. Before Gianni could heal us."

"We had it when I was shot," Gianni said.

Franki moaned.

Vinnie analyzed the motley group assembled there. No one had the energy—or the knowledge—to deal with this.

Yet he had no choice but to try.

"Okay," Vinnie said. "Gianni, you're going to have to open him up and keep the blood back. Keep every slice as small as possible, but remember, we're going to have to get our hands in there. Franki, Nico, you're going to have to share your energies with him. Toni, Donni, you're assisting me. Everybody washed and gloved?" When they all nodded, he looked at Coz. It was a toss-up at that point as to who was whiter—everyone's coloring was way too pale. He so didn't want to be in charge of this one. A quick pull on his own dagger told him without Mike, their chances weren't good.

JO PEEKED IN the window. Everyone seemed to be glowing, even her sisters to some degree. Everyone, of course, except for Coz. He was still out cold. It was probably for the best. The last thing they needed was for him to come to while Gianni ripped his flesh open.

It killed her that she didn't know what was going on in there, except for the sliver of a view she managed through the windowpane. They all spoke in hushed whispers, so either things had turned really serious, or they didn't want her to know what was going on. Or both.

Probably both. After all, this latest dilemma in a series of shitty dilemmas was on her.

If she couldn't help in there, she would help from the hall. She whipped her phone out of her pocket and scrolled through her contacts. Dialing a number she'd never used before, she was pissed when she got voicemail.

"Mike, it's Jo. I don't know where you are or what you're doing, but we need you over here. Pronto. I got Coz shot and it's not looking good. They're operating now, but they need you. I thought you were always watching. Where the hell are you?"

She disconnected without a goodbye.

She peered again through the window and saw Toni holding her phone up for Vinnie to view. It looked like she'd done a web search for a diagram of stomach anatomy.

That didn't bode well for any of them.

Unable to do anything else, Jo rooted through her purse. At the bottom, she found a tiny leather pouch and grabbed it. Unzipping it, she took the beads out and held the crucifix in her right hand. "Lord, I know I don't deserve a miracle, but it's not for me. Jesus, please carry Coz through his surgery unscathed. Mary, I beg of you, intercede on my behalf."

She continued staring through the window as she made the sign of the cross, then she began praying the rosary. With every confused look the brothers exchanged, she gripped the beads tighter. With every panicked glance her sisters shared, a tear rolled down her cheek.

Still she prayed.

Was she the only one who noticed that Gianni, Franki, and Nico weren't even steady on their feet any longer? She reached toward the doorknob but pulled her hand back. And again.

She didn't want to interrupt, but she didn't want things to get worse.

Resolved, she grasped the handle and was about to twist.

"What are you doing, Josephina?"

Mike had finally chosen to make his appearance.

She gasped and dropped both the doorknob and the rosary. "Damn it!

Why do you always ghost in like that?" She bent and picked up the beads, kissed them, and looked for the one she'd been on. Then she held it with her right thumb and index finger while grabbing the doorknob with her left hand. "Never mind. Get inside before it's too late. They need you."

"Why aren't you inside?"

"I was banished to the hallway. Who cares? Get inside!"

"They need us both." He gestured to the medical room. "After you."

She stomped her foot, but there wasn't time to argue. She flung the door open and walked into the room ahead of Mike.

All eyes turned to her as she crossed the threshold.

"I thought you were waiting outside," Vinnie said. It was definitely more of a demand than a statement.

She chose to ignore him. "Look who I brought with me."

"Oh, thank God!" Toni said.

"You do not look well, Giovanni. Dominico."

Jo stood near Coz's feet and assessed the situation. Toni was near his head, near where the monitors blinked and beeped. Vinnie stood to Coz's right, where he had easiest access to the wound. Gianni and Nico stood across from him, holding their daggers against Coz's heart and clasping their free hands together. Franki and Donni stood behind them, linking fingers with each other. Donni had her free hand on Nico's shoulder, and Franki had hers on Gianni's. The four of them, five if Coz counted, formed a ring, sharing as much power as they could and channeling it all toward Gianni's control of blood and Coz's dominion over death.

It didn't appear to be working.

There was an awful lot of blood on the table and floor, more than she thought Gianni would be able to have Coz reproduce. Coz was even paler than he had been when she had left the room. The rest of the ring looked barely able to remain upright, let alone lend any energies to anyone.

"Josephina. Join us."

She hadn't realized she had grown roots. Mike had already washed his hands and donned gloves, so she hurried over to the sink and began scrubbing her own hands. This was probably the only basement she'd ever been in that had foot-operated soap dispensers and water spigots, but nothing surprised her with the Brotherhood any longer. Their facility was kitted out for every eventuality.

Once washed and gloved, she joined them at the table where Mike had taken over. He already had the bullet removed and was instructing Vinnie and the others.

"You could not see the bullet because it was lodged behind the appendix."

"Where's the appendix again?" Vinnie asked.

"It is this tiny organ right here. Or it was. It is shredded beyond repair now. We will have to remove it."

"Are you sure that isn't his gallbladder?"

"A human can live without either organ, but the gallbladder is up higher, near the liver."

"I thought the liver was this big thing down here."

"That is part of his large intestine. Vincenzo, I would be happy to give you a lesson in human anatomy, but perhaps now is not the time?"

Jo thought she saw the slightest hint of luminescence on Vinnie's skin, but it was gone so fast she wasn't certain that was what she saw.

"Just do whatever you need to. It'll work, right?"

"Yes, Vincenzo. The appendectomy should be all it takes to save his life. Let us begin."

Mike worked efficiently, locating and lifting the mutilated tissue out of the abdominal cavity and isolating it from the rest of the organs. A series of clamps and scalpel maneuvers later, the remnants of the appendix were removed and added to the pan with the bullet.

"Giovanni, are you capable of sealing up the peritoneum, or shall I suture it?"

"Hmm? The what?"

Mike gestured inside the abdominal cavity. "Right here. The peritoneum."

"I've got enough left in me."

"Can you do that, and seal his muscle tissues, replace his lost blood, and heal his skin?"

Gianni pursed his lips and let out a stream of breath. "Yeah, I got it."

"No. I will suture this tissue. It is delicate work, and we have the right materials. Recharge for the moment. We will need all of your powers shortly."

Gianni nodded.

"Vincenzo, if you would assist, please?"

"What do you need me to do?"

He ignored him. "Josephina, you as well."

"Okay."

"No, stand here, beside Vincenzo. I need this hand free to move."

She moved over and stood beside Vinnie.

"Vincenzo, hold this clamp at exactly this angle." He adjusted Vinnie's hand on the clamp. "Do not move."

Vinnie nodded.

"Josephina, please prepare—" he gestured again "—that needle with that absorbable suture. I will use the purse string technique."

"Is that the best way?" Vinnie asked.

"It is what I learned over the years."

"Learned from where?"

"In your vernacular, I studied medicine in a former life. Now let us get to work. Is the needle ready, Josephina?"

She nodded.

"Giovanni? Some suction."

She handed him the needle, and the blood moved away from the peritoneum just enough so he could work. He proceeded to suture the opening closed in tiny, precise stitches. Watching his fingers move around in such small, exact loops mesmerized her, but it only took a glance into Coz's stomach cavity to bring reality rushing back.

She wasn't sure how long Mike worked, but she knew it took a while. Vinnie's hand shook from holding the clamp in one awkward, stationary place, but he didn't complain. Gianni looked wiped. Finally, Mike tied off the last stitch, and Gianni slumped against Nico. Coz's blood oozed back into the area where Mike had just been working.

"Give me the clamp, Vincenzo."

"Are you sure?"

"It is now or never. It is time to release it and see if our efforts succeeded."

Vinnie handed the tool over in an awkward exchange, and Jo noticed how he struggled to even move his fingers after holding the clamp for so long. Trepidation probably added to the choppiness of his movements.

When Mike had the clamp, he looked around the room, then met Gianni's gaze. "A little suction, please, Giovanni?"

The blood again cleared from Coz's abdominal cavity. When Mike released the clamp, everything held. There was a collective release of breath that Jo didn't even realize the group had been holding, and again Gianni relaxed and allowed the blood to flow through Coz's body again.

"All right, Giovanni. There is just some tissue and skin, and you are done. Can you handle that? We will all lend you our energies again."

Gianni didn't answer. He just closed his eyes and focused, as did the rest of the group. Vinnie lay his dagger over Coz's heart to add his power to the mix, and grabbed Coz's hand with his other hand. Mike, his dagger at his heart, clasped Vinnie on the shoulder. Jo watched, fascinated, as Coz's wound began to seal. First random tissues knitted, then his abdominal muscles fused. Gianni trembled, and the other brothers swayed on their feet, but Coz's skin simply wasn't coming together.

Fearing they were going to need to stitch him closed, she fumbled with the needles and sutures on the surgical table. God, what had she done? This was all her fault, and now poor Coz suffered—they all did. Since Gianni had come into his powers, not one of them had been left with a cut to heal, let alone a scar. And now Coz had both. Mike was going to have to stitch him up, and he'd have a horrible recovery. And a nasty scar. And she knew all about scars.

Hot tears began to well in her eyes.

To add to their problems, he started coming to. He began to moan and move on the table. The tears rolled down her cheeks, falling on Vinnie and Coz's interlocked hands.

Coz screamed so loud and hard, the window of the door shook. His body bucked and turned rigid.

Finally, he bolted to a seated position, his abdomen sealed over with a nasty scabbed line. Jo jumped back in shock.

Coz's brothers all collapsed to the floor.

VINNIE WASN'T SURE how the hell they had pulled it off, but as he lay sprawled on the bloody floor looking up at his brother, he knew Coz would be okay. They all would.

His power of strategy had given him the warm fuzzies when Jo brought Mike in. He didn't know when the hell the guy had studied medicine, but he didn't give a surgeon's shit on a Saturday. It saved his brother. He'd worry about the particulars later.

He looked over at G. *Merda...* the guy looked wasted as all fuck. Franki cradled his head in her lap and stroked his hair. Other than rest and high-iron food, that was probably the best damn thing for him.

Nico didn't look much better than G, but Donni was taking care of him. Toni had rooted through her bag and had passed out granola bars to the guys, and Donni was breaking off small pieces and giving them to Nico while he rested against the wall. Coz was doing his best to get a granola bar, but Toni kept fending him off as she explained everything that happened to him in soft whispers. The guy must be doing okay if his appetite was back.

Vinnie gnawed at his own granola bar. Next to rice cakes, granola bars were ambrosia. Next to anything else, they sucked. He smoothed out the wrapper to see what the hell he was gagging down—carob and flax? Who the hell ate carob instead of chocolate? And flax tasted like fish. But he was starving, so he took another bite of the pressed paper bar dotted with fake chocolate and faux fish seeds.

As he choked down the health bar, he scanned the room. Everyone was with someone except for him, Jo, and Mike. Jo stood in the corner cleaning the surgical equipment, and Mike lingered in the doorway. He gestured with his head for Vinnie to join him and stepped into the hallway. Tired as Vinnie was, he got up and followed him out.

"That was a closer call than I would have liked, Vincenzo."

"I'd like to say we had it under control, but if you didn't show up, we would have lost Coz. At the very least. Maybe G, too." He ran his hand through his hair. "Where were you, anyway? We needed you."

"That is immaterial. I fear that this compound is no longer safe."

"Because Sal figured out John built this place?"

"No, not that. Before now, he believed John built this home for a man who won the lottery. He never gave it a second thought."

"Then what's the problem? Security here is state-of-the-art."

"Vincenzo," Mike sighed, "I do not believe the attack on Josephina was the end game. Had she been eliminated, they likely would have celebrated our grief, but I believe they merely were trying to get close. Close enough to plant a tracking device on her."

"No way. They could do that anytime at work."

"How? You are always with her, and her vehicle is always closely inspected before she gets into it. The attack in the woods left her vulnerable to be traced. Did anyone check her before allowing her to return to the compound?"

Vinnie thought. "No. We were so relieved she was safe that we rushed her back here."

"And she was easily found at the cemetery, was she not?"

"They were probably casing the grounds."

Mike shook his head.

Vinnie ran his hand through his hair again and started pacing in the hall. "Fuck. Her grandmother. Jo went straight to her house."

"Carmina is safe. Her house is always under surveillance."

"By who?"

Mike waved the question off. "She was never an unknown to them. If I have to move her, I will. If I move the girls, I believe Carmina will be safe."

"They could use her as leverage."

"Vincenzo! Your obligation is to the Medici line, not Josephina's maternal grandmother. This compound needs to be evacuated. You have one hour. Take only what you need and go. I will make sure everything left behind is properly dealt with. And make sure you check Josephina for the tracking device, but do not destroy it. We can use it to our advantage. Our opponents cannot know that we know, or we will lose our window of opportunity."

"I'll need a minute to use the dagger. We need a strategy. I don't know where to go."

"I have a list of addresses for you."

"Where are we going?"

"You need to visit Sal's brothers."

"We've been looking for them. We can't find them. Surely you knew that."

"I did. And you did not need to find them. Not then. It was not the time before. It is now. I have their locations, and I will give you the list. Right now, though, I have my own preparations to make. I will see you in one hour's time. Be ready to leave then."

"You've known where they were this whole damn time?"

But he spoke to the air. Mike had already projected away.

Fucker.

Oh, well. He didn't have time to be pissed. Or he'd have to multitask. At the moment, he had to go tell everyone the latest bit of good news.

9

WHEN VINNIE STEPPED into the room, he noticed no one had moved except for Jo. She had finished cleaning the equipment and had moved on to scrubbing down the floor, a task far easier accomplished with a high-powered hose. Something about seeing her on her hands and knees wiping up his brother's blood tugged at his heart, but he didn't have time to dwell on his emotions.

Time was a luxury none of them had.

"Listen up, people. We have to bug out. The compound's been compromised, and time's tight. Pack a small bag—only the necessities—and be ready to leave in an hour. Mike will be back then with details for us. Move out." Vinnie stood by the door, moving his arm in a circle and snapping his fingers like it would get them going any faster.

Nico and Coz got to their feet, and Donni and Toni helped them out the door. But Gianni didn't budge, and Franki sat with him, unmoving. Jo stood and began cleaning up.

"Just leave it, Jo. Mike said he'd take care of the house. You need to get ready."

She blinked, but didn't answer him. She did put the bucket and scrub brush down, though.

"What do you mean, compromised? And why are you suddenly in charge?" Gianni asked.

"Can't we address your concerns on the road?"

"Not when I don't even know how we're getting on the road."

"The compound's been made. We need to get out of here before Sal musters a big enough force to try and take it. All right?"

"How'd they get our location, V? Our phones aren't traceable, and we never come here if we think we're being followed."

"It was my fault. You can bitch me out later, okay? We have to pack. Would you please go?"

"We're not done."

"Noted."

Gianni hefted himself up, and he and Franki left. Jo started to follow them, but Vinnie grabbed her arm. "I need a minute."

"There's nothing to say."

"There's plenty to say, but I don't have the time right now. That's not what this is about."

She sighed and dropped her head, unwilling or unable to meet his gaze another moment. "What do you want, Vinnie?"

He barely heard her, thought he heard a tremor in her voice, but couldn't let himself deal with it at the moment. It wasn't the time or place. "Come to the office. We need Nico's equipment."

It didn't escape his notice that he hadn't let go of her arm. For just a second he wondered if it bothered her, then realized he didn't care. The heat of her skin under his hand, the silkiness of her flesh beneath his palm—he'd probably cost himself the chance to ever have that again, any more than what he had at the moment, so he would savor the innocuous contact for the short span he had it.

He pretty much dragged her up the basement stairs and into Nico's computer haven. At that point, he had to let go of her arm. He needed both hands to root through the equipment until he found the wand he was looking for. "Arms out."

"Last time I did that, you basically stripped me."

"There's a big difference between undressing a woman and rearranging her clothes. When we have more time, I'll show you."

She crossed her arms in front of her and raised an eyebrow.

"Sorry. That was probably inappropriate."

"I'll say."

"Jo, we don't have time for this."

"What do you want?"

"I wasn't lying to Gianni. The compound being compromised is my fault. Mike thinks when Dante had you, he planted a tracking device on you. I never checked you out before sending you home, so—"

"Oh, no!" She grabbed his arms. "I went to see Nonna!"

"I already thought of that. Her location was never a secret and has always been watched."

"Really? I didn't see anyone when I was there."

"That's kind of the point." When she didn't budge, he continued, "Look. If Mike thinks she's in danger, he'll get her out of there. But in the meantime, we need to find the tracker on you."

For the second time, Jo stood in front of Vinnie with her arms out to the side. Vinnie waved the wand over and around her, listening for the change in tonal frequency. It happened when the wand passed over her left hip. When he focused his efforts on determining the exact location of the tracker, it seemed to be coming from her back pocket.

She looked at him and raised her eyebrows. "Well?"

"You can put your arms down. There's only one I can find. Back left pocket."

She reached her hand in her pocket and pulled it back out. It was empty. "I didn't find anything. Are you sure?"

"Check again."

She did. "Nothing."

"Mind if I try?"

"There's nothing in there."

"I have a wand here that says otherwise."

"I just bet you do."

He sighed. "We don't have time for this. Do I have to turn you over my knee or something?"

"You wouldn't."

He put the wand down and deliberately spoke in a low voice. "Try me."

She wiggled her knees a little like she was stomping her feet inside her shoes. "Fine. But you won't find anything. I think I would have noticed if Dante was stroking my ass to shove something in my pocket."

"Hmm. You would think so, wouldn't you?" He stood behind her and placed his right hand on her right hip. He smiled to himself when he heard her sharp intake of breath. Also breathing in, he was again hit with the potency of her scent. She smelled like lavender, not so different from when she'd used his soap. Closing his eyes, he allowed himself a moment to just absorb the fragrance and feel of her.

She cleared her throat, bringing his concentration back to task. He slowly slid two fingers of his left hand into her left pocket and traced the outline of the seam.

"What are you doing?" she asked, breathless.

"Checking the edges of the pocket. Just being thorough."

"Could you please hurry?" Her voice squeaked a little, and she cleared her throat. "We don't have much time."

"Your wish is my command." He shifted and put the rest of his fingers in her pocket. He could feel her body tremble under both his hands, but he didn't mention it aloud. His knuckles skimmed the denim that separated their flesh, and he suppressed a groan. Why did he keep torturing himself?

Shoving his fingers to the bottom of her pocket, he traced the outline carefully until he felt a small, flexible object. Jo would have thought it was something hard sewn into the seam of the pocket, but he recognized it for what it was. Wiggling his fingers into position, and ignoring Jo's protests, he managed to snag it and pull it free.

"Are you quite through?"

He put the tiny object in her palm. "I'll save the 'I told you so' and just ask you to put it on the desk when you're done looking at it."

"I felt that." She poked at the corner of it. "I just thought it was part of the pocket, though."

"I'm aware. Can we get going now, please?"

"It's so tiny."

"I know."

She bent it between two fingers. "And flexible."

"Yes."

"It kind of looks like a circuit board, but smaller. And bendy. And apparently not as delicate."

"I'll have Nico give you the 4-1-1 later. We've got to go."

"How do you destroy it?"

"We don't. Mike has plans for it."

"Like what?"

He took the device and put it on the desk. "You talk too much. Go pack!" He grabbed her arm—again—and dragged her up the stairs, depositing her at her door. "We're down to forty minutes. Make them count."

He went to his room and started stuffing random articles of clothing in a large duffle. Not knowing how long it would be until they hit a store, he figured a toiletry kit was probably a good idea. Throwing some things in his case, he lingered a moment when he got a whiff of his soap. He was going to have to buy a new brand. *Merda!* He couldn't keep going all girly and gooey every time he smelled soap. Finishing off the toiletry kit, he headed back to his room. He didn't expect company while he was packing, but it didn't look like he had a choice in the matter.

Jo and Gianni sat on his bed.

"Don't the two of you have anything better to do than watch me pack?"

"Jo told me about the tracker."

He shot Jo a dirty look before turning away. "This can wait until Mike gets here. I need to pack." He walked to his sock drawer and pulled a few pairs out. That bought him all of fifteen seconds.

"You said it was your fault, V."

"And it was. For a number of reasons. One, she's my responsibility. Two, she snuck out on my watch. Three, Dante planted the tracker on her when I should have been keeping her safe. Four, when we got her back, I'm the one who sent her home before checking to be sure she was clear. It's on me. So get off her back. And you can ride mine later."

"Stop talking about me like I'm not here," she said.

Vinnie threw his socks into his bag.

Jo grabbed his arm. "It's my fault. I'm the one who snuck out. None of any of this would have happened if I had just listened."

"How about you guys go finish packing, and we can argue over this later?"

"We're done," Gianni said. "Our stuff's downstairs. Franki's putting a few last minute things—"

"You'll be waiting for my sister until Mike drags her out the door," Jo said.

"Well," Vinnie interrupted, "I'm not done, so if you don't mind, can we talk about this later?"

"You pack. We'll talk."

"G. Get out."

"No. As we were saying, you aren't solely to blame."

"Fine. Now go."

"What's your problem, man?"

Vinnie stalked to his dresser and pulled open his top drawer. "You want to watch me pack my boxers, watch. Got a good eyeful?" He waved a handful of underwear toward them. "They're black cotton Armani, if you must know." He started throwing them in his bag.

"Maybe I should go," Jo said.

"If that's what he was really pissed about, I'd agree. But I've never known him to care about underwear before."

"Can't I just have five fucking minutes alone in my room to pack in private?"

"Here." Gianni held out his hand.

"What's that?"

"Since secrets are so important to you, I thought maybe you could keep one of mine." He handed Vinnie a small box.

Vinnie opened it and saw a diamond ring.

"It was my mother's. I plan on giving it to Franki when the time's right. I don't want her to find it before then, so I can't keep it, and I can't give it to any of the girls because she might go into their things at some point."

"I'll hold it for you." Vinnie looked away, his gaze landing on a box on his dresser.

"Oh. I get it."

"What?" Vinnie looked at his brother.

"Jo," Gianni said, "can you wait downstairs for us?"

"If you're going to argue about me again, I—"

"No," Gianni said. "I promise I'll include you in all the yelling and lecturing that concerns you."

Jo walked to the door, gave them each one last look over her shoulder, then walked out.

Gianni went to Vinnie's nightstand and picked up the wooden box. "You wanted us out because you didn't want us to see you pack this."

Vinnie snatched it out of his brother's hands. "Don't start with me, G."

"Look, we already had a knock-down, drag-out over that box when the girls first moved in here, and I know you don't want to tell me the gory details. But I also know it means a lot to you. I wouldn't have said anything if you had packed it, and Jo wouldn't have even noticed if you just grabbed it while you were packing. By making a big deal of it, you're the one drawing attention to it."

"You're the one making a big deal about it, not me." He wrapped a t-shirt around it and shoved it into his bag. "I think I'm as ready as I'm going to get."

"Vinnie—"

"Topic. Over."

"When are we going to talk about this?"

"We aren't. Let's go see if Mike's here yet."

Gianni sighed. "And you want to tell me how I got replaced as lead on this excursion?"

"Your ass was down for the count. And I'm the king of strategy. It was a two-fer. Now let's go."

JO HATED HERSELF for being an eavesdropper. But she had come to hate herself for so many things over the last couple of days, what was one more? She had been certain Vinnie was going to talk about her. He had been so mean and dismissive in the medical room, it was only logical that he was going to be candid with his brother when she wasn't around. So when she left his room, she lingered, hoping to overhear the straight truth. She never expected him to reveal personal information instead of mission details.

Granted, he didn't reveal a lot. Only enough to make her want to know more, in fact. But still, she knew almost nothing about him, and her life was an open book to him. Snooping wasn't right, but it somehow seemed fair, in a warped kind of way.

When he and Gianni got ready to leave his room, she dashed down the stairs. So when they got to the ground floor, she was out of breath.

"What's wrong with you?" he asked.

"Thought I left my purse in the basement. Ran down to check." Crap. Did she leave her purse in the basement?

"Did you find it?"

She patted her front pockets.

"You're not going to find it there," Gianni said.

"Phone," she said, and darted off. She ran downstairs and checked the basement for her purse. She made the sign of the cross for thinking that sometimes lies were a good thing. She needed to go to confession. Grabbing her purse, she checked all the rooms quickly for anything anyone might need. Satisfied that she was the only moron who left anything behind, she walked upstairs, breathing back under control.

"Do you have everything now?" Vinnie asked. He was standing at the top of the stairs waiting for her. She knew he saw that she returned with her purse, but she chose not to acknowledge it and was grateful he didn't make a comment.

"Yep. Phone. Purse. Luggage and laptop are packed. Cords for everything are in—"

"Fuck." He turned and walked out of the hallway, and she followed behind him. "Nico! Are you packing the equipment, or do we each need to bring our own computer?"

"Don't you have a separate laptop for MDH work?"

"Yeah, but I thought if you were bringing a bunch of systems, I'd just borrow one of yours."

"Bring your own. I have enough shit to pack." He turned back to what he was doing, mumbling about camera feeds and monitoring equipment, routers and laptops, peppering in a few choice expletives about Vinnie in the process.

"Damn it. I thought I was done." Vinnie ran upstairs, and a few minutes later he came down with a computer bag. Cords stuck out of it where the zipper didn't close. Jo suppressed a smile and watched him put it down. He muttered about phones and iPads until Mike came in. Then he zipped the bag, tossed it on the pile with the rest of the luggage, and launched into strategy-mode.

"We're pretty close to ready. The tracking device is on the desk, and most of the bags are here. We just need to figure out what vehicles we're taking, who's driving, and of course, where we're going."

"Ah, Vincenzo, that is the easy part," Mike said and continued walking through the house.

A tall, good-looking man entered the room. He and Vinnie looked at each other and big grins broke out on both their faces.

"Vin!"

"Danny! How the hell are you?"

The two of them stepped into a one-armed man-hug.

"Good, man. I'm good. You?"

"No complaints."

"Not what I hear, otherwise I wouldn't be here."

"Yeah, well, if I bitch, who's going to listen?"

"You got a point."

"So what are you doing here?"

"Well, me and some of the boys are going to help Mike clear the place out. They aren't here yet."

"How'd you get here first?"

"I brought your ride." Danny held up a set of keys and dangled them in front of Vinnie's face.

Vinnie ripped them out of Danny's hand and walked to the door. Jo heard him yell, "Oh, hell no!" and watched Danny burst into laughter.

"Hey, man, I had to drive the damn thing here. Surely you aren't too good to drive it away? It's fully loaded."

"Mike! G!" Vinnie took off through the house looking for someone to bitch at or back him up.

Jo's curiosity got the best of her. She went to the door and looked outside. An extended black conversion van sat in the driveway.

"Seats nine, easily. Guys their size, probably more like eight. It's got every option you could think of. Even a few custom additions. Everything but a nitrous boost. And knowing Coz, he'll add one when no one's looking. It's the only way you could all ride together. It's comfortable. And not bad looking." He smirked. "For a van."

His smile was a little too big. She understood why Vinnie ran screaming through the house. She and her sisters, except for a couple of crappy work trucks, drove nice vehicles. The guys almost exclusively drove Italian sports cars. What was in the driveway looked like a step up from the A-Team's ride. A luxury step, but still. A van?

"Beggars can't be choosers," Danny said. "Let's go find Mike. He has a lot to tell you, and you don't have much time left."

"Lead the way." She gestured and followed him out of the foyer.

VINNIE AND HIS brothers were with Mike in the kitchen. Vinnie argued to the point that he grew hoarse, but Mike refused to give, saying they all needed to stay together.

A van. He was stuck with a fucking *van*.

Things just kept getting better and better.

Maybe one last try. "Two vehicles are still better than one."

"Vincenzo, enough. I am going to have the tracking device moved in the opposite direction of where you are headed. Hopefully that will send Salvatore's men on a wild goose chase. Meanwhile, I will lead the group here in clearing the compound. The eight of you will head to the first of the addresses I am sending you. Go see Marcus. Find out whether he is involved in Salvatore's plot. If not, try to glean any information he might have. Now, not another word. It is past time that you leave. I will be in touch." He spun on his heel. "Daniel, this way," he called over his shoulder and walked out.

Danny had just walked in, only to be told it was time to go. He shrugged. "Good luck, guys." He followed Mike out of the room.

Vinnie looked at Gianni. "There you have it, then." His phone vibrated. It was the addresses Mike promised to send. "Son of a bitch."

"What?" Jo asked. She had followed Danny to the kitchen.

"All this time. All these searches. Marcus was within an hour's drive."

Jo grabbed his phone and looked at the location. "That'll take longer than an hour."

He looked at her. "Depends on who's driving."

WHILE THE GUYS loaded the luggage in the back of the van, they engaged in a brief debate on who would drive. By the time they finished packing, they still hadn't come to an agreement. And they looked almost as bad as they had after Coz's surgery.

"That settles it," Franki said. "You're all benched. One of us is driving. Just climb in the back. No arguments."

"It's our van, for what it's worth," Gianni said.

"Yeah," Vinnie said. "If anyone's going to be mistaken for a child abductor, it should be one of us."

"Oh, it's not that bad." Jo gave the van a once-over. "It's actually a pretty nice van. Danny told me it's fully equipped. Get in, sit down, and shut up."

Vinnie raised his eyebrows.

"Guess she told you, huh?" Coz said. "I, for one, don't care who drives. I'm beat, and I'm glad to not have to do it." He opened the door and climbed in the back.

Vinnie glanced inside. The roof had been raised so there would be plenty of headroom. The back of the seating area was windowless, as there was a separate luggage compartment behind it. Instead of a plain wall, that panel sported a large LCD monitor. A small pass-through window in the front let the passengers stay in contact with the people in the front seats. Everything was kitted out in wood grain and tan leather. The seats formed a large semicircle around the back, side, and front so it looked like a seventies lounge in there. He watched as Coz sat back against one of the seats along the side of the van, sank in, and moaned. Vinnie figured the seats must be pretty comfortable.

Donni took the keys from Vinnie. "Just relax for a while. I know you could use the rest. We've got it. Come on, Toni. You're up front with me. Get the address from Vinnie to put in the GPS."

Toni got the address and followed Donni to the front of the van. Vinnie didn't have a choice. Everyone else had already entered the van—Nico beside Coz, Franki and Gianni in the backseat, and Jo beside Nico but in corner between the front and side. He climbed in and closed the van door. He looked around, but there was only one place left to sit comfortably—the seat beside Jo, behind the driver. Donni started driving before he sat, and he scrambled to sit before he fell over.

"Ah, heated seats with massage," Coz said. He was asleep before they reached the end of the driveway. Nico passed out a short time later. Soon Franki and Gianni leaned into each other and dozed in each other's arms. That left Jo and Vinnie, awake and for all practical purposes, alone.

And with Donni driving, they had probably two long hours ahead of them. He flipped on the massage and heat functions and closed his eyes.

"Are you going to pretend you're asleep so you don't have to talk to me?"

"I'm not pretending I'm asleep," he said. "I'm trying to go to sleep."

"Fine."

"What's that supposed to mean?"

"It means I'm fine with you sleeping instead of talking to me."

"That's not what your tone says."

Her eyebrows went up. "And what's my tone say, Mr. Expert-On-Every-thing-Having-To-Do-With-Jo?"

"I never said I was an expert on you. Far from it, in fact."

"You're the one who knew I shouldn't go off by myself. You're the one who took charge in the medical room and sent me out. You're the one who knew about the tracking device when I couldn't find it. You know it all."

He sat up and leaned forward, resting his arms on his knees. Then he turned toward her. "First of all, anyone of us, your sisters included, knew enough to tell you not to go off by yourself. If you had thought your actions through, you would have known better, too. Second, yeah, I found the tracker and you didn't. I knew what to look for. So what?"

He watched her pick at nonexistent lint on her jeans. He hated it when she wouldn't look at him, wouldn't talk to him, but this wasn't a conversation he wanted to have in hushed tones in the back of a conversion van, so he didn't force the issue. Instead, he leaned back and closed his eyes again.

"What about the surgery?"

He sighed, but didn't open his eyes. "What about it?"

"Why'd you kick me out?"

"Look. I was pissed, and I took it out on you. I'm sorry. Is that what you wanted to hear? Fine. I'm sorry, okay?"

"It was more than that."

That time he did open his eyes. His gaze bore into her. "You really think you needed to see that? After seeing him get shot, did you need to see him die, too?"

"So you claim you kicked me out to protect me?"

Her voice got louder, kind of squeaked on the last word. He figured Donni and Toni eavesdropped, but he didn't even care anymore. The whole damn van could wake up. She could take out an ad during the Super Bowl. None of it mattered. "I didn't lie earlier, and I'm not lying now. I was mad, and I took it out on you. That was wrong, and I'm sorry. And I didn't want you to watch Coz die if I couldn't save him, because I knew you'd blame yourself. It's my job to protect you, and that's what I do."

"So you were doing your job?"

"Yes."

"That's the biggest bunch of bullshit I think I've ever heard you say."

"What?"

"You weren't protecting me. You *blame* me. Say it. Say you think it's my fault."

"Why are you pushing this?"

"Why aren't you strong enough to admit it?"

"Strong eno—What the hell's wrong with you?"

She pulled her sleeves down and crossed her arms over her chest.

He suddenly understood. He didn't have to punish her during the surgery. She took care of that all on her own.

And for a lot more than just Coz getting shot.

He leaned over and planted a quick, soft kiss on her lips.

"What do you think you're doing?" Her voice got higher with each word.

"Winning the argument. Now leave me alone. I want to sleep." He leaned back in his seat and closed his eyes. A weariness fell upon him down to his very soul.

"What about—"

"Later, Jo."

She was quiet for a moment, then right before he was out, she whispered, "Have you heard anything about Chuck?"

A kernel of guilt tugged at his conscience. He'd been so focused on his brother, he hadn't given the foreman a second thought. Of course his welfare weighed on her. He mumbled, "We'll get Nico on it when he gets up." And with the swaying of the van and the comfort of the seat, a restful sleep claimed him for the first time in longer than he could remember.

10

JO DIDN'T BOTHER trying to talk to Vinnie as they rode along. He fell asleep within minutes of closing his eyes, or he pretended to. Either way, she seemed to be the only one awake in the back of the van, rendering her essentially alone. She could have leaned through the pass-through window and talked to Donni and Toni, but she treasured the silence. It gave her time to think through the events of the last couple of days. Try as she might, she couldn't put the blame for any of it on anyone but her.

Her attack.

Coz's shooting.

Chuck's shooting.

God, Chuck. How would she ever get over the guilt of what she did to him? He was the only person who had always been there for her, and how did she repay him? By getting him shot. Probably killed. What kind of friend would leave another behind like that?

Her eyes stung with welling tears, but she didn't close them, choosing instead to feel the burn and deal with the pain.

Pain she knew. Pain she understood.

She glanced up front, then looked around the back of the van. The twins, whom she'd known and loved all their lives. Franki, her older sister and best friend. Gianni, her sister's whole heart. Nico and Coz, warriors and dear friends. And Vinnie, her protector. Her—

No. So many—too many—descriptions of him danced through her mind. She shut the thought-carousel down, refused to give voice to any terms spinning through her head.

It would be easiest if she put everyone out of her mind. That way, when she left—and she would take the first opportunity presented her to run—she wouldn't have to acknowledge what she left behind. Those seven people were her life, and she endangered them all. She could best protect them by isolating herself from them.

Sure, when she struck out on her own, she set events in motion that got Chuck killed, but that was because everyone was still in her orbit. If she could run and not be followed? She might actually save some lives. It wasn't running away. It was protecting her loved ones.

Just had to bide her time until she found her opening to go.

VINNIE WOKE UP after the most restful nap he'd taken in months. He didn't open his eyes right away, but rather enjoyed the soothing sway of the van as they headed toward the address Mike had given them for Marcus. He wasn't sure how long they had been driving, so he didn't know where exactly they were, but given the condition of the road, he figured they were off the interstate and on either a small town or country road. They had to be close.

Or lost. They could be lost.

For the moment, though, he'd keep faith in the GPS system and assume they neared their destination.

Eyes still closed, he listened to the sounds inside the van. Someone grunted and moaned when the van hit a particularly hard bump. That had to be Coz, still feeling the effects of his surgery. Someone snored slow and soft, almost more of a hum. That was Nico. A broken nose from a fight when they were young gave him a deviated septum. Huh. Wonder why he hadn't taken care of that, now that he could manipulate bone.

Franki and Gianni spoke in hushed whispers. What a surprise—they made plans for another fucking anniversary celebration. G had turned into such a sap since he'd come into his red dagger powers. God willing, when Vinnie's full powers hit, he wouldn't suffer the same fate. He'd rather be powerless than a pussy. His passive strategy-power wasn't that great, anyway. Made him feel like a little bitch, when all he could do was think and his brothers could act. Sure, strategy was necessary. But he felt just as comfortable relying on his instincts.

Music drifted to him from the front of the van. Donni and Toni had a pop station on the radio. He hated pop music. They played it low, thank God. They also talked quietly to each other, so he tuned out the song and focused on their conversation. Vinnie had to fight the urge to smile—they were talking about his boys. Their voices were so similar he couldn't tell which mentioned Nico and which mentioned Coz, but everything they said was favorable. Some of what they said bordered on the X-rated.

He tuned them out. Some things just shouldn't be overheard.

The only person he couldn't get a read on was Jo. She clearly wasn't talking to Franki and Gianni, and the boys were sleeping, so she wasn't passing the time with them. Her breathing was so quiet, it was unlikely she was asleep. What was she doing? What had she done during the ride? That was too much time to let someone like her sit and stew. They'd all be better off if she didn't have time to think about things.

Damn it, he shouldn't have slept and left her alone with her thoughts. That could only spell trouble for him—potentially for all of them.

"How long are you going to pretend to be sleeping?"

Busted. One mystery solved. She spent her time keeping tabs on him.

"I'm not pretending to sleep. I'm resting my eyes."

"You sure you're not just avoiding me?"

He cracked open his left eye. She looked calmer than when he'd fallen asleep. He opened his other eye and turned to face her. "If I was avoiding you, I wouldn't be sitting beside you."

"And where would you be sitting? The luggage compartment?"

"I would have just driven and shoved you back here, away from me."

"If you had driven, you wouldn't have been able to sleep."

"Then you admit I wasn't avoiding you. I was just catching up on some shut-eye."

"You're incorrigible."

The van made a sharp right hand turn, jostling everyone in the back. Jo fell into him, which normally he wouldn't mind in the slightest, but it wasn't really the time or place for those kinds of thoughts. Franki ended up in Gianni's lap, but she might have been there to begin with. His concern focused on Nico and Coz, who pitched forward into the empty floor space, waking them both up. By the sounds Coz made, the tumble aggravated his stomach wound.

"Sorry!" one of the twins shouted back.

"What the hell, Don?" Jo called up to her sister.

Vinnie helped Jo right herself and then pretty much threw Nico back onto his seat. Then he dropped to Coz's side and looked him over. Before getting him up, he needed to know he wouldn't hurt him. "Hey. You okay?"

Coz touched his side and raised a bloody hand. "Looks like I ripped it open."

Gianni had reacted almost as fast as Vinnie. He probably would have been on the floor sooner if he hadn't had to untangle himself from Franki first. "Let me see."

Vinnie lifted Coz's shirt up while he braced himself. "Doesn't look as bad as it feels, I bet," Gianni said. "Lucky for you, the doctor is in, and he's rested."

Franki put her hand on Gianni's shoulder. "Are you sure you can use your powers again? You were pretty drained. And last time it didn't even work right."

Coz grabbed Gianni's wrist. "Just get a needle out and stitch it. I'll be okay."

"You don't know that," Gianni said. "You could've ripped the internal stitches, too."

Coz closed his eyes and threw his head back against the seat cushion. "I'll be okay, man."

Vinnie looked at Gianni. He still didn't look one hundred percent. Before Gianni and Coz argued any more, he intervened. "Simmer down. Here's what's going to happen. I'm going to use my strategy power to see if Gianni is strong enough for this. What I see is what we'll do. No arguments."

Gianni's jaw muscle twitched and Coz opened his eyes long enough to glare at him, but he didn't care. He grabbed his dagger and looked at the possible outcomes. Gianni would wilt if he healed Coz, but there would be no long-term problems from the effort. It seemed that without it, Coz would be in serious trouble. The bleeding was internal, too. Before he released his dagger, he was slammed with another vision—Jo sneaking away and getting caught. He didn't recognize where they were when she made a break for it, but he did see her death if she left.

Damn it, that girl infuriated him. He'd have to be on the lookout and prevent that.

He released his dagger and sent Jo a glare that would have made most men wither. Instead, she crossed her arms over her chest and turned to talk to the twins. So he turned and talked to his brothers. "Sorry, Coz, but you're bleeding internally. G can fix you up. He'll be a little tired after, but there won't be any serious implications from his efforts, so you can relax." He looked at Franki, who was about to speak. "You can all relax. Coz needs this and G will be fine. Case closed."

Gianni looked smug as he concentrated on Coz's injuries. Soon, Coz's coloring improved and there wasn't even a scab or scar where the wound was. His skin was as smooth and unblemished as before the gunshot.

"Thanks, Gianni." he said.

Gianni leaned against the sliding door and propped his arm on his raised knee. "Anytime, man."

Vinnie needed to put a stop to that line of thinking, pronto. "No. Not anytime. You have this savior complex, like you're some kind of god, and that renders us all invincible. Cut the shit, G. You know these efforts are draining, and at some point, the energy required for a save could be too much. You'll use your gifts judiciously, or you'll need my permission to even seal a paper cut. And everyone needs to be more careful so situations like this stop happening. Are we all clear?"

"Did I die and leave you in charge?" Gianni asked.

"Am I or am I not in charge of strategy?" When Gianni didn't answer, Vinnie continued. "You don't see what I see, and you don't know what I know. There are serious implications to using these powers, and I can see what they are. So, when it comes to overexertion, you're damn right I'm in charge. Deal with it."

"Or what?"

Gianni wasn't usually that belligerent, but he was obviously tired and trying to save face in front of Franki. Fuck image, though. Lives were on the line. "Or I make you deal with it. The way you looked earlier today, the way you look right now, it wouldn't take special powers to knock you out. I could just breathe on you and you'd fall over."

"Fat fu—"

"God, Gianni!" Franki said. "Stop. Just stop. You still didn't recover from earlier, and you're wiped out again."

"Coz needed help."

"Not at your expense, I don't," Coz said.

"I don't have a problem with him helping you," Franki said to Coz. Then she turned to Gianni. "Of course I want you to save your brother. Any of them, or any of us. But not when Vinnie says it'll be too much. Promise me you'll listen to him."

"I know my limits, Franki."

"Promise." She grasped his hand and looked into his eyes.

"I'll let V have a say. That's all I'll promise."

Franki looked at Vinnie, desperation and fear on her face.

"I'll keep an eye on him." Sure. What was one more responsibility? "Now, how about we all get off the damn floor?"

They scrambled back to their seats. Vinnie looked at Jo. She crossed her arms and stared at the floor where Gianni and Coz had been. Then he looked across the van to where Gianni and Franki whispered. He took a deep breath and let it out slowly.

Merda.

How long before he had to intervene in someone *else's* life.

Or how long it would be before he missed something else and someone got hurt. Or worse.

The van rolled to a stop and Donni called over her shoulder, "We're here!"

The eight of them climbed out of the van, and Vinnie stifled a laugh. Coz had jumped out first and bent over, touching his toes. Then he squatted, jumped, and did a few lumbar twists, all with a smile on his face.

"Feeling better?" Vinnie asked.

"I feel awesome." He turned to Gianni. "Thanks, man. How you doing?"

"I don't really feel like jumping right now, but I'm solid."

Franki threaded her arm through Gianni's and clung to him. Gianni reached for her arm, looking like he was going to brush her off him, but apparently thought better of it and patted her hand instead. Vinnie held in another laugh, and Gianni glowered at him.

"All right," Jo said. "Let's get on with this."

"So," Coz said, still stretching and twisting, "are we all going in, or should we send a smaller group at first?"

"Marcus was Vinnie's mentor," Nico said. "Maybe he should test the waters."

Vinnie gritted his teeth and turned away, acting like he was assessing the building. The last thing he wanted to do was spend time alone with Marcus, even for a little while. "Honestly, I think it would be beneficial if we all went. More people to assess his reaction, you know?"

"Is that strategy or gut telling you that?" Gianni asked.

"Does it matter?"

"You're Mister Strategic-Power," Gianni said. "You just made a huge speech about listening to you when it comes to courses of action. I'd like to know if I'm relying on your instinct or your power."

Prick.

Gianni knew he and Marcus often had tension. None of them had the same rapport with their mentors as Gianni had had with his, but then again, look where that got Gianni. Sal had betrayed him and all the Brothers because Gianni had been blinded by their relationship.

At least Vinnie wouldn't be swayed by his emotional connection to Marcus.

He didn't have one.

"I don't give a flying fig about the plan or either of your opinions," Jo said. "We're here to meet the guy and decide whether he's involved, so I'm going. Besides, I've seen enough of this van for one day. So, where to? House or school?"

Vinnie looked around. They'd parked in a gravel lot outside a martial arts training center. The school looked less like a commercial structure and more like a giant converted barn. On the hill high above the building stood a big white clapboard farmhouse, complete with wraparound porch. A rustic path carved into the wooded hillside connected the properties.

Vinnie deferred to Gianni's leadership position. "What do you think, G? House or school?"

"You're the strategist. You tell me."

"Fuck you. Will you get over it, already?"

Franki squeezed his arm and whispered in his ear. He sighed. "Fine." He scanned the parking lot. "Let's start at the school. There are two vehicles out front. Maybe he'll be inside."

Vinnie scanned the parking lot. Both vehicles were minivans, which he doubted Marcus would be caught dead in. He likely lived in the house on the hill, and he wouldn't have driven when he could just walk. Hopefully he'd be inside, teaching a class or running a meeting.

Vinnie headed toward the door, and the others followed. It looked like he was taking point on this one, despite his desire to remain in the background.

The group slipped inside. Vinnie looked around. What looked like a rustic barn on the outside was actually a state-of-the-art training facility on the inside. They stood in the lobby near an unmanned check-in desk. Behind it, two adults waited in a generous seating area facing two glassed-enclosed areas. One was a fully equipped gym, complete with weight equipment and cardio machines, the other was a training area full of mats, sparring dummies, and racked weapons where a white belt class was going on. Young children from what he guessed were ages four through nine worked on front snap kicks.

He smiled, thinking back to when he was a white belt. He didn't have parents waiting for him in the lobby, though.

When the class wrapped up, the two youngest children bowed to their master and ran out to the people in the lobby, who helped the kids with shoes and bags. The rest of the class filed out of the room and walked through the lobby toward the door. As they walked past Vinnie and his brothers, many of them bowed. Instinct kicked in and the brothers bowed back, but Vinnie couldn't figure out how the students knew to bow to them. They weren't wearing their uniforms, so there was no way the kids could know the brothers were black belts and due such respect. After all the students were out the door and in the waiting cars, the instructor came out to greet them.

"It's such an honor to have you here!" He bowed to them. He was an Asian man, short, but broad and muscular in stature. His face beamed, and he vibrated with excitement.

The guys bowed back, and the group exchanged looks with each other. Finally, Vinnie spoke up. "I'm sorry. You seem to know us, but I can't place your face. Have we met?"

"Not until today. Wow. I can't believe you're here. All four of you." He stuck out his hand and took each of theirs in turn, pumping their arms with vigor.

"There are eight of us," Gianni said.

"Excuse me. Where are my manners? Hello, ladies. I'm Kevin, Kevin Tran. It's nice to meet you." He shook hands with all the sisters.

Jo returned his handshake, but held on, staring him squarely in the eye. "So, how do you know these men?"

"They're legends here."

Jo dropped his hand and looked at Vinnie.

He shrugged at her and turned his attention back to Kevin. "We've never been here before. How could we be…." He let his voice trail off. Saying the word 'legends' was just too ridiculous.

"Follow me," Kevin said. "I'll show you."

They walked down a hallway outside the weight room, passed a closed door labeled private, and stopped in front of an awards case. In addition to a number of trophies, plates, and medals, there were photos of Marcus's prize students. The shelves held pictures of black belts ranging from young and tiny to middle-aged and muscular. Right in the center of the case were pictures of the four brothers in various stages of their martial arts training. The center photo was one Marcus had taken after they achieved their fourth degree black belts. Also in the case were competition photos and lists of all their achievements at tournaments over the years.

Coz whistled. "Would you look at that?"

"We were what there?" Gianni asked. "Twenty-four?"

"You guys were," Nico said. "We were twenty-two."

"Man," Vinnie said, "we look so young."

"It wasn't that long ago," Jo said.

"Why do you guys look so different?" Franki asked. "You were so cute then."

"I still am, thank you very much."

Franki smiled and kissed Gianni on the cheek.

"That was a lot of miles ago," Vinnie said.

"You won a hell of a lot of awards," Jo said. "All of you."

"Mike told our trainers he wanted us tested by people outside the school," Vinnie said. "He figured we knew the fighting styles of the other students, so they were easier for us to beat. He wanted us to spar people we hadn't ever seen before, to see if we were up to the challenge."

"Did you ever lose?" she asked.

"None of them ever lost in competition, except when they had to spar with one another."

All eight of them turned to look at the man speaking behind them.

Marcus stood there in his *dobok*, a solid black instructor's uniform. Vinnie knew he was a seventh degree black belt, yet his belt was unadorned with his name or rank stripes. Mike believed embroidered belts and patch-adorned *doboks* should be for competition or show only, so everyone involved with the Protectorate trained wearing only plain uniforms and black belts at practice. Even the instructors had followed the policy. Apparently Marcus carried the philosophy with him to his own school. The uniform didn't matter, however. Vinnie knew from experience that even in the soft cotton practice uniform, the material would snap when Marcus threw a kick, block, or strike.

Or would it? It hadn't even been a year since they had last seen each other, yet Marcus looked so different. His hair had grayed around the temples, and he had developed worry lines on his face. He looked older, much older than when they'd parted.

"Vinnie." He swept him into an embrace.

Vinnie clapped him awkwardly in a one-armed hug, but Marcus didn't let him go. He was assaulted with a flood of memories he didn't want to have. He remembered how hard Marcus had tried to make him feel welcome when Mike transferred him from the Italian orphanage to the New York school. Try though he might, given the events surrounding their move from Italy to America, he couldn't bring himself to bond with anyone else. He had Gianni, Nico, and Coz, and he wasn't about to let anyone else in.

But Marcus never quit trying. There were so many times he got Vinnie one-on-one and tried to draw him in, discuss his life, get him to talk... But Vinnie never opened up. Even when he could see his silence hurt Marcus. He just couldn't help it.

And things hadn't changed. He pushed himself away from his mentor and tried to ignore the disappointment on his face.

Marcus turned to the other three men and embraced each of them. Vinnie noticed that Marcus seemed much more relaxed with his brothers than he had with him. And despite the fact that Marcus was under investigation, the guys all seemed happy to be greeting him, too.

"It's great to see you guys," Marcus said after his last hug. "Kevin." He looked at him and nodded down the hall. "Go set up for the next class, please." He returned Kevin's bow, then Kevin bowed to the brothers in salute. They bowed back, then Kevin hurried down the hall, talking to himself. Only then did Marcus turn to the girls. "And it's nice to see you again."

"Again?" Jo asked. "We've never met."

"Met, no. But I know who you are. Who you all are. Your father was so proud of you girls. He talked about you all the time." All of the sisters got tears in their eyes at the mention of their father. Only Jo brushed them away with an irritated swipe of her hand.

Marcus patted Toni on the arm when her tears spilled over. "And I did watch you grow up, although you didn't realize it. I knew so much about you, it was like watching my own family."

Vinnie saw how warmly he greeted everyone—so kind and happy. And they all seemed to be falling under his spell. He refused to be taken in, though. He was there to investigate, and he was going to do his job. Even if no one else would.

"So, what brings you by? I thought we weren't allowed contact anymore."

"Things have changed," Gianni said. "What do you know about—"

"Uh, Marcus," Vinnie interrupted.

Marcus turned to look at him, and Vinnie recognized the look he was hit with. The drawn-down brow, the piercing eyes, the grim set of his mouth. Marcus knew Vinnie was about to unload some kind of deception on him, and he wasn't buying it.

So instead, Vinnie went with the truth. Or a modified version of it.

"We have a lot to talk about, both with you and with each other. But it's been a long day, and we need to get the girls settled in. Just point us to the nearest hotel, and we'll catch up with you in the morning."

"Hotel? Don't be ridiculous. You're family. You're all family. You'll stay with me at my place. It's the farmhouse on top of the hill."

"You don't have to—" Vinnie started.

"Enough, Vin. Come on." He led them back down the hall to the door marked "Private" and opened it. Inside was a large office, complete with a massive walnut desk, leather chairs, a large couch, and several bookcases. When Marcus went to his desk, Vinnie looked at the shelves. Interspersed among several reference books were weapons in display cases and personal mementos. He saw several pictures of him and his brothers, one of John's family, and a framed letter or two. It was too much to take in. He turned his attention back to the desk.

Marcus had already retrieved something and offered it to him. "Here's my house key. Let yourself in. Alarm keypad is right inside the door and the code is twelve-oh-seven. Make yourselves at home. I'll be along after this last class. Unless..."

"What?" Vinnie said.

"Unless some of you want to stay and help instruct. It's my black belt class. I'm sure they'd love to meet you."

"Sounds like fun," Nico said.

"Count me in," Coz said.

"Are you sure?" Toni asked him, glancing at his side.

"Hell, yeah. I'm itching to get in a workout."

"What about you guys?" Marcus asked. "Gianni? Vinnie?"

He sounded so hopeful saying Vinnie's name. Not happening.

"G and I will get the girls settled. You have fun."

Marcus walked them to the door. "Just drive up that road there. It'll take you right to the house."

"We'll grab our bags and come back in," Coz said.

"We don't have doboks, but we've got workout clothes," Nico said.

"Don't worry. I've got it covered. You can change in here, or there's a locker room down the hall. We'll see the rest of you in about ninety minutes." He didn't really give them the option of protesting. Coz and Nico stayed inside and the rest of them found themselves in the parking lot and assessing the "road" he pointed out. It was really more of a long gravel driveway. Vinnie had assumed correctly earlier when he guessed the path up the hill would take them to Marcus's house.

"Do you think this thing will make it up the hill?" Donni asked. "It's pretty steep."

"Give me the keys," Vinnie said. "I'll drive."

She handed them over, and everyone got in. Jo stayed in the back with everyone else, leaving him alone in the front. Fine by him. He needed a minute. He was pissed. Pissed Nico and Coz stayed. Pissed he had to be there at all. Pissed about the alarm code. Just generally pissed.

His brothers had to have noticed, but didn't say anything. Marcus's alarm code was Vinnie's birthday. What the hell was he supposed to make of that?

JO HAD TRIED to sit in her earlier seat, but the twins squeezed in beside her where she and Vinnie had been sitting, forcing her into the corner. With every bump Vinnie hit, she slid around the seat until she was sitting where Nico had been. Vinnie didn't seem to be having any issues driving the huge van up the gravel drive, but the ascent was steep. She felt like she was pitching toward the back of the van, so she grabbed the seatbelt. If she did keep sliding, it would keep her from hitting the floor. When they hit another bump, she clutched the seatbelt to stay seated. She looked up to find Gianni smirking. When she glared at him, he just smiled at her plight. He didn't seem to be having the same trouble she was. Even her sisters were pretty stable.

Must have something to do with the side seat.

Or maybe it was because she had her head up her ass and wasn't paying attention to what she was doing.

Vinnie had seemed different since they arrived. More quiet, more contained. Kind of like something bubbled under the surface and he fought to contain it.

Surely he wouldn't agree to their staying there if Marcus wasn't safe. Would he? It was his job to assess threats, but it was his job to keep them safe, too. Marcus had seemed so nice. But it could be all an act.

She planned on watching Marcus carefully. Guess she'd just have to watch Vinnie, too. One of them was bound to show his cards, and then she'd have a better idea of what was going on between them.

"We're here," Vinnie said through the pass-through.

They clambered out of the van and stood looking at the farmhouse. It was so much grander than Jo had thought when they were down in the school parking lot. The high roof had a steep pitch and many dormers in it. She figured there was a decent-sized attic up there, and not the ones used for storage, but the kind that was safe to walk around in and create other rooms. Potted plants adorned the wraparound porch, and there were two swings plus several cushioned wicker chairs. A few side tables sat between the furniture and held citronella candles.

The windows were large and without mullions, providing lots of natural light and leaving the views unobstructed. And the view, at least the one she could see from the front of the house, was amazing. West Virginia had beautiful mountainsides, and Marcus had chosen a spot that looked over a valley. She could see for miles. There were a few tiny towns they had probably driven through, and the rest was hillside after hillside of forested land, with trees peeking out from between misted gullies. She imagined rocking on one of the swings, bundled in a sweater and drinking coffee while watching the sunset. With a spectacular view like that, she could sit there for hours.

The guys unloaded the luggage, and her sisters started grabbing bags. She joined in, and the group climbed the porch stairs. Vinnie put the key in the lock. They opened the door to the beeping of the alarm. She walked into the foyer and looked for the keypad. "Anyone remember the code? I forget it."

Her sisters all shook their heads, but the guys answered in unison. "Twelve-oh-seven."

She typed it in and the beeping stopped. "Is number recall part of your warrior training?"

"It was an easy number for us to remember," Gianni said.

"Why?"

"It's my birthday." Vinnie barely unclenched his jaw to get the words out.

"Oh, I love birthdays," Donni said. "Too bad yours is so far away. I'd make a big meal and a cake…"

"Sounds great," Toni said. "Do we have to wait for Vinnie's birthday, or can we collect now?"

She giggled. "Surely one of us has a birthday soon. Who's next?"

"For us, Coz," Gianni said. "But not until October. What about you guys?"

Jo busied herself going through a bag she had carried in. She didn't like where this was going.

"Well," Toni said. "Jo's is soon, but—"

"So let's do a big bash for her," Gianni said. "I'll help cook."

"Thing is," Donni said, dropping her voice, "Jo doesn't really do the big celebration thing."

She could feel everyone's eyes on her, so she kept rooting in her bag. Surely something in there was better than where the conversation was headed.

"She's doing it this year," Vinnie said. "Right, Red?"

She looked up and met his gaze, then turned back to her bag.

"Buck up, *bella,*" he said in her ear. She hadn't even heard him approach. "We could all stand to unwind a little. Take one for the team."

"So, when is the shindig?" Gianni asked.

Donni looked at Jo and shrugged, then turned to Gianni. "Less than a week. We should probably start planning."

"Why can't we just have a party whenever we want?" Jo asked. "If you all want a big spread and a cake, we could just do it now. No use in waiting."

"Then your birthday won't seem special," Gianni said.

Damn it.

"I can't believe we never discussed birthdays before," Franki said. "So Gianni, when's yours?"

"It was in May. It's a long way off."

"May? Why didn't you say something? I'll have to make it up to you."

Jo rolled her eyes. Great. Another anniversary those two would be celebrating. Wonder if she'd have any luck convincing Donni to throw Gianni a belated party instead.

She looked up and saw Vinnie staring at her. Nope.

Looked like she would be getting a party, whether she wanted one or not.

11

"**WELL, WHAT DO** you guys think?" Vinnie asked. "Order food? Unpack?"

"Unpack?" Jo said. "Isn't that kind of forward? We don't know him, or his house, or his expectations."

The guys laughed. The girls all looked perplexed.

"You need to understand," Gianni said. "We're family. That would be like feeling out of place at your parents' house."

"We aren't family," Jo said, gesturing to her sisters and herself. "We just met him. Besides, are you really comfortable with him? What if he's—"

"No point saying anything out loud that you'd rather no one knows about," Vinnie interrupted.

He mouthed 'surveillance' at the group, and the girls nodded.

"Okay," Gianni said. "The ladies don't feel comfortable finding rooms yet, so why don't we deal with dinner?"

They all drifted into a spotless kitchen outfitted with high-end professional appliances that gleamed as though never used. The warm wood floors and cabinets were equally pristine.

Donni tossed her purse on the soapstone counter and opened the refrigerator. "That's odd. It doesn't even look like he lives here. No leftovers, no takeout containers. Not even enough veggies in the crisper to make a salad. Nothing is thawing for dinner tonight." She opened the deli drawer. "I can't even make a good antipasto platter with what he has here."

"He probably goes out every night," Gianni said. "We'll likely have to order something."

"Order what? From where?" Toni asked. "We don't know what's around here. And if we did, we wouldn't know what was good and what wasn't. I haven't eaten today, and I'm not wasting my one meal on fast food or a bunch of crap."

"Someone's cranky when she doesn't eat," Jo said.

"I'm not cranky. I'm particular."

"Maybe you should just eat meals at regular intervals like a normal person," Franki said. "Then you wouldn't have to worry about a missed one or a lousy one once in a while."

"I eat your cooking and I don't complain."

Franki glared at her. "Then taking a chance on an unknown restaurant here shouldn't be an issue."

"Ladies," Gianni said. "Donni and I can go shopping for food. The rest of you, get comfortable." He kissed Franki and guided Donni toward the foyer.

"Do you have a store in mind?" Donni asked him. "We passed two grocery stores not far from here."

Gianni closed the door before Vinnie heard his answer. Didn't matter. He wasn't the one shopping, thank God. He was, however, the one left in his mentor's home with three curious women.

"Well, I know you don't want to unpack yet, but do you want to at least explore the house, get a feel for it?"

"Do you think Marcus would mind?" Toni asked.

Vinnie snorted, but his phone vibrated before he could answer. He checked the display—a text from Gianni.

Passed car on driveway. Keep eyes open. Want me back?

Why the hell was a car on Marcus's driveway?

He texted back. *Checking. If u don't hear from me in 5, come.*

"Something wrong?" Franki asked. "Is Gianni okay?"

"Follow me." He led them into the family room and spied a staircase. "I need to check something. Wait upstairs until I give you the all clear. If something happens, call G."

"Wait," Jo said.

"Now, Jo." He started pushing them up the stairs, then turned back toward the family room. He drew his gun and his dagger and crouched down, trying to avoid the windows.

He crept to the foyer and looked out one of the sidelights. No car in the driveway, which meant either the driver had turned around or had recognized that someone other than Marcus was at the house and parked down the drive so as not to be seen. Given that it would have been far easier to turn around in the school parking lot than to get up the driveway, his money was on the latter.

Not seeing anyone or any movement in front of the house, he reset the security alarm and made his way through each room, glancing out the windows to look for intruders.

Backing into the kitchen, keeping his eyes trained on the doors in the dining room that led out to another porch, he bumped into someone. Spinning around, dagger fisted in striking position, he found himself face-to-face with Jo. Armed with a butcher knife, she was also ready to strike. Unlike him, though, her eyes were wide with terror.

"What the hell are you doing?" he whispered at her.

"I was coming to help."

"I could have killed you."

"I could have killed you, too." Her voice had a slight tremor to it, but she no longer looked frightened. Her brows and lips were both drawn down in an expression he'd learned well—annoyance.

"Get back upstairs with your sisters."

"You're not my boss."

The whisper-yelling grew louder, and he worried they would scare their intruder away. Or run out of time. He didn't want Gianni returning for nothing. "In matters of safety, what I say goes."

"I'm coming with you."

"Damn it, Jo," he said. Her crossed-arm stance told him she wouldn't budge, and he didn't have time to argue. "Stay behind me. And if I tell you to do something, do it. Got it?"

She shrugged.

He clenched his teeth and bit back a retort. Then he set off toward the kitchen door, Jo right on his heels. He saw movement just beyond the tree line. "Gotcha."

"Who? What do you see?"

"Keep your head down and go disarm the alarm. Once I'm outside, rearm it."

"Where are you going?"

"We don't have time for this. Go!"

She crept down the hall, and he went back to the dining room. Soon he heard the beep indicating that he was free to open the door. He snuck outside and into the trees bordering the side yard. With any luck, he'd be on the guy before he made a move toward the house.

Vinnie moved silently through the woods. By his estimate, he was about thirty yards away from where he had seen the person hiding when his foot snapped a twig. He ducked behind a tree and didn't move. After waiting a few minutes, he was about to continue on when he heard a rustle behind him. Unsure how the guy got behind him, he moved into position. The guy headed right toward him, but he'd get the advantage.

He reholstered his gun, leaving one hand free for grappling, and waited… a little longer… a little longer… He heard the guy breathing right behind him.

One more step…

He tightened his grip on his dagger and raised it. Spinning around the trunk, he threw the intruder against the tree and put his dagger against his throat.

Her throat?

"Who are you?" he asked.

She didn't answer. Her pupils dilated and she huffed shallow breaths, but she didn't cower. Props to her for standing her ground with a weapon at her throat.

She was fit for her age. Mid-forties, maybe? He studied her face, noted the tiny lines around her eyes and lips. Maybe she was older than he initially thought. As he stared at her, he could see her trying to figure out how to counter his grip. Maybe she was one of Marcus's students.

That didn't explain why she was up at his house, though.

"I'm going to lower my hands, and you're going to start talking. I don't like what I hear, I'm putting this dagger to use. *Capisce?*"

She nodded.

He lowered his hands and stepped back one step. The woman assessed him for only a fraction of a second, then tried to take his legs out with a sweep kick.

He saw it coming the whole way. It took him no time to jump over the kick and, using her own weight against her when she was on one leg, take her to the ground, pinning her. "What'd I tell you?"

"You said you were going to use the dagger if you didn't like what I said. Looks like I'm not the only one who lied."

"A, you didn't say anything, so I didn't lie. And B, you're out of chances. Start talking, or I'm ending this conversation my way."

There was more noise in the brush, and Vinnie took his eyes off the woman to see if more trouble was coming. Jo stepped out from behind a tree. "Vinnie! What are you doing?"

"Help! Help me! He attacked me! Rape! Rape!"

When Jo hesitated, Vinnie said, "Come on, Jo. You know I wouldn't force myself on a woman."

She squinted at them both, and once again crossed her arms over her chest, the butcher knife still grasped in her hand. The woman under Vinnie kept struggling.

"No, it's not that," Jo said, shaking her head. "She looks familiar."

"So?" Vinnie focused on the woman. "Who are you?"

The woman stopped thrashing and threw her head back on the ground. "Fine. My name is Tina. I'm an instructor down at the school."

"That doesn't explain why Jo thinks she knows you. Or why you're here."

Tina gritted her teeth and turned her head.

"Start talking, lady" Vinnie said.

She sighed. "Marcus asked me to meet him here."

"Here?" Jo asked. "That doesn't make sense. He's down at the school right now. Why would he send you here?"

"That's none of your business."

"I'm the one with the weapon here," Vinnie said. "I'll decide what's my business and what isn't."

"I'm not saying anything else. You want answers, ask Marcus."

Vinnie looked at Jo, who just shrugged. Then he yanked the woman to her feet. "Fine." He sheathed his dagger and pulled out his gun. "Walk."

He guided them out of the woods into the cleared lawn area behind Marcus's house. Gianni ran out the back door, dagger in hand and gun drawn. "You didn't text, so we turned around."

"Sorry. Took longer than I expected," he glared at Jo, "but I've got it covered."

"Who's that?" Gianni talked to Vinnie over the woman's head like she wasn't even there.

"Name's Tina. That's all she's said so far. She doesn't want to talk until Marcus is here."

"Let's call him, then," Gianni said.

"He won't answer when he's in class," Tina said.

How the hell did she know so much about Marcus and his schedule? Maybe she worked with Sal and had Marcus under surveillance. Or maybe Marcus was up to no good, and she was in on it.

Maybe he should just wait and gather facts before jumping to conclusions.

"He should be coming soon, anyway," Jo said.

"All right," Vinnie said at the backdoor. "In you go." He pushed her inside then shoved her into a kitchen chair. Huh. The alarm didn't ring. "Jo, did you set the alarm before you left?"

"Yeah."

"Here's my gun." He handed it to her. "Watch her." He nodded to Gianni, and they started to leave the room.

Franki ran down the stairs waving her arms. "Wait! It was me! It was me!"

Vinnie and the others stopped and looked at her. Donni and Toni came down, too.

"Sorry," she said. "I saw Gianni get here, so I turned off the alarm and went out to meet him. But he ran around back before I got to him, so I came back in and went back upstairs."

"Damn it, Franki," Gianni said. "You could have been hurt."

"So could you!" she said.

"Enough," Vinnie said. "We have more pressing issues at the moment."

Vinnie and the others looked at Tina.

"Don't I know you from somewhere?" Franki asked.

Tina stayed silent.

"You, too?" Vinnie asked. "Has she been following you?"

"We would have seen her," Gianni said.

"No." Franki tapped her chin.

"She used to go to our church," Donni said.

"That's it!" Jo said. "You used to sit by the organ."

"So what are you doing here?" Vinnie asked.

Tina didn't answer, just glared at him. After a long period of silence, she cocked her head to the side. "You aren't what I expected. By a long shot."

"Who sent you?" Vinnie asked. "Obviously it wasn't Marcus. Or was it?"

"What's that supposed to mean?"

"We'll ask the questions." Vinnie stared at her. He stared at her through narrowed eyes while he tried to decide their next course of action. "What do you mean, we aren't what you expected?"

"I think that statement is self-explanatory."

"Why'd you expect anything from us? We don't know you."

"I told you. I work at the school. I've seen the trophy case, heard the stories. You're a far cry from your reputation. What do you think Marcus would think of your behavior?"

"What do I think?" Vinnie asked. "I'd imagine he'd appreciate us looking out for his house!"

She snorted.

"And what does that mean?"

But she remained silent.

"Look, lady… Tina," Vinnie said. "We need to know what's going on."

Still she said nothing.

Vinnie exchanged looks with Gianni. G shrugged, looked toward the door, and pointed to his watch. Vinnie glanced at the time. If this encounter was an innocent misunderstanding, Marcus should be along any moment. If not—

Vinnie didn't want to think about the alternative.

Jo walked around Tina's seat and motioned to Vinnie to follow her. He gestured to Gianni, and his brother stood guard over the woman, dagger out and ready to strike. Satisfied, Vinnie followed Jo to the dining room.

"Why don't you and Gianni leave and let us talk to her?" Jo asked. "We can probably get more out of her if you two aren't here."

"Are you crazy? Leave you alone with her? She's at least a second degree black belt. She'll kick all your asses and be out the door before you know what happened."

"We've been training with you for months. I took kickboxing for years before that. I think four of us can handle one black belt."

He didn't want to say it aloud, but he seriously doubted it. Tina was strong, fast, and most importantly, seemed smart. Very smart. She knew how to track, how to defend herself, what things were safe to say, and when to stay silent. She was well-trained by someone.

"Give us a shot," she said.

"Not. Happening."

She sighed, but Vinnie just dragged her back into the kitchen before the argument could continue. He looked up when he heard the front door. Marcus and the guys were back.

"Guess the point is moot," he said to Jo.

It didn't stop her from being angry with him, though. Her eyes blazed and her nostrils flared, and he looked away.

Just one more sin he'd have to atone for later.

The three guys walked into the kitchen, deep in conversation, but when Marcus saw Tina sitting in the chair and Gianni's dagger out, he stopped speaking in mid-sentence and ran over to her.

"What the hell is going on here?" He put himself between Gianni and Tina.

"We passed her on the driveway," Gianni said.

"But she hid her car and sneaked up here," Vinnie continued. "She was in the tree line out back, scoping out the property. We tracked her, and she fought. Brought her in, but she's not talking."

"Let her go. Tina, get up," Marcus said. He held up his hand to cut Vinnie off before he could say anything else. "No, Vin, it's okay. She was only doing what she was taught. What I told her to do."

"What?" Gianni dropped his dagger about an inch.

But Vinnie had already put the pieces together. He sighed. "Drop it, G. She's his girlfriend."

Gianni immediately lowered his dagger. "You came to that conclusion pretty damn quick."

"It's true," Marcus said. He offered his hand to Tina. She took it, and he pulled her to her feet and into his arms.

"I'm sorry," Vinnie said. "We didn't know. We were just trying to protect the girls. And your property."

Tina eyed him coolly. "You have a funny way of protecting people and things. You were on the offensive. That's not a typical defense."

"The best defense is a good offense," he said.

"That's the other way around."

Marcus chucked her under the chin and tipped her face to look at him. "They were doing what they were trained to do, babe. Just like you did. No one was hurt, nothing's damaged. Let's just move on from this, hmm?" He kissed her quickly and pulled back, searching her face.

Just like that, she relaxed and extended her hand toward Vinnie. "I'm ready to put this behind us. Let's start over, shall we?"

Vinnie struggled not to gape at her. Why did all the women in his life change opinions so damn fast? He constantly struggled to keep up with their logic. He didn't always get along with his brothers, but at least he knew where he stood with them.

There was no point in wondering, though. Guys had wondered that for centuries and gotten no further than he did figuring it all out. He took her hand, and they shook to their truce. Gianni and Jo did the same.

"So," Donni said. "Gianni and I were going shopping for dinner. Can we give you a lift to your car?"

"Oh, don't go," she said. "I brought dinner for Marcus and me, but there should be plenty."

"For eight additional people?" Gianni said. "We don't want to impose."

"It's not an imposition. I just did a massive grocery run. I'll go get the car, then we can eat."

"I'll drive you," Gianni said. "I know it's not far, but it's the least I can do."

"Deal."

Vinnie watched them leave, pointedly ignoring Marcus, who seemed to be struggling for words. The last thing he wanted at the moment was the heart-to-heart talk his mentor seemed interested in having. Before Marcus broached the conversation, Vinnie asked, "So, how did you two meet? And why do the girls recognize her from their church?"

"So suspicious. It's not a big deal. We met when I was guarding John. She was always at the church, always alone. I found her attractive, so I approached her. We started dating about six months before John died. When I moved here, she followed."

Vinnie didn't want to talk about Marcus and his romantic life. While the rest of them caught up, Vinnie excused himself and left the room. The girls could eat up the romantic details of that story. He needed a moment alone.

IT WAS A NICE evening, so they decided to eat *al fresco* instead of in the house. Jo sat back after a large bowl of Caesar salad and a piece of grilled chicken and sipped her wine. Everyone seemed to enjoy themselves, and after the tense beginning, got along beautifully. Tina had apparently recovered from her earlier encounter, and she and Marcus were the perfect hosts. They alternated between telling amusing stories and asking their visitors questions.

If the eight of them hadn't gone there with an ulterior motive, the evening would have been fun and relaxing.

Well, probably. Maybe not for her. She had a lot eating at her.

Jo tried to put things out of her mind and enjoy the easy company, but the best she could muster was taking in the scenery. The sun set, painting the sky with vibrant splashes of color interspersed with the softest pastels. The first stars winked at her from above the treetops. She chose the brightest, the one she noticed first, and made her silent wish.

I wish for Chuck to be safe and well.

She fought back tears. The last thing she wanted to do was ruin everyone's evening. And frankly, that was all that would happen if she stayed. Every minute sitting there, composed and engaged, became more difficult to endure. Before she lost it, she had to escape.

Jo stifled a fake yawn and stretched her arms over her head. "I'm going to start cleaning up." She stood and grabbed her plate. "It's been a long day, and I'm getting tired. I'd like to get the dishes done and the food put away, and then, if you don't mind, I'd like to go to bed."

Marcus and Tina stood before she finished speaking. Everyone else started to get up, too.

"Don't you worry about a thing," Tina said. "I'm just going to toss this stuff in the dishwasher. It won't take more than a couple of minutes."

"Really, I'd like to help. You've been so kind," Jo said.

"Don't be ridiculous," Marcus said. "You must be exhausted. Let me show you all to your rooms."

"We can help," Donni said. "At least, I can. I'm not really tired."

A chorus of voices agreed with her.

"How about I show you all where you can stay," Marcus said, "and then anyone who isn't tired can come back down?"

"I really feel like I should help clean up first," Donni said.

"Go," Tina said. "I'll be done before you're back. There's really very little to do. Then you can tell me more about that chicken marinade you mentioned earlier."

"You got it." Donni stood with the others.

Marcus led them into the house. Everyone grabbed bags and followed him up the stairs. "This house has five bedrooms. I have four rooms I can offer, plus a foldout in the office."

"If we all double up," Toni said, "we should be fine. We don't want to impose on your workspace."

Jo swallowed a sigh and a bitter retort. With Franki and Gianni sharing a room, she became the odd duck. No way would she ask Vinnie to take the uncomfortable space. So she'd either be on the floor in the twins' room or on the foldout. Given the choice, she preferred the foldout.

Marcus stopped at the top of the stairs and pointed to the left. "That's the master suite, if you need me. Right in front of us is the hall bathroom. Towels are in the linen closet behind the door. There's also a bathroom in the basement and showers down at the *dojang*. With this many people, we're all going to need to use any facilities available."

They all nodded.

"All the other rooms are this way."

He turned right and gestured to the first door on the left. "Two twin beds are in here."

Jo peeked in the room, tastefully decorated in olive and camel.

"That's us," Coz said.

"Thanks," Nico said. He and Coz stepped inside and put their bags down.

"That's the only room with two beds," Marcus said. "Right across from them is a queen bed."

"We'll take that," Donni said.

"Thanks." Toni entered the room, followed by her twin.

Jo glanced after them. The room was decorated in a similar fashion to the first one, but in ice blue and cream.

"Down the hall, the rooms each have a king," Marcus said.

Franki looked at Gianni. "I should stay with Jo, so we all have a place to go."

"Yeah." He kissed her on the nose.

"Don't worry about me," Jo said. "You guys take one room and give Vinnie the other. I'll stay on the couch downstairs." That might just give her the opportunity she'd hoped for to sneak away.

"Marcus and Tina have done so much already," Franki said. "You don't want to kick them out of their workspace and have yet another bed to make up."

"Don't be ridiculous!" Marcus said. "It's no imposition."

"I don't plan on opening the bed, Franki. I'll just sleep on the couch part of the couch."

Marcus guided Franki and Gianni into the room on the left. "I'll take care of it. Get settled."

Franki raised her eyebrows, but she followed orders. She and Gianni entered the room and started unpacking.

"I'm not staying up here," Vinnie said by the door of a bedroom decorated in oxblood and tan. "If anyone's taking a couch, it'll be me."

As inviting as the room looked, Jo wasn't interested. "I'm the one who didn't want to share with Franki or the twins. I'll go."

"Not going to happen."

"Well," Marcus said, "while you two argue over the room, I'll go make up the foldout."

"Please don't," Jo said. "Just give me a sheet and a pillow. I'll be fine."

"I'll be fine," Vinnie argued. "Don't do any more than you already have, Marcus. Just leave the stuff on the couch. I'll take care of it."

Marcus waved and stepped into the hall bathroom, coming back out with sheets, a blanket, and a pillow. "This stuff will be in the office for… one of you." He chuckled and walked downstairs.

"Vinnie, please. I'm tired and I want to be alone. I don't need a bunch of people all around me."

"You aren't sleeping alone downstairs."

"You're joking, right? God, get over yourself, okay? Marcus trained you guys, he trained Tina in case something would happen here. Do you honestly think this place isn't as secure as the compound? It's probably locked up tighter than the White House."

"Still…"

"Vinnie." She grabbed her bag and headed back to the stairs. "I need some distance right now. Don't push me."

He stood there, staring at her as she began her descent. When she was on the last step where she could still see him, she looked back. He was just turning to go into his room.

Downstairs, Marcus was leaving the office when she got to the door. A peek inside confirmed her suspicions. He made up the foldout for her.

"Thank you, Marcus. But you really didn't need to go to all that trouble. I would have been fine sleeping on the sofa."

"And what kind of host would that make me?"

She smiled.

"Truth be told," he continued, "I figured you'd win the argument. That's why I made up the bed. If I had thought Vinnie would be the one down here, I would have just put the linens in here and let him decide what he wanted to do."

"No, you wouldn't have."

He cracked a smile. "You're probably right. But it doesn't matter now. The bed's made up for you. And now I'll leave you to it. If you need anything, I'll be awake for a bit longer. And you know where everyone is sleeping. Don't hesitate to ask if you need something."

"Thanks, Marcus."

He patted her on the arm. "Goodnight, Jo."

"'Night."

He walked down the hall, and she closed the door.

Finally, some peace and quiet.

She locked the office door, drew the brown thermal shades, flipped on the ceiling fan, and turned off the light. The room was cloaked in darkness, the only sound the whirring of the blades, the only light from the pale moon shining through the skylight. She stripped and stood under the fan, enjoying the feel of the circulating air caressing her skin, cooling her until gooseflesh rose all over her body. Her eyes soon grew accustomed to the darkness, and she could make out her surroundings. Digging in her bag, she pulled out a big, baggy nightshirt and slipped it over her head, letting the soft cotton warm her chilled flesh.

She climbed onto the bed and peered around the room. She could make out a massive desk and bookshelves behind it. It looked like a flat screen nestled between the shelves across from her bed. Maybe she should ask Marcus for the remote control. It was obvious she wasn't going to be doing much sleeping. A shame, really. She'd prefer to be rested when she left in the middle of the night. But if she went and asked about the remote, she'd run the risk of having to talk to people again, and she just wanted to be alone.

Uninterested in turning on the light, she got up and groped the desk surface and some of the shelves. After a half-hearted five-minute search for the remote, she gave up and went back to the bed. If she tried hard enough, maybe, just maybe, she could get some sleep.

Instead of sleep claiming her, she was hit with a crying jag.

It was no use trying to stop herself. She accepted it would last a while, so she lay there while the tears soaked her pillow.

12

VINNIE TRIED TO sleep. God knew he needed to get rest when he could. Instead, he lay there, listening to the laughter floating up the staircase.

How could they all be carrying on with Marcus and Tina? Especially after all that had happened? They should be taking stock of events and investigating Marcus for signs of involvement. Instead, everyone sat in the kitchen enjoying themselves.

Everyone but Jo. And him. Him and Jo.

Man, it didn't take long for his thoughts to turn there. But he refused to dwell on her.

He lay there, unable to sleep, thoughts churning over and over in his head.

They needed to find out about Jo's vision.

And they needed to confirm what happened to Jo's foreman.

He wouldn't mind learning more about Enzo Palmeri, either.

And whether Marcus threatened Jo's safety.

Huh. Everything came back to Jo. Even when he tried to put her out of his mind, she was there.

A quick glance at the clock showed he'd lain there for hours, thinking the same thoughts over and over. He strained his ears, listening to his surroundings. Everyone must have gone to bed, because the house was silent. He could hear the occasional cricket or barn owl, and the whirr of the ceiling fan. The air conditioner kicked on, humming softly in the background.

Fuck it.

He got up and threw on a pair of shorts. One way or another, he and Jo were settling things.

He opened the door and slipped out into the hall. From Gianni's room came a deep muffled voice followed by a feminine giggle. He and Franki were probably celebrating some other stupid anniversary. Or creating a new one to celebrate later.

Thinking about it only soured his mood.

Vinnie sneaked down the stairs, trying not to make a sound. He and Jo were going to have a long, frank discussion, and he didn't want anyone to interrupt them.

He stopped in front of the office. The door was ajar, and a dim light shone through the opening. Rapping quietly on the door, he let himself in. The light came from a desk lamp, which cast a soft glow in the room. Exploring the office might be a good idea—could have done so earlier if Jo had let him have the office foldout—but he'd have to save it for another time. He had more important issues to deal with at the moment.

Jo was gone.

Vinnie tamped down the icy panic that roared through his veins and took a deep, calming breath. There was no way something could have happened without him hearing. He hadn't slept all night. But she had sneaked out before. Maybe she ran again. Or, if luck was with him, maybe she was in the kitchen.

He left the office and turned down the hall when he heard a creak on the front porch. A quick glance at the alarm system showed it to be disarmed.

Damn it. He didn't even have a weapon.

It took only a second for him to cross the foyer and open the door.

Jo sat on the porch swing, one bare toe pushing her back and forth, the chains emitting a tiny squeak every time she swung forward.

Relief flooded his system, followed by agitation. He resisted the urge to lecture her about safety. Again. He also fought the desire to take her in his arms, confirm she was safe, and comfort his fears. No, he'd do neither. It was time to clear the air, nothing more.

She didn't look at him, but must have sensed his presence in the darkness. "Don't just stand there. Come over here or go back inside."

"I thought you'd run."

"I considered it."

"Why'd you stay?"

She didn't answer.

"You shouldn't be out here alone. It's not safe."

"It's fine. I'm fine."

"Still…"

"Look, I couldn't sleep. I came out here for some fresh air. Are you going to join me or not?"

He crossed the porch. She stopped the swing long enough for him to join her on the seat. When he began rocking, she tucked her leg under her.

"Jo, we need to talk."

She still didn't turn to him. "Do you know any constellations?"

"What?"

"Constellations. Star formations. Do you know any?"

He thought a moment and said, "Just a few of the major ones. Why?"

"My dad used to have a telescope. On clear nights we would spend hours star-gazing. Being out here, watching the night sky, it makes me feel closer to him."

He decided to give her a while before he pressed for information. At least she was talking.

"See that one?" She pointed to her left. "The one that looks like a stretched out W? Do you know that one?"

He shook his head.

"That's Cassiopeia, the queen. I always liked that one. She's easy to find."

"What else do you like?" he asked.

"If you follow the center of the W and draw a line, you'll run into the tail of the Little Dipper and the middle of the handle of the Big Dipper."

"I see them. Those are pretty much the only ones I know. Those and one other. What else?"

"Follow the tail of the Little Dipper down through that cluster of stars." She pointed, guiding his gaze with her fingertip. "See that really bright one?"

He nodded.

"That's part of Lyra. That small angular figure eight." She drew the pattern in the air, tracing the stars. "And see those other two bright stars there and there?" She pointed at two other stars about as bright as the first. "Those two plus the one in Lyra make up the Summer Triangle."

"Wow. You really do know your stars."

She shrugged.

"I always liked Orion."

"The hunter? Figures."

"What's that supposed to mean?"

"Nothing. See that one? It looks like a dipper but has a trapezoid attached to it and two lines coming off the bottom?"

"There?" His gaze followed her finger.

"Yeah. That's Hercules, the strong man. Maybe that's more to your liking than a queen or a triangle."

He turned to her. "I think they're all beautiful. When I was... never mind."

"What?"

"It's just nice that your dad took the time to teach you all this. Anytime I looked at the night sky, it was just to wish on a star."

"Did your wishes ever come true?"

This time he didn't answer her.

"I wished on a star tonight."

"What'd you wish for, Red?"

"I can't tell. Then it won't come true."

"Ah."

"It probably won't anyway." They rocked a bit in silence. "What did you wish for as a child?"

He stayed quiet.

She turned to face him. "Do you want to talk about it?"

He smiled at her through the darkness. "Actually, I came out here for you to do some talking."

"There's a shock."

"Come on, Jo."

"What could I possibly have to say?"

"Don't even go there. I'm offering an open ear, a dry shoulder."

"I don't need either."

"Okay, then. You don't want to share your feelings, you can share some information. Tell me about the vision."

"Now's not really the time for business."

"God, you're infuriating. You won't talk about Brotherhood business, you won't talk about how you're feeling. All I've gotten out of you tonight is an astronomy lesson."

"That doesn't have to be all you get."

He raised a brow. "Excuse me?"

"No business tonight." She turned her body toward him, readjusting her legs under her on the swing. "You want to know what I'm feeling? I'm feeling numb, empty, wrung out. Entirely spent. What I really need is… is… God, are you going to make me say it?"

"Say what?" He couldn't have been more confused if Nico had been explaining programming code. Been there, done that, felt equally lost as he did at the moment. "Tell me what you need, and it's yours."

"How about I show you, instead?"

His head hurt. For the life of him, he couldn't imagine what she was going to show him. They'd already looked at the stars, they weren't in the house, and the entire property was just shadows and silhouettes in the middle of a dense West Virginian forest. If she wasn't going to say what she wanted, he'd have to let her guide him. "Okay. Show me."

She got off the swing, and he started to rise, too, but she pushed him back down. Then she stood in front of him, placed her hands on his shoulders, and straddled his lap.

She started to lower her lips to his, but he put his finger against her mouth. "Jo. Stop. This isn't what you want."

She pulled back from his hand. "Don't tell me what I want. You aren't in my head. You don't know."

"But I *do* know, Jo. I know the last time we kissed, you put on the brakes. I know you're hurting over Coz and Chuck. I know you're scared about Dante, and probably your vision, too. And I know you'll hate yourself—and me—if we do this."

"You're wrong. This is what I need."

"I'm not going to take advantage of you like this."

"I'm not drunk, or sick, or out of sorts. I know what I'm doing. And what I want to be doing. I'm the one who will be taking advantage of someone tonight. And if it's not going to be you, I'll just go inside and find somebody else."

It was his turn to pull back. A slap would've hurt less.

"So, I'm that easily replaced?"

"I don't know how else to say this, Vinnie. Just for tonight—no strings. I need you. I need to be held, to be loved. I choose you, but if you say no…" Her voice trailed off, leaving him to fill in the rest of the sentence.

He didn't like the implication. At all.

"Jo, I've thought about this. A lot. You know I have. But I didn't think our first time would be like this. Lots of ways, but not like this."

"Not first time—just *our* time. Our time is now. Don't turn me down."

Her vulnerability was as obvious as the tears in her eyes.

"Why me?"

"I'm not discussing this now. Are you in or out?"

"If you can tell me—and mean it—that you won't go looking for someone else if I say no."

"Kind of a no-win for me here, Vin."

"You're wrong. Answer the right way, and it's a win-win."

She sighed and closed her eyes. "I was lying, okay? I wouldn't have gone after anyone else." She opened her eyes. "But I wasn't lying about needing this. I need you tonight."

"Are you sure? I can just hold you. All night long if you want, and we never have to do anything else."

"I know what I want, Vinnie. I was honest with you. Now it's your turn. What's it going to be?"

As wrong as it felt, it still felt right. Honor be damned. He took her face in his hands and tipped her head toward him.

She seemed so fragile, nearly breakable. He planned on taking things slow. Figured gentle would be the best way to go. Not that he minded. When it finally happened—and he had been ninety-nine percent sure from the beginning it was going to happen—he had planned on savoring every moment of it.

Plans change.

Jo fisted her hands in his hair and pulled him to her. She claimed him with a searing kiss, exploring his mouth, tongue laving and circling his in fevered heat.

It only took a second for his brain to click off and match her pace.

Her nails raked down his back, and the chills she caused melted away with the heated rush of his blood. She smelled like lavender, the bouquet drifting to him on the breeze as he ran his hands up her thighs.

He could get high on her scent.

Or her touch.

Or her taste.

His mind reeled, caught up in the assault on his senses. She dipped her head to his neck and ran her tongue over his Adam's apple, across his collarbone, and up to his ear. A hiss escaped him. She bit his earlobe, her teeth nibbling on the sensitive flesh, her breath moist and hot against his skin.

His hand skimmed higher. Still higher. *Il mio dio!* All she had on was her nightshirt, and nothing underneath. Her skin was soft as rose petals. Smooth, silken. He felt his control slipping away but couldn't stop. He palmed her hips, his fingers cupping her firm backside. When she moaned, he knew he'd found a sensitive spot, one he wanted to explore in greater detail.

"Jo," he said, voice raspy and hushed, "let's take this inside."

He lifted her to her feet and stood, hands still cupping her. The plan was to walk her to her room, but she had other ideas. Instead of stepping with him, she reached for his shorts and yanked his waistband down. The combination of her hands grazing him and the breeze touching his newly exposed skin took his defenses away. She pushed him back down on the swing, and straddling him again, took him inside her.

She set a ferocious pace, each thrust punctuated by a throaty grunt. The swing creaked under their frenzied motions, the squeaking chains keeping tempo with their ragged breathing and pumping hips. All thoughts of foreplay rushed out of his head as fast as the blood did. Squeezing her, riding a wave of pure lust and desire, he lost the tenuous hold he'd had on the small amount of control he possessed. She took him up and over his threshold, smiling against his neck as he came down from his climax.

She climbed off him and straightened her nightshirt, then, probably because he sat there stunned and unmoving, pulled him to his feet and adjusted his shorts so he was covered again.

"Well, thanks. I needed that. Goodnight." She lifted her hand in a wave and turned toward the door.

Before she could walk away, he grabbed her arm and pulled her back around. "What the fuck was that?"

JO WAS FLUMMOXED. Despite the darkness, she could see the anger on his face, in his eyes. A wild animal, barely contained.

For the life of her, she didn't know what had happened. They'd agreed on a quick tryst, and that's exactly what they'd had. In fact, it had been better for her than it had been with any of the other men she'd slept with. Could it be that he didn't enjoy himself? She thought he'd finished, but she didn't have much experience with those things. Maybe he wasn't satisfied.

"I'm sorry, Vinnie." She hung her head, unable to meet his gaze.

He was silent for a moment, then spoke in a much softer voice. "Jo, look at me." When she didn't—couldn't—look at him, he tipped her head up so he could see her. "Jo?"

She couldn't breathe, couldn't speak. Tears welled in her eyes—again. She'd slept with him to mask her pain, not add to it.

"Hey." He pulled her into his arms.

She fought to get her breathing under control. If he didn't let her go soon, she'd hyperventilate and pass out. Not the end of the night she was looking for.

He pushed them apart a few inches and looked at her again. "I thought we were going to make love, Jo."

Her brows drew down. Isn't that what they just did?

"You can't possibly be satisfied after what just happened."

She shrugged. "Why not? Isn't sex about gaining satisfaction?"

He sighed and ran one hand through his hair. "Jo, what just happened here can barely be called sex."

"What would you call it, then?"

He grunted. "Mindless fucking."

Was that bad? Was she just bad at it? Stepping back to gain some defense against him, she crossed her arms over her chest, protecting herself. "Well, I don't know what you consider sex, then. This is how I've always done it, and I've never had any complaints. Until now, anyway."

"God, Jo. *Porca troia!*" He ran his hand through his hair and cursed some more under his breath. Then he sighed. "I'm not complaining. I'm fine. You were fine. Too good, actually. I'm worried about you. Your needs."

Her eyebrow arched. "My needs? I needed sex. I got it. I was quite content, until you pointed out how I messed that up, too. So now, if you don't mind, I'm going to bed."

She turned, but again he grabbed her and stopped her from leaving. Jo looked at his hand on her arm, then up into his face. "Get your hand off me."

"No."

"Excuse me?"

"I said no. I promised to make love to you tonight, and that's what I'm going to do."

The word 'what' died on her lips as he scooped her into his arms. She squealed and slapped at him. "Put. Me. Down!"

"I will." He opened the door, entered the house, closed and locked the door behind him. Walking to the keypad, he said, "Set the alarm."

"Put me down and do it yourself."

Instead, he hefted her over his shoulder into a fireman's hold and punched in the numbers. She pounded on his back, but he gently slapped her bare bottom. She hadn't expected that. Or what she felt when his hand connected with her flesh. When she wiggled—not sure whether she was trying to escape or trying to get him to do it again—he repositioned her in his arms again and entered the office where she had a makeshift bed.

"I'll scream."

He put her down. "I'm counting on it."

She wasn't sure how she felt about that, either, but her heart fluttered in her chest, betraying all thoughts of reason.

He locked the office door and put his hands on her arms, pushing her back into the room. Then he grabbed the hem of her nightshirt.

"Please, don't." The tremor in her voice belied her fear, but she couldn't control it.

"I'm not going to hurt you."

"I… I've never…"

"What?" He searched her face, but she looked away.

Why had she turned the desk lamp on before she left the room? The damn thing was still on, and she didn't want him to see her embarrassment. Or her apparently never-ending supply of tears.

"I—" But the words wouldn't come. His fingers stroked her neck, then came under her chin and tipped her head toward him. "Tell me. You can tell me anything."

It tumbled out of her in a rush, like a waterfall plummeting to depths far below. "I've never had sex with my clothes off."

"Wait… what? Were you a virgin before tonight?"

She saw the incredulity on his face and rushed to explain. "No, no. I don't mean—" She sighed. "You know." She dropped her voice. "I've only ever removed the clothes that were necessary. No one's ever seen me naked before."

She saw the shock on his face and tried to turn from him.

He pulled her to sit beside him on the bed and once again spun her head toward him.

"How can that be? How can you…?" His voice trailed off.

"Easy enough." She looked at her hands, clasped tightly in her lap. Her fingers were wringing each other, but she couldn't stop them. It was like she was watching someone else's nervous tick and was powerless to stop the movement. "I never wanted anyone to look at me. And no one's ever complained."

"Tell me about them."

"What? No."

"Tell me. I don't understand."

She sighed and surrendered to him. There was no way he would drop the subject, so she figured she might as well get it all out in the open. The words tumbled out in a rush. "My first time was in college. At a frat party. We ducked into the only private space we could find—a closet. It was dark, there wasn't much room and we were drunk, so it was over pretty fast."

"No one's first time should be so void of passion."

She couldn't bear the sympathy in his voice, on his face. "Who the hell said it was *passionless*?"

He cocked a brow.

"It was no big deal. I wanted to get it over with, and I certainly didn't want him staring at me. I got what I wanted."

"But not what you deserved."

She ignored him. "That way worked for me. Works for me. I prefer sex that way. When I decide I need a release, I go in search of one. That's how it's always been."

"You just hook up with random guys in random places?"

She knew he was growing upset. In case it was because of their encounter, she decided to set his mind at ease. "No, they weren't random. And with the exception of tonight, I've always used condoms in addition to the pill. No unplanned pregnancies, no diseases." His relieved sigh didn't escape her notice. "And for the record, I get tested regularly. It's not like there have been a lot of guys, anyway."

"What do you consider a lot?"

She scowled. "I don't see you sharing."

"I'll tell you whatever you want to know."

"What's your number?"

"I believe I asked you first."

She harrumphed and crossed her arms. "After the first guy, three more. And then you."

"But you never took your time and did it right?"

"Who's to say what's right? It's been just fine. For me." She ran her hands through her hair. "After the frat boy, there was a bartender in the stockroom, a waiter in a different stockroom, and someone I took my general contracting license exam with."

"In a stockroom?"

"No. In a car."

He shook his head. "So that's it, just fully clothed in four in tiny spaces. And now a porch."

"No. Not fully-clothed. Mostly clothed. And yes. You make five. Well, five and a half."

"I'm sorry." He kind of laughed the words out. "How do you have a half?"

She turned away again and fought off a new wave of tears. "Chuck and I... tried once. I thought maybe I could be more open with him, but..."

Again he turned her head back toward him. "But what?" he asked quietly.

"But I got uncomfortable even when he started undressing me. I was okay when he undressed, but I just couldn't go through with it. He ended up holding me for most of the night. That's when we knew we couldn't ever be more than the best of friends."

"He was a good friend, Jo."

She sighed the tears away and straightened her shoulders. "So there's my story. You know my number, and you know why I can't give you any more than what I gave you on the porch. I'm sorry it's not enough."

"Jo." He took her hands in his. "You're enough. I feel bad because I wasn't enough for you."

"What are you talking about? You were wonderful."

He shook his head. "The problem is that your scale is off."

"What?"

"If you're comparing what we just had to what you've had before, the bar was set so low that it might have seemed wonderful to you. Here, tonight, I'm going to show you what wonderful really is."

Her breath caught. "What? What do you mean?"

He leaned in, his breath heating her to her very core, and whispered in her ear. "We're going to make love, Jo. The right way. Right here. Right now."

Before she could respond, he nuzzled her and started kissing her neck. He moved her collar aside and trailed his lips over her collarbone, up her throat, and along her jaw line. She trembled under his ministrations, thoughts tumbling out of her head like white water rapids over a mountainside.

As his tongue traced a path from her neck toward her mouth, panic poured through her. "At least turn off the light."

He murmured "hm-mmm" against her throat, and she took that as a no. She wriggled under him, trying to stand up, but all she managed to do was free the edge of her nightshirt.

Vinnie wasted no time. He grabbed the hem and started slowly raising it, letting his knuckles graze her overly-sensitive flesh. Tiny bursts of electricity zinged over her skin everywhere he touched. She was charged, alive, and vibrating under his hands. Lord help her, his fingers had done nothing but caress her back. What would it feel like if he—when he—explored her body.

She was ready for more, ready for what he offered.

But, no. She wasn't. She couldn't.

He nipped at her lower lip.

Oh, God help her. She was. She could.

He must have sensed her change in attitude, because he pulled away from her and continued to inch the soft material up her stomach, past her ribs. She sucked in a breath as he let the hem brush against her breasts. The sensation shot through her torso and pooled in heated agony low in her abdomen.

He smiled and continued letting the material dance lightly across her skin.

She threw her head back, abandoning control to him. When a moan escaped her, he continued pulling the garment until her arms were pinned above her head.

Horrified at her behavior, at what he'd see, she fought to redress. He held her hands tightly wrapped above her.

"Jo?"

She shook her head, clamped her eyelids shut.

"What happened? Why are you fighting me?"

She couldn't breathe. Spots flashed behind her eyelids, and she feared losing consciousness. Instead, she opened her eyes wide and tried to look past him to the door. "Stop. Let me go."

He didn't look at her body. He searched her face, tried to make eye contact. She could only be grateful his gaze didn't roam. She fought for breath and tried to hold back yet another rash of tears.

"Tell me what's wrong. Let me help you."

She shook her head furiously as her body began to tremble.

He lowered her arms to her side, the gown dropping with it, and she curled into a fetal position on the bed.

He lay beside her, brushing wisps of hair away from her face. She recoiled from his touch, but he didn't stop. Slowly, her racking sobs turned into short, silent whimpers.

"Jo. Please talk to me."

While she hadn't been able to give in to his demands, his soft plea undid her. "I don't want you to see my body."

"Why on earth not? You're beautiful."

She balled the blanket in her fist and whispered, "Because I've abused it. I'm... I'm hideous."

He tried to turn her head toward him, but she wouldn't budge. Finally, he stroked her neck and whispered, "Is this the secret you've been trying to keep from me?"

She couldn't say another word, so she just nodded, tears soaking the blanket in her hands.

"I hate to tell you this, then, but you've been wasting your time."

Her breath caught in her throat, momentarily ceasing her sobs.

The slight change in her demeanor must have urged him on, because he said, "I know about the scars."

She bolted upright and turned to look at him.

"What? How did you know?"

"Remember when you tried to help Gianni in the woods?"

She thought back to the day she followed Gianni, tried to reason with him. He had begun using his power on himself, once even slicing so much of his flesh that it seemed he'd been scourged. After his repeated displays of self-mutilation, she'd gone to him and told him part of her story—the part she hid from everyone. She'd become a cutter after her trouble with Enzo, tried to match the pain on the inside with pain on the outside. It was only because her family had intervened that she was still alive. But she bore the scars—many, many scars—of her temporary break from reality. That was why she didn't want anyone to look at her. But to think that Gianni betrayed her trust...

"I can tell by the look on your face that you want to strangle him. Before you go off the deep end, you should know he kept your secret. He never said a word."

"Then how did you know?"

"We had surveillance out there, part of the security system. I was at the monitor when you talked to him. I'm sorry I didn't turn away, but I was worried about him, too. That was a brave thing you did to help him."

She shook her head. She was many things, but brave wasn't one of them.

"Still," she said, "you haven't seen. That's worse than just knowing."

He cleared his throat and looked away. She sneaked a peek at his face, and she thought he might be blushing. "What?"

"I've seen," he muttered.

"Excuse me?"

"Not on purpose. But I have seen, and I think you're breathtaking."

She didn't know if she should be flattered or pissed off. She went with the easier of the two emotions. Anger.

"What do you mean, you've seen? Do you have surveillance in my room, or in the bathrooms?"

"Do you really think so little of me?"

She didn't answer. She needed more information first.

"The night you spent in my room? After the bar?"

"You said you didn't undress me."

"And I didn't. But the next day, I went to my room after I thought you were up and gone. You had apparently fallen back asleep." He played with the blanket for a moment, then he looked at her.

"I had showered." She could barely get the words out.

"If I had known you were in there, I wouldn't have barged in. And I covered you so no one else could walk in on you."

She could feel the heat rising to her cheeks. For what seemed like the hundredth time that night, she blinked back tears.

"Jo. Please look at me."

Finally, she turned her head about a fraction of an inch.

He pulled her the rest of the way around. "You're beautiful. Just the way you are. Inside and out."

And the tears spilled over, running down her cheeks.

He wiped them away with the pads of his thumbs. "If you still can't bear for me to see you, tell me now. We can always try again another time."

She looked down. "Another—? What if I never want you to see me?"

"Too late," he said.

She looked up, her mouth dropped open in shock.

He seized his opportunity and kissed her.

13

SO THIS WAS what being kissed senseless meant. He'd kissed her twice before that night, and twice before she'd been shaken to her core. But this was a whole new level of passion for her.

He consumed her very essence. As his tongue explored her mouth, his body pressed against hers, the only thing between them a thin film of material. Her hands raked over his bare back, nails teasing the skin, fingers digging into the ripple of muscle. She had to remove that barrier and feel his heat against her.

Pushing back from him, she noted the concern on his face. It was quickly replaced with appreciation and longing when she reached for the hem of her nightshirt and lifted it over her head. She trembled, wondering if she made the right decision. Wondering if her courage would last.

He took it from her and tossed it to the corner of the room, far out of her immediate reach.

Probably didn't want her getting any ideas about recovering herself. But as soon as she met his gaze, her fears vanished. She'd never experienced what he was offering, and she was primed to take it.

Thinking he'd pull her back into the kiss, she started to lean toward him, but he held her at arm's length. Despite her desire, discomfort inched up her spine, tightening her scalp in a tingling sensation of shame. Lifting her hands, she tried to cover her scars.

He grabbed her hands and held them out to her side.

Then the corners of his lips lifted. "Exquisite."

And just like that, the burn of desire replaced the heat of shame.

He lay her back on the foldout and knelt beside her. Then bending, he lifted her arm to his mouth and pressed his lips to a scar on her bicep.

It felt like current surging from his lips through her blood. No man had ever seen her scars, let alone touched them with such reverence. His lips skimmed over the surface of her skin, stopping to kiss each one of them. The heat from his breath, the softness of his mouth… she was stuck in a limbo of arousal, unable to retreat, unwilling for it to stop.

He trailed his kisses along her collarbone, lingered in the hollow of her throat, and continued across the other collarbone to her shoulder. Every scar he found he paid close attention to, tracing it, nuzzling it. She found it hard to breathe, not because of his weight draped across her, but because of his nearness to her, his focus on her body… the very heat of his skin against hers.

His mouth continued to explore, moved from her wrist to her hipbone. She hissed in a breath and tried not to quiver, not to tremble.

"Mmmm," he said.

She felt the sound rumble in his chest and throat before it vibrated on her body, but it didn't prepare her for the erotic sensation. A moan escaped from her lips, an involuntary answer to his hum against her skin.

Certain he was about to move between her legs, she parted them for him, all too eager for his attention to move on. Instead, he chuckled, pulled her legs together, and moved down one leg, then to the other, kissing the scars he found on her thighs.

She reached down and threaded her hand in his hair, the soft waves like strands of silk between her fingers. It was too much. "Please, Vinnie."

He turned and looked up at her, his tongue tracing a glistening path down toward her knees.

"Please," she begged.

He looked toward her. "Please, what?" His voice was low, husky. Before she answered, he returned to her shin.

"You know what." She was breathless, close to panting.

Again he ignored her. There were no scars on her feet, but that didn't stop him from kissing her ankles and sucking on her toes. She fisted the blanket with both hands, holding herself down so she didn't fly away.

"Jo." He trailed his fingers along the arch of her foot. "Turn over."

"Hmmm?" She could barely form a sound through the haze of sensation. He rolled her onto her stomach and brushed his lips over the nape of her neck.

"What... what are you...?"

His tongue laved the length of her spine, lingering in the small of her back.

"Relax. We're not moving on until I've shown you how beautiful you are," he said between kisses. "Every. Square. Inch."

His fingers trailed down her thigh, lingered on the back of her knee, while his lips pressed lower on her spine. Lower. Lower still...

His attention was torturous, unbearable, exquisite. Her buttocks trembled, sensitive to every lick, every nibble, every kiss. Unable to endure another caress, she flipped over onto her back and reached toward him. "You've shown me, I believe you. Please? Now?"

"Not even close." He pulled her into a seated position, drew her lower lip between his teeth, bit down gently until she squirmed. He kissed the corners of her mouth, traced her lips with his tongue.

She gasped, opening her mouth for his further exploration, and he took full advantage of the opportunity, slipping his tongue inside, meeting her stroke for stroke, need for need.

He tasted minty, of toothpaste or mouthwash. The cool tingling mixed with her hot greed, the collision of senses condensing into a storm of passion. She turned the tide and tipped his head, claiming his mouth in a searing kiss, tongue plunging into his mouth and taking all he offered.

His hands skimmed down her arms, lingered at her elbows, then came up and cupped her breasts. As he kneaded her sensitive flesh, her breath caught. He took that opportunity to pull his mouth away from hers and trail kisses over her face and down to the hollow of her throat. His thumbs brushed over her hardened nipples, making them throb and tighten further.

Throwing her head back, she granted him easier access to her neck, and he sucked at her pulse point. She couldn't see, couldn't hear, couldn't speak... just floated on the crest of the waves of sensation.

She had to touch him. Her fingertips danced across his back, over his broad shoulders, and down over the ridges of his biceps and triceps, which flexed with every flick of his fingers.

More. She needed more.

Her hands flitted over his chest, and she stopped to trace circles on his breastbone where there was a smattering of downy hair. She moved her fingers down to his stomach, feeling the ridges of his abdominals. Her nails traced the grooves between each sculptured muscle, trailing lower and lower, skimming through the soft hairs under his navel that led the way to her goal. Her heart pounded. Every stroke of her fingers over his body made it harder for her to breathe, to think, to feel. And she loved it.

She tucked the fingers of one hand under his waistband while the other cupped him through his shorts. His arousal pressed through the material, a spot of his excitement dampening the soft cotton. She rubbed the wetness, circling the tip of his erection in slow, deliberate strokes. His hiss gave her immense satisfaction. Spurring her courage, she tugged at the garment. "Take these off."

He stood and pulled her with him. "You."

She met his gaze, then pulled the shorts down, watching them puddle at his feet until he stepped out of them. His erection popped forward, large and throbbing. Caressing him, she was again satisfied when he moaned.

He moved her hands aside. "Not yet."

There was no time to pout. He sat her on the edge of the bed, lowered her to the mattress, and nudged her legs apart. He knelt and kissed the inside of her thigh by her knee, then higher. And higher.

His mouth finally reached her most sensitive spot and she groaned, thrashing her head. Scents of soap, sweat, and arousal mingled into an erotic bouquet that engulfed her. He lapped at her folds before circling the sensitized bundle of nerves, sending her into new levels of ecstasy. His fingers skimmed over her stomach and again reached her breasts. He fondled them again, alternating between softly squeezing them and gently pinching her hardened nipples, all while he laved her sex. She clutched his wrists, not wanting him to stop, not knowing if she could take much more.

Something was happening. Something new, exhilarating. A tingling ache built low in her abdomen, growing and expanding. Filling her up from the center out or emptying her by drawing energy from the ends of her hair to the tips of her toes. She didn't know where the feeling started or ended, but she knew she couldn't bear it.

He pulled one hand away and she whimpered. Suddenly he plunged his fingers inside her, stroking her while flicking his tongue on the sensitive nub above his fingers.

It was too much. The pressure built and burst, exploding through her body. Shattered, she wailed as she rode cresting wave after cresting wave of pleasure, rising and falling with each stroke of his finger, each circle of his tongue, until the flood slowed to a tingling pool of satisfaction.

He stood between her legs, his sex throbbing, the tip glistening. She didn't think she could take anymore, but couldn't deny her desire.

Leaning over her, he positioned himself and pushed slowly into her, filling her. She groaned at the fullness, the friction a blindingly glorious sensation. He thrust into her, first slowly, then quicker, establishing a rhythm she was only too happy to meet. The pressure built again, this time faster and fuller, but she knew what to expect and pumped her hips harder, desperate to reach her release.

Vinnie thrust harder, then he grunted, stopped. Arched and strained. A heat surged through her, overloading her senses. He twitched a bit, and she looked at him. Head back, neck cords taut and leg muscles quivering, she couldn't take her eyes off him. He was magnificent. She bucked against him, making him groan, then he draped his body over her, managing to thrust farther into her, slow and deep, while he nuzzled her neck.

And with one last exquisite stroke, he forced her over the edge again, the explosion engulfing her and sending her on a mindless ride into oblivion.

HE FORCED HIMSELF to roll off her, worried about her supporting his full weight.

"Mmmm. Where're you goin'?" Her words slurred, and she reached one hand toward him, her eyes still closed.

She was either well satisfied or near death, and he didn't think it was the latter. He slipped his arm under her and pulled her close to him.

She nestled against him and rested her head on his arm. "That was different."

"Just different? Not spectacular, mind-blowing, life-altering?"

"Fishing for a compliment?"

"I don't need one. Your screams told me all I need to know."

"Screams?" She propped herself up on her elbow and looked at him. "I didn't scream."

"Oh, but you did. Twice. Just like I said you would. In addition to various moans, whimpers, and gasps."

Her whole face felt warm. She might remember a moan or two. Or more. Maybe. But she vehemently denied it. "I did not. I'm a quiet lover."

"Maybe with your one night stands, but not with me." He grinned.

"I did not scream. Or anything else."

"Well, there's no way to prove it now. We could go again and record it."

She started to roll away from him.

"Get back here." He tucked her against him again. "I'm just kidding. Kind of."

He stroked her back, loving the feel of her soft skin under his construction-roughened hands. After a moment, her fingers skimmed over his stomach, and he knew she wasn't going anywhere. He closed his eyes and inhaled deeply, trying not to quiver under her touch. He hadn't realized how sensitive he was after sex, and he didn't want her to know the effect she had on him.

"Vinnie?"

"Hmm?"

"That was the first time I ever—"

"I know, *bella*. I know."

"No, I mean, not the clothes thing. The other thing. I never had an…"

He wasn't surprised. Given her experience with sex, it was unlikely she'd had an orgasm before him. He was truly honored to have been her first.

And second.

"Anyway… It was spectacular, mind-blowing, and life-altering."

He turned toward her and smiled, traced her lips with his thumb. "No, you are." She closed her eyes and settled her head on his arm. He kissed her eyelids and the tip of her nose. Her lips parted on a soft sigh, and he pressed his mouth to hers.

She reached to pull him deeper into the kiss, but he stopped her. "Get some sleep. You need your rest."

She smiled, snuggled next to him, and dozed off.

Vinnie lay silent and still, unable to sleep, trying to figure out their next step.

He crawled out of bed at five the next morning, careful not to wake Jo. It would be best for both of them if he got upstairs before anyone noticed where he'd been. Besides, he was running late for his call to Pasquale.

His shorts were still on the floor where he's stepped out of them. A smile spread across his face at the memory. He bent to retrieve them, and when he looked up, Jo was awake.

"Are you sneaking out on me?" She clutched the sheet to her and lifted it higher as she waited for his answer.

Still undressed, he sat on the bed, hoping his nakedness would make her more comfortable. He leaned over and kissed her softly on the lips. "You don't really think you're getting rid of me that easily, do you?"

"You don't owe me anything. Besides, you were the one rushing out, not me."

"Where's your phone?"

"What? Why?"

"Just give it to me. Mine's in my room."

She wrapped herself in the sheet and crossed the room. He slipped on his shorts while her back was turned and held his hand out for the phone when she came back to the bed.

"I guess I'll go get dressed," she said.

"No need. I don't expect to be too long."

"I'm not sitting here naked while you have clothes on."

"Fine." He striped the shorts off and threw them at her. "Now we're both naked. Deal with it."

She groaned but didn't dress.

He dialed and glanced her way. "Hope you have an international plan."

"What?"

"Pasquale?" he said into the phone. He noticed her look of surprise when he started speaking in Italian to his assistant in Italy. She almost dropped the sheet. Almost. Good thing she didn't. He needed to focus.

At first he felt a little strange. He'd never been naked while talking to a man on the phone. But not long after explaining the number on his caller ID and the need to be brief that morning, he forgot all about his lack of clothes.

Soon he forgot his need to be brief.

Merda, Pasquale turned incompetence into an art.

How fucking hard was it to get a man to sign a contract? Every time Vinnie talked to the CEO of Gemmora and smoothed things over, Pasquale talked to them and made things worse. Vinnie had finally convinced Gemmora they didn't need to see Gianni, and instead of Pasquale getting the contracts signed, he came back with a demand for a sit down with all the VPs. And the CEO. They'd all met before. It was totally unnecessary. And totally Pasquale's fault.

He argued with Pasquale so long he lost track of time. As sunlight started creeping through the skylight, he focused on where he was. He'd hoped to save Jo the humiliation of everyone knowing he spent the night with her, but he was cutting it close. Tired of getting nowhere with Pasquale and in a hurry to get upstairs, he barked a list of orders at the fool and ended the call. Despite the disconnection, his mind worked on overdrive processing the problem.

He ran his hand through his hair and did some fast figuring. There was no way to make the merger work unless the Gemmora people met the executive team, and there was no way to do that unless they came to the States. And he doubted that was going to happen. He let loose a string of curses and flung himself back against the pillows.

He jumped when something grazed his thigh. *Madonna mia*, he'd forgotten he was in Jo's room. How the hell did he lose sight of something so important?

"I'm sorry," he said. "Work issues."

"Sounded bad. Anything I can do to help?"

He toyed with the edge of the sheet, much more interested in his fingers grazing her skin than the linen. "If you don't mind me being caught in here, I can think of a great stress reliever."

She batted his hand away. "I do mind people knowing you were in here. Go. Now. Before anyone gets up and sees you."

He knew she was right, but couldn't resist a parting barb. "Now who's blowing who off?" He slipped his shorts on, kissed her, and walked to the door.

"Vinnie?"

Grabbing the handle, he turned and looked at her.

"Thanks for a wonderful night."

"There's more where that came from." He grinned and left the room.

It wasn't until he was up the stairs that he realized she never agreed to more than one night.

"WHAT THE HELL was I thinking?" Jo threw on her nightshirt and dug in her bag for toiletries. She didn't often talk to herself, but this was a special occasion. She'd fucked up, big time. "More where that came from? What have I gotten myself into?" She grabbed clothes and added them to her collection of things for the shower. "No. No. No no no. No."

She shook her head, then took a deep breath. "No." Then, marginally settled, she left the room.

After the night she'd had, she was a little sore and needed a nice hot shower to wash the aches away. The house was quiet. It didn't appear that anyone was up yet, so she crept down to the basement, hoping to be bathed and dressed before anyone woke.

The bathroom was done in calming blues and grays. Cadet blue and steel in the slate floor complemented the dove-colored walls and midnight blue linens. She opened the shower door and cranked the brushed nickel lever to hot. While waiting for the water to come to temperature, she undressed and looked in the mirror. Her scars had faded to white as the years passed, but to her they always stood out against her fair skin, pale reminders of the pain she'd endured, battle scars of a war waged against herself. A war she always felt she'd lost.

Yet she'd shared her defeat with Vinnie, and he hadn't run. No, he'd loved her anyway, and she had liked it. Positively reveled in his attention.

What had she been thinking? She certainly didn't deserve it.

Disgusted with herself, she turned from the mirror. No matter how hard she stared, her reflection wouldn't change. It would continue to leer back at her, mocking her through the steam in the room.

She stepped into the shower and let the hot water sluice over her skin. She couldn't wash away her scars, nor could her scrubbing bring back the afterglow of the night before. It was already long gone, replaced by the ubiquitous revulsion. She lathered more vigorously than usual, the scent of lavender doing nothing to calm her frayed nerves. Resigned, she stood under the spray, allowing the water to rinse away the soap, but not her resolve. She wouldn't get that close to him, to anyone, ever again.

Never should have succumbed to that crying jag and stepped out to look at the stars. Should have just packed and run away like she had originally planned.

The water pressure dropped, probably someone upstairs started showering. She turned off the water and stepped out, releasing a cloud of steam into the already hazy room. At least she didn't have to look at herself again. Grabbing a towel off the rack, she buffed her skin dry then got dressed. Once she was covered, she felt marginally better. She gathered her things and opened the door.

And was greeted by all three of her sisters.

Nosy bitches.

"Shower's free." She tried to step around them.

Franki blocked her way. "Not so fast."

"What?"

"Give us the scoop," Donni said.

Jo looked at the three of them. They all had Cheshire smiles she wanted to smack off their faces. She again tried to walk around them, but Toni stopped her.

"Come on, Jo," she said. "We know about last night. How'd that happen?"

"And how was it?" Donni asked.

"We know how it was," Franki said. "Everyone in the house heard."

Jo's mouth dropped open. "The whole house is talking about me?"

"I don't know about that," Franki said.

"But you just said…"

"I don't know if anyone else is talking about it. I only said the whole house *heard*. We certainly heard you. One more 'God!' and I think He might have appeared."

Again her mouth dropped open. She had to consciously close it and choose her words very carefully. "What, precisely, did you hear?"

"You know exactly what we heard. You were there," Franki said. "We'll ask the questions."

"Yeah," Toni said. "Like, what brought you two together?"

"And how was it?" Donni asked. "Although, I'm sure we can guess based on your howling."

Her face flamed as she realized Vinnie had indeed made good on his promise. Apparently she had screamed. A lot. And not just some moans that didn't leave the room.

Damn it.

"Come on." Franki grabbed Jo's hand. She led everyone to the game room, where leather sofas lined the walls around a black felt pool table. She plopped on one of the couches and pulled Jo with her. The twins sat on the floor near her feet. "Are you okay?"

Jo still clutched her toiletries to her chest, and Donni reached up and pried them away from her. She must have been squeezing them pretty hard, because her hands and arms were numb when they were empty.

"Jo?" Donni prompted.

"I don't know. I really don't want to talk about it. Not until I've figured out what I think about it all."

"You don't want to talk about anything these days," Toni said. "You're going to burst if you keep holding everything in."

"Then I burst. It beats the alternative."

"Making yourself sick trumps sharing with us?" Franki asked. "We're your sisters. If you can't talk to us, who can you talk to?"

"I don't want to talk to anybody. Can't you just drop it?"

"If you don't want to talk about the bad stuff right now," Donni said, "why don't you tell us about the good? Last night was good, right?"

Jo thought for a minute before answering. "Last night was good at the time. Now I regret it."

"Why?" all three sisters asked together.

She sighed. This was yet another topic she'd like to bury, not belabor. "Because last night I was caught up in the moment. Today I'm thinking clearly, and I know it was a mistake."

"Did he use you?" Franki stood.

"No. Nothing like that. If anything, I used him."

"Then what's the problem?" Franki asked. "Given the sounds coming out of your room, I think you should use him more often."

Not wanting to face her sisters any longer, Jo covered her face with her hands. Her cheeks were warm to the touch, and her head hurt.

Franki and the twins laughed. "Jo, relax." She pulled on her arms, but Jo resisted. "We're just teasing you. You weren't that loud. The only reason I heard anything was because I came downstairs for a glass of water. You didn't wake the house or raise the dead. I asked Gianni if he heard you, and he didn't."

Jo dropped her hands and stared at her sister. "You asked *Gianni*? Why would you do that?"

"I tell him everything. We don't have any secrets."

"Besides," Donni said, "given how close Vinnie is with his brothers, he's probably going to tell them about it, anyway."

"You aren't helping." Jo rubbed her head.

Franki reached over and pulled her hands away from her face. "I know we torment you. That's just what we do. But you know we're here for you, right?"

Jo nodded.

"We're worried about you. You've been off for a while now. Talk to us."

"Yeah, Jo." Donni agreed with Franki.

Toni patted Jo's leg.

Jo grabbed fists full of hair and rocked in her seat, the buttery leather softly squeaking under her weight.

"Jo?" Franki asked.

She shook her head. The pressure in her chest was suffocating, the lump in her throat impassable. Talk to them? She couldn't even bear to think her thoughts, let alone speak them.

The vision.

Enzo.

Dante.

Chuck. God, Chuck!

She sniffled, images slamming into her one after another, a multi-car pileup she couldn't avoid.

Coz.

Papa.

Mama.

Carla.

Vinnie's secret box.

Vinnie.

Madonna mia! What had she been thinking?

"Jo… Jo!" Franki pulled at her arms until she dropped them to her lap. "I don't know what's going on in your head, but you need to talk to someone. Tell us what's going on."

She looked at her sister, registered the concern on her face. Franki hadn't looked at her like that since—since the cutting.

Now she was worrying her family.

She shook her head again. "Too much," she whispered. "Too many things."

"Pick one."

Jo turned from Franki to the twins. They were mirror images of alarm and anxiety. It wasn't likely she was getting out of that room without giving them something.

But *what?*

Chuck was off limits. They were grieving her parents as much as she was. Enzo was old news to them. And the night before? That was too raw.

She'd give them just enough to go away. *If* she could get the words past her lips.

"The morning with Dante?" She took a deep breath. She could do it. Just spill it fast, like ripping off a bandage. "He scared me."

"We were all scared for you, honey," Donni said.

"No. That's not what I mean. He... he reminded me of..."

"Did he touch you?" Franki's voice was cold, hard.

"He was just too close." She couldn't tell them about his hands on her breasts, his thigh between her legs, his breath on her neck. "It brought all the old fears back."

"Of course it did, sweetie," Toni said, rubbing her leg. "But you're safe now."

She shook her head. "You don't understand. I—I had to erase that. That's why I turned to Vinnie."

"And of course he was ready and waiting." Franki leaned back and crossed her arms over her chest.

"No. No. It wasn't like that at all. He kept saying no. He said it wasn't right. I forced the issue."

"So you aren't good enough for him?" Franki stood up.

Truer words never spoken. "God, no. He didn't say that. Doesn't think it. He said he wanted things to be special between us, not just a roll in the hay."

"That's great," Donni said. "So what's the problem?"

"Yeah," Toni said. "I've seen the way you look at him when he isn't watching you. That's good news."

Franki sat back down. "Spill it."

"It's just not what I want. I used him, and now it's all messed up."

"Given what I heard last night, it doesn't seem messed up at all. I think things are just where they should be."

Jo glanced at her arms.

Franki grabbed her hand. "Were the scars a problem for him? Or did you hide them?"

"I didn't have to tell him. He knew. And it wasn't an issue." For him, anyway.

"So what's the deal?"

"I just can't!" Jo sprang to her feet and dashed up the stairs. She ran to her makeshift room, locked the door, and threw herself onto the bed, only to realize she wasn't alone.

14

VINNIE TOOK A cold shower. Not entirely by choice. It seemed he was the last one in the bathroom and the hot water was nothing but a promise. Besides, the cold water certainly didn't hurt. Just thinking of his fingers brushing over Jo's skin was enough to heat his blood—got it moving right out of his head and pooling a hell of a lot lower. He thought sleeping with her would make the desire more bearable.

It had made it worse.

How the hell was he going to get through the day without touching her?

And what if it was a one shot deal? What if there were no more nights to look forward to?

He had to talk to her. They'd left things too up in the air.

Vinnie toweled his hair dry and slung the towel around his neck. He looked in the mirror. There was no steam to cloud his vision, just a few errant water spots on the glass. Reflected back at him were the dark taupe wall, the ivory towels on the iron rack, and a scruffy bastard with a slight resemblance to him.

He'd been so busy over the last few months that he'd really let himself go. Sure, his muscles were probably even more sculpted now, but the rest of him looked like shit. His five-o'clock shadow was hours past five and shades darker than shadow. He rubbed his face, listening to the rasp of his palms over the stubble. He'd have an actual beard if he didn't shave within the day. He pulled his lower lids down. His eyes were bulldog-bloodshot with purple circles under them. Shouldn't he look relaxed and well-sated? Sure as hell didn't. Far from it.

Running his fingers through his damp hair, he sighed. He needed a fucking haircut. The ends curled around his ears and over the towel. They'd touch his collar when he dressed. When had he last had a trim? Who the fuck knew anymore? If he didn't get one soon, though, he'd have to tie the mess back to keep it out of his face.

Bet Mike would love his VP of Legal to be sporting a ponytail and face grunge. Just the thought made him laugh, but he knew it looked bad. He'd make time for a cut, hopefully that afternoon.

Before calling Pasquale again. Right after talking to Jo.

He took the towel off his shoulders and wrapped it around his waist. At least he had time for a shave. He lathered his face and brought the blade up.

And stopped cold.

His hand trembled, remembering Dante's hand holding a blade to Jo.

He closed his eyes, fought to center his thoughts. After a few deep breaths, he opened his eyes, gritted his teeth, and swiped the razor over his face.

In his hurry, he cut himself a few times.

But nothing like what Jo had endured.

Cursing a blue streak, he cleaned up. Then he forced the thoughts out of his head. He had things to do. Having forgotten any clothes, he was forced to leave wrapped in the ivory terry. Like it mattered. A body was a body was a body.

Except for Jo's. Hers was something special.

There was no reason for stealth, anyway. If everyone had showered already, they were probably downstairs.

He entered the hall just as Tina closed her door.

Perfect.

"Morning," he said and turned toward his room. He'd made her blush and didn't want to linger.

"It is a good morning, isn't it?" she said.

He turned and looked back at her. She just smiled and started down the stairs. What the hell was *that* all about?

Shaking his head, he entered his room. All three of his brothers were there waiting for him.

Coz was sprawled in the brown leather recliner. Nico leaned against the padded headboard, booted feet dangling off the side of the bed. Gianni looked out the window, blood-red drapes pushed wide open, tan roman shade raised to the top. The sunlight streamed through the glass, cutting a swath of brightness across the striped comforter.

"You comfortable?" He closed the door behind him.

Gianni turned his back to the window and stared at his brother. "Extremely, thanks."

"So what do you want? I need to get dressed."

"Don't let us stop you."

Vinnie dropped his towel and strode to the window, pulling the blinds. "You guys want to ogle my naked ass, fine, but the whole damn mountain doesn't need a show." He turned toward his luggage which he hadn't unpacked and bent over, rooting for boxers and clothes for the day.

"God, Vin," Coz said. "You're shoving your ass in my face." He scrambled to put the foot of the recliner down, then he stood and walked over near Gianni.

"No one invited your ugly mug in here. You don't like it, get out." He threw his clothes onto the chair Coz vacated and stepped into his boxers. Then he sat and started putting on socks.

"Well, we would, but we have business," Nico said.

"I already talked to Pasquale. I'll figure it out."

Gianni crossed his arms over his chest. "Figure what out?"

Vinnie stood and put on his jeans. Zipped them, but left them unbuttoned. "If that's not why you're here, what business are you talking about?"

"You and Jo."

"Jo?"

"We wanted to make sure you know what you're doing. If this thing goes south, we still have to work with her."

"You've got to be fucking kidding me. You're screwing her sister, and you're lecturing me about the consequences?"

Gianni's jaw ticked. Then again. And a third time. "We're not just hooking up. We're together. It's different."

"You don't know shit about what's going on between me and Jo. Who told you anything happened, anyway?"

No one answered.

Vinnie pulled a black t-shirt over his head. "So no one. You're just assuming. You know what they say when you assume." He turned his back on his brother and searched for his boots, spied them beside the chair.

Gianni grabbed his arm and spun him back around. "We aren't done discussing this."

Vinnie looked at his hand on his arm and flung it off. He spoke in a soft voice. "You don't want to do that again."

Gianni stepped forward, stood toe to toe, nose to nose with his brother. "Or what?"

Nico and Coz moved between them, Nico grabbing Gianni and Coz pushing Vinnie back.

"Look," Nico said. "This is getting out of hand. Fast. We're not here to argue."

Vinnie and Gianni stared each other down around their brothers.

"We just wanted to talk about it," Coz said.

Vinnie tore his gaze from Gianni and looked at Coz. "Seems more like some twisted intervention than a discussion. And I want an answer. Who said anything about us?"

Gianni sighed and reopened the blind so he could look out again. "Franki told me last night."

"Last night? How the fuck did she even know?"

"She went down for a glass of water and heard you."

Vinnie tucked his shirt in, then he grabbed a belt, threading it through the loops of his jeans. "It's not her business. Not yours, either."

"V, Jo's a runner. She's already unstable. A mistake like this and we could lose her. Completely. "

Vinnie dropped his hands, the ends of the belt hanging down and the waistband still unbuttoned. He sat and grabbed his boots. "You know, G, given your history, I'd think you'd be careful throwing around words like 'unstable'. She's upset and under a lot of stress. That doesn't make her a nutcase."

"She's still a flight risk, man," Coz said.

"You feel that way too, Nico?"

"We're worried about her running again. This thing goes wrong, and we could have another Dante situation. And if we don't get to her in time…"

Vinnie tied his boots, ducking his head down so they couldn't see his face. The thought of anyone laying hands on her scared him more than was rationally possible.

"V? We're worried about you. And her. And our ability to protect her. And the rest of them."

He stood, buttoned his jeans, and fastened his belt. "I'll take care of it."

"You guys aren't serious yet. Break it off before it blows up in our faces," Gianni said.

Fat fucking lot he knew. "And if I won't?"

"Don't let it fucking explode."

He glared at Gianni, who stared right back at him. Then he flicked his wrist and headed for the door.

"What was that?"

"What?" Gianni asked.

"That wrist thing."

Gianni shook his head. "Just cleaning up another one of your messes. Get a new razor. Or a steadier hand."

They filed out of his room. As they left, Nico clapped him on the back then closed the door behind him. Vinnie glanced in the mirror. G had healed all his shaving nicks.

He plopped down on the bed and wondered if his brothers were right. He was losing control of everything.

Had he made a mistake with Jo? Was too late to go back?

Could he if he tried?

JO RAISED HER hand to her chest. "Oh! You scared me, Marcus."

He was sitting in a chair by the window. He'd raised the blinds, and the sun coming in the window backlit him, making his expression impossible to read.

"Sorry. I just wanted a moment to talk."

"Sure." She began folding the bed back into a sofa.

"Just leave it, Jo. Have a seat."

He made her nervous, so she continued. "It'll just take a sec." Marcus was silent while she collapsed the frame into the couch and replaced the cushions. She sat and crossed her hands in her lap, tightly interlacing her fingers so he couldn't see her hands tremble. "Okay." Thank God her voice didn't falter. "What do you need?"

"I don't mean to embarrass you, but I know what happened last night."

Good Lord. Was the whole world aware of her sex life?

"Oh, um. How did... I mean..." She felt her cheeks flame, but fought to maintain her composure.

"This office is right under the master bedroom. Sometimes sound travels through the vents."

Her cheeks burned hotter. Had he only heard their actions, or had he heard their discussion, too? Please God, let it only be a moan or two. "I'm sorry. It was inappropriate of me to take advantage of your hospitality like that."

"Don't be ridiculous. That's not why I'm bringing it up."

"Then, why?"

He sighed. "Vinnie is... His past is one of... Let's just say he doesn't let people in easily."

"He's not the only one."

"I heard you this morning after he left. That was a lot of no's given the night you'd just had."

How much had he heard? If he heard her talking to herself in the morning, did he hear her whispered confessions the night before? She didn't speak. Instead she waited for him to reveal more.

"I know it's difficult on you, being part of this prophecy. Your father struggled with his role. And he worried for you girls."

She blinked back tears. This man knew her father in ways she never would.

"He never wanted this to affect you. He certainly never wanted you to be unhappy." He sighed. "But he wouldn't want you to upset your guardian, either, just to shield your own feelings."

She tried to read him, but his expression was cloaked by the shadows covering his face.

"I didn't hurt Vinnie."

"No. Not yet. But you need to know, if this continues and you push him away later, you might destroy him. If you aren't ready for a relationship with him, you need to tell him now. Before it's too late."

"What happened to him? What's left him so vulnerable?"

"That's his story to choose to tell." He rose and stepped toward her. Even without the shadow cloaking him, she couldn't read his face.

"About what you heard? Was that just this morning, or did you hear me talking last night, too?"

"I heard your discussion. And what came of it. And I heard what happened after Vinnie's phone call this morning. If there was anything else, I didn't catch it."

"I think that's enough, don't you?"

He pulled her into a bear hug. "I'm not going to say anything. But if you need a fresh perspective, or just a sounding board, I'm here."

He left her standing in the office, the sunlight making the room look more cheerful than she could possibly feel.

VINNIE HEARD THE people in the kitchen before he got there. It sounded like everyone was having a great morning. Too bad he wasn't. He strode to the archway and looked at everyone gathered for breakfast. Nico and Coz perched on barstools at the island. Everyone else, except Marcus and Jo, sat around the table. Wonder where the hell she'd run off to.

No one noticed him standing there, and he thought about turning around, avoiding them and going to find Jo. Then he felt a strong hand clap him on the back, and he turned to see his mentor staring at him. "Going into the lion's den?"

Vinnie didn't answer.

"Tina ran out early this morning for more groceries. We're fully stocked. Come grab a bite."

He followed Marcus into the kitchen and over to the coffeepot, avoiding eye contact with anyone. All conversation abruptly ceased, then started again, softer and less animated. He held his mug out for Marcus to fill. He kept his back to the room and felt seven sets of eyes on him. Not one to hide from a fight, he turned and leaned on the counter. All the chatter died away and everyone averted their gazes. That's when Marcus turned to look at him. Damn it. Bastard never walked away from a confrontation, either.

"Do you guys have plans for the day?" Marcus addressed everyone although he stared at Vinnie.

"We need to have a meeting at some point," Gianni said, "but we're pretty flexible otherwise."

"How would you feel about guest-teaching today? Maybe doing a demo? Kevin's off, and I could use the help."

"You have any advanced students?" Coz asked. "I need a good workout, and these losers sure aren't giving me one."

Nico punched him on the arm so hard his barstool tipped. Coz just laughed and munched on a piece of bacon.

"I've got classes today ranging from the tiny tots all the way through my advanced black belt class. And two weapons classes. Take your pick. Any or all, it's up to you."

"Sounds like fun," Gianni said.

Franki put her hand on his arm and whispered to him, "Are you sure you're up to it?"

"You seriously asking that after last night?"

Vinnie fought to keep his disgust off his face. Why'd he have to be standing close enough to overhear this conversation? He took a sip of coffee to hide his expression behind his mug. "I was thinking about getting a haircut." His voice trailed off when Jo entered the room, but he quickly recovered. "But I can probably put it off a day."

"When you go, can I go with you?" Jo asked. "I'm overdue for a trim, too."

Everyone looked up at her, probably unaware she'd entered the room. Her presence didn't surprise Vinnie. He felt her before she even crossed the threshold. She looked beautiful, her skin nearly radiant under the soft incandescent light of the kitchen. The shadows under her eyes didn't concern him too much. He knew why she didn't get much sleep. The memory pleased him, and he took another sip of coffee to hide his smile. Putting the mug down, he said, "Sure. When my plans… firm up, you'll be the first to know."

She blushed and turned to Marcus. "Don't suppose I could join in a session or two? I could use a good workout."

He rooted in one of the drawers and came out with a brochure for his school. "Look the schedule over. You're welcome to join any class you're comfortable with. It's summer, so classes run all day, not just the evening."

"You know," Coz said, "all you girls should get in a couple hours today. Just because we're not at the compound doesn't mean you shouldn't train."

Toni groaned. "I was trying to think of this as a vacation."

"Vacation doesn't mean let your health go."

"It does to me. No work. No exercise. Just bad food and relaxation."

"Then you've been vacationing wrong. Pick a class, Toni. Or I'll pick one for you."

She walked over to Jo and peeked over her shoulder. "Don't suppose I could just join a beginners' class?"

"Funny," Jo said. "I was thinking I'd like to take all the advanced classes. Definitely Weapons II and the black belt class."

"Do you girls have uniforms with you?" Tina asked.

Toni smirked, a hopeful look crossing her face.

"None of us brought *doboks*," Gianni said.

"No matter," Marcus said. "We sell them, so I have a full range of sizes. Getting you all fitted shouldn't be a problem. My treat."

"Great," Toni sighed, all of her hopeful expectation replaced with resignation.

Jo said, "Great!" at the same time as Toni. She seemed much more enthused.

The crowd started to shuffle out of the kitchen amid jokes and martial arts discussions. Vinnie picked up his mug and hid another smile. He couldn't think of a more innocent way to get Jo in his arms again.

JO THREW A few kicks in her new uniform, just to get used to the feel of it. Marcus and Tina had given all the girls white uniforms and black belts, despite their lack of formal martial arts training. Gianni felt their skill levels were on par with a first degree, so Marcus took his word on it.

She'd never worn a uniform before, so she threw some kicks to test it out. The formality of the uniforms intimidated her, but she got a rush when she was able to make the crisp material snap. As she had tied her belt, she'd felt herself slipping on the mantle of warrior.

Jo didn't need Vinnie. She was a force all on her own.

Then she saw him step out of the locker room in his uniform. The guys all got full black *doboks* because they were instructing. Most students would find him intimidating. She found him hot. Sizzling, more like it. If he touched her, she'd melt.

Or explode.

Her earlier resolve to keep her distance evaporated as fast as the saliva in her mouth. Staying away from him was going to be harder than she thought. She looked around the room to distract herself.

Gianni huddled in the corner with Franki, pretending to help tie her belt. They weren't kidding anybody. He just wanted his hands on her.

Coz and Nico stood with the twins, reviewing some finger locks. Jo wondered if she should join them. She was rusty on locks. She didn't know what they planned on covering in all the classes, but she was up for anything. As long as she wasn't paired with Vinnie. Despite the extracurricular activities of the night before, she had pent-up energy. Nearly vibrated with it. She needed to blow off some steam.

Working with Vinnie would make things worse, not better. She wasn't sure she'd be able to stick to her resolve if she was paired with him. It felt far safer to ogle him from a distance.

He'd be instructing, though, not part of the student body. She was safe. Ish.

Vinnie approached her, and rather than launch herself into his arms, she bent down to stretch. This so wasn't what she had in mind for her next encounter with him. There was something about seeing him in warrior-mode, though. Something… delicious. She only needed to control herself for a few minutes. Once class started, she'd throw herself into the workout and wouldn't have to focus on denying the pull she felt to him.

"Hey," he said. "You sure you want to do all the classes? Maybe you could do some snooping while we're all down here."

All business, huh? Well, she could maintain her composure, too. "If you recall, I'm the one who asked to come along. If I backed out now, it would look suspicious."

"I thought you might be tired or sore after last night."

She stood and put her hands on her hips. "Did you think that? How thoughtful. But I'm fine. You, on the other hand, look exhausted. Maybe you should go back up to the house."

He cocked an eyebrow and a smile slowly crossed his face. "I'm fine, thanks. See you inside." He turned and strode into the *dojang*. Without warming up, he executed a five-forty kick over the bag—jumping off, kicking with, and landing on the same foot, spinning one and a half times in the air. His foot easily cleared the top. Wonder what he could do when he was warmed up?

Well, she knew that answer to that, didn't she?

What the hell had she gotten herself into?

While they were on their way down the mountain, Marcus had suggested the girls join the guys for all the classes. He said they'd be an extra set of eyes and hands for the younger, less experienced students, and when the advanced classes started, they could just join the group. She and the guys agreed it would be good for them to get a solid day in. Toni and Donni looked mutinous. Franki just linked her arm through Gianni's. She'd be happy wherever he was.

But given the nearly sadistic grin on Vinnie's face, she was rethinking spending the day there. The workouts were supposed to work off some of her tension, not add to it.

WELL, IT DIDN'T look like he'd have time for a haircut that afternoon. And it didn't seem likely there would be house-snooping, either. He couldn't do anything about his hair, but maybe he could dig up some dirt on his mentor. If he could break off from a class, he could check out the office and the rest of the facilities.

But looking at Jo's flushed face, the sweat glistening on her neck and chest, he knew he wasn't skipping out. Spying on Marcus would have to wait.

They worked with a kids' advanced color-belt class. Most of them were a belt or two away from testing for black, and all of them were excited to have the guest instructors. While he and the guys walked around, adjusting positions and answering questions, the girls sparred with some of the students. The kids had on full gear and the girls didn't have any pads on, so it was supposed to be light contact. Jo had worked up a sweat, but there was a light in her eyes that he hadn't seen in months.

Last night not included.

The kid she sparred looked like he was kicking a little harder than he was told, but Jo kept blocking him. Vinnie headed over to referee and saw Jo land a light ax kick on top of the kid's head. Nice timing. The kid retaliated with a full-force side kick to her gut. She hadn't landed her foot yet and was unable to block, so she took the brunt of the kick, totally defenseless, and crumpled to the mat.

Vinnie's peripheral vision faded and he laser focused on the kid. Reaching them in two strides, he picked the kid up by his chest protector and held him, nose to nose. "What the hell are you doing? We said light contact! She doesn't have pads!"

"I'm sorry, sir. I lost control! I didn't mean anything by it!"

Vinnie shook him. "You mean you wanted to teach the girl who was beating you a lesson?"

The kid stammered, his feet dangling a foot above the mat.

"Taekwondo is all about control. You lose it, and you lose. Got it?"

"Yes… yessir."

Vinnie dropped the kid. "Laps. Now. Keep your gear on."

"How many, sir?"

"I'll tell you when you're done. Count them out when you pass this corner."

The kid took off, and Vinnie turned to help Jo up. She'd already stood, but her hand rubbed her stomach. He glanced around the room. Everyone had stopped sparring and was staring at him. "Back to work, people." When the group's attention went back to practice, he turned to Jo. He grabbed her, holding her at arm's length and looking her over.

"Are you all right?" he asked.

"You're being too hard on him," she said.

"One, sir!" The boy just passed the corner and counted his first lap.

"Too hard? Are you kidding me? If he wasn't such an oaf, he could have hurt you. If one of us had landed that kick, you could have had organ damage!"

"Well, I wasn't sparring you, I was sparring him."

Vinnie glared at the kid as he ran laps.

"And," she continued, "you wouldn't have kicked that hard."

"He shouldn't have, either."

Jo put her hand on Vinnie's arm. He was shaking, and her hand helped still him. "You said yourself, this is all about control. You need to rein it in."

"You could have been hurt. Bruised intestines. Broken ribs."

"And Gianni and Nico could have fixed it."

He pulled her into an embrace. "They aren't always going to be there."

"Well, they're here now. And I don't need them, anyway." She pushed off him.

He reluctantly let her go. "What's the ass-hat's name?"

"Jeremy."

As the kid rounded the corner, Vinnie said, "Come here, Jeremy."

The boy turned around and ran back. "Sir."

"Do you have something you want to say to Miss Jo?"

"I'm sorry, ma'am. I don't know what I was thinking."

"You weren't thinking," Vinnie said.

Jo shot him a dirty look and turned back to Jeremy. "Be more careful in the future. Some of the girls here are pretty tiny."

"Yes, ma'am." He looked at Vinnie.

"Fifty pushups, v-ups, and squat thrusts. Then you can rejoin the class."

"Yes, sir."

He dropped to the mat and began calling out pushup reps.

"I'll be ready when you're done," Jo said to Jeremy.

"No," Vinnie said. "I'll finish sparring with him." It didn't escape his notice that Jeremy faltered in his reps.

"Vinnie," Jo said.

"Go get a drink, Jo. I'm taking your place."

Jo went to the door, turned back to the room and bowed, then spun and walked out.

Marcus approached Vinnie as Jeremy moved on to v-ups. "A word, Vinnie?"

Vinnie kept his focus on Jeremy as he walked to the corner with his mentor.

"You do realize that once you're gone, I still have to work with these kids. Provided they don't leave. Or sue me."

Vinnie tore his gaze away from the boy and looked at Marcus. "What are you saying?"

"You need to be a little more patient. This is my *livelihood* you're playing with."

"You never would have let me get away with shit like that."

"You're family. I could treat you differently than these kids. And I was training you for war, not competition."

"He hurt her."

"And you dangled him in the air. I have to answer to his parents, all the parents, for that."

"She's my responsibility."

"And everyone here is mine. Get it together or get out."

Marcus walked away toward Jeremy. He stopped, turned back toward Vinnie. "I'll spar him. You take a break."

"Yes, sir." Vinnie bowed, and Marcus returned it. Before he turned away, Vinnie said, "For the record, Marcus, I have no family. Never did." He strode to the door and bowed before leaving.

15

JO TOWELED OFF and looked around. She didn't want to go back in the gym until the class ended, so she had twenty minutes to kill. She didn't have enough time to run up the hill and check out the house, but if Marcus kept his office unlocked, she'd have enough time to pop in there and poke around.

As she headed down the hall, Tina approached her. "How are you, Jo? Do you need an ice pack or anything?"

Tina's appearance startled her, but she composed herself. "Do you all walk so damn quiet?"

"Sorry. I didn't mean to scare you. I was worried."

"I'm fine. I just had some water and now I'm going to sit in the locker room for a bit, just until the class is over."

"Do you want some company?"

"No need, thanks. Really, I'm fine."

"If you're sure. I'll be in the office if you need anything."

Jo tried to hide her disappointment. "Okay. Thanks, Tina."

Tina ducked into Marcus's office and Jo kept walking, committed to the story of heading to the locker room. Once Tina closed the door, Jo bypassed the locker room door and walked straight over to the trophy case.

With no one in the hall, she had more time to examine the awards and photos. Vinnie must have been born handsome. Even in the years when he should have looked disproportioned or gangly, he had been good-looking and well-built. They all were, really, but she couldn't tear her gaze from his photos. There was one of him as a white belt standing by a trophy that was almost as tall as he was. There were pictures of him with gold medals, blue ribbons, silver cups. In some, Marcus or his brothers were with him, in others he was alone. But even in the ones where he stood with family or friends, he held himself apart, not quite blending into the group. She hadn't noticed that the day before.

Thinking about it, Vinnie kind of held himself apart from everyone when they were all together, too.

If the guys had to be broken into pairs, she'd put Nico and Coz together and Vinnie and Gianni. That's how they usually broke apart for sparring drills, and their ages were more comparable. They probably grew up as two sets of best friends before Mike adopted them all. But while Nico and Coz were pretty tight, Vinnie and Gianni seemed to have grown apart a bit. Maybe they were never as close and Nico and Coz. Maybe it was Gianni spending all his free time with Franki. Maybe it was the fight they had a few months ago that never truly got resolved.

But the pictures… Why did Vinnie hold himself apart? And would he eventually distance himself from her if she let him in?

Not that she planned on it, anyway. She still had plans to run. He didn't figure in her future.

"What are you doing?"

Jo jumped and clamped her hand on her mouth to keep from calling out. She was so deep in thought that she hadn't noticed Vinnie approach.

"Sorry," he said.

"Why are you here? Don't you have a kid to humiliate?"

"I wasn't trying to embarrass him. I was trying to teach him a lesson."

"So why aren't you with him now?"

"Marcus is trying to teach me a lesson."

"I see. So you decided to scare the bejeezus out of me?"

He laughed. "Bejeezus?"

She sighed and smacked him on the arm. Rock. Solid.

And he wasn't even flexing.

"Actually," he said, "I was going to poke around the office while I'm on break. But I saw you standing here."

"And?"

He shrugged. "You drew me here."

She didn't know what to say to that. The hallway had seemed smaller with him in it. It was positively suffocating after that proclamation.

When she didn't say anything, he turned away. "I'll be in the office. Give me a signal if someone comes."

"Wait!" She grabbed his arm. "Tina's in there."

"What? Damn it."

"I know. I was going to go in there, but she ruined my plan. I thought I'd hang out here until she left, then I'd go in and see what I could find."

"We only have about ten minutes, and she's still in there. If she doesn't leave soon, there won't be enough time."

"Probably isn't enough time, anyway." She turned back to the photos.

He stood behind her, his mere proximity heating her. She grabbed her neckline and tried to fan herself with it.

"Warm? You need a drink?"

"I'm okay." Liar. "Vinnie, can I ask you something?"

"Shoot." He leaned against the wall.

"What's the deal with you and pictures?"

"What do you mean?" He crossed his arms over his chest.

"Look at them," she said. "You seem to stand away from everyone, even in the group photos."

He didn't look at the case. "I'm in the middle of the photos half the time. How the hell am I holding myself apart if everyone's around me?"

"Look." She pointed to each in turn. "A step in front. A step behind. Off to the side. This one, everyone has their arms over each other's shoulders, and you're just standing there. What's the deal?"

"No deal. Just bad poses, I guess." He pushed off the wall. "I'm headed back. You coming?"

She reached for him, but he avoided her touch. "Stay. Come. Doesn't matter to me." He turned and strode down the hall without a backward glance.

JEREMY'S CLASS HAD gone and the next one filed in. Vinnie made good use of the few minutes of downtime he had by kicking the bag. Five rapid-fire roundhouse kicks with his right leg.

Bang! Bang! Bang! Bang! Bang!

A quick stance shift then the same on the left.

Bang! Bang! Bang! Bang! Bang!

He got lost in the rhythm of his foot smacking the vinyl, in the cadence of his thoughts.

Need. To. Know. She's. Safe.

Really. Should. Keep. My. Distance.

Who's. G. Think. He. Is?

Why's. She. Analyzing. My. Pics?

Why's. Marcus. Giving. Me. Grief?

Damn. Marcus. Damn. Mike. Too.

When he felt a hand on his shoulder, he spun around, ready to strike.

Nico stepped back, eyebrows raised. "Time for class to start."

"Sorry, man."

"You tight?"

"I'm fine."

Nico looked him over, then turned his back to him and joined the brothers in the front of the class. Vinnie went and stood with them, then self-consciously shifted closer to Gianni, wondering if he was "holding himself apart" in some way. When Gianni looked at him, he shuffled back again. Damn woman got in his head.

He only vaguely listened to Marcus make introductions to the students.

The students bowed to each of them as Marcus mentioned their names, and when they bowed to him, he returned the gesture. But his focus was on the back line. This was one of the weapons classes, and the girls were in line as students instead of assistants. No chance of him keeping clear of Jo this class. It was his job to work with all the students.

This first weapons class was with the less advanced belts. Jo had paired off with Franki, and they both held their own. He and Gianni both seemed to hover by them more than anywhere else, but hey... they had to stand somewhere, right?

He knew his presence affected Jo because her movements got stronger and faster. When Franki missed a block and Jo hit her with a kali stick, they took a break. Gianni went to check on Franki's arm. Jo left for a drink. Vinnie suppressed a smile and made his rounds through the rest of the class.

The next class was also a weapons class, but it was for advanced belts. They started with the bo staff, but they worked on forms instead of sparring. He couldn't help but notice how relieved Franki looked. Vinnie walked through the rank and file, correcting positions and adjusting stances. Then he stopped in front of Jo. Her movements were fluid, forceful, graceful. Beautiful. Just like her.

He couldn't help himself. He needed some reason, any reason, to touch her. So he kept stopping her to make minor tweaks to her form. By the time the class ended, she couldn't manage more than a "Thank you, sir," through clenched teeth.

Vinnie turned his back to her and started walking to the front of the room. She swept his feet with the staff and knocked him to the mat.

"Oops. Sorry sir. I was trying to tuck the staff under my arm, and it swung out of control."

Out of control, his ass.

He stood, adjusted his *dobok*, and snatched the staff from her hands. "Twenty laps when class is dismissed." He strode to the front of the class without looking back.

When the students left, Jo started her laps. With a smirk on her face.

He went back to pounding the shit out of the bag.

She was just finishing when the next class lined up. It was a black belt class. Once again, the girls stood in the back. He met and held Jo's gaze. She raised her chin.

Defiant little brat.

Marcus introduced the Brothers again, and then began class. After he conducted the warm ups, he declared they'd be working on holds and broke the class into pairs. He couldn't have known, but he partnered them the same way they practiced on their own—Gianni and Franki, Coz and Toni, Nico and Donni, and him with Jo.

It was going to get interesting.

"This a problem for you?" she whispered as Marcus gave his instructions. "Maybe you'd like to stand a foot away."

He sighed. She wasn't going to let the photo issue go.

"I guess you're staying this close, then?"

She tried to push his buttons, but he ignored it. Or tried to. Instead, he said, "You didn't mind me being close last night."

Her cheeks colored, and she looked away.

Instead of a second smart-ass retort he wanted to throw at her, he said, "We're supposed to start with rear choke holds. Do you know what to do, or should I review it with you first?"

"You know damn well I know what to do."

"Then turn around."

"Why do you get to attack?"

His hold on his temper was tenuous at best. He bent down, putting his face an inch from hers, and lowered his voice to a whisper. "Because I'm your teacher. Turn the fuck around."

Thank God she turned her back to him and kept her mouth shut.

"Okay. This time we'll go slow, just to review." He put his hands on her neck, his arms outstretched and elbows locked.

Jo didn't listen. She went full speed, lifting her left arm and spinning counter-clockwise, knocking his arm out of the way. She continued the turn and threw a right elbow strike to his face. When he bent over, she administered three knees to his midsection. It was only because of his reflexes that he avoided the full force of her attack.

"Great work, Jo!" Marcus said. "Class. Watch this. She executes a perfect defense." He gestured for them to repeat.

Vinnie was livid. She didn't listen when he said to go slow, and he wasn't ready for the full speed attack. He especially wasn't prepared for her grin and Marcus asking her to do it again. He didn't have any pads on, and she didn't fight with light contact. His cheekbone stung. Good damn thing she missed his nose. It was also a good thing that she went for his abs instead of his groin. If the class wasn't watching them, he'd throw her on her ass.

Instead, he glared at her, clenched his teeth, and set up to demonstrate again.

She fucking smiled before turning her back to him.

When they executed the hold and release again, he was ready and avoided the brunt of her elbow and knees. She wasn't quite as vicious with Marcus watching, anyway.

"Good job," Marcus said. "Class… Just like that. Begin."

"You sure you don't want me to attack this time?" she asked with a false innocence. "I obviously have it down. Maybe you need to practice."

"That's okay. I'm good. Let's move on to something else."

"Whatever. I'm game."

"We'll do a rear hair grab."

"Wait. I thought that was for people with long hair in ponytails. My hair's too short."

"Didn't you just this morning say it was too long?"

"It's too short for this."

He spun her around and grabbed a fist full of her hair with his right hand. "Still think it's too short?"

She struggled fruitlessly against his hold. He knew she didn't know the release, and he kept a tight grasp of her tresses. Vinnie pulled her to him and she stayed still, her back against his chest. He could feel her distress. She panted, her body's heat radiating off her and seeping into his skin, warming him.

He went from wanting to teach her a lesson to just wanting her.

Her breasts heaved with every breath she took. He had a perfect view from above her down the V of her *dobok*. Her chest glistened with a thin sheen of sweat. He noticed how soft her hair was between his fingers. Closing his eyes, he took a deep breath. Damn. There was that scent again. That fresh lavender smell.

The Jo smell.

He released her and she spun away from him. It didn't escape his attention that she was flushed and and breathless. She licked her lips.

She was aroused.

She was also pissed, and he briefly wondered how she would retaliate. He had bigger problems, though, than her anger. Just one big problem, really. And he hoped his uniform was loose enough to keep it hidden.

"What the hell was that?" She still hadn't caught her breath.

"What?"

"You know what." She inhaled deeply, then her breathing leveled out.

"I don't know what you're talking about. I was just working on a new hold for you."

She glared at him. "Show me how to get out of it."

He stifled a laugh. He thought about not showing her, just so he'd have some leverage, but he'd never hold her like that for real. Not in anger, anyway. And he needed her to be prepared for any attack. Besides, one of the others could always teach her if he refused. And he definitely didn't want her working with someone else.

"Okay. For this one, pay attention to the hand the attacker grabs you with. It's crucial. Chances are he'll be right-handed and will grab with his right, but just reverse the moves if he grabs with his left."

"All right."

He reached out with his right hand and grasped a fist full of her hair. "You have to control his grabbing hand, or this won't work. I'm holding you with my right hand, so reach up with your left hand and take hold of my hand."

"I won't be able to pull you off with my left hand. I couldn't get you off with both hands."

He smiled at the unintentional innuendo and continued on with his instruction. "This isn't to strip my hand. It's actually to hold it in place."

"Why the hell would I want to keep your hand there?"

"I'm about to show you. Reach up with your left hand and grab hold."

She did as he said.

"Now put your right hand up in a middle block."

She raised her right arm, her triceps parallel with the floor and her forearm bent up in a right angle.

"You're going to step forward while spinning clockwise, to the outside of my arm. The goal is to get my arm straight as you spin. Then deliver a back fist. If you're holding my hand tight and have my arm extended, you'll be hitting my straightened elbow. Deliver the back fist hard while controlling my arm, and you should be able to dislocate the elbow or break the arm, freeing yourself."

She spun slowly, increasing the space between them until his arm was straight. Then she tapped the back of her fist against his extended elbow.

"Perfect," he said. "Let's try it a little faster."

They continued practicing the hold. Vinnie was proud of how quickly she picked up the techniques he showed her. Once he felt she was competent on the rear hair grab release, he switched hands and grabbed with his left. She didn't notice and moved the same way, only to discover she was out of position and his arm merely bent at her strike.

"Sorry," she said. "I wasn't paying attention. I let my mind wander."

"Here that's not so important. In real life, that could be the difference between living or dying."

"I know! I said I'm sorry."

"What were you thinking about?"

"Never mind. Let's do it again."

He had a feeling he wouldn't like where her thoughts had been. "Not enough time. Class is ending."

"Already?"

He recognized a dodge when he heard one. Why wouldn't he? He, too, was a master at avoidance. "Listen, Jo. We need to talk about last night."

"No we don't. I need to line up." She jogged to the back of the room and stood in line beside her sisters.

He walked to the front of the room to join Gianni and Coz. "Where's Nico?"

"Sick," Coz said.

Vinnie heard the implied air quotes around the word. "G?"

"He's up at the house. Marcus pulled Tina in to work with Toni when he left."

"Good. I wanted to get in his office earlier, but she was in there. Glad she was occupied, or she might have followed him. I don't think she trusts us."

"Would you? We nearly killed her."

"She wasn't very forthcoming about who she was and why she was there."

"Neither were we."

"Whatever." They bowed to the group and the black belts were dismissed. Many of them stopped to chat before filing out, and Vinnie lost his chance to talk to Jo. She had run out the door when Vinnie was cornered by the stragglers. He was certain she'd be long gone before he was done with the small talk, so he resigned himself to making polite conversation with the remaining students.

His talk with Jo would have to wait.

JO COULDN'T SEEM to shake Tina. She left the *dojang* with them and hung out with them in the locker room while they changed. Apparently she was going to escort them back up the driveway. Donni excused herself and went into a stall. Tina looked at her, but obviously couldn't follow. When Donni came out, she was tucking something into her pocket. Tina stared at her, then ushered the girls out. She made small talk on the way up the hill, but Jo didn't bother listening. Her thoughts raced ahead of all of them while she lagged behind.

"Penny for your thoughts?" Donni asked. Jo hadn't even noticed that she drifted back with her.

"They aren't even worth that much," Jo said.

"Tina really watches us closely, huh?"

"Yeah. I think she doesn't trust us completely. Probably shouldn't be surprised by that." They kept meandering up the hill. Tina and the others got farther and farther away. She seemed to be on a mission to reach the house. "Wait. What about Nico?"

"I texted him we were on our way. You know, so he could stop snooping and go lie down like he said he was going to do."

"Huh. I hadn't even noticed him leave."

"You were otherwise occupied." Donni waggled her brows.

Jo smacked her arm. "Shut up. Vinnie taught me a new lock release."

"Mmm-hmm. Call it what you like. You were in his arms for the better part of the last hour. And you both looked like you were enjoying yourselves."

"I was enjoying myself. I love working out."

"You love something."

Jo sighed.

"Still not going to tell me what you were thinking about?"

"Nope."

"Doesn't matter. Nico said tonight they plan on having the meeting you've been putting off. They want answers. We all do."

Great. This trip was just getting better and better. "I'd rather hear what Nico found out."

"I don't think you're getting a choice."

"Race you to the top!" Jo took off running. She passed Tina and her other sisters in about thirty seconds and just kept going. Donni didn't follow, and she was grateful. They wouldn't have been able to talk, anyway. Sprinting up the hill would make conversation impossible. But she wanted to be alone.

Her lungs expanded as she pushed herself harder. She welcomed the lactic acid burn in her thighs. It had been too long since she was free to be alone and get in the zone. For months, she had been running with a partner, working out in a group. Running up the driveway, she felt free.

Then the panic set in.

Her heart pounded, her palms grew sweaty. Every time she broke away from her family, someone got hurt. She stopped and turned around to wait for everyone else. After about two minutes, her pulse rate rose. Finally Franki, Toni, and Tina came around a bend.

"What got into you?" Franki asked.

"Really," Tina said.

"I was going to race Donni up the hill. I guess she didn't follow. I was waiting for her. Didn't she even catch up with you guys?"

"No," Toni said. She looked behind her. "I don't see her. She shouldn't be that far back, though."

"Go on ahead," Jo said. "I'll wait for her."

"I'll wait with you," Toni said.

"I think we should all stick together," Tina said.

"Why?" Jo asked. "This is a private drive. There shouldn't be any danger."

"Just some animals…" Tina trailed off.

"It'll be fine. Go on. I'll wait for her, and we'll be along soon."

Tina wavered. Franki and Toni started off. After a brief pause, she followed.

Jo only waited until they rounded a bend, then she took off back down the hill. Donni should have caught up by then, but she was still nowhere in sight. The path was too well established for her to have gotten lost.

Dear God. Did she disappear? Did someone get her?

Images of Dante morphed into images from high school. Nameless, faceless men attacked her, one after another. In the woods with a knife. On the bed with a camera. It didn't matter. She was in a mental prison, being violated over and over. She continued running blindly down the hill, not even bothering to push branches and limbs out of her way. She was more worried about the knife, the hands, the stares.

She was near the bottom of the hill when Donni took her place in her mental hell. It was her sister being attacked. Voices echoed through Jo's mind, mocking her, blaming her for Donni's demise. She slid the last ten yards down the hill and stood, helpless, teeth chattering and body trembling.

Jo needed to help her sister. But where was she? How could she help?

Why did she always cause everyone around her pain?

Someone grabbed her wrist and training kicked in. She shrieked—part out of surprise, part to draw attention to her attacker—and twisted her hand in the grip. She slipped her wrist out between the person's fingers and thumbs, then she immediately threw a straight palm strike to her attacker's nose. She felt the bone break even before she registered the crunch sound, and the man grabbed his face.

"Son of a bitch!" he yelled.

"Jo. Jo!"

The sound of Donni's voice broke through to her. She grabbed her sister's hand and started pulling her toward the gym. "Run!"

Donni shook her head "no" as arms came around Jo from behind, holding her in a bear grip. She tried throwing her head back to head butt this second assailant, all the while screaming, "Run, Don! Run!"

To her horror, Donni didn't run. Instead, she approached her. She reached for Jo's face and held her head still. "Jo! Stop!"

Jo kept thrashing, kicking her legs and bucking her body. When the first attacker put his hands down, Jo stilled, watching the luminous form approach her.

Blood poured down Vinnie's face, covered his hands. Instead of wiping his hands off, or holding his now swollen and very crooked nose, he raised his hands and continued walking slowly toward her. "Jo? It's me. Vinnie. Are you with me?"

She shook her head to clear it. Her eyes felt too wide, and they stung. She blinked a few times to clear her vision. Vinnie, Donni, Gianni, and Marcus stood around her. The arms hadn't released her yet, so she assumed that was Coz standing behind her.

"Where are you, Jo?"

She took a quivering breath. "Here. I'm here. In West Virginia. With you."

"Good girl. We're going to let you go now. Don't fight, okay?"

She nodded.

"And don't run."

"Okay. I'm okay."

Vinnie nodded his head, and the arms slowly let go. Coz stepped cautiously to her side, his hands also raised.

She crumpled to the ground, and Donni rushed to embrace her. "What happened, honey?"

"I—I couldn't find you. I thought someone—" She took a deep breath. "And Dante. Knives. Cameras. I couldn't find you—" Body-racking sobs tore through her.

Donni rocked her. "Shh. It's okay. We're all okay."

"Oh, my God! Vinnie! I'm so sorry!"

"No worries. I should have been ready to block or duck. I wasn't expecting it. Totally on me."

"How can you say that? I did it." Tears streamed silently down her face, but she had stopped sobbing. Vinnie didn't wipe his blood away, so she refused to wipe her tears. Small penance, but it was all she had to offer.

"It's fine, Jo. Nico can fix it. I'm more worried about you. What were you running from? Is everything okay?"

"Not from. *To*. I was running to find Donni. I just... I guess I just freaked. It won't happen again."

"Damn right it won't. We're talking all this out. Tonight. You can't hold all this in anymore."

"I don't need to talk. I'm fine."

"Bullshit."

She knocked Donni's arms off her and scrambled to her feet. Most importantly, she stopped crying. "Really. It's all good."

"My nose says otherwise."

"I'm really sorry," she whispered.

"Let's go, everyone," Vinnie said.

"One second." Gianni grabbed his arm. He looked luminescent for a moment, then Vinnie's nose stopped bleeding. Then Jo noticed a stinging sensation on her face, arms, chest, and legs. She looked down, surprised to see tiny trails of blood all over her. Scratches—all gone. Marcus's eyes widened, but he stayed silent. So did she.

She noticed Vinnie shoot Gianni a hard stare, but she was grateful he'd helped Vinnie and didn't care he was made Gianni exposed his power. That was the least of their worries.

"Okay. Now can we go?" Vinnie asked.

Without another word, they all formed an unofficial circle around her and started up the hill.

What a freak she was. And because she couldn't contain herself, she was being forced to talk it all out. Barring some unforeseen issue, she'd be front and center after dinner, baring her soul to the seven people she desperately wanted to avoid sharing her horrors with.

Maybe Nico would have turned up something juicy, and she wouldn't be on the hot seat.

And maybe the whole Medici-descendant thing was just a bad dream.

If it was, it was time to wake up.

Guilt, humiliation, and dread made her feet plod up the hill. She looked around at the foliage that apparently scratched her on her way down the hill. The irony wasn't lost on her. She was walking her own personal green mile.

16

VINNIE AND THE guys left Donni to handle Jo and Marcus to do whatever Marcus did. They went upstairs, Vinnie grabbed a towel from the bathroom, and they walked to Nico's room. Vinnie opened the door without knocking.

"What the...?" Nico jumped. He slammed his laptop shut and shoved it under his pillow before turning around.

"Just us." Coz plopped down on his bed.

"How you feeling?" Vinnie wiped at his nose and stepped further into the room. Gianni brought up the rear and closed the door behind them.

"Better than you, apparently."

"I could use a little help here." Then Vinnie lowered his voice. "In case anyone's listening, though, I thought you should act like this is draining for you. You know, because you were 'sick' and came up here to rest."

Nico spoke softly, too. "Given how you look, it might be draining regardless. What the hell happened?"

Vinnie put one finger to his lips and gestured to the door. There was a shadow outside it. He spoke louder again. Clearer. "Are you sure you're well enough to do this?"

Nico grabbed the remote and turned on the television. He didn't look at what was on, he just cranked up the volume. "I think I just ate something funky. I'm okay to help you out."

"Where's your first aid kit?" Vinnie asked.

Gianni leaned toward him and whispered, "What's the point of this ruse? Marcus already knows."

"He knows about *you*. Part of what you can do, anyway. He doesn't know anything about Nico. Or the rest of us."

"I think they'll notice when you don't have raccoon eyes and a splint on your schnoz."

"Shut up. I'm not going around unable to breathe till we leave here." He dabbed at his nose again.

"Maybe you should," Gianni said, "if you're worried about what he learns."

"Doesn't matter, anyway," Nico whispered. "I couldn't find anything on Marcus. Zip. Zilch."

"What about Tina?" Coz asked.

"Yeah. She's been a real pain in the ass since we got here. Hard to dig up any dirt when she's hovering everywhere."

"Well, you did try to kill her," Coz said.

"Why does everyone keep saying that?" Vinnie asked. "I didn't try to kill her. If I wanted her dead, she'd be dead." The thought sickened him. He would have killed her to protect Jo. And that was something he would have to live with.

He prayed it never came to that.

"You know you sound ridiculous right now," Gianni said, distracting Vinnie from his morose thoughts. "All nasally and stuffy."

"Bite me, G."

The guys all laughed.

"Anything on Tina?" Vinnie asked.

"Not much. And I mean that in a bad way. I can't find anything on her until three years ago. And she's been making calls to burner cells."

"Shit," Vinnie said.

"Yep," Nico answered.

Vinnie saw the shadow leave and was about to ask Nico to fix him up. Without warning, though, his nose snapped back together.

"Fuck!" he yelled and looked at the door again. The shadow didn't return, so he continued to talk without whispering. "*Testa di cazzo!* How about a heads-up next time?"

Nico just smiled. "You're welcome."

"Quit squawking, V," Gianni said. "You ready for me to finish this up?"

"Go ahead." The pain of the break repair had already receded. Then Vinnie felt the pressure in his sinus area release. He looked in the mirror. Other than the dried blood, which he scrubbed at again, his face looked normal. No swelling. No black eyes. In fact, his nose might be a bit straighter than it had been. "Thanks, guys."

Gianni shrugged. Nico said, "No prob. Now what happened?"

Vinnie plopped down at the foot of Nico's bed. Gianni sat at the foot of Coz's bed, and the four of them faced each other.

"Vinnie got his ass kicked by a girl." Coz shoved him.

Nico looked like he tried to suppress a smirk. He failed.

"That's not exactly how it went down." Vinnie straightened and punched Coz in the arm.

Coz chuckled and leaned back against the headboard.

"What happened?"

"Jo. She completely flipped. I don't think she knew where she was or what was going on. She babbled about…" Vinnie trailed off, realizing the guys didn't know about her high school issues.

"What?" Nico asked.

"I told her she has to talk about it all tonight. For now, it's enough to say she was flashing back to some ugly shit."

"Flashbacks? Like PTSD?" Nico said.

"After everything?" Vinnie said. "Her history. Chuck. Coz getting shot. Dante attacking her… Would it be a stretch to think she's coming unglued?"

"None of us can heal the mind," Gianni said. "What are we supposed to do about this?"

Vinnie had been thinking about that on the way up the hill. "I think she just needs to air her dirty laundry. If we can get her talking instead of bottling everything up, we can probably control her stress. If not, we're going to have to seek help."

"I don't think PTSD gets better just because someone talks once about their experiences," Coz said.

"Don't you think I know that?" Vinnie said. "I've looked for a strategy here. This is the only thing that comes up. And whether she gets better or not, she has information we need. She has to talk. I'll keep working on it."

"And the two of you?" Gianni asked.

"That topic's off the table to you guys." He glanced at the television to avoid everyone's stares. Romeo and Juliet was on. The suicide scene. Vinnie closed his eyes and sighed.

"I hope you know what you're doing," Gianni said.

"Yeah," Vinnie said. "Me, too."

JO CREPT DOWN the stairs. She had gone to Nico's room to check on Vinnie but moved when she realized they were talking like Nico was really sick. It was likely they had seen her feet at the door. Or maybe they were worried about surveillance. It was Marcus's house, after all.

So she stepped away from the door and stayed plastered against the wall right beside it. Once she moved, their tone went back to normal, and she could just make out their conversation over the sound of the television.

They started discussing Marcus and Tina. Useful information there. Although she didn't know what she could do with it, other than being more careful around them. And she was already pretty damn careful.

She found it really fascinating when the discussion turned to her. To his credit, Vinnie didn't tell her secret. But he basically promised that she'd share it later. That was around the time he said she was crazy. And right before he wouldn't discuss their relationship with his brothers.

Relationship.

What a laugh. They didn't have a relationship. They'd had a fling. One that she'd been determined to end.

So why did it hurt so bad to know he was just using her for information? I'll keep working on it. Those were his exact words. She wasn't even a "her" to him. She was an "it," a thing to manage.

She needed a break. She couldn't talk to her sisters. She definitely didn't want to talk to the guys. And there was no way she was going to talk to Marcus or Tina.

What she really needed was a heart-to-heart with Nonna, but reaching out to her would only put her at risk. And could potentially give away their current location. She'd already made so many mistakes that jeopardized her sisters and the Brotherhood. No way would she chance another.

No. What she needed was a clean break. Distance. Alone time.

Despite her desire to run, she was in the middle of nowhere. Running would mean they'd follow, and that would only put everyone in danger, because somehow her departures kept having negative consequences. No, she needed a congested area where she could disappear into the crowds and her family couldn't follow.

And Vinnie couldn't follow.

God, they were right about one thing. She had a shit-ton of bottled up stress.

She usually relaxed by working out. But the taekwondo classes earlier had tired her out, and that was before she ran up and down the hill a million times. She didn't have the energy to exercise her stress away. Clearly that option hadn't worked so well today, anyway.

So she did the only thing she could think of. She let herself into Marcus's office—her bedroom while she was there—and opened up her laptop. In seconds, she was logged into the NBD network, checking emails and looking at their pending projects.

She worked for a while, preparing a schedule from permits through final walkthrough for an upcoming house in The Woodlands subdivision, then she confirmed the timeline for the house she'd left Chuck in charge of.

Chuck.

She blinked back the tears before they could fall. There wasn't time for grieving at the moment, especially as she hadn't received confirmation of his death.

Like she needed it.

No! There was hope, at least until there wasn't any. Maybe Nico could search hospital records, see if he'd been taken anywhere for treatment. See if he couldn't find something somewhere. She swiped at a tear that escaped and took a deep breath. Poor, sweet Chuck. They needed to find him. She needed to make things right.

Jo shook off the despair and got back to work. She'd have to get in touch with Dean and let him know the project was his.

Clicking through the directories, she came to her own personal folder and opened it. There was a video file titled "Play me now" at the top of the list. What the hell? She hadn't saved anything like that on the server. It positively screamed 'malware.' Maybe Seth or Samantha had put it there. They often shared jokes.

But usually through email.

Although they did have access to all the sisters' folders. Franki had changed their status to be able to get into the personal directories when the girls went to live at the Brotherhood compound. She was worried the company would need something and none of the sisters would be available to access a necessary file.

She wasn't wrong.

Still, she didn't want people saving stuff to her folder. She liked having control of what was there.

Pulling out her burner phone, the one Nico had given them before they left for West Virginia, she dialed the office.

"NBD. This is Samantha. How may I help you?"

"You're there late."

"Jo! How are you? Where are you? Is everything okay? What's going on?"

Jo chuckled. "Hey. Slow down. How are things there?"

"Things here are fine. A little stressful, but fine."

"Why? What's up?"

She sighed. *"No one can find Chuck. Production's going to shut down if we can't get a foreman in there. Are you available?"*

Jo once again had to swallow her grief. It hurt to speak past the lump in her throat, but when she continued, she was fairly certain Sam didn't notice her sorrow. "It's my fault. Chuck needed some time off. I should have let you know."

"Oh. Oh, okay. Um... is he all right?"

"Just had to deal with some personal issues. Don't worry." She closed her eyes. God, she hated lying. And she hated what she lied about even more. "I want Dean to take over. I have a schedule ready for him. I'll email it to both of you."

"I'll keep an eye out for it. Hey, Jo? Are you coming back soon?"

"I don't know. We have some issues of our own to work out first."

"We miss you."

"Miss you, too."

"Seth's coming in with an armload of something. I'd better go get the door for him."

"I'll hold. I have a question for you both."

Dean Martin crooned through the phone while Jo waited. It wasn't long until Sam was back on the phone. *"Hey. We're back. I have you on speaker."*

"Hi, Jo. How's it going?"

"Hello, Seth. We're fine. Any problems on your end?"

"Nothing I can't handle."

"If you get stuck, email Franki. We'll get back to you."

"I still don't know why we can't have your numbers."

"I don't have time to explain it again. Listen... did either of you save a file to my private directory on the server?"

"Not me," Seth said.

"Me, either."

"Are you sure? Maybe by accident?"

"I don't think so."

"What's it called?" Sam asked.

"Never mind. Seth, keep us in the loop. Daily emails. Sam, I'm sending you and Dean the schedule now. Give him a call. If there are questions, email me."

"Okay," Sam said.

"Gotta go. Take care." She hung up on their goodbyes.

There was little information she could ascertain from the file without opening it. With the mouse hovering over the icon, all she could get was the type, file size, and date modified. The video was only one day old. Or was edited one day earlier. There was no creator information. She ran it through a virus scan, and it came back clean.

Throwing caution out the door, she double-clicked on the icon.

When the media player popped open, she gasped, unprepared for the opening image.

Chuck was center-screen, suspended on a wooden cross. His shirt was covered in blood.

When her hand stopped shaking, she clicked the 'play' arrow.

Dante walked into view and put his face in the camera. It filled the screen, blocking Chuck's image, but she could still hear him in the background. Someone was doing something to him. He screamed once, again. Then he panted and gasped for breath before falling silent. The entire time, Dante just grinned into the lens. Finally, he broke his silence.

"Are you enjoying the show? Oh, I'm sorry. I bet I'm blocking your view. Let me just step aside for a moment..." His image left the screen and she could see someone circling Chuck, standing behind him so his face was hidden from the camera. Suddenly Chuck's body bucked and he howled, an agonizing, heart-wrenching sound to hear, even through the speakers. When his body stopped thrashing, he panted for air.

Dante stepped into the side of the frame, still leaving her clear access to Chuck's image. *"I bet you thought your favorite foreman was dead. Yes, we know all about your relationship. And no, he's not dead. Not yet. See, we have a few special tricks up our sleeves, too."*

Chuck bucked again and yelled.

Dante turned away from the camera and faced his captive. *"Say hello to your boss, Chuck."*

Chuck turned his head to the camera, but didn't open his eyes. Probably couldn't, as they were bruised and swollen. He shook his head, his movements slow and labored, and spoke just clearer than a moan. *"No... don't...."*

Dante walked away from the camera and stood right in front of Chuck. *"How chivalrous. He's trying to protect you, Jo."* He patted Chuck's cheek, and Jo flinched more than even Chuck did. *"Chuck, you stupid fuck. You should be worried about yourself, not your girl."*

Tears fell down Jo's cheeks as she reached for the screen, touching Chuck's face, his battered body.

Dante held his hand out to the man behind Chuck, then turned toward the camera again holding something in his hand. *"Do you know what this is, Jo?"* He brandished it with a flourish. *"It's a cattle prod. It's enough to cause excruciating pain, but not enough to kill. At least, not at first."*

He held the charged end to Chuck's heart. After a few seconds of wailing and bucking, Dante pulled it away. Chuck fell still.

"Hmm. Looks like we have some work to do here. In the meantime, know this. Chuck will tell me where you are, or he will die. If you want to spare him any more pain, call me." The screen went dark and a number appeared.

The video was over. Jo ran to the bathroom and threw up. When her stomach was empty and she could do nothing but heave, she pulled herself to her feet. Shaking violently, she steadied herself on the counter and splashed water on her face.

It was bad enough when she thought Chuck's death was on her hands. How would she ever cope knowing about him being tortured? Because of her?

It was too much. She returned to her room and picked up the phone. She typed the number in, but couldn't bring herself to hit *send*. What if she made things worse? She couldn't trust her decision-making skills any longer. Instead, she stored the number and, grabbing her laptop, went to find Vinnie.

She found her sisters and The Brotherhood in the kitchen.

"Dinner will be ready in about an hour and a half," Donni said. "We've got a couple pot roasts going, and Marcus is going to grill veggies."

"That gives us time to talk," Vinnie said. "We're going out back for some privacy. No excuses this time."

Jo didn't answer. She stood there, trying to figure out what to say.

"Hey." Franki said. "What's wrong?" She and Vinnie both started toward her, but she clutched the laptop to her body like a shield and held her other hand up to stop them.

"I'll go out back with you, but I have something to share."

"We know," Vinnie said. "You've got a lot to share. Time's up."

"That's not what I mean."

"Okay," Franki said. "What do you mean?"

She shook her head. "Outside." And she walked out. She didn't need to look behind her to know they all followed.

Searching the back yard, she decided the safest place to go would be the middle of the clearing. She couldn't be certain Marcus didn't have a discreet mic by the picnic furniture, but she was pretty sure he didn't bug the lawn.

She sat on the grass and everyone sat in a circle around her. "I know you're expecting me to explain what happened today. Which would dig up a lot of history. I know you want to know about the vision, too. And I promise, I'll tell you all. Soon."

"Jo," Gianni said. "We've given you enough time already. We need to know this stuff now. Definitely sooner rather than later."

"I get it. And I agree. Mostly." It had been a long time since seven people glared at her at once. She didn't care for it. "But this is more important."

"What could possibly be more important than learning about your vision?" Franki asked.

"And about your erratic behavior lately," Gianni said.

"This." Jo turned her laptop screen to face the group and played the video. She couldn't watch it again, but recognized the sounds, and saw her reactions mirrored on her sisters' faces. The guys stayed stone-faced and silent.

"My God!" Toni said when the video was over.

"Chuck...." Donni raised her hand toward the screen, much as Jo had stroked it earlier.

"That's the guy from Italy," Franki said.

Vinnie's head snapped up. "What? What guy?"

"Our stalker," Franki said.

"What are you talking about?" He turned to Jo.

"It was a long time ago. Way before we met you. Before Papa died. The twins were still in school. Franki and I went to Italy for a couple of weeks. A few guys followed us around. We weren't even entirely sure we were being followed until we got back to the States. We were chased out of the airport."

"And you didn't think to tell me?"

"It didn't seem important."

"Jo, you need to tell me these things!"

"I get that now."

He sighed, ran his hand through his hair. "Okay. The video. Where did you get it?"

"It was in my folder on the server at work."

"And you opened it without checking with me first?" Nico said.

"I ran it through the virus scan software. It was clean."

"Jo," Nico said, "it's probably a Trojan horse. They've likely already tracked your location and are on their way."

"I thought the virus scan would protect us."

Gianni stood. "We need to leave. Now. Everyone go pack up. We're on the road in fifteen."

Everyone started to get to their feet except Jo. "What about our mission here? We haven't even had a chance to spy on Marcus and Tina properly yet."

"Nico got enough info while he was here today. We'll have to base our assumptions on what he's learned." Vinnie pulled her to her feet and they started walking with the others.

"Actually, I got more than just some info," Nico said. "I left a few goodies behind that will keep feeding us intel."

"You didn't tell us that," Coz said.

"I don't tell you everything. Let's get moving. I want to check out that file once we get on the road."

Jo listened to the exchange in silence. Once again, it seemed everyone was pitching in to clean up her mess. She needed to find a way to break the cycle.

Or just break away.

VINNIE COULDN'T REMEMBER the last time he had been that scared. He'd never been afraid of Dante. He was just a weak-ass punk.

But Dante seemed to be targeting Jo.

And given how she kept running, he knew it was only a matter of time until Dante caught up to her.

What if Vinnie couldn't get to her in time?

Would Dante kill her?

Torture her first?

Rape her?

Even as anger tinged his vision red around the edges, his blood pumped cold and slow through his body, washing him from the center out in icy terror.

He'd never loved anyone enough to react this way.

Merda! Love? Where the hell'd that come from?

He looked at Jo. Her hair almost glowed in the brightness of daylight, strands of blonde highlights shining in the sun. She'd been outside for months working on NBD's construction projects, yet her skin was still pale. He'd had her in his arms grappling and in much more intimate ways, and he knew that body was lithe, supple, strong.

Yet as she trudged along to the house, she looked delicate, fragile.

Beaten.

He needed to do something to get that spark of life back in her. But what?

Too bad he didn't have time to figure it out. Marcus stopped him on his way back in.

After everyone had gone to pack, the two of them stood alone in the kitchen.

"Vinnie, sit for a minute." Marcus gestured to the barstools at the island.

"Didn't G tell you? Something's come up. We need to bug out. Now." He tried to pass him, but Marcus grabbed his arm and nodded toward the stools.

"It'll just take a minute. If I know you, you're traveling light and didn't even unpack. You can be ready to leave in under a minute. Just give me a fraction of your time."

Vinnie wavered.

"It's important."

He sighed and sat on the stool.

Marcus joined him. "I've been wanting to talk to you for a while now, but I wasn't sure it was my place. When you showed up, I took it as a sign. I thought I'd have a chance to ease into it, but I'm out of time. After what you said to me in class today, I know this talk's long overdue."

Vinnie stood. "I don't have time for a heart-to-heart."

Marcus grabbed his arm again. "This won't take long. Promise."

Vinnie allowed himself to be pulled back onto the stool. "One minute."

"I need longer."

"Clock's ticking."

Marcus sighed. "You've kept people at a distance since you were young. I tried to become the father that Mike should have been—"

Vinnie snorted.

"—but you didn't seem to want that kind of relationship. You were always closed off."

"Yeah, well…" But he had nothing to say. Marcus was right. He was closed off. It was easier. There was no point in growing attached to anyone. When people tired of him, they left. His parents hadn't wanted him. Mike's "adoption" was a joke. The guys would eventually go their own ways. That's what happened to friends and siblings. Gianni was already drifting. He had always been prepared for that. It only stood to reason that if the people who should have been closest to him were out of his life, or would eventually be, why would Marcus be any different?

"Look. I need you to understand a few things. One—I've always been here for you, and I always will be. It only takes a phone call. Two—You and Jo are made for each other, but you're also cut from the same cloth. She holds people at a distance, too. If you want her, and you'd be a fool to throw her back, then you're going to have to be the one who opens up first."

"Is that it?" Vinnie's chest was tight. "I gotta go."

"One more thing. You need to set things right with your mother. That's the only way you're going to be able to move forward."

"What do you know about my mother?"

"Everything. I know she didn't dump you on the doorstep of the church like you tell everyone. And I know she would love to be part of your life. Let her in."

"You don't know anything." Vinnie got up and turned toward the hallway.

Marcus stopped him one last time. "Be careful." He pressed something into Vinnie's hand and walked out of the room.

Vinnie opened his palm. It was a card with all of Marcus's contact information. Marcus had circled his private mobile number and written *'Call anytime. I'll be there.'* beside it.

Vinnie crumpled the card in his fist and tossed it in the trash.

Before he made it the whole way out of the kitchen, he stopped, hung his head, and sighed.

He strode over to the trash and retrieved the card. Smoothing it out, he stuffed it in his pocket, then went to gather his things.

17

EVEN THOUGH MARCUS had delayed Vinnie, he was the first person in the driveway. The guy had been right—he'd never bothered to unpack. It was easier for him to live out of his bag if he didn't know when he'd be leaving.

Jo came out next, and they stood there in strained silence. He found that looking at her hurt, but not looking at her hurt, too.

What a fucking pansy he was. And he made fun of G? *Merda.*

He turned to her. "Look, Jo—"

"Don't. I shouldn't have opened the file. I shouldn't have gone to the cemetery. I shouldn't have skipped out the morning Dante found me. You don't have to rundown my list of sins. I got it."

"That wasn't what I was going to say."

She finally met his gaze. "What, then?"

Yeah, jackass. What? He didn't know what to say. He just hadn't been able to tolerate the silence.

He was saved by Nico and Coz coming out.

"I think I got everything," Nico said. "If I missed something, I'll have to buy it once we get there."

"Get where?" Vinnie asked.

"Mike texted," Nico said. "Don't you ever check your phone?"

Vinnie pulled out his phone. Sure enough, he'd missed a text.

"How the hell does he know when we need information?" Coz asked.

"You know how," Vinnie said. "It would have been nice if he had made himself known, though."

"You'd think he could just check this stuff out on his own," Coz said.

"I don't think it works that way," Vinnie said. "If he's not—what's the word? Corporeal?—If he's not corporeal, he can only eavesdrop. He can't physically dig around. That's why he sent us."

"Bullshit," Coz said. "He can transport and get corporealized whenever he wants. He just needed to get us out of the compound and didn't know where else to send us."

"Corporealized?" Nico said.

"What? It's a word."

His brothers continued bickering, but Vinnie tuned them out. He'd seen Jo's reaction to Coz mentioning them needing to leave the compound. She blamed herself for it, hated herself for it. He needed to get her mind off it and focused on something else.

He interrupted Coz and Nico. "Maybe there's more to it. Maybe we're supposed to be learning something as we do this."

"All I learned is that Mike's making this harder than it needs to be," Coz said.

"Hope he's not listening to you right now," Nico said.

Coz scowled, but he didn't say anything else.

Donni and Toni came out. Their bags bulged even more than when they first packed at the compound.

"Shit," Coz said when he looked at the bags. "I know you didn't go shopping. Or did you steal something?"

"No, we did not steal anything," Donni said. "The only extra things we have are our *doboks*."

Nico laughed. "They aren't that big!"

"We didn't have time to properly organize everything," Toni said. "I don't even know if we got everything."

"If you missed something, we'll replace it at our next stop," Gianni said. He and Franki had finally come down, and Gianni threw their bags in the back of the van. "Load 'em up."

Marcus and Tina came out to see them off while the guys stowed the rest of the luggage.

"It was a pleasure to meet you all," Tina said.

"Bet you didn't think that originally," Coz said.

Tina looked at Vinnie and smiled. "Yes, well… We all make mistakes. All's well that ends well, right?"

Tina shook hands with all the guys and hugged the girls. Marcus hugged everyone, holding Vinnie just a little longer than everyone else.

"I guess you can't tell us where you're going," Tina said.

Before anyone answered, Marcus said, "We know. Security. Can you at least contact me once in a while? Let me know you're safe?"

He'd been looking at Vinnie, but Nico answered. "We'll see what we can do."

Amid a chorus of thank yous and goodbyes, they climbed into the van and left. Gianni drove, and Franki sat up front with him. Donni and Toni took their seats in the back, and everyone else kept their seats from the drive down.

At the bottom of the steep drive, Vinnie said, "G? Stop here a second."

"What for? We need to get moving."

"We need to sweep the van. And all of us."

"You don't think…?" Franki said.

"I don't know. But I'm not taking any chances."

Nico hopped out and grabbed a wand. He checked the whole exterior and interior of the van, then he swept all the passengers and luggage.

"That's five minutes we'll never get back," Gianni said.

"Did you trust Tina?" Vinnie said. "I know I sure as hell didn't."

"It doesn't matter now," Donni said. "We're tracker-free and on the road."

"Where are we headed, anyway?" Franki asked.

"Atlantic City," Gianni said and pulled onto the road.

"Atlantic City!" Franki said. "That's what? Six hours away?"

"Depends who's driving," all four men said together.

Toni scowled. "So we have six hours to kill."

Gianni just laughed. "Whatever. Anyone want to hear some Zeppelin?"

"I want to hear Jo," Vinnie said. "We've waited long enough, and there's nothing else pressing at the moment."

Jo looked at him, positively pleading with her eyes. He felt sorry for her, but they couldn't wait any longer. She had to tell them what she knew.

After everyone agreed with him, Jo sighed, resigned, "Fine. Where do you want me to start?"

THERE WAS SOME debate as to what she should cover first, so she made the decision for them. Holding up her hand, she said, "Stop, okay? I'll figure it out as I go."

The group quieted down, and Jo took a deep breath. Then she began.

"First, I guess I should explain why I was getting my drink on the other night." Was it really just a few nights ago? Time flies when you're ruining everyone's fun. "See, all my usual subs were on other jobs, so I had to call in Palmeri. Instead of him staying clear, he started hounding me. It got to be too much, so I went to Giuseppi's to blow off some steam."

"And why is Palmeri a problem?" Nico asked. "I ran his name when Vin gave it to me. Nothing suspicious came up."

"Palmeri is a problem because we have history." She paused, trying to figure out how much to include. Finally, she shrugged and plunged ahead. "In high school, he took advantage of me. At least, I thought it was him. Doesn't matter now. The whole school…"

She couldn't bring herself to say more. When no one said anything, she continued. "I guess it doesn't really matter who it was or how many people knew. At the time, I reacted… poorly… to the situation. All these years later, I still hadn't moved past it. And when Palmeri didn't avoid me but actually came after me at the site, I panicked."

"Came after you?" Gianni asked. "Came after you, how?"

"Is that why you were so upset when we found you with Chuck that afternoon?" Nico asked.

"Like I said, he kept trying to get me alone. I was afraid of what he wanted, but it turns out he just wanted to talk. To explain."

"Fuck," Coz said. "There's no explanation in the world to explain taking advantage of a girl."

"It doesn't matter now. After my meltdown that one night at dinner, Vinnie took me to meet him."

She noticed Vinnie's hands clenched into fists, but he stayed quiet.

"I hope you kicked his sorry ass," Gianni said.

"He handled the situation," Jo said. "Enzo won't be a problem anymore."

Vinnie reached for her hand. She didn't want anyone to see that display of affection, didn't even know if she was ready for it, but she needed something—some human contact, some external reserve of strength. Despite what anyone might think, she took his hand. He squeezed it, and she continued.

"Anyway, I'm sorry about what I said at the bar. I hope I didn't reveal anything during my drunken rant. But I don't think anyone of any consequence was there. And I'm sorry about my freak-outs over Enzo. That one did have consequences." Her hand fluttered to her unmarred throat as she thought about Dante. She owed the guys big time for saving her life.

"After everything that happened with Enzo, I just needed a break from everything. I felt trapped. So I cut out early one morning. That's when Dante found me. I'm sorry about that, too."

"You were the one hurt that time," Coz said.

"Initially, yes. And you all exhausted yourselves to fix the problem. And then I made things worse. I got you shot." She looked down at her feet, then continued in a whisper. "I got Chuck shot. I thought he was dead. But it's so much worse."

"Hey," Donni said. "It's not over yet. As long as he's alive, there's a chance."

"And he's tough, honey," Toni said. "If anyone can get through what they're doing to him, he can."

"It'll be okay, Jo," Franki said from the front of the van.

It didn't escape her notice that none of the men said anything. And their silence spoke volumes. They believed as she did—Chuck's torture might last a long while, but he wasn't getting out of there alive.

"Thanks," she managed to say to her sisters. Vinnie squeezed her hand again. "So that's my story."

"Not by a long shot," Gianni said. "What happened to you when you broke V's nose?"

"Yeah," Nico said. "I didn't see it. Tell me what went on then."

She sighed. "Donni and I had... oh, I don't know. An argument of sorts."

"About what?" Vinnie asked.

She felt her cheeks heat when she thought back. Donni had been teasing her about him. There was no way she was admitting that. So she confessed to the other part. "About telling you guys this story. I don't let people in my business. You can't understand how uncomfortable this is for me. It's bordering on the wrong side of violation."

"We don't ask you these things to hurt you, or to take advantage of a vulnerability," Vinnie said. "We need to know this stuff to better protect you."

"I don't see you sharing," Jo said.

"My life's an open book," he said.

"Liar," she countered.

"Besides, you aren't protecting me. I'm protecting you."

"Don't you and your brothers watch out for each other? You don't share with them, either."

"You're getting off topic," Vinnie said. "So you and Donni fought. What happened next?"

"I ran away from her, but then I started to worry, so I went looking for her. By the time I was at the bottom of the hill, I was convinced Dante had her and was hurting her like he did me."

"But you didn't even know where you were," Coz said.

"Not at first. I was kind of stuck in my head. That's when I hit Vinnie."

"So how do we make sure panic won't send you deeper into your thoughts the next time?" Gianni asked.

"I don't know. I feel like I've just gone to confession. You know, somehow lighter in the soul? I think letting all this go and sharing it all with you was a good first step. If I don't have to hold this all in, then I won't be so screwed up."

"I guess we'll see," Gianni said.

"There's one thing you haven't let go of yet," Vinnie said.

She looked at him. She knew what he was going to say, but having to say the words aloud was going to be harder than any of the stories she'd told yet.

"The vision, Jo. Let's have it." His voice was hard, firm.

She tried to pull her hand away, but he only held it harder. Tears blurred her vision, but she didn't let them fall. She bit her lip and tried to stay calm, but panic rose in her chest, hot and burning like bile after a bender.

"We can't prepare for what you saw if we don't know what it was," he said, his voice a little softer but still insistent.

"I don't know where we were," she began, her voice barely audible over the sounds of the van.

Vinnie squeezed her hand, urging her to continue.

She took a deep breath. "I'm at a site I don't recognize. Dante's there."

"Dante!" Franki said.

"It took me a while to even realize it was him. Not until after the woods. But it's him. He's going to detonate some kind of bomb. Vinnie shows up, but that only makes him laugh. Then he sets off the bomb. I expect to be blown apart, but somehow I'm drowning." She took a shaky breath. "And Vinnie's gone. I get him killed."

She couldn't hold it back any longer. The tears poured out of her, and Vinnie dropped her hand. The isolation broke her heart.

Then he pulled her toward him and held her, rocking her and whispering soothing sounds in her ear.

Relief flooded over her that he didn't abandon her, followed immediately by a wave of panic. He didn't abandon her! That meant the vision was still viable. She was going to get him killed.

Jo pushed away from him and looked into his eyes. "I can't be responsible for your death. I can't! It's too much!"

"Shhh." He put his finger over her lips. "None of that. I'm not going anywhere. Now that you told us, we can make sure that doesn't happen. Just like Franki and Gianni."

"But her vision came true! It just didn't make sense to us until it happened."

"But we misinterpreted it, Jo," Franki said. "I'm sure you're doing the same."

"No. No, I'm not."

"Doesn't matter," Gianni said. "Now we know what we're dealing with. We can work with it just like we did before."

"No!"

"And the same could happen here." Vinnie ignored her protests. "You said I wasn't there when you're drowning. That doesn't mean I died. That just means you can't see me. I'll get to you."

"You can't know that!"

"Jo," Nico said. "Now that some time has passed, do you recognize the site?"

She thought for a moment. "No. It felt somehow familiar, but I don't think I've ever been there."

"And are you sure you were drowning? If there was an explosion, then there would be fire. Maybe you're choking on smoke?"

"No…" She revisited the vision again, then shook the image off. "It's definitely water. I don't know where it came from, but it's water. I'm covered with water."

"Are you sure you're drowning, then?" Coz asked. "Any chance you're just under water and able to get to the surface. Safely?"

"I… I don't know. I felt like I couldn't breathe."

"If you're under water, you can't breathe," Franki said. "That doesn't mean you won't get to the surface."

"I don't know." She knew they weren't going to give up until she felt better, so she said, "I guess I'll figure it out when the time comes. Am I done now?"

"Yeah, *bella*. You're done," Vinnie said. "Just relax now. G?" he called up to the front of the van. "I think we should stop for food soon."

"And I want to go somewhere with a computer," Nico said.

"What? You don't have enough hardware with you? Can't you just set up a hotspot?" Coz asked.

"I want to dig up some info on that file Jo got. And I don't want to do it from my station. Just in case."

Jo sat back and looked at Vinnie out of the corner of her eye. He looked calm, but looks could be deceiving. He was probably already trying to find a way to keep her safe. But she determined it wouldn't come to that. She wouldn't be responsible for him getting hurt.

She'd find a way to keep them all safe.

VINNIE WAS ENJOYING some down time. He didn't get to relax often, so when he did, he took full advantage of it. At the moment, he was content to sip his wine and just listen as everyone else talked.

Because it was evening, they hadn't thought stopping at a library would give Nico much time. And barely knowing where they were—let alone where any Internet cafés might be—they had opted to eat at a restaurant right beside a twenty-four hour copy center. Nico had devoured his food in record time then left to work his magic. The rest of them, Vinnie included, lingered over their meals.

Franki and Gianni were in their own little world, whispering to each other and laughing softly. Coz chatted with Toni about something she had done during training earlier. By the look on her face, Vinnie thought Coz must have told her they'd be spending extra time on it. He'd never seen a girl exercise so much yet loathe it with the passion she did. If she wasn't working on an NBD project or training with the group, it seemed she was in the pool or on a treadmill. Only Jo seemed to work out more. Of course, Jo seemed to thrive on it.

Jo and Donni discussed Seth and Samantha and other NBD employees. He felt bad pulling them away from work and home, especially so soon after losing their father. Really, for all intents and purposes, they'd lost their mother, too. Given everything they were going through, he had to hand it to them. They adjusted really well.

Well, all of them did except Jo.

He saw her struggle everyday with the lack of freedoms, the lack of privacy. And every time she took some time and space for herself, someone got hurt. Or worse.

Depriving her of her independence wasn't something he relished. He loved her autonomy, her liveliness. Her spunk and drive. It killed him to snuff it out of her.

But it was a temporary necessity.

He prayed they'd get to the bottom of the whole Medici mess before her spirit broke irreparably.

He could at least do that for her.

He took another sip of wine. Nico plopped down beside him.

"Are you guys ready?" Nico said. "We should get going."

Vinnie threw money down on the table and they all got up. "Learn anything new?"

Nico glanced around. "In the van."

They left the eatery, filed into the van, took the same seats as they'd had earlier, then Gianni pulled out.

"Okay," Vinnie said. "Let's have it."

"We've got a problem."

"No shit," Coz said. "Want to be more specific?"

"The number on the video is a burner cell. It was purchased five miles from the compound."

"So Dante was able to track us," Coz said. "Good thing we left when we did."

"Anyone heard from Mike?" Vinnie asked.

"Other than when he sent us a new location?" Gianni asked. "Not me."

Nobody else had, either.

"So we don't know how the compound is or if Dante got anything useful out of it," Vinnie said.

"That's the other problem," Nico said. "I don't know if they got into the compound. I don't know if Mike had it cleared out or if they've been through all our stuff. What I do know is Dante and Sal are working with a hacker. A damn good one."

"How do you know?" Donni and Toni asked together.

"I can't trace the file. I have no idea where it came from or how it got on the NBD server. I mean, obviously the system I was on was complete junk with little power and none of my apps. I could probably learn a little more from my own equipment, but I don't think we should risk it."

"Can't you scrub it somehow so it's safe?" Vinnie asked.

"If I couldn't learn what I wanted off the copy center's computer, then I can't be sure I can keep our location hidden if I try it from mine. We can't leave ourselves open to some backdoor exposure. I'm worried there's some kind of tracer on there that I might miss, and it could lead them right to us."

"Couldn't that have already happened on my system?" Jo asked.

"I thought of that earlier. That's why I left your laptop behind at Marcus's."

"What am I supposed to do without a computer? What about all my files?"

"Your system is backed up daily to an offsite server, so after I'm sure your files are safe, I'll download them for you on the new laptop I'm going to get for you. If you're emotionally attached to your old system, I'm sure we can get it off Marcus when this is all over."

Jo crossed her arms and sat back, but she didn't say anything.

"What about Marcus?" Donni asked. "If they did Trojan horse her laptop, he'll be in danger."

"Unless he's involved," Nico said. "We still aren't sure. And if he's innocent, we have to trust that he's prepared to defend himself. He knew the risks when he signed up."

"But he's retired!" Toni said.

"Not by choice," Gianni said. "Besides, in this life, you're never out for good. Not really."

Vinnie took in the exchange, then turned to Nico. "Marcus. Jo's computer. Those aren't really the big problems."

Nico shook his head.

"Then what?" Jo asked.

"The hacker," Nico said. "They've got a hacker."

"A good one. As good as ours," Vinnie said.

"Maybe better," Nico said. "Fuck. Never thought I'd be saying that."

"Me, either," Vinnie said. "Meanwhile, no one open anything—emails, texts, files of any sort—until Nico clears it."

"I don't think anyone's better than you, Nico," Donni said. "I know you'll figure it out."

"Hopefully before it's too late," Nico said.

Vinnie couldn't agree more. They'd just lost one of their advantages.

18

VINNIE SLEPT THROUGH most of the ride to New Jersey. When he woke, he looked around the van. String lights around the ceiling cast a soft glow throughout. Jo had curled into a ball and faced the corner. It was like she didn't want to associate with anyone. He got that. But it still hurt him to see her that way. She was a vital part of his group, and he wouldn't let her pull too far away without dragging her back.

Metaphorically or physically.

A quick glance over his shoulder told him that Franki was most definitely not asleep. He hoped to God Gianni didn't wreck the van given that his attentions were… divided. He smacked Gianni on the back of the head and turned back around. Gianni grunted from the slap, then he whispered something to Franki. He heard her muffled, "Oh, my God!" and was satisfied that Gianni focused solely on the road again.

Determined to put that image out of his mind, he scanned the rest of the group. Donni and Toni leaned against each other and dozed. They looked like bookends with nothing between them. Nico and Coz also slept. Once again, Nico snored. Every now and then he would go from small, soft snores to a loud snort and Coz would elbow him, causing him to slump further in his seat, which made the snoring worse. Vinnie wondered how long it would be before Nico fell on the floor. One, two more bumps? Instead, Nico pushed himself back up and turned toward Coz. Three bumps later the two leaned against each other just like the twins did.

A small chuckle beside him caught his attention.

"I thought you were asleep," Vinnie said.

"I thought you were," Jo answered.

"I was. I woke up."

She turned to face him. "You almost look well-rested."

He cocked his head to the side. "We really going to do this?"

"Do what?"

"Small talk."

"I poured my heart out earlier tonight. I don't have anything else to say."

"Maybe not about Brotherhood business. What about our private business?"

"Private business?" She laughed. "We don't have any private business. Everyone knows what happened."

"That doesn't mean the situation is resolved. We need to talk about it."

"There's nothing to say, Vinnie."

"I've got plenty to say."

"I don't want to hear it. I thought I was clear. I needed someone that night. For one night. That's all it can be."

"You think that's all it can be? Or that's all you want it to be?"

"What's the difference?"

"A pretty damn big one. One has to do with possibilities, the other with decisions. For me, the two are in line. It sounds to me like for you, they're worlds apart."

She looked at her watch. "We should be there soon, don't you think?"

"Don't change the subject, Jo." He grabbed her face and turned it toward him. "I need to hear you say it."

She yanked her head back, wrenching away. "Say what?"

"What you want. Not what you expect, or what you think would be best. What do you want?"

"What I want doesn't matter. Like I said, that was a one-time thing."

"It doesn't have to be. We have a good thing going here. Or we can, if you let us. What are you so afraid of?"

Her eyes widened and she recoiled like she'd been slapped.

They were already whispering, but he lowered his voice even more. "What is it? What's wrong?"

She shook her head and batted her eyes like she was blinking back tears. "If you have to ask, then you aren't even ready for a relationship."

Before he could answer, she turned around. "Hey Franki? We almost there?"

"Yeah. Less than a mile, I think," she said.

"Wake everyone up," Gianni said.

Jo got up and shook the twins awake. She put her finger to her lips to tell them to be quiet, then she nodded toward the guys.

The twins stifled a giggle while they stared at the two men snuggled together.

Jo sat back down and took out her phone. She clicked a picture of them, the flash illuminating the back of the van.

"Was that lightning?" Coz mumbled.

"Dunno. Shh," Nico said.

"Rise and shine, boys!" Vinnie called.

Both men started to stir. Soon both blinked sleep out of their eyes. Then they turned to see where they were.

The two of them leapt away from each other. Everyone else in the back of the van erupted into laughter.

"What—what the fuck were you doing?" Coz yelled.

"Me? What the fuck were you doing?"

"What's going on back there?" Gianni called.

"I'll show you when we get out." Jo waved her phone. "I have a picture."

"Gimme that!" Coz said.

"Not on your life. That might be this year's Christmas card."

"Don't worry," Nico said. "I'll hack in and delete it from her cloud drive."

Coz shoved him. "That won't get it off her damn phone."

The van stopped. "We're here," Franki said.

As they climbed out of the van, Nico pulled Vinnie aside. "You'll delete that off her phone, right?"

"Geez. Lighten up. It's a joke."

"You suck. You know that?"

"Don't blame me because you're a cuddler. I like my space when I sleep."

"You didn't last night!" Nico called and darted out of Vinnie's reach.

He turned and looked at Jo. Even in the dark he could see she blushed. Of course she had heard. When the hell would he catch a break?

JO'S FACE STUNG with shame as she walked around the van. She'd been so lost in her thoughts and wrapped up in teasing the boys that she hadn't really paid any attention to where she was. That changed quickly. She stopped short and tipped her head skyward.

They were in front of a several-stories tall, high-end hotel and casino on the boardwalk. "Are you sure you have the right place?"

"This is what Mike texted us," Gianni said.

"So why are we here? Is Enrico or Paolo a gambler?" Jo asked.

Vinnie smirked. "Not the way you think."

"What's that supposed to mean?" Jo asked.

"Mike sent us a few pertinent details. Apparently Enrico made a risky investment with his retirement bonus," Nico said. "A risky, high-end investment."

"What?" Franki said.

"This is his casino." Vinnie nodded toward the door. "Let's go see if they have any rooms."

Jo's sisters looked as shocked as she felt. Donni's eyebrows arched, and Toni's mouth dropped open. Franki just stood, still and speechless. Jo recovered first, shrugged, and headed for the door. "Might as well get on with it." She led the way inside.

The lobby impressed her. A fountain dominated the center of the space, the gurgling water soothing to her ears. Large Romanesque columns, faux-aged to look eroded at the tops, formed an aisle into the hotel proper. To the right and left of the columns sat stone benches with poofy cushions on them, interspersed between tall plants which offered privacy for the people who might choose to sit. The walls had a stone texture to them, and the whole place looked like an old Italian garden.

At the end of the aisle was an elevator door painted to look like an iron gate with an atrium behind it. To its right were double doors, also painted like the elevator. Printed above them was the word CASINO. The doors must be sound-proofed, because Jo couldn't hear a single noise from beyond. Across from the casino doors was the registration desk. While Donni and Toni 'ooh-ed' and 'ah-ed' over the décor, she headed toward the counter. Everyone followed, even the twins, although their discussion didn't stop.

"Hello, and welcome to The Grotto," the cheerful desk attendant said. "The restaurant is closed," he continued, gesturing to a hallway off to his side, "but the bar is open. And of course, the casino never closes."

"We're not looking to drink or gamble," Jo said.

"We'd like to rent some rooms," Vinnie said.

"I'm sorry. We're full up."

"Are you sure?" Gianni held up a hundred dollar bill. "Hotels usually save a few rooms for emergencies. And this is an emergency."

The agent looked at the bill in Gianni's fingers like he wanted to devour it. "Again, sir. I'm very sorry. We're booked to capacity. You aren't likely to find anything on the boardwalk this week. The week before and the week after Independence Day are usually booked a year in advance. Maybe if you try something inland?" He still hadn't made eye contact with anyone. He was fixated on the money.

Vinnie pulled out a second c-note. "Would you mind looking again?"

The man's eyes moved back and forth between the two bills. "Ah…" A ringing phone cut off his response. He tore his gaze away from the money and glanced at the display. His face drained of color.

"One moment, please," he murmured to them. Then he picked up the receiver. "Hello, sir. How can I help you?"

Jo watched him carefully while she wondered how much of a tip would be necessary to secure even one room for the eight of them.

The attendant turned and looked at the security camera, then he typed something with frantic fingers into his computer. "Yes, sir. I'll take care of it right away." He pulled some key cards out of a drawer. "No, sir. I wouldn't dream of it… Thank you… Good night, sir." He clicked off the call then dialed a four-digit number. "Cameron? Please bring the cart around… This is a special exception… Now, Cameron."

He hung up the receiver and smiled at their group. "I am so sorry for the delay. Cameron will be right here with a luggage cart, and he'll show you to your rooms."

Gianni and Vinnie moved their money closer to the attendant, but he shook his head and held up his hands. "Oh, no. Thank you, sirs, but I couldn't."

"Really," Vinnie said. "For your trouble."

"No trouble at all, sir. I'm sorry about the delay."

Jo looked around their group. They all looked as puzzled as she felt.

"Let me give you a credit card, then," Gianni said and reached for his wallet.

"I'm sorry, sir. Your money is no good here. Your entire visit is to be compensated. It's been arranged."

Vinnie's eyebrows shot up. "Excuse me?"

"You're comping our stay? The whole stay? For all eight of us?" Gianni asked.

The bellhop arrived then with the luggage cart.

"Finally, Cameron. Get their bags." The guys shrugged and headed for the parking lot to grab their things..

"No, no. Let us do that." The attendant rushed out from behind the counter to stop the men. "Just give Cameron the keys. He'll load the cart and see to it that your vehicle is safe with the valet."

"I carry my laptop." Nico followed Cameron out to the car, and when they returned to the lobby, all the luggage was on the cart, except for Nico's laptop, which he held himself.

"Well, ladies, gentlemen," the attendant said. "If you should need anything during your stay, anything at all, just call down. My name is Mitchell. Ask for me directly. If I'm off duty, request Charlene or Fred. One of us will certainly be available, and we'd be happy to help you with whatever you need."

Vinnie offered the money one last time. Cameron looked at the camera behind him. The red blinking light seemed to be saying "no" in some kind of code. He shook his head. "No. Really sir. It's my pleasure." He handed Cameron the key cards and whispered something in his ear which sounded to Jo like, "Under no circumstances are you to accept a tip." Cameron frowned, and Mitchell tried to discreetly elbow him.

Jo noticed, anyway.

"I hope you enjoy your stay here at The Grotto," Mitchell said as they walked toward the elevator.

When the doors opened, they all filed in. Jo marveled that the elevator could accommodate the nine of them plus an overflowing luggage cart. But the elevator was massive. She pondered the logistics behind an elevator that size, then turned her attention back to Cameron.

He swiped one of the key cards in a card reader. "You'll need to do this to reach your floor." He pushed forty-nine, one number shy of the top.

"Gee," Vinnie said. "Do you think maybe Enrico knows we're here?"

"What was your first clue?" Gianni asked.

"Enrico?" Cameron asked. When everyone looked at him, he blushed and looked at his shoes. "My apologies. I didn't mean to eavesdrop."

Jo looked at Franki and mouthed, "Are you kidding me?"

Franki just shrugged.

The elevator was the smoothest Jo had ever been on. She studied the elevator permit looking for information and decided to ask Mitchell about the brand and installation. If he didn't know, she was certain he'd bend over backward to find out.

They were at their floor much faster than Jo expected. Her knees didn't buckle, her belly didn't flop. The car just eased to a stop and the doors opened without a sound. Cameron gestured for them to exit the elevator, and he followed with the cart.

He turned left and went the entire way down the hall. "Mr. DeSanto. Miss

Notaro. This is your room." He opened the door, handed Gianni two keys, and wheeled the cart inside. Gianni and Franki followed him in and assisted him in getting their bags. Cameron tipped his hat and started to leave when Gianni grabbed his arm, offering him a tip. "No, thank you, sir. This is my pleasure."

Gianni cocked a brow. "Thanks," he said and shut the door.

Cameron headed back the way they'd come and stopped at two doors across from each other. "Ladies," he said, looking at the twins. He opened the door to their room, handed them their cards, and wheeled the cart inside. In no time he tipped his hat and exited the room. "Mr. Micelli? Mr. Cozza? I was told to put you right across the hall from these ladies. This is your room." He opened the door and wheeled the cart in. They guys followed.

Jo looked down the hall. It was empty except for the elevator and one remaining door. "Um, Vinnie... there's only one room left."

"Yeah. I noticed."

"Did you do this on purpose?" She heard the squeaky tone of her voice, but she couldn't get it under control. No way she could be alone with him in a hotel room.

"And when would I have done that? The bellhop doesn't even know who Enrico is. He and the guy at the desk both turned down our tips. How could I have arranged this?"

"Well, I can't share a room with you."

"What choice do you have? That's all that's left."

"I'll stay with the twins."

"This far from me? I don't think so. You're my responsibility. You need to stay near me."

"Nico and Coz are there."

"Leaving you one warrior short if you go down there. And I'm not sharing a room with them to make things easier on you. Nico snores. And apparently both of them like to snuggle."

"Vinnie! You can't possibly expect me to share your bed?"

"I shared yours last night."

It was preposterous. She stammered and stuttered, but words failed her.

"Relax, Jo. We'll see how the room looks. I'll crash on the couch or send down for a cot."

That made her feel only marginally better. They might not be hip to hip, but they'd still be in each other's space. How would she keep her distance when they were on top of each other? What if they really ended up on top of each other? She'd told him that wasn't what she wanted, but if they were in such close quarters for a long time, she didn't know if she'd last. And even if she did, he was still invading her privacy. How would she sneak away if he was right there?

Damn it.

Cameron came back out and wheeled the now-almost-empty cart down the hall, past the elevator, and to the only remaining door. "Mr. Falco. Miss Notaro. Your room." He started to put the card in the door, but Jo reached out and stopped him.

"Um. Excuse me. There's been some mistake." Vinnie leaned against the doorframe and crossed his arms. She looked at him, swallowed, and continued. "We aren't together-together. We're just traveling together. Do you have another room available?"

"I'm sorry, ma'am. These were our emergency rooms. Henry told us to give them to you, and to split you up like this."

"But..."

"This is all that's left, ma'am."

She sighed. "Could you at least send up a cot or something?"

Cameron smiled. "Let me show you inside, ma'am. I think you'll find the accommodations satisfactory."

Jo bit her lip and Vinnie pushed off the wall. Cameron opened the door, handed each of them a card, then wheeled the cart inside. Vinnie gestured for Jo to precede him, so she entered the room.

Her purse fell off her shoulder and hit the floor with a thud.

To call it a room was like calling caviar fish. She stood at the top of three marble-tiled stairs that led to an expansive suite. The sitting area had a fireplace with a cabinet above it. Cameron walked over to it and opened the doors to reveal a large, flat screen television. There was a table and chairs on the other side of the room beside a bar that divided the living area from a small, state-of-the-art kitchen. Cameron walked over to the windows and opened the curtains. The wall was floor-to-ceiling glass panels, and two of them opened to a balcony overlooking the ocean.

"There is a bedroom through this door," he gestured to the right, "and another to the left. Each has its own private bath. Will this be satisfactory, then, ma'am?"

She'd have as much privacy as she did at the compound. Maybe more, if she just stayed holed up in her room. "This will be fine, thank you."

"Shall I take your bags into your bedrooms?" he asked.

"No," Vinnie said. "I've got it."

"I'll just leave them here, then." He unloaded the cart and tipped his hat. "Enjoy your stay at The Grotto."

Vinnie offered his hand to shake Cameron's, and the bellhop paused for a moment before raising his. As they shook, Jo saw a look flash over his face.

"Sir. I really appreciate your generosity, but I can't accept it."

"For you and Mitchell. I insist. You wouldn't want to turn me down, would you? That would make me very unhappy."

Cameron wavered. Vinnie pushed the cash into his hand. "You've made me happy. Very happy." He looked over at Jo, and she turned away. "Believe me."

She snuck a peek at the bellhop. He glanced down at his hand and then back up at Vinnie. "Thank you, sir!"

"Good night, Cameron."

Cameron tipped his hat. "Sir. Ma'am." And he scurried out of the room.

Jo tried to look at anything except for Vinnie, but for some reason he seemed to be taking up the entire suite. Finally she cleared her throat and walked toward her luggage. "I'll just take this stuff to my room, then. Do you have a preference?"

He sat on the back of an overstuffed sofa and stared at her. "I think you know I do."

"I mean a preference for what room you take." He didn't say anything, so she continued. "I guess without having seen either of them, it's hard to say."

Her voice trailed off at the end. He still didn't move or say anything. "Well, why don't you check out the rooms and pick one?"

He raised an eyebrow and crossed his arms.

"You don't want to look at them?" His gaze drove her crazy. It felt like he looked right through her clothes and took in every inch of her flesh. "Okay, then. I'll just take this one." She walked over to the door closest to her, opened it, flipped on the light, and stepped inside.

She'd built homes and commercial buildings for some extravagant clients, but she'd never been in a place as opulent as that room. Her eye was immediately drawn to the chandelier above the bed, the crystals twinkling with reflected light. The bed beneath it looked larger than any king-sized she'd ever seen and was covered in a plush gold brocade comforter. Four fluffy bed pillows rested against the headboard, and several throw pillows in shades of vermillion, gold, and sage sat in front of them.

On one of the nightstands was a crystal lamp and a phone. On the other was an alarm clock and a plate with truffles. A fireplace similar to the one in the common area took up wall space near the balcony door. Above it was another cabinet-covered flat screen. A red and gold striped loveseat faced the fireplace, flanked on either side by green wingchairs. A platter with chocolate-covered strawberries and two champagne flutes sat on the coffee table, and an ice bucket with a bottle sat in arm's reach of the settee.

Fresh flowers were spread throughout the room, and classical music played out of the in-ceiling speakers. The door to the bathroom was partially opened, and she could see a giant basket of toiletries sitting on the counter beside a folded white terry robe and slippers.

The whole room screamed romance.

She turned around and bumped into Vinnie.

"I didn't hear you come in."

"I'm not in. I'm still at the door."

"Well." Once again, she didn't know where to look to avoid him, so she tried looking straight ahead. One look at his broad chest had her looking lower. Not her best idea ever. She looked up and met his piercing gaze, his brown eyes boring into hers, searching her for secrets she wasn't ready to reveal. She settled for looking at her feet.

"Okay. Well. Hard to believe they got all this food and the flowers up here before us, huh?"

"Impossible." His tone hinted that he wasn't talking about the truffles.

She cleared her throat. Didn't stop her voice from squeaking a little, though. "Now that you've seen this room, do you want it or the other one?"

"Which one do you want?"

The décor of the room they were in called to her. She longed to jump on the bed and snuggle into the pillows, savor a truffle and a strawberry then pop the cork on the champagne.

But every time she pictured herself staying there, she wasn't alone.

"Let's take a look at the other one." Anything to get him out of that room, to put some distance between them.

She crossed the common area to the other bedroom door. It was a mirror image of the first, except the reds and greens were midnight blues and icy lavenders. Every detail was mimicked, right down to the number of truffles on the plate.

This room didn't say romance.

It said *sex*.

The darker palate brought out a more visceral, passionate response in her. She was certain Donni would have a thousand reasons why those colors elicited that response, but she didn't care. She was so hot, she thought about sleeping on the balcony.

Turning around, she found Vinnie. Right there. Again.

"So, do you want the blue one?" she asked.

"Which do you want?"

"I'll... I'll take the red."

"The red looks comfortable."

"You think so? Would you prefer I take the blue?" She moved the collar of her shirt and fluttered it a bit to try to get some air. Even though the fireplaces weren't lit, it was sweltering. She took a step away from him, trying to get some air and some distance, but with each step back she made, he advanced a step toward her.

"What do you think of the blue?"

What did she think of the blue? She thought it was decadent. Delicious.

Or maybe that was the man standing in front of her.

"I'll take the red," she said.

"I think I'll join you."

"You're not invited."

He cocked a brow, but didn't answer her.

"Yes, I know big ole He-Man can bust the door down and get to me." She was flustered and started rambling. "But you won't. You have more honor than that. You're here to protect me, not molest me."

He raised both brows, and she realized that coming from her, he'd have been offended by her statement. But she hadn't meant it that way. Funny, but with Vinnie, she thought about her high school trauma less and less.

To smooth things over, she babbled on. "Not that I think you're capable of molesting someone. I'm mean, I know you could, you just wouldn't." If her foot went any farther into her mouth, she'd choke on it.

Maybe that wouldn't be such a bad idea. It might shut her up.

"I mean, I trust you. Not enough to share a bed, but still…"

When a grin started slowly spreading across his face, she gave up.

"I'm going to bed now. Goodnight." She pushed past him and started toward her bedroom.

"Jo," he said, his voice a soft caress to her ears.

She stopped but didn't turn around.

"Before this is over, you'll change your mind."

There was no way she was answering him. She entered her bedroom and closed the door. Leaning against it, she sighed.

Damn it. He was probably right.

19

JO TRIED EVERYTHING to relax. The large bathtub had jets, so she soaked in the hot, bubbly water. After that, she took a quick shower then wrapped herself in the luxurious but too-large robe left for her. Nowhere near tired, she cuddled up on the loveseat and helped herself to the strawberries. Then she caved and popped the cork on the champagne. The bubbles and foam rose quickly in the glass, and she had to take a few fast sips to keep it from overflowing. The fizz tickled her nose and danced across her tongue, only invigorating her more. She poured a second glass… and then a third.

She was pleasantly buzzed when she killed the bottle.

As she shifted on the settee, the robe slid off her shoulder, deepening the V opening. She trailed her fingers over her skin along the edge of the robe. Sighing, she tipped her head back and closed her eyes as her hand skimmed her collarbone, her throat, her jawline.

Although her hand was soft and warm, she couldn't stop thinking about a rougher, hotter hand that had been on her recently. Teasing. Touching.

She squirmed in her seat, crossed her legs, and the robe fell apart, exposing the top of her thigh. Untying the belt, she opened the robe and ran her fingers up her leg, over her hip, across her pelvic bone and onto her stomach. She rubbed small circles on her skin, feeling her abdominal muscles quiver beneath her hand. The fluttering lightness of her touch combined with the warmth and effervescence of the champagne she'd drunk were a synergistic combination, causing the heat in her stomach to pool lower then spread throughout her body. Desire consumed her. She was burning, electricity pumping through her veins and sparking everywhere her hand stroked.

She needed him.

Climbing to her feet, she wove her way to the bedroom door, never bothering to retie the belt.

He hadn't gone to bed yet. Rather, he stood at the open balcony door, leaning his shoulder against the jamb and looking out over the inky ocean.

She walked up behind him and wrapped her arms around his waist. His chest expanded from a deep breath, but he didn't say anything. So she broke the silence. "Did I surprise you?"

"No. I told you you'd come to me."

She giggled. "No. I mean now. You didn't know I was behind you until I wrapped my arms around you. Right?"

"Wrong."

"Huh? I was quiet."

His finger traced a pattern over her knuckles. "No, *bella*, you weren't. Besides, I knew the second you opened your bedroom door."

"Did not." Her voice was muffled against his back.

"Just like I know your robe isn't tied and your bare skin is pressed against me."

She sighed and pushed off him, reaching for and missing the ties of her robe. "How could you possibly know that?"

He turned around to help her with the belt, his fingers lingering only a second on her skin as he pulled the material across her body. When he'd tied it closed, he met her gaze. "I know everything about you."

"Then you know what I want tonight."

"I do." She reached for the belt again, but his hand gripped hers and stopped her. "And I'm not giving it to you."

Her hands fell to her sides. "But you said I'd come to you. And I did."

"Of that I'm well aware."

"Maybe you don't really know what I want."

"I know. And the answer's no."

"But… why not?"

"Because you're drunk, Jo. I would never take advantage of you like that. If you weren't drunk, you'd know that."

"I'm not drunk."

"You're not sober."

"Pleasantly tipsy." She reached one hand up and put it behind his neck, threading her fingers through his hair. With her free hand, she reached up and traced his lips. So soft.

He kissed her finger then put his arms on hers, forcing them down to her sides. "Let's get you to bed."

She grabbed his hand and started toward her bedroom.

"To sleep, Jo."

"But I'm not tired."

He sighed. "Me, either. Not any more than I usually am, anyway. Probably shouldn't have slept in the van."

They were in her room now. She led him over to the bed, but he somehow steered her to the loveseat. He sat in the chair beside her.

"Why don't you sit beside me?" she asked.

"I'm fine here."

She got up and straddled him, this time entwining both her hands in his hair.

Her robe was falling open again, and the bottom had split very high to accommodate her spread legs. Even slightly buzzed she could follow his gaze, and it traveled all over her flesh. He stared so hard she swore she could feel him touching her wherever he looked.

And she thought she was hot before.

A smile crept across her face, and she started to lower her mouth to his.

He put his hands under her hips and grabbed her thighs. She thought she'd broken him down, but instead he stood, lifting her, and deposited her on the settee again. Then he sat beside her. "I can sit next to you." He put his arm over the back of the loveseat and crossed his foot over his knee, almost like he wanted to protect himself from her advances.

She leaned against him, and his arm slid down across her back, his hand resting on her shoulder. The robe opened dangerously far, and she wriggled like she was trying to get comfortable, knowing his eyes would be drawn to her exposed skin.

He sighed and began trailing circles over her bared shoulder. "Maybe I should make coffee."

She shifted in his arm so she could rest her cheek against him while tracing her own pattern across his chest. "I don't want any coffee."

"Maybe I need some." He extricated himself from her and went to the bar.

She followed him and climbed onto the stool, allowing the robe to fall open again.

Instead of making coffee, he poured himself a bourbon and rested his hands on the bar. He closed his eyes and hung his head.

"What's wrong?" She rubbed her finger around the rim of his glass.

"You're kidding, right?"

She shook her head, then put her finger to her mouth, tasting the traces of liquor she'd wiped up.

"Jo, you know I want you. I've wanted this probably since the first time I saw you. I want you more every day."

"So what's the problem?"

"You're killing me."

Her eyes popped open. What was he saying?

"Do you have any idea what you're doing to me? How hard it is to see you naked but know I can't touch you? To feel you next to me but know I have to step away?"

"So don't step away."

"*Merda!* If I don't, I'm no better than Palmeri!"

She recoiled like she'd been slapped.

"Jo." He reached for her. "Jo, I'm sorry."

She slid off the stool and fumbled to close her robe. This time he let her do it on her own. "I think I'm ready to sleep, now." She walked to the door and opened it for him. "If you wouldn't mind."

He walked toward her and reached out, but she pulled away, so he dropped his hand. "I am sorry. But I'm not wrong. You'll thank me later." He left, pulling the door closed behind him.

Thank him? For what? The heat of her flaming cheeks was only slightly cooled by the trail of tears down them. She was doubly humiliated. Once for offering her body to him, only to have him reject it. And once for having shared her most intimate and painful secret with him, just to have him throw it back in her face. Mortification wasn't a strong enough word.

She curled into a ball on the bed, covered herself with the enormous blanket, and fell asleep.

VINNIE HAD BEEN swearing at himself for the better part of two hours. He was a heel. Scum. The lowest of the low.

As if telling her those things wasn't bad enough, he actually defended himself for saying them.

Maybe if he could just keep his damn mouth shut, they'd get along better.

His mattress was probably quite comfortable, but it felt like a bed of nails. Guilt and shame pricked him from head to toe, and he rolled and punched his pillows. Didn't matter. It was unavoidable. He wouldn't be getting any sleep. Not until he talked to Jo.

When he heard a rustling in the common area, he grabbed his dagger and his gun. He was about to get out of bed when there was a soft knock at his bedroom door.

"Vinnie? Are you awake?" Jo's voice was barely above a whisper.

He hurried to stow his weapons. "Come in."

She cracked the door open, but stayed in the doorway. The light in the common room was on, backlighting her, casting her features in shadow while making her appear to glow. She looked like an angel.

"What's wrong?" he asked. "Are you sick?"

"No." She shook her head. "I just wanted you to know that I'm sober now. I know what I did. And what you did. I don't think I can sleep until I apologize, so I came to say I'm sorry."

He turned on the lamp then started to get out of bed, only to realize he was naked. Thinking better of it, he readjusted his blanket. "I'm the one who should apologize. I'm supposed to be taking care of you, not making you feel worse."

She waved her hand like she was brushing his words away. "I just wanted to clear the air. I'm going back to bed now."

She turned to leave, and he knew if he let her go, he'd never get her back. "Jo. Wait." She spun around. He didn't have the time or privacy he needed to dress without risking upsetting her, and he knew she wouldn't appreciate him approaching her naked, so he wrapped the sheet around his waist and stood. He crossed to her and grabbed her hand. "Let's talk."

"It's very late."

"Please, Jo." He pulled her over to the loveseat and sat. This time she was the one who chose the chair.

He ran his hand through his hair. Shit, he was a lawyer. Words should come easily to him. Instead, he was probably going to open his mouth and shove both feet into it.

He spun to face her better. "I can't tell you how sorry I am for earlier. I was an insensitive ass." He grabbed her hands. "I don't know why you feel you owe me an apology, but know that you don't. You did nothing wrong. It was me. I handled the situation badly."

She started to pull her hand away, but he wouldn't let her.

"Do you think you could forgive me?" He used the pad of his thumb to rub her wrist.

She yanked her hand away. "I don't know what you want from me!"

He leaned forward, rested his elbows on his knees, and tried to meet her gaze, but she looked down at her lap. "Jo." He waited for her to look up, but she never did. "I think you do know what I want from you. I've been clear about that."

She gripped her hands together. He feared she'd crush the bones if she kept squeezing but sensed touching her would probably make matters worse.

"I can't give you what you want."

He sighed. "Did you ever hear anyone say that drinking doesn't turn you into someone else, but brings out who you really are?"

She finally looked at him. "What are you saying? You want me to go get drunk again?"

"God, no. I need you sober for this."

"For what?"

"For what your uninhibited-self came to me for in the first place."

Before she could ask another question, he was on his knees in front of her, pulling her head down to kiss him.

She tasted of chocolate, rich and decadent, creamy and smooth. When he had seen the strawberries and the truffles, he had fantasized about feeding them to her. As his tongue explored her mouth, though, he couldn't think of a better way to share the confections.

He tipped his head, taking the kiss deeper, and both heard and felt her moan. His heart pounded in his ears, each beat threatening to deafen him to her every murmur or whimper.

And he wanted to hear it all. Each gasp, each yell. Every call of his name and every plea to the Lord.

He traced her mouth with his tongue and nipped at her lip, then he pulled away and stood, his sheet falling to the floor. He noticed her gaze flicker over his arousal before she started to scramble to her feet. Instead of letting her stand, he scooped her up and carried her to the bed. Once he lay her down, he knelt beside her and reached for the belt of her robe.

Her hand clamped on top of his.

"What's wrong, *bella*?"

"The last time I was upset and looking for comfort. Earlier tonight, I was drunk and out of control. Now I'm… I'm just very aware."

"I wouldn't have it any other way." Again he reached for her robe.

"I'm not sure I can do this."

He sat and pulled her up so she faced him. "At the risk of making you angry again, I need to point a few things out to you."

She started to talk, but he put a finger to her lips, silencing her. "First, you may have been looking for comfort on the porch, but when I took you inside it was about something else entirely. Second, you weren't sloppy drunk earlier. You were just uninhibited. Relaxed. And this was definitely what you wanted. Third, you most definitely can do this. I'm certainly not going to force you, but if you admit what you want—what you really want—you'll know I'm right."

"I think… I think I want to keep my robe on."

He shook his head, saddened that she was back to her old insecurities. Or that maybe she'd never truly shed them. "I couldn't get you to keep it on earlier. What's changed?"

"Sobriety." She clutched the robe tighter together.

"Jo. You know I've seen you, all of you, more than once. You're stunning."

She shook her head. Tears welled in her eyes. He was losing her, letting her wallow in a past injustice.

He bent and kissed her tears away. Kissed her forehead, the tip of her nose, her chin, and each cheek. Then he kissed her gently on the mouth, savoring the softness of her lips.

"You don't need to hide anything from me. Never."

She dropped her hands, but the robe stayed closed.

"Why don't we just see how this goes? If I do anything you don't like, just let me know."

She nodded. "We can try that. Only…"

"What?"

"Can we turn off the light?"

He sensed her desperation was nearly as strong as his own. She just lacked the confidence.

He was determined that none of it would matter to her for much longer.

"Whatever you need."

Vinnie switched off the lamp.

"And can you close the door so no light is coming in?"

He stifled a sigh. "Sure." Getting up, he crossed the room and closed the door. The only light left in the room was a crack of moonlight from the improperly closed curtains. He made his way over to the bed and stretched out beside her.

"How do you do that?" she asked.

"What?"

"Walk around naked. Completely comfortable with how you look."

"Is there a reason I shouldn't be?"

"No! No, that's not what I meant. I just wondered…"

"Look, Jo." God, he wished he could see her face, read her eyes. "I love the way you look. I adore every dimple, every freckle, every contour of muscle. And yes, even every scar. I look at you and see only beauty, whether you're bundled in a robe or naked in my arms. You're a feast for all my senses. I love the sounds you make. I love the smell of your soap on your skin. The way you feel in my arms and taste on my tongue. And yes, Jo, I love the way you look. So, I'll take you any way I can get you. But I would prefer to see you."

She rolled away from him. It was maddening, not being able to see what she was doing, how she was feeling. He heard a soft rustling, then a small click. The room was bathed in a soft glow from the lamp on the nightstand, and she stood before him, robe unbelted.

He smiled and offered his hand to help her climb back on the bed.

"I need to take this—whatever this is—a step at a time. Baby steps." She bit her lip, closed her eyes, and slipped off the robe, allowing it to pool at her feet.

"This is a perfect first step." He pulled her into his arms. She trembled under him. Knowing she wasn't cold, he needed to get her mind off her body.

And he didn't need his power of strategy for that.

He tilted his head and slanted his mouth over hers. She opened her lips on a sigh and he slipped his tongue inside. She still tasted like chocolate, but the taste was fading. He reached over her, grabbed a truffle off the plate on his nightstand, and held it to her lips. When she opened her mouth for a bite, he pulled it back. Her brows furrowed, but he didn't tell her what he was doing, he just let her experience it. He brought the truffle back to her face and traced her lips with it.

It was no longer cold, but room temperature, and it melted all over his fingers, all over her mouth. He moved the candy again and watched, fascinated, as the tip of her tongue peeked out. She licked the melted ganache off first her top lip, then the bottom. "Mmmm," she murmured, and closed her eyes. He brought the chocolate back to her mouth, but this time he slid it past her lips. She opened her mouth and took his offering, letting it melt on her tongue.

While she savored that bite, he rubbed his chocolate-covered thumb over her collarbone, then bent down to lick it clean. She shuddered under him, and he grazed his teeth over the area. When she sucked in a breath, he sucked on her neck. She settled even further back into the pillows, moaning. Each sound she made vibrated against his mouth, spurring him on. She grabbed the back of his head, holding him in place, and he didn't mind in the slightest. He laved her neck, trailed kisses along her jawline and across the sensitive skin under her ear, then nuzzled her hair. Lavender.

He suppressed a shudder of his own and pulled back. His finger still had chocolate on it, and he teased her with it, waving it over her eyes, her chin. Finally, he put it to her lips. She opened her mouth and sucked on the candy-covered digit. Every pull on his hand shot a wave of desire through his body straight to his already throbbing erection. Just picturing the other things she could be doing with her mouth, teeth, and tongue put him dangerously close to embarrassing himself. He pulled his finger out of her mouth.

Before it dried, he ran his finger across her left breast, then he blew on it. The combination of his touch and the air cooling the wetness made her already rigid nipple grow even harder. She trembled, and he licked his own finger, repeating the process on the right side. Her back arched, thrusting her breasts closer to his hands. Knowing what she needed, he bent down and sucked her nipple into his mouth, scraping his teeth over the sensitive skin. He took her other nipple between his fingers, pinching and rolling it as she squirmed beneath him.

She felt incredible under him. Each draw of his mouth, each pull of his fingers—every action of his was met with stronger and stronger reactions from her. She writhed, moaned. Her hands reached up and fisted in his hair, holding his mouth exactly where he wanted it to be. Then she clasped his back, only to lift up her palms and scrape her nails down his flesh. He'd be marked later, but couldn't have cared less. The slicing sting urged him on.

When he started to move, she grabbed his hips, nails digging in to hold him in place, but he broke her hold and slid down her belly, his tongue following the natural contour of her stomach straight down the center. He didn't have to move her legs, didn't even have to ask. She opened for him, positively writhing with need. His tongue circled the engorged bundle of nerves as his fingers slid into her. She was hot, wet, and so ready for him. She bucked, pushing herself closer to him, her moans growing closer to screams.

She was warm and sweet, and he lapped at her while stroking her, curling his fingers to take her even higher.

"There, there! Yes! Vin, don't stop!"

Hearing his name in her breathless voice spurred him on, and he moved his tongue and fingers faster. She grabbed his free hand and pulled it toward her chest. He found her nipple and pinched it while humming against her.

Her insides squeezed his fingers just before she cried out.

"Oh, God! Yessssss!"

He continued stroking her, slowing his pace as he brought her down gently. Her face was flushed and her eyes were bright under half-closed lids, but she wasn't covering herself. Instead, she lifted her arms to him.

He grabbed her with one arm and rolled over, taking her with him. She straddled him and took him in her hands. The hiss escaped him before he could swallow it, and she smiled. Instead of positioning him at her opening, she stroked him.

God, she felt incredible. He grasped the sheets and tried to watch her but didn't have the control. Seeing her hand sliding over him, his erection dark and throbbing against her pale fingers, was just too erotic a sight. Leaning back, he closed his eyes and felt. Her hand started at the base of his shaft, squeezing, building pressure, then slid up toward the tip, her fingers circling the ridge, then skimming back to the bottom again. She kept the same pattern up, stroking then tickling, but increased her pace. His pulse thundered in his ears again.

It felt good. Too good. His whole body was a torrent of conflictions, tensing from the force of restraint, relaxing under her lavish attentions.

He grabbed her hips, lifted and pulled her forward. She didn't release him, but rather positioned him at her entrance. Like he needed guidance. With one stroke, he plunged fully into her and began driving at a frenetic pace. He was so close to release, but he needed to send her over the edge first.

He looked at her, riding him. Her skin was flushed, her eyes were closed, and her breasts bobbed with each stroke. He cupped them, causing her to moan. Then he skimmed his fingers over her pebbled nipples, and she threw her head back, thrusting harder against him. He grabbed her hips to help her, and she let go, calling his name as she pulsated around his shaft.

The tremors were more than he could bear. As she rocked against him, he tightened, exploded, and followed her into oblivion.

JO WAS PLEASED to see Vinnie sleeping. She worried he didn't get enough rest, and it was her fault. As they lay together, a tangle of limbs and sheets, she absorbed his warmth, his solidity. She was safe, nestled there against him.

But safety depended on proximity. She might be safe because she was near him, but no one was safe around her. If she wanted to protect her loved ones, she needed to be on her own.

Vinnie awoke feelings and desires in her that she didn't even know she had. Ones she definitely didn't want. Not then, not when their lives were in jeopardy.

She tried to extricate herself from his embrace, but he met every shift in her body position with one of his own. Even in his sleep, he made sure she stayed where he wanted her.

Surely at some point he'd let her go.

And then she'd go.

20

VINNIE WOKE TO find Jo still in his bed. Still in his arms. He could definitely get used to that. As much as he enjoyed watching her sleep, he had work to do. Careful not to wake her, he unraveled himself from her warm body, grabbed his cell, and went to the common area of the suite to call Pasquale.

Twenty minutes later, it was all he could do to keep from throwing his phone against the wall. There was no avoiding it. The guys were going to have to go to Italy to assure the acquisition went through. He stood at the balcony door watching the sun rise over the ocean. Funny how such a peaceful scene could be viewed from such a pissed-off perspective and still look good. Sighing, he leaned against the doorframe and shot a text off to Mike and his brothers.

He sensed her before he turned to meet her gaze.

"It's a good thing we aren't facing another building," she said.

"Hmm?" She looked so good, tousled from sleep. He could barely concentrate on what she said, let alone answer her with words.

Her gaze skimmed over him from head to toe. "No one would be able to concentrate if they saw you standing there like that."

When he left the bedroom, he hadn't bothered grabbing any clothes, and standing there, he'd completely forgotten he wasn't dressed. Looking at Jo standing there, robe tied loosely at her waist, hair mussed from the pillow, cheeks pink from rubbing her face, he became hyper-aware of his nakedness.

And knew from her rapt attention that she was more than aware, too.

Before he could go to her, he received a succession of texts. Despite wanting to take Jo back to bed, he read his messages. And frowned deeper with each one.

Jo crossed the room and wrapped her arms around him. "Looks like last night is over. I'm going to go get dressed."

As she pulled away, he caught her hand and spun her around. When she looked at him, words failed him. Instead of saying how he felt, he slipped into work-mode. "Don't take too long. We've got a schedule to keep."

"What schedule? I need a shower, and I thought I'd order breakfast, and—"

"We're meeting Enrico in twenty minutes."

DANTE DIALED HIS boss and prayed for voicemail. When Sal picked up on the third ring, he bit back several curses and launched into his carefully rehearsed report. "I hate to say it, but they aren't here."

Only one sentence in, and the questions started.

"What do you mean?" Sal's voice was soft, but the tone couldn't disguise the menace behind it. "You said the intel was solid."

"It is. Was." Dante fumbled for the words, his speech all but forgotten. "The intel was good. They were here. We just missed them."

Sal was silent for a long moment. "What's your next move?"

"I'm going to see if our contact has more info."

"See that you do. Then tie up the loose ends."

Dante shuffled his feet, but couldn't quite bring himself to say what was on his mind.

"Dante? Do you understand?"

"That's going to be kind of hard to do."

"And why is that?"

"Because the damn school is closed. Everyone's fucking gone."

"I hope you have a contingency plan, because I'm not taking the blame for this failure. You can answer to the boss yourself."

The silence on the line when Sal ended the call sounded way too final for Dante. He began working on his contingencies.

JO WASN'T SURE what to wear to a meeting with a casino owner who was a former Brotherhood member. He obviously knew her father, and likely her and her sisters, so there was an element of familiarity there, even if not from their end. But he was also a trained killer and a possibly shady businessman, and that put her on edge. What did one wear to meet an assassin-slash-benefactor?

She washed herself clean of the evidence of her night in Vinnie's bed and decided on black capris and a white blouse. That was pretty much the nicest outfit she'd brought, anyway, and it was for church.

It was only after she was dressed and ready that she realized she looked like a waitress, but it was too late to do anything about it. She met Vinnie in the common area.

He scanned her head to toe, and a slow smile crept across his face.

"What?"

"I was just thinking about the last time I saw you in a button-down shirt."

She blushed, remembering how he altered her wardrobe the day they met McGuire at the station. "Don't get any ideas about me distracting Enrico."

"Like I'd share your body with anyone."

"You did before."

"First, I only let him look, not touch. Second, that was before we—" He paused, furrowed his brow. "Before. And I didn't like it then."

His gaze, his comments, his tone sent tingles all through her. "Before what?"

He never answered her questions. Instead, he opened the door. "Let's go."

They walked out into the hall and met up with Donni as she exited her room. Coz and Nico opened their door just as Toni stepped into the hall.

"I guess we're all ready," Vinnie said.

Were they staring? They all stared. Jo fought not to squirm under the intense scrutiny from all the people in the hall. To get the focus off her, she said, "Franki and Gianni aren't here. You know how she's always late. I'll go get her." She broke clear of the pack and started down the hall.

"I'll go with you," Donni said.

"Me, too." Toni followed them.

"We can all go," Coz said.

"No!" the twins said at the same time. Donni continued, "Just get the elevator. We'll be right there."

Coz shrugged as Jo turned away from them and hurried down the hall.

Donni scurried after her. "So?"

"So, what?"

"How was it?" Toni asked.

Jo knocked on Franki's door. "I don't know what you're talking about."

Franki opened the door. She was putting earrings on, but at least she was dressed and had her makeup and hair done. "Oh, my God! You're glowing. You slept with him!"

"Again?" Gianni said, walking up behind her.

Jo didn't answer anyone. She just turned and headed back toward the elevator. By the yammering behind her, she knew they all followed. To tune them all out, she hummed to herself. She didn't recognize the melody, but the lyrics expressed her hatred for their invasion of her privacy.

She smiled at her little secret, felt her frustration abate. A little bit.

When the elevator doors opened, Mitchell was standing there. "Good morning! I'm here to escort you to the penthouse."

"We need an escort?" Nico asked.

"Just as you need a keycard to access this floor, you need one to get upstairs as well. Your card will only get you to this floor, so I've been sent to retrieve you." He held the doors open and gestured to the inside. "If you would?"

They filed in. Mitchell swiped his card and pushed the 'P' button. The ride up was swift and the landing gentle.

When the doors opened, Mitchell stepped out and pointed at double doors down the hall to his left. "Those are Henry's offices. Just go in and his assistant will direct you."

"Henry?" Jo whispered to Vinnie.

Vinnie shrugged and shook his head.

"What's that door?" Nico asked, pointing to a set of double doors down the hall in the opposite direction.

"His private quarters. Please, this way." They followed him down the hall.

"Here we go," Coz said.

Jo still wasn't clear what the guys' relationships were with their mentors. She knew Gianni had been close with Sal, but that ended in disaster. Vinnie didn't seem that close with Marcus, but he didn't really seem to let anyone get too close. Nico and Coz, though? She didn't have a clear read on them. And Nico's response didn't really help her. She needed to stop dwelling on her own issues and do what they were there for—assess the mentors for risks.

They stepped into a comfortable reception area. A plush, deep indigo carpet silenced their footsteps. The walls had a Venetian plaster treatment and were the color of fog and pearl. Mounted on the opalescent walls were paintings of Renaissance women.

"If I didn't know better, I'd swear these were by Titian." Donni approached one of the works and peered closely at it. "The brushstrokes. The color. But none of these is a work of record. Damn good imitations, though."

"If Jo was heavier and her hair was longer," Toni said, "she could be the model in these."

"The resemblance is uncanny," Vinnie said.

Jo turned to look at him and felt herself flush. He stared at a painting of a voluptuous redhead, lying in a grotto that looked much like the lobby décor. She was completely nude and reached for someone out of the frame, her face portraying the rapture of a woman in love. Well loved. It wasn't a stretch to figure out what Vinnie was thinking. Her only recourse was to stare at the floor and pray no one looked at her until her blush subsided.

She was saved by the receptionist entering the room. "Right on time. Good. He's expecting you. This way." She grabbed a folder from her glass-topped desk and walked through another set of double doors. Jo was only too happy to follow.

Behind the doors was the biggest private office she'd ever seen. An entire wall of shelving lined the right wall, adorned with books, awards, photos, and artwork. A seating area was to the left. Two sofas and four chairs in luxurious fabrics surrounded a massive wooden table, reminiscent of the Brotherhood table, with a darker marquetry star in the center. Off to the side was a large marble-topped bar covered with selections of top shelf liquor.

A door in the corner likely led to a private washroom. And in the center of the office was a magnificent walnut desk, clean except for a phone, a lamp, and a laptop. Beyond the desk was a wall of windows letting in a spectacular view of the ocean.

But what captured Jo's attention was the man seated at the desk, talking on the phone. He was more impressive than the room he held court in, with dark, wavy hair, tan skin, and a designer suit that seemed custom-tailored to his muscular physique.

Hotel mogul Henry Moore. AKA ex-Brother Enrico Moretti.

He cut off the person he was talking to and ended the call. Then he pressed a button and the laptop receded into the desk, leaving the surface almost clear. Standing, he walked around the desk to greet his guests with arms open wide.

"I never thought I'd see the day when you boys were in my hotel. And you brought the girls!" He pulled Nico into a hug and clapped him on the back. "I definitely never thought I'd see these lovely young ladies again." He embraced each of the men in turn, then pointed to the seating area. "Shall we?"

They all filed over to the sitting area. Enrico lowered himself into one of the chairs, crossed his foot over his knee, and leaned back. Resting his elbows on the arms of the chair, he lifted his hands and gestured for them to sit. "Park it, huh? We've got things to discuss."

Jo glanced at her sisters and the brothers. They all looked as thunderstruck as she felt, sporting combinations of wide eyes, open mouths, and furrowed brows. They sat, but still none of them had said anything other than some murmured pleasantries.

"Oh, come on now, Nico. Surely you've put some of these pieces together."

"Exactly what pieces do you mean?"

"Are you telling me you missed all the signs?"

Vinnie leaned forward. "All what signs?"

"*Merda.* I haven't been to bed yet and I'm more alert than you. You're not thinking twenty-first century." He looked at Nico. "Surely a computer genius like you is on top of things."

Nico just cocked an eyebrow.

Enrico sighed. "It's one of our busiest weeks, yet I had rooms for you all. Doesn't that make you wonder?" When no one answered, he continued. "Okay, honestly, I always have these suites free, just in case some VIPs show up. But you saw your welcome baskets, the chocolate, the champagne. I obviously knew you were coming. Don't you wonder how I knew? Doesn't it concern you that your enemies might know, too?"

"How did you know we were coming?" Jo asked, afraid to pursue the ene-my-angle at the moment. Enrico might just fall into that camp, and even the guys seemed unprepared for an attack.

"Finally, someone with the brains or courage to ask the right questions." He reached into his pocket, pulled out his phone, and typed something on it. Then he spun it to face them.

It was a Twitter stream all about them and their visit to West Virginia.

"What the hell is that?" Vinnie asked, grabbing the phone and scrolling. Jo leaned over to see it, too.

"That," Enrico said, "is Kevin Tran's Twitter stream."

There were tweets about how excited Kevin was to have met his idols, photos of them instructing, and even pictures of each of them broken into couples—Gianni tying Franki's belt, Donni and Nico working with kali sticks, Coz showing Toni a finger hold, and Jo in Vinnie's arms trying to execute a release. That last photo really caught Jo's attention. Her feelings for him were written all over her face for anyone to see. And apparently the entire Internet had seen them.

"Who's viewed these?" Vinnie asked Enrico.

"Hard to tell. But I can tell you who commented on them."

Enrico scrolled deeper into the stream, and Gianni grabbed the phone. "Who's @DTest?"

"I don't think it's D-test," Enrico said. "I believe it's supposed to be 'detest.' You know, like, to hate?"

Nico grabbed the phone and clicked on the user name. "There's no name. Just DTest again. And the pic is just a tattoo. I'll have to hack into the account for more information."

"Don't bother," Vinnie said, looking at the picture. "I know who it is."

"You do?" Nico said.

"I'd know that stupid skull tattoo anywhere. I've seen it enough. And the scar running through what would be the cheek? I put it there."

"Fuck," Gianni said.

"What?" Jo asked. "Who is it?"

"Tosta," Vinnie said.

"Dante Tosta?" Toni said. "The one who—?"

"Yes," Vinnie interrupted. "That Dante Tosta."

Jo tried to shake off the chill shooting up her spine, but despite her efforts, she still shivered. Dante Tosta was actively tracking them.

"So now you're caught up," Enrico said. "I've still got my sources, but sometimes the easiest way to get information is to just look online."

Nico muttered something under his breath. Jo didn't hear what he said, but by the scowl on his face, she got the gist. And it wasn't good news.

"That still doesn't explain how you knew we were coming," Vinnie said.

"Read through the stream," Enrico said. "One of Tran's comments was that his heroes took off. His boss's girlfriend told him they were headed to see an old friend. If you had just seen Marcus, it's not a stretch to figure you'd be coming here next."

They all watched Nico scroll through the stream until he stopped and shook his head.

"For the record, and to move this little pow-wow along, I'm not involved."

Jo studied his face, but she couldn't tell if Enrico was telling the truth or not.

"So, I figure you have about a day on Dante. I have a picnic lunch and blankets packed for you. I know you'll need to talk and won't trust me not to have your rooms bugged. Go down to the beach, eat, talk, make plans. Let me know if you need anything." He handed Nico his card. "That's my personal cell, so you won't have to jump through hoops to reach me."

Enrico stood, his intent to dismiss them clear. "Don't be strangers." Walking to his door, he opened it for them. He hugged the guys and shook hands with the girls. "The basket will be waiting for you at the concierge desk, when you're ready. Beach access is right across the boardwalk." He looked past them to his assistant. "Maria? Hold all my calls." He walked out with them.

Jo couldn't help but look at the paintings in the waiting area as they passed through. Enrico must have noticed, because he said, "Breathtaking, aren't they?"

"Yes," Jo said, her voice barely above a whisper.

"I always was partial to redheads." He looked her over from head to toe.

Vinnie stepped between them, and something like a growl came from him. Enrico chuckled.

"Who did them?" Donni asked. "The artist has Titian's style perfectly, down to the coloring and brushstrokes."

"Good eye. But why, might I ask, do you assume they are imitations?"

"Because there's no record of these pieces."

He left them standing at the elevator and continued down the hall. Speaking over his shoulder, he said, "That doesn't mean they aren't authentic."

Donni gasped. Jo just stared at him until he walked into his private rooms.

VINNIE HURRIED EVERYONE along. He had a bad feeling he couldn't shake, and he didn't want to waste any more time than necessary.

A quick trip to their rooms for a change of clothes, another brief pause at the desk for the picnic supplies, and they were at the beach.

Despite it being a busy holiday week, the beach was nearly deserted, most of the guests likely spending their time in the casinos, sleeping off their busy night, or gone further down the boardwalk to browse in the little shops and eateries. The guys spread the blankets while the girls got out the food, and after Nico swept the contents for listening devices—and found none—they sprawled out and polished off their meal without any conversation at all.

When they finished, Gianni looked at Jo. "You aren't going to want to hear this, but I have a few things to say before we get into Brotherhood business."

To her credit, she didn't bolt. She looked like she wanted to, but she stayed.

"First, I know you and V have been… getting close."

"That's none of your business, G." Vinnie sat and faced him. "Or anyone else's."

"As leader of the Brotherhood, it is my business. Because I have to make sure she's not messing with your head."

Jo snorted.

"What's that supposed to mean?" Gianni asked.

"Nothing," she said. "Don't worry, Gianni. There's nothing between me and your boy that you need to concern yourself with."

Vinnie narrowed his eyes.

"Well," Gianni said. "Maybe the two of you need to discuss that. Work out whatever this is. And I mean work it out. Don't just sweep it under the rug. Which brings me to my second point."

"Which is?" She crossed her arms.

"We need to talk about you constantly bolting."

"I get it, okay? I know Coz's injury is on me. And so is Chuck. I almost died, too. And you're worried about Vinnie because of me. I get it. We don't need to belabor the point anymore."

Gianni opened his mouth, but Franki cut him off. "You know, Jo's been on the hot seat for a while now. There are some things I'd like to know from your perspective."

"What?" Gianni asked.

"Carla's box. You were supposed to tell us something about it, but we got interrupted. Fill us in."

"Actually," Vinnie said, "it was Mike who was going to fill us all in. Nico, you have any idea what he wanted to discuss?"

"No. He hasn't been in touch about any of that."

"I had hoped to join you at Marcus's home, but unfortunately your time there was short. As will be your time here." Mike's voice came from behind Vinnie, causing him to jump. The others looked equally surprised.

"Do you have to do that?" Vinnie asked.

"Yes. Now, I believe you have questions regarding Carla and the information she left for you."

Vinnie rubbed his temples. He had a raging headache, and it got worse every time someone spoke. Clouds rolled in, obscuring the sun, and he was grateful he could stop squinting from the glare. The few other groups of people scattered about gathered their things and left, leaving the nine of them alone on the beach.

"I have a few questions," Jo said.

"Me, too," Donni said.

Toni nodded.

"Perhaps it would be best if I just tell you what I know."

"That would be a first," Vinnie muttered.

Mike looked at him, but continued on to the topic at hand rather than addressing his insubordination. "Did it not occur to any of you to examine the box itself?"

"What's to examine?" Gianni asked. "It was a box. It had a diary in it. A letter. A trinket or two."

"It was more than just any box. There was a secret compartment in it."

"What was in it?" Jo asked.

"Names. Dates. Carla's guess at the hierarchical structure of Legatus."

"Did you bring it?" Nico asked.

"No. You do not need to examine it. I will send you all the information I gleaned from her pages."

More secrecy. Of course. Vinnie's head throbbed.

"I believe Vincenzo and Josephina have some things to talk about. And you all need to get ready to depart. We will continue this discussion at your next destination."

"Which is where?" Coz asked.

"Please go pack. Your current location, I fear, is once again compromised. I will forward you the details of your next destination."

"You're here," Gianni said. "Why can't you just tell us?"

But Mike was already gone. Damn it.

"Look, Mike's right," Vinnie said. "Jo and I do have a few loose ends to tie up. Go get your things together, and we'll be along soon."

Vinnie pitched in to help pack up while Jo stood at the water's edge, looking out into the ocean. When everyone left, he walked up to her and put his arms around her waist. When she tensed, he released her. "What's that all about?"

"What's what all about?" She didn't turn around.

The tight rein he had on his temper snapped. "So we're back to this. Physical comfort when it's convenient for you, but don't get too close."

She spun to face him. "Too close? That's rich. You expect me to bare my soul, but you keep all kinds of secrets. Even from me. If I even matter at all."

"First, I defended you. I didn't let them push for details on Enzo. Second, of course you matter. Where's that even coming from? And third, I told you before, I'm an open book. What secrets am I supposedly keeping?"

"What's the deal with the box?"

"How the hell should I know? Mike'll tell us when he's ready."

"Not that box. Your box. The one you and Gianni were fighting over."

The first drops of rain began to fall, cool against his skin but doing nothing to chill his temper. "What do you know about that?"

"I know enough to know you're keeping secrets."

"That has nothing to do with you."

"Then I guess I have nothing to do with you."

"Fuck, Jo." He pushed wet hair off his face. "That's kind of extreme, don't you think?"

"No, I don't think so. You know everything about me. Every personal thought, every private action. You've seen me in ways no one ever has. But you don't share anything about yourself. How am I supposed to be intimate with a man I barely know?"

His head pounded, his stomach churned. Each drop of rain felt like a countdown to an inevitable explosion. He took a deep breath and tried to think of a way around her argument, but for once both his instincts and his power failed him.

"That's what I thought." She turned back toward the ocean.

"Jo, wait. You're right. I agree with you. I should be more forthcoming. Ask me anything."

She turned to him and raised her eyebrows.

"Anything else."

Jo shook her head, flinging water droplets into the rain. "I'm not going to stand here getting soaked for no reason. I know I'm just a job to you. Consider yourself fired." She started walking toward the hotel.

He grabbed her arm and spun her around. Words failed him, but his body did his talking for him. He crushed her against him and claimed her mouth in a searing kiss. He didn't feel the rain any longer, didn't hear the ocean over the roaring of his pulse in his ears. She didn't fight him, but surrendered to him, and he nearly drowned in the sensations. When he pulled away, it took him a moment to notice that the storm had passed as quickly as it had popped up.

"Why do you think that? How can you say those things after everything?"

"Look," she said, "this is going nowhere. I'm wet, I'm mad, and we're in a hurry. I'm going up."

"Jo, wait."

She looked at him, but he couldn't bring himself to tell her the story. "Come here." He pulled her to him and cradled her in his arms, her back pressed against his chest while they faced the water. As tranquil as the scenery was, he was in turmoil.

"Vin? The only things on me that are dry are my feet, and if we keep standing here, they'll get soaked, too. Let's just go."

He looked at the breaking waves and the rush of the water onto the shore. He didn't know how he knew it, but he was certain they wouldn't get wet. "We're safe here. We won't get wet. Well, any more wet than we are now."

"The water is creeping up all around us. It's only a matter of time before—"

"We won't get wet."

She sighed.

"I promise. Just let me hold you for a minute." He could feel her tension in the rigid way she held her body, but she didn't pull away. She just kept staring at the waves. And somehow, he was right. The water lapped around them but never touched their feet.

"How did you know the water wouldn't rise here?"

"I don't know. My power, I guess. I can just tell it's not going to come here. If it's going to, I'll know, and we'll move."

"That's a weird thing to use strategy on."

"I didn't even realize I was. I just knew I was safe to hold you here."

She pushed away from him. "Well, safe or not, time's up."

Unready to talk about his own history, he could do nothing but follow her up to the hotel. As they walked away from the shoreline, he looked back. The water rushed to where they'd been standing, washing away their footprints. He hadn't expected that.

They rode in silence up the elevator. When they got to their floor, she turned away from their suite.

"Where are you going?"

"I just need to talk to Franki for a minute."

"I'll go with you."

"Don't be ridiculous. Gianni's there if I need protecting. Go pack. We're already behind all the others."

"I never unpacked. I can be ready in a minute."

"Then go take your minute. Because I need one of my own. Without you."

He hesitated for just a second before agreeing. She headed for her sister's room, and he went down the hall. After closing the door behind him, he looked out the peephole. Jo hadn't knocked on Franki's door. She'd gone back into the elevator.

Damn it.

He bolted for the elevator but was too late. There was a brief moment when he considered taking the stairs, but the elevator was so swift that it could be to the bottom and back before he got even half way down. So he waited, knowing she was getting a huge head start.

By the time he got to the lobby, it was as he feared. She was long gone. He grabbed Mitchell by the lapels. "Where'd she go?"

"Who, sir?"

"Don't stall. Jo. The redhead. Where'd she go?" When Mitchell looked around, Vinnie shook him. "Now! She's in danger."

"Okay. She asked about car rentals. We don't have any on premises, to I sent her to the closest one. It's by the airport. She asked me not to say where she went, and she hopped into a cab."

Vinnie let him go and rushed out the door. He hailed a cab, asked to go to the nearest car rental, and then called Gianni.

He answered the phone without a greeting. "You ready?"

"Listen. You and Franki need to pack up our suite and then you can leave without us."

"Why? What the fuck's going on?"

"Jo split."

"We just talked about that!"

"I know. I'm going after her. Text me the address of our next stop, and I'll meet you there." He ignored the string of curses from the other end. "G? Not now. Just send me the address."

"I don't have to. You know where it is. Mike's place."

"What? In New York?"

"Yep. We're going home."

Home. Great. "Just take care of our stuff. I'll meet you there."

"Do you need any help?"

"No, I got it."

"Keep me posted."

Vinnie hung up. The driver had stopped at the rental place. He threw the fare at the cabbie and looked through the window. Jo was at the counter. Instead of confronting her there where she could cause a scene, he walked around back to the car lot.

21

JO SCANNED THE paperwork in her hand. She was looking for a silver Impala. That shouldn't stand out on the road. Once she picked a destination, she'd blend into to the highways and the guys would never find her. Her phone. She'd have to ditch her phone so they couldn't track her GPS. He first stop would be a store, where she'd grab a burner and some provisions.

Lost in thought, she didn't pay attention to where she was going. As she pushed the door open to walk into the parking lot, it bounced off a man on the other side of it. "Oh! I'm sorry!" Her keys and papers fell to the ground. They both bent to retrieve them. "I wasn't watching where I was going, and I—"

She stopped when she noticed who she spoke to. "What are you doing here?"

"I think a better question, is what are you doing here?"

"Damn it, Vinnie." She snatched her rental agreement and keys from him and stormed into the parking lot. "You know why I'm here."

"And you know why I'm here." He followed her.

"No, I don't. You being here defeats the whole purpose of me being here."

"Sorry, Red, but I'm just doing my job."

"Well, stop doing it so well. I fired you, remember?"

"For some reason, I don't think this is what you fired me from."

"Well, from this, too. I need to go. Stop interfering."

"Stop running away, and I won't have to stick so close." He paused. "Unless you want me to."

"Go away." She unlocked the driver's side door.

"You better open this door."

"Or what?" She got in the car and shut her door.

"Open my damn door, Jo."

She started the car and turned on the radio. "Sorry. Can't hear you."

He clenched his fists. "Now, Jo."

She shook her head and gestured to her ear. "What'd you say?" She put the car in reverse and backed out of the space. Way out. He stood there, staring at her. He'd be mad that she stranded him, but she would get away. It was all for the best. They'd be safer without her.

He clenched his jaw and shook his head.

Yeah, he was definitely going to be angry with her. But she had to do it. She put the car in drive and hit the gas.

He didn't move.

Was he crazy? Was he seriously playing chicken with her? Didn't he realize he'd lose against a car? Maybe she should swerve. Or stop. Or surely he'd move at the last second, right? She took her foot off the gas. Waited.

He didn't move.

Her foot hovered over the brake. She looked down at the speedometer.

Thump.

She stomped on the brake pedal. He clung to the hood and glared at her through the windshield. She'd hit him! Or the crazy moron had jumped onto the car. Either way, she'd lost.

She put the car in park and bolted out. "What in the world is the matter with you?"

"I told you I was going with you. How was up to you."

"You can't ride to—well, I hadn't decided where I was going yet. But wherever that was, you can't ride there on the hood of the car!"

He strode over to the open door and pressed the unlock button. "Then maybe you should have unlocked my door." He walked over to the passenger side and got in.

"But you weren't invited!"

"Get in the damn car, Jo. We're late."

Defeat crushed her hopes as full and final as dynamite demolishing a building—swift, complete, and with mountains of debris. She climbed in beside him and put the car in gear. "I didn't want to go with you."

"Looks like you don't have a choice. Head to the toll road and go north."

"Where are we going?" She pulled out and made her way toward the toll road like he asked. "This car has GPS. We can put the address in."

"We don't need to." He leaned back, closed his eyes, and rubbed his elbow.

She bit her lip. He'd probably banged it up leaping onto the car. Yet another injury that was her fault. Of course, if he hadn't followed her, his elbow would be fine. Oh, well. She couldn't dwell on that. It was what it was.

And it was her responsibility.

"Did you program the address into your phone?"

"No."

"Then how will we know where to go?" They came to the toll road and she headed north.

"I'll tell you where to go."

"And how will you know?"

"Because we're going to Mike's place."

She sucked in a breath. "You mean, your home?"

"If you want to call it that. Sure." He dropped his arms. "The way you drive, it'll take about four hours."

"What's that supposed to mean?"

"What?"

"The way I drive?"

"I'd make it there faster, but it'll take you about four hours."

She pushed down on the accelerator. She could drive just as well as he could.

One speeding ticket, three hours, and twenty minutes later, they were in East Hampton, New York. In Mike's driveway.

"YOU GREW UP here?" Jo asked as they cleared the second of three gates on the long private drive.

"Only from fourteen on. Before that, I was at the home in Italy."

"The church orphanage, right?"

He clenched his jaw and looked out the window at the tree-speckled undulating lawns. He didn't want to be here, and he certainly didn't want to be taking this stroll down memory lane. But instead of talking to her during the drive and trying to get through to her, he'd spent the time seething—and nursing his injured elbow, as Nico wasn't there to fix it—and shutting her out. He figured their alone time was just about up, and he was going to lose her again unless he started talking. The last thing he wanted to talk about was his childhood, but he probably owed it to her, even if he was mad at her.

"Yeah. The church. San Crisogono."

"And then Mike adopted you four and brought you here?"

He sighed and rested his head against the window. Closing his eyes, he muttered, "Something like that."

"Well, that's what Gianni said."

The car slowed down and he opened his eyes. They were at the third gate. "Look into the camera. They'll let you through."

She rolled down her window and stuck her head out. The third gate swung open and she pulled the car through.

"Follow the path to the right."

She took the fork that headed right. "We're not done talking about this."

"We are for now."

She pulled behind the conversion van and got out of the car. They stood in front of a sprawling ivy-covered stone mansion. "Holy crap! This makes the compound in Pennsylvania look like a tenement. I can't believe this is your home."

"It's not my home. It's Mike's home."

"He adopted you. He raised you. Of course it's your home."

He took a deep breath. He so didn't want to open that can of worms. "Let's just go in and find out what's going on."

She stood in the driveway, staring at him. "What's with you?"

He didn't answer. Just grabbed her hand and pulled her inside.

Nothing much had changed since he'd last been there. When was that? He didn't keep track anymore, but it hadn't been long enough. The white Italian marble floors in the foyer still gleamed. The wide, curved, dark oak stairs with iron balusters and polished rails still dominated the hallway. The same impossibly-detailed paintings he'd always been afraid to touch still hung in the same places on the same walls. Plush and ornate rugs he'd never been comfortable treading on covered the floors. Houseplants in elaborately-carved statuary he'd always been terrified of breaking still stood on either side of the doorway.

To him, this place had always been more of a museum than a home. But then, he'd never been welcomed here as family. Not like everyone else had.

Jo looked around, eyes wide and mouth slack. "This is amazing. It would have been so much fun here. Sock-skating down the hallway. Sliding down the banister. And that's just the foyer. I bet your room rocked. Can I see it?"

"Damn it, Jo!" Franki barged into the foyer, followed closely by her sisters and the rest of the Brotherhood. Vinnie, in no mood for any of it, sat on the stairs. "We were worried sick. And you just got done saying you understood."

"I do understand your view. But why can't any of you understand mine?"

"What?" Franki said. "Your privacy is being violated? Boo-freaking-hoo. Deal with it. There's a lot more at stake here than your bathroom schedule."

"No, damn it. I'm not talking about my privacy. Although I miss it." She turned her back on them and ran her hand through her hair. "I'm talking about everyone's safety!"

"We're safer if we stick together," Coz said. "Then we can protect you."

"Funny, coming from the guy I almost killed."

"You almost killed him because you went off on your own," Gianni said.

"If I had been alone, he'd have been fine. So would Chuck."

"If you had been with all of us, he'd have been fine. And so would Chuck," Gianni said. "This isn't up for debate. Tell her, V."

Vinnie held his head in his hands. "I'm tired of talking. She knows what we have to do. If I have to keep chasing her, then I'll go off alone and chase her. But I'm done arguing. Just leave her alone. What's our next move?"

"You have to explain how important it is that she stay with us," Donni said. She knelt in front of him and took his hands. "It's more important now that ever."

He looked at her. Tears were in her eyes.

God, he hated it when women cried.

Toni stood behind her looking equally upset. "Yeah. Use your power of strategy. Convince her to stop running."

"Why?" he asked. "What's wrong now? What changed since New Jersey?"

Nico held up a passport book. "The girls left these at the compound. Mike collected them and brought them here when he cleared out. We have a plane to catch." He tossed a book at Vinnie. "You should keep Jo's. Just in case."

"Are we going somewhere now?" Jo asked. "It's almost night. We'll never get a flight at this hour, especially on such short notice."

"Not a problem," Gianni said. "Already got that covered."

"Well, where are we going?" Jo asked.

Vinnie didn't even need to use his powers to know the answer. "Italy."

JO LOATHED EVERY aspect of flying. Getting through security and waiting at the gate was usually a huge hassle. Flying was an even bigger hassle, being squeezed into seats like coins in a wrapper, every one of them arranged just so or they wouldn't all fit. And if the flights weren't booked solid, squeezing all the people they could into the plane, the airlines felt shortchanged. So they wedged people into each flight, shoulder to shoulder, front to back, just so they got their money. She felt claustrophobic on flights. She could only imagine how the guys must feel.

But they surprised her. Again. Flying with the Brotherhood wasn't anything like that.

For starters, because they didn't even enter the airport property.

"Where are you going?" Jo asked Vinnie, who drove with his usual disregard for the speed limit. "You missed the exit."

"No, I didn't."

"The exit for JFK was—" she turned her head. "Well, it was way back there."

"We're not going to JFK. We're going to an FBO nearby."

"An FBO?" Franki asked.

"Fixed Base Operator," Gianni said. "It's a smaller airport where MDH stores its jet. There's a lot less hassle flying out of a smaller airport."

"We should be a lot more comfortable than we were in the van," Vinnie said. "It seats ten."

Jo looked out her window. Huge compound. Multiple properties. Six-figure sports cars. Private jet. Every time she thought she had a handle on the kind of lifestyle Vinnie led, she had to reassess. It wasn't that they weren't in the same league. It was that she wasn't aware of what his league even entailed.

She needed an equalizer. Something to make him feel more accessible to her. Maybe if he'd talk to her about his childhood. But she wasn't really entitled to those details. They didn't exactly have a relationship, after all. She was just a means to an end for him.

So she'd put an end to trying to figure out what they had. Instead, she'd sit back and enjoy the benefits for the time being.

Just entering the FBO property was more pleasurable than entering a regular airport. They drove straight to the jet, handed their bags to attendants who immediately stowed them onboard, and after barely flashing their documents to someone who gave them nothing more than a cursory glance, they boarded the plane.

Jo was immediately ensconced in utter sumptuousness.

The jet was divided into two pods—four seats in the front and six in the back. Vinnie was talking to an attendant in the front pod, so Jo walked to the back sunk into a supple ivory leather seat. The plush cushions were beyond comfortable and she snuggled into the one in the back right corner, as far as she could get from the front left seat that Vinnie had paused by. Unfortunately, he was only giving instructions to the flight attendants, because instead of sitting down, he made his way to the back pod and sat in the seat facing her. Before she could say anything, one of the attendants approached.

"Can I get either of you anything? Water? Soda? Champagne? Beer? A snack, perhaps?"

"This is your last chance for service, then you're on your own," Vinnie told Jo. "They're disembarking before we take off."

"I'm fine, thanks." Jo mustered a smile for the attendant. If she'd be looking at him for the entire flight, she doubted she'd be enjoying the luxury of her surroundings for much longer.

"Thanks," Vinnie told the attendant, "but not for me. I might get something after we level off."

Everyone settled in. The twins stayed in the front pod with Coz and Nico. Franki and Gianni joined Jo and Vinnie in the back, taking one of the two sets of seats that were joined together. No one asked the attendants for anything, so they left the jet.

The copilot made sure the door was secure, then he joined the pilot in the cockpit and closed the door to the cabin. Unlike with commercial flights, the pilot's voice came over the intercom immediately to tell them to prepare for takeoff, and they began moving. They were in the air before she knew it, and Jo closed her eyes, the rhythmic hum of the engines and the soft sway of the jet in the wind lulling her to sleep.

The pilot's voice on the intercom jolted her awake about fifteen minutes later announcing they'd reached their cruising altitude and could take their seatbelts off.

"Sure didn't take you long to doze off," Vinnie said in a low voice, leaning forward so no one else could hear.

"I guess I'm a little tired. I didn't get much sleep last night."

He grinned. "You didn't seem to mind then."

She crossed her arms over her chest. "Well, I mind now."

"Suit yourself. I thought you'd want to discuss Marcus and Rico."

"Shouldn't we do that with everyone?"

He nodded toward Franki and Gianni. "They're already falling asleep.

And there are only two more seats back here, so unless two people want to sit on the floor, we aren't getting the group together. I just wondered what your opinions were."

"My opinions? I think Marcus knows a lot about your personal history that you're trying to keep quiet. Want to talk about that?"

"Go to sleep, Jo. We'll talk when everybody's together."

"That's what I thought." She shifted in her seat until she found a comfortable position but doubted she'd drift off anytime soon. Her thoughts reeled with questions about Vinnie.

Why did he keep holding himself apart from his family and friends?

What was the deal with the box?

And what did he really mean when he said "he was working on it" with respect to her?

Where did they stand?

Jo refused to open her eyes because she didn't want to give him the option of speaking to her again, and she fell asleep somewhere over the Atlantic. She barely stirred when they landed in London to refuel, and when they got to Italy, she was invigorated and ready to start the day on a new continent.

DANTE SAT IN the lobby and watched Mitchell discreetly pocket the bills he'd slipped him. He assumed he was trying to avoid the cameras. Probably didn't want anyone to know he'd been talking to him. Just as well. He didn't want anyone to know he'd been there.

He leaned against one of the stone pillars, out of view of the security cameras covering the lobby, and took out his phone.

"Sal, It's me. They were here, but we missed them. Most of them left in a van, but two of them headed for a rental car place. What do you want me to do? I can probably get the GPS info from the rental car place, figure out where at least two of them are."

"*There's no need. We know where they are.*"

"How?"

"*Think*, testa di cazzo. *They've already gone to two of my Brothers. Where do you think they're headed next?*"

"They'll go see Paolo."

"*Get your ass to Italy. We're getting everything in place now. I expect you to be in on the execution.*"

The line went dead. Dante pocketed his phone and made his way to the exit. He had a plane to catch.

VINNIE ENJOYED WATCHING the girls' wonder at the private jet experience. He was used to having Customs on site and easily passing through the FBOs—all the brothers were, they traveled so often—but it was a new experience for the girls, and they were thrilled with the expedience of the process. Franki and Jo had been to Italy before, but the twins had never been out of the States. They were all amazed that they didn't have to land in Rome but went straight to Florence. Just another private jet perk. The twins seemed a little sad that they weren't going to see some of the more famous sites on the drive through Rome, but who wanted the hassle of the three-hour drive? When this was all over, they could tour the whole country together.

Was he seriously considering spending family-time with all of them now? *Che cazzo?* What was wrong with him?

Nico was busy making sure everyone had all their bags and paperwork. The Customs officials barely glanced at them. In fact, they'd been through that FBO so many times that they knew the officials by sight. Coz made small talk while Nico obsessed and Gianni helped the overwhelmed girls through the process. They didn't need to wait in the passenger lounge. Mike had arranged to have four cars waiting for them. Vinnie grinned. He was looking forward to being behind the wheel of something fast and sleek again.

"Come on, let's go," Nico said.

"Can we see Mama now?" Jo asked. The girls all parroted her.

"We have to check with Mike. I don't even know where she is," Nico said. "But right now, we have a schedule to keep. Let's go." He herded everyone along and kept muttering under his breath.

Vinnie kept his sarcastic comments to himself as he watched Nico obsessing over his computer equipment and Internet something-or-others. He'd been muttering a steady stream of incoherent babble since they landed. Vinnie didn't envy him. With the Italian government having shut down Internet communication in the country, his work was going to be a lot more difficult.

"I wish we were here under better circumstances," Gianni said, "but we're going to have to be careful while we're here. I don't know how much of the country you're going to get to see."

Donni started to pout, but Franki spoke up. "But while we're here, shouldn't we start working on the building?" Her face fell, and her tone dropped. "Or were we just working on that as a diversion?"

"No, it wasn't a ruse," Gianni said, "We really want a new corporate building. If we decide it's safe, and if there's time, we can show you the site."

"When do you think we can break ground?" Jo asked.

"Even if we think it's safe, we'll have to secure the permits, and you'll have to meet some local crews, learn how we do things," Gianni said. "It's going to take some time."

Jo huffed and crossed her arms. Vinnie smiled. Gianni could deal with her attitude for a while.

"What do you think, Vinnie?" Jo asked.

He didn't need his powers to know not to touch that one. "Come on, let's go. We have a long drive ahead of us."

Jo glared at him when he avoided her question, but she didn't say anything.

"Where are we going first?" Franki asked. "MDH Headquarters? Another living compound?"

"Actually," Gianni said, "Mike wants us to go straight to San Crisogono."

Vinnie hadn't seen that coming. He walked to the metallic blue Lamborghini Hurácan, grabbed the keys from the visor, and popped the trunk. "Good thing we were traveling light." He threw his duffle inside. "Here, Donni, give me your stuff. We can wedge our smaller bags behind the driver seats." He didn't miss the hurt look on Jo's face, or the confusion that passed across Donni's, but before anyone could object, he grabbed Donni's bag.

Jo crossed to Nico and tossed her stuff in the back of his Gran Turismo. "Good thing I travel light. You should have plenty of room for your stuff." She got in his car before anyone could argue.

Donni got in the car with Vinnie. "What gives?"

Everyone pulled out, but he sat there for a moment, gripping and regripping the steering wheel. He was certainly in no hurry, and the way he drove, he'd have no trouble catching up. "I didn't want to talk about it with Jo. I'm definitely not discussing it with you." His phone vibrated with an incoming text. He glanced at it. It was from Nico.

Don't lag behind. We shouldn't get separated.

"Well, why don't you tell me about San Crisogono, then?" Donni said.

He glanced at her, then pulled out, leaving tire marks on the ground behind them. She got the hint. They drove the rest of the way in silence.

The San Crisogono orphanage was under the direction of Sister Catherine, although Miss Teresa was the one who had primarily raised the boys. It was on the southern edge of Florence, on land maintained by the *Chiesa di San Leonardo in Arcetri,* or the San Leonardo Church.

Vinnie remembered the property itself being pretty enough. The orphanage, convent, and church were small stucco buildings enclosed by a wrought iron fence. They sat on a seldom-used country road surrounded by olive groves.

He had grown to loathe the trees, having to hand-harvest the damn olives for much of his young life every fall and winter. Sister Catherine seemed to take great pleasure in sending him out to the trees whenever she was irritated with him. Which was just about every day. He tried to stay on her good side, but unlike all the other boys—who she left almost solely to Miss Teresa's care—she kept a close eye on him. And didn't like anything she saw.

He sat inside his car outside the orphanage while everyone else got out. Sister Catherine stood on the stairs, talking with Mike and surveying the large group assembling before her. He sighed, dreading the whole experience.

"Well, look who's dawdling." She spoke in perfect English, in deference to her guests.

Vinnie closed his eyes and took a deep breath. He was a grown man now. She held no power over him. Yet her first words to him were derisive, and they cut to his core. Clenching his jaw, he unfolded himself from the car and rose slowly, hiding his true feelings behind his body's massive, and seemingly impervious, veneer.

He sneered at her. "Sister."

"It's Mother, now. Mother Superior."

"Got the title to go with the complex, huh?"

"Vincenzo," Mike said. "Show some respect."

She smiled.

Vinnie just shrugged and looked over at the door as it banged open.

"*I miei ragazzi!*"

"Teresa," Mother Catherine said. "In English."

"My boys! You're back!" Miss Teresa ran down the steps, not even noticing the girls. She threw her arms around Gianni, Nico, and Coz, who each gave her huge hugs, then she stopped at Vinnie, tears in her eyes, and put her hands on his cheeks. "You're home."

"This was never 'home' to me," he said softly. "Just a place to lay my head."

She blinked. "I tried to make it a home for you."

He put his hands in the pockets of his jeans and shrugged again.

Running her hands over him, like she was making sure he was really there, she finally put her arms around him. "I'm glad you're here. We have much to discuss." The she pulled his head down and kissed him on the cheek.

Vinnie hated that she caused a scene, hated that everyone stared at him. He reached into the car for the sunglasses he had discarded and put them back on his face. They offered little in the way of protection from everyone's gaze, but they were the only mask he had.

"Come on, everyone," she said and grabbed his hand. "Let's go inside."

He pulled away from her but followed the herd. He felt like a lamb being led to the slaughter.

The guys didn't have to be told what to do. Keys were thrown in the bowl by the backdoor and they went straight to the sink to wash up. The girls smiled and followed along.

Miss Teresa had put out a huge spread of food in the dining hall—cheeses, meats, peppers, tomatoes, tapenades, artichoke hearts, of course there were the ubiquitous olives from the groves outside, fruit, and fresh baked bread. She'd also baked a few different types of cookies and Vinnie's favorite chocolate torte. There was coffee—blessed Italian coffee—and carafes of water. No wine at the orphanage.

"Where are all the kids?" Donni asked.

"The sisters have taken them on a field trip," Miss Teresa said. "It's just us until dusk."

Vinnie was about to take a seat when Miss Teresa grabbed his hand. "Can we talk in the kitchen? I have plenty for you to eat in there."

He glanced around the room. Everyone looked at them. Everyone, that was, except for Sis—Mother Superior, who for once didn't look like she wanted to butt into his affairs. God, he couldn't believe he was back here. He swore he'd never set foot in this place again.

"Here's fine for me, thanks."

"I need a word with you. In private."

Even Mother Superior looked at him.

"Not interested."

"It was not a request, Vincenzo," Mike said.

"You know," Vinnie said, the pressure too much to take, "I don't have much of an appetite, anyway. I'm going for a walk." He strode out of the room and headed for the olive groves.

Was he punishing himself? Was that why he went into the godforsaken groves? Maybe. He'd certainly acted like a child and an ass. But he wasn't ready for a one-on-one with Miss Teresa. He wasn't ready to be there at all. They had work to do. They didn't have time for a social call. Especially one he didn't want to make. Didn't *need* to make.

Soft footfalls caught his attention, and he turned around. Jo approached with a sandwich and offered it to him. "Asiago and *soprasatta* with fried peppers. Teresa said it's your favorite."

"I said I wasn't hungry." His stomach growled.

She handed him the sandwich, which he couldn't resist. As he devoured it, she said, "So, are you going to tell me what's really going on?"

"What are you talking about?"

"Don't waste my time, Vinnie. You didn't want to ride with me because you didn't want to talk about this place. You're hiding in an olive grove because you don't want to talk to your housemother. Just spill it, because I don't think we're leaving here until we get past whatever this is."

He swallowed his last bite of sandwich and sat down under an olive tree, resting his back against the trunk. She sat beside him.

"Remember a while back? Before Gianni had control over his powers? You guys were just moving into our compound and he and I got into a fight?"

"Yeah."

"I was mad because I thought he was going through some of my personal stuff. He wasn't. It was all a misunderstanding. But I thought he might have figured out something about me that I didn't want him to know."

"Like what?"

He sighed. "The box. From my nightstand." He looked at her.

She waited, no censure in her expression.

"That and a pin inside it are the only things I have from here. They're from my birth mother."

"I thought you didn't know who your birth parents were."

"I've been lying, okay?" He ran his hand through his hair. "My whole life is one big lie after another. I told the guys that I was left here as a baby, but that's not entirely true. I was here with my mother the entire time."

She shook her head. "What? I don't understand."

"Teresa. *Miss* Teresa is my mother." He closed his eyes and rested his head against the tree trunk.

Jo put her hand on his arm. "Vinnie. I… I don't know what to say. How do you feel about that?"

"How do I feel about that?" He looked at her. "How the hell do you think?"

"I don't know."

He guffawed. "Funny. I guess I don't, either. Mad. Confused. Embarrassed. I could never be adopted out of there because I wasn't available to be adopted. I don't even know how I ended up with Mike."

"What do you mean?"

"The guys aren't really my adoptive brothers. Mike didn't adopt me. I don't know how he even legally got me out of the country. She must have given him consent or something, I don't know. But I'm not a Buoni."

"Are you sure?"

"I'm a lawyer. I know how to check adoption records. I don't have one. Plus, when we left here, Sis—Mother Superior gave us all files containing necessary paperwork. There's no adoption certificate. The guys all have one in their files. I don't. I was never adopted."

"Maybe Teresa couldn't get your birth father to sign off. Did you ever try to find him?"

He scoffed. "There's none listed."

"Well, maybe that's what she wants to talk to you about."

"I don't want to hear anything she has to say."

"It could be important, Vinnie. You know very little about your mother, nothing about your father. This could be your last chance to get the answers you've wondered about your whole life. Don't walk away because you're angry. Or confused. Or whatever you are."

"What would you be? How would you feel if you'd been living a lie your whole life?"

"Well, for starters, they're your family. I wouldn't have lied to them at all."

"That's just it. They aren't my family. Not really."

"Don't be an ass. They are. Blood isn't what makes them call you their brother. Why would a piece of paper be any different?"

He took a deep breath and looked at her. "What if I don't like what I hear?"

"You'll never know unless you go and listen to what she has to say." She kissed him lightly on his lips, then she stood and offered her hand. "Come on, let's go."

"I'm so tired of being told what to do in this olive grove." But he let her pull him to his feet.

As they walked back, they came to an old well. Jo stopped by it. "Give me a coin. You can make a wish for a good outcome."

He smiled and shook his head. "Not in this well. They still use it."

"What?"

"The spring underground is what irrigates the groves, and the small garden the nuns have behind the convent. And sometimes, if necessary, you can still gather water by hand if you'd like." He showed her how the hand pump mechanism operated. "You don't want to throw money in there."

"Oh. Okay. Well, make a wish anyway, and let's go inside."

He paused for a moment, but for the life of him, he didn't know what to wish for. She looked at him, a tentative smile on her face, so he took her hand and followed her inside.

Teresa sat at a small table in the kitchen, picking at invisible lint on her apron. He heard voices coming from the dining hall, where the meal was presumably still going on. She jumped up when they entered and brushed tears off her cheeks.

"I'll just go join the others," Jo said. "If you'll excuse me." And she left Vinnie alone with his mother.

She cleared her throat. "Sit. I'll fix you something to eat."

"I'm fine. Jo brought me a sandwich."

She sat back down and resumed fussing over her apron. "Will you join me? I'd like to talk to you."

He sat at the table, the same table that had been there when he was a child, and the memories flooded back to him. Scrubbing the table and floor while she taught Gianni to cook. Folding laundry while Nico did homework. Polishing flatware while Coz cleaned oil off something mechanical for the groundskeeper. It wasn't fair. So much wasn't fair. But he was there for answers, not blame. So he kept his anger in check and waited.

"I had hoped to have this conversation with you one day. When you left, I feared you'd never come back, and I'd never get to tell you everything I wanted.

Now here you are, and even though I rehearsed this a thousand times, I have no idea how to begin."

He felt no pity for her, so he did nothing to ease her way into the conversation.

"Maybe you want to ask me some questions?" she prompted.

Did he ever.

But still he waited.

"Okay. I get this is hard for you, too. Maybe you don't want anything from me. I at least owe you your story."

He knew his story. What more could she add? About to get up, a tingling, a sense that he'd want to hear her out kept him seated. He crossed his leg over his knee and stared at her.

"I was here at the convent, studying to become a nun. I was finishing postulancy and was about to enter novitiate when I met your father. I'd never even given another man a second glance. I was so sure I wanted to dedicate my life to God."

Curiosity got the better of him and snapped him out of his silence. "If you were here, how did you even see a man? The convent keeps its novices well-hidden to prevent temptations like that."

"Your father has a way of showing up in the most unexpected places. At the most unexpected times. I kept meeting him in the groves. Or in the garden when I was supposed to be meditating. It was love at first sight. For both of us."

"Then why didn't you leave the convent?"

"He didn't ask me to, and I couldn't ask him to take me away. I had mentioned our future a few times, and every time I did he seemed sad, like it wasn't something he could give me. So I stayed quiet, and I stayed here. Even after—well, we had a long discussion, but nothing was really settled. I was officially a novice at that point, but I was also starting to show, and your father disappeared."

She sighed. "When Sister Catherine found out, she immediately unenrolled me from the program. Then she went to Father to have me removed from the property, but he said he'd recently received a charitable donation for the orphanage from an anonymous patron and thought someone in my predicament would benefit from a job, not an ousting. So he hired me to be the headmistress at the school."

Teresa glanced at the door and lowered her voice. "I know your father was behind all of that, otherwise I'd have been cast out. I was grateful for the job, because I had nowhere else to go. Unfortunately, Sister Catherine was my immediate supervisor, and she resented my being given the opportunity. She believed it wouldn't do to have a former novice raising a child at the orphanage where she worked, so I was sequestered until you were born. When I finally began my job, you were to look like another abandoned child, not my own baby. I know I shouldn't have agreed to her terms, but I was alone and frightened and had no other way to support you. Her way, I got to keep you with me and watch you grow. I had no idea she was going to scrutinize my every move and punish you every chance she got."

"What about my father? Why didn't you look for him after you saw what life was like here?"

"I didn't know where or how to begin. And I didn't have the resources. Then, as time marched on, I just grew to accept things as they were."

"I never did."

"I know. And I'm sorry."

"That's not enough."

She brushed tears off her cheeks. "But he came back."

"What?"

"Your father. He came back when you were a boy. He saw what was going on, and he vowed to make it better for you."

"And let me guess. Mike came and took us away, and he never got his chance. Story of my life. Always too little, too late. Or did he send Mike to clean up his mess?"

She crossed to him and stooped in front of him, took his hands in hers. "Oh, my sweet boy. Are you really that damaged when it comes to family? Can you really not see it?"

"See *what*?" He pulled back from her.

"I came and took you away to honor my vow," Mike said from the doorway.

Vinnie looked at Mike, then Teresa, then back at Mike.

Mike walked into the room. "Do not misunderstand me. I had plenty of selfish reasons to take you with me, as well. But I always honor my obligations."

Vinnie's jaw dropped.

All reason escaped him, all rational thought was gone. And too bad, because all he was left with was raw, churning emotion. Emotion was Gianni's thing. Gianni could process this.

He couldn't.

"Fifteen years," he whispered. "I've been with you for fifteen years with questions and doubts. And today—" his voice ramped up to a roar, "—today you tell me I'm your fucking *obligation?*" He grabbed his keys and stormed out before Mike could say anything more.

22

JO LOOKED AROUND, startled and confused.

Mike held Teresa, who sobbed uncontrollably into his chest.

"What's going on in here?" Gianni asked as they all came running in from the dining hall.

"I knew it," Mother Superior said. She crossed her arms and looked at Teresa with smug satisfaction. "I told you thirty years ago it would come to this. You never should have stayed here."

Teresa broke from Mike's arms and dabbed at her face with her apron.

"And where would you have had her go?" Mike asked. "She had no one."

"She should have had you."

"What the hell is going on?" Gianni asked again.

"Giovanni, watch your language," Mother Superior said.

"If someone doesn't tell me what's going on, right now—" Gianni said.

Jo crossed to Teresa and touched her arm. "Are you all right?"

"Fine, dear. Thanks."

Jo bit her lip. She felt like crying, too, for the secret Vinnie had carried and for whatever hurt him before he left.

Teresa squeezed her hand.

"It's okay. They're going to hear about it, anyway." She sighed. "Has Vinnie never told you I'm his mother?"

"What?" the guys all said at once.

"I guess not," she said.

"The pin," Gianni said.

"What?"

"I saw your pin in a box he had. I knew I recognized it. Your guardian angel pin. You always wore it. I just couldn't remember where I had seen it before."

"Yes, well, we had family matters to discuss," Teresa said.

"Namely the issue of his paternity," Mike said.

"You mean he knows who his father is and didn't tell us about that, either?" Nico asked. "Why would he keep that a secret from us?"

"Because he didn't know until now," Teresa said.

"So why's he so mad?" Coz asked.

"Because I am his father."

Jo wasn't sure she'd ever heard a room get so quiet so fast. Then it erupted into chaos. She couldn't focus on any of it. She grabbed a random set of keys from the table and went outside. As she expected, Vinnie's car was gone, but there was still a dust cloud down the road where he had clearly driven off in a hurry. If she was lucky, she could catch him. She pressed a button on the key fob and Gianni's Ferrari unlocked.

Nice.

She slid into the car and took off after Vinnie.

He hadn't gone far. He had pulled over about two kilometers down the road. Jo found him leaning on the hood of his car. He wore his sunglasses again, so she couldn't see his face, but by the set of his jaw, she could tell he was angry. She pulled in behind him and walked over to him.

"So," she said, "you met your dad."

He scoffed. "Apparently I met him fifteen years ago."

She touched his arm. He stiffened but didn't pull away.

"Now you know how he got you out of the country. Now you know why he didn't adopt you."

"Yeah, legally he didn't have to jump through any hoops. Great. Glad it worked out for him."

She rubbed his arm.

"You know, Gianni relied on Sal to be his father-figure when we went to the States. He told me that even though Mike adopted us, he apparently wasn't going to be there for us as anything more than a financial backer, so we should rely on our mentors." He snorted. "How right he was. I never told Gianni I wasn't even adopted, but what a joke that turned out to be. His mentor turned out to be a psychopath, and I learned not to let anyone in."

"You let your brothers in."

"Not too far. Just farther than anyone else."

"What about me?" she asked.

He looked at her.

She reached up for his sunglasses, but he pulled away.

"Vinnie, I never let people in, either. I always pushed them away. But you know everything about me. Everything. I've given you more of me than I ever thought I'd share with anyone. And that's what you claim you want for us. So it's time for you to decide. Are you going to let me in or push me away?"

He leaned back from her. "Are you seriously going to ask me this now? Today? After everything else?"

She took a deep breath and shook her head. "I am. It might not be fair. It might hurt or be scary. But I have to. And you have to. Because I'm here for you, Vin. I laid myself bare for you. Can you give me the same?"

She saw him tremble. Without seeing his eyes, she didn't know what he was feeling, and she was so afraid he was angry with her for the ultimatum. The longer she waited, the more certain she was that he was going to get in his car and leave. Instead, he took his sunglasses off. His eyes were red-rimmed. When he spoke, his voice was hoarse. "I don't know who I am. I don't know what I have to give you."

She touched his cheek. "I know who you are. And you have plenty to give me."

Well, how about that? Not only had she decided not to run, she'd decided to give them a chance. Didn't see that coming.

He grabbed her hand, pressed a kiss to her palm. Then he let her go and looked away. "All this time, and he never told me. So many chances... Do you know what that means?"

"I know."

He threw his arms around her and buried his face in her neck.

She held him and rubbed her hands on his back. She couldn't believe that someone so strong, so powerful, could be so vulnerable, so wounded. "Vinnie, it's okay."

She continued holding him for a long while. Then he pulled away and turned from her. "I spent the first part of my life thinking no one wanted me. When I was fourteen, I found out I was with my mother all along, and she was fine with giving me up. And I spent the next fifteen years foolishly thinking that someday I'd find my father and he'd want to make up for lost time, only to find out that I'd been with him for just as long, and he'd lied to me, too. Don't you get it? My parents didn't want me. They kept me close to work with them, for them. But never to love them or be loved by them. That's the ultimate rejection, the utmost betrayal. You're asking me to let you in, to love you, to trust you. How can I love anyone completely when I don't even know what love is?"

"Do you really think that?"

"That's what he said. I was his obligation." He dragged his toe in the dirt on the side of the road.

She watched him. Despite his massive size, he was just a little lost boy kicking pebbles into the grass. "Vinnie," she said, like she was approaching a temperamental child, "that's not how I see it at all."

He stopped scuffing his feet, but didn't turn around.

"I think your mother took the deal not for cheap child labor, but for the ability to keep you with her. It sounds like she had nowhere else to go. It was a lousy deal, but apparently the only one she had. With no money, no home, and no family to turn to for help, what was she going to do? No one was going to hire a pregnant woman. She wasn't going to be able to support herself while she was pregnant, let alone once you came along. She just made the best of a bad situation."

He shrugged.

"And when Mike took you to the States? Yes, caring for you was an obligation. But that doesn't mean it wasn't something he enjoyed. And you heard him chastise me before. He said you guys were more to him than just warriors."

"We're assets."

"That's not what he meant. I'm sure you mean the world to him. He may have adopted your brothers, and he probably loves them in his own way, but you're his blood. He did more than just provide for you. He gave you opportunities most people can only dream of."

"That's not what I wanted from a father."

"So he didn't know how to be a dad back then. That doesn't mean you can't have a different relationship now."

"I wouldn't know where to start."

She tugged on him until he faced her. "Well, you can't start standing here on the side of the road."

"I should just go."

"Is that what you want?"

"Yes. No. I don't know." He sighed. "I have responsibilities."

"So you want to stay with me because I'm an obligation?"

He shook his head. "God, no." He grabbed her arms. "Don't ever think that."

She stared at him and tipped her head to the side.

He dropped her arms and rubbed his face. Finally, he took out his phone and sent a text. A few seconds later, he got a reply.

Jo raised her eyebrows and waited for him to explain.

"I asked Gianni if they were still at the orphanage. He said they left and texted me the address. Looks like we're headed to our new base of operations. Follow me."

"Are you going to be okay?"

"Do I really have a choice?" He got in his car, turned around, and pulled to the side, waiting for her to do the same.

As she proceeded to get in the car and follow him, she realized he never did tell her that he was willing to commit to her.

THE RIDE TO the address Gianni had sent was uneventful, but Vinnie was grateful for his GPS system, because he'd never been on those roads. He wasn't even sure some of what he was on were roads. They arrived at the destination twenty minutes later, another massive property. And he thought he'd been to all the places Mike owned. Apparently not. Just one more surprise for the day.

What didn't surprise him was the layout of the property. They had the high ground. It sat at the top of a craggy hillside and was easily defensible. They'd see anyone who tried to approach kilometers before they got near the place.

Looking down the way they'd come, he could even see the orphanage and all the property surrounding it. He couldn't believe he'd never seen the house on the hill before. From the ground, the olive trees must obscure the view. Or he just never bothered looking. And it was something to see. The home itself was a massive stone structure sitting on hectares and hectares of land, and Vinnie was certain that, despite the traditional Mediterranean façade, he'd find nothing but modern amenities inside.

He and Jo had arrived last. There was a church van out front. He suffered a momentary bout of dread until he realized they'd left his brothers—for lack of a better word—without enough vehicles. They must have borrowed the saint-mobile. Better them than him. He was sick to death of vans.

Hopefully a matronly driver hadn't tagged along.

Stepping out of the car, he joined Jo in the driveway.

"You ready?" she asked.

He didn't comment because he didn't know. Instead, he sneered like it was a stupid question and gestured for her to walk inside.

Vinnie wished he felt as confident as he let on. He didn't want to see his— could he even say it?—his parents.

No. It sounded ridiculous.

He walked inside to pretty much what he expected. Marble floors, expensive artwork, high-end textiles. He was certain he'd find top of the line furnishings and state-of-the-art electronics as he made his way room to room.

It was just like every other property Mike owned. Fully kitted-out. Tastefully done. Heavily secured.

At the moment, he loathed every square millimeter of it.

Gianni met them in the foyer. "You tight, V?"

"Yeah, I'm solid."

"Because I swear, when I dropped that box and found that pin, I didn't know. I never put it together."

"It's cool, G. Let it go."

Gianni threw his arms around Vinnie in an awkward hug. Vinnie appreciated the sentiment behind the gesture, but he so didn't want to deal with this shit. He patted his brother's back.

"So we're good, right?" Gianni said.

"We'd be better if you'd let me go."

Gianni stepped back. "You know you have to talk about this. It's not good to hold this stuff in."

"You're the heart, G. You're emotion. I'm the mind." Vinnie tapped his head. "I don't need to get in touch with my feminine side. I'm fine."

Gianni's eyes narrowed before he turned away and looked at Jo. "Do something with him, would you? We can't have our strategist less than one hundred percent going into battle."

"Battle?" Jo asked. "We have a lead?"

"Nothing concrete," Gianni said. "And seeing as our strategist isn't thinking clearly, that's going to put us at a disadvantage. But we're here for a reason. So we need to be prepared. Speaking of which," he turned back to Vinnie, "we haven't done any dagger drills in a while. Feel like a session?"

"I could use a workout." He rotated his neck and felt the tension in his muscles. A workout might be just the thing he needed.

"Go change. There are about a thousand bedrooms upstairs. Find one without bags in it and it's yours. Just try to stay close to the stairs so we're all clustered together. No reason to spread out all over the place. Meet down in the gym in fifteen. It's down this hall and to the right. You'll find it." He pointed to the left, opposite of what Vinnie assumed was the kitchen, and headed in that direction.

"Yo, G?"

"Yeah?"

"Who drove the van here?"

Gianni sighed. "If you're asking if Mike or Teresa are here, they aren't. They figured you could use some time and space."

"I was just asking. Wondered how we're going to get it back to them, is all."

"Yeah, sure you were." Gianni walked down the hall, out of sight.

Vinnie grabbed the heaviest of his and Jo's bags and headed for the stairs. "Let's go check out the upstairs."

She grabbed their smaller bags and followed him up. He looked in a few rooms and could immediately tell who was sleeping where.

Nico had computer equipment all over his bed already and was across the hall from Donni, who had managed to decorate her vanity. Her room was beside Toni's. She'd somehow already found fresh flowers from somewhere and had a vase of them arranged and sitting on the nightstand.

Coz was across the hall from her—beside Nico—as was obvious from the black bag thrown at the foot of the bed. And absolutely nothing else.

Gianni and Franki were in the room beside Coz's. They didn't have to look for the largest bedroom, because all the rooms were generous. Their things were already mingled together and strewn about.

Vinnie stood outside the next open door. He hadn't thought about this. Were they sharing a room? Did he ask? That would be the polite thing to do. Or it would be way too forward? Or just show how clueless he was? Did he just assume one way or the other? If he acted like they were staying together when they weren't, she'd think he was a presumptuous ass. But if he made the move like they weren't and she thought they were, he'd embarrass her and make things really awkward between them. If he asked, she'd know he didn't know, which could really make her mad if he was supposed to know already. By her silence, he had a feeling he was supposed to know.

He had a headache.

So he settled on stalling. "I don't think I want to share a wall with Gianni and Franki."

"Ugh. Me either."

"Well, that eliminates that room." He looked at the other empty rooms. "Do you have a preference?"

"I haven't noticed any bathrooms. Did you see any?"

He looked up and down the hall. "We haven't passed any." He stepped into the closest bedroom and looked around. That room had a bathroom attached. A pretty damn nice bathroom. It had dual vanities, a soaking tub with a window above that overlooked the gardens below, and a shower big enough for a small family. He opened a door that he assumed was to a linen closet, but it opened to another bedroom. Walking through that room, he stepped out into the hall. "Surprise."

Jo jumped and turned. "Is that one big suite?"

"Not really. The bedroom has a Jack-and-Jill bathroom. I just walked through the other bedroom."

"Well, why don't I take this bedroom by Toni and you take the bedroom on the end? We can share the bathroom."

One awkward situation averted.

"Sounds good to me." He brought her bag into her room and she handed him his smaller one. "Want to walk down together?"

"Sure. I'll be ready in about five minutes."

"See you in the hall."

AS VINNIE GOT ready for his workout, he was acutely aware that Jo was right next door. It was all he could do to not throw open the bathroom door and take her on the cold, hard tile.

But that wasn't the kind of workout he needed right then.

Well, it wasn't the only kind he needed.

And it certainly wasn't the kind he was getting.

By the time they found the gym, his thoughts were mostly focused on the exercise he was supposed to be concentrating on. Usually workouts began with at least some form of weightlifting, just to get everyone's heart rates elevated and muscles warmed up, but Vinnie vetoed that idea. "Work out on your own time," he said. "Let's get this show started." So they broke immediately into descendant/protector partners and started martial arts training.

Since the beginning, Vinnie had been paired with Jo, and he always worked her hard. Usually she loved it. This time, though, he pushed past her limits. He was in his own zone, fighting his own demons. He punished her, throwing combinations she'd never seen at speeds she couldn't possibly defend. Even he lost track of how many times he'd pinned her, thrown her, or made her tap out. But it wasn't her. Not really. He lost sight of his actual opponent thirty seconds into the session and battled someone—something—entirely different the whole time. Every kick was aimed at the injustices he'd suffered. Every strike was him lashing out at his pain. Every choke hold was him strangling the people who wronged him, who cheated him out of what should have been, could have been, a happy childhood. Finally, after one particularly grueling restraint, Gianni and Coz had to pull him off Jo because her hands weren't free to tap out.

He fought against the men holding him, rage urging him to continue his battle. He only stopped fighting when he saw the fear in Jo's eyes.

It stopped him cold.

"Let me go." They stopped struggling against him, but didn't release him. Everyone in the training room stared at him. "I'm fine. Let me go." His voice was calm, measured, controlled. He saw Nico reach for his dagger, probably to control the temperaments in the room, but he waved him off. "Really, Nico. You don't need your powers. I'm okay."

Nico dropped his hand.

Vinnie stooped in front of Jo. "Are you all right?"

She nodded, but Vinnie noticed her eyes were wide and she hadn't blinked since he started looking at her. He reached for her hand. She flinched, but allowed him to take it.

"Jo, I'm so sorry. I don't know what came over me. I—I have no excuse."

She stroked her thumb over his knuckles. "I'm okay. But I think I've had enough for today. Maybe I'll skip weapons training, if that's all right with you?"

He closed his eyes and brought her hand to his lips. He didn't care who saw him do it. "You're all off weapons practice for today. You should go rest. We'll only be another hour or two."

"No. I still want to watch. We'll sit off to the side." She walked over to join her sisters. They all started whispering at her in hushed and frantic tones. Perfect. Just what he needed. A hostile audience. He rubbed his eyes. With no way to get out of it, he resigned himself to the fact that he was in the hot seat this time, not Gianni, and he'd just have to deal with it.

The guys gathered a bunch of weapons and headed for a set of glass doors.

"Where are you going?" Vinnie asked.

"After what happened with Gianni manifesting fire last time," Nico said, "we can't train with our weapons indoors anymore. The regular ones, sure. Well, probably. But not when we use our powers."

"We're going to the atrium," Coz said.

Vinnie followed them out the doors and into the atrium. Except it was like no atrium he'd ever seen. If this was a courtyard surrounded by columns, he wasn't sure where the outer boundary of columns were.

"It's really more like a garden," Gianni said. "Or a series of them."

"You think?"

"Mike calls it an atrium to downplay its size," Nico said.

Kind of the way the UK calls the Atlantic Ocean a pond.

Vinnie stood on a large covered terrace and looked out to the horizon. The grounds were stunning. Closest to him was a pristine lawn. Behind that, a long path flanked by stone sculptured fountains led to an enormous hedge maze with a fountain in the middle. Off to either side was another water feature, looking more natural, more grotto-like. And beyond it all lay woodlands. As they had approached the house, Vinnie hadn't noticed the gardens because the house was so large and had obstructed his view of what lay behind it. But standing there, he realized the house wasn't the apex of the hill. The lands behind it were. There had to be at least twenty hectares of pools and fountains, waterfalls and statuary, lawns and topiary, hedgerows and natural flora. And Mike—his *father*—owned it all.

Maybe it was the elevation, but he found it hard to breathe.

He followed his brothers out onto the lawn.

His brothers. For the first time, he didn't feel like a lying hypocrite calling them that. And of course, that was followed immediately with doubt. Maybe they didn't like it, though. Everything finally felt equal to him, but for them? Everything had changed.

Damn Mike for doing this to him.

JO SAT WITH her sisters and watched the men work with their weapons. They had spaced themselves far from each other—there was certainly room on that lawn—and had begun working with broadswords. They all looked beautiful, and lethal, as they performed a routine, or what they called a form, with them.

But she only spared the other men an occasional glance. For the most part, her attention was locked on Vinnie. He was equal parts grace and agility, beauty and power. He mesmerized her—one second crouched low to the ground the next fully extended, spinning in the air. Flexing muscles, sweating body. Hair damp with perspiration, eyes burning with concentration.

She'd seen him in a similar condition before.

When he separated the swords and started working with one weapon in each hand, she leaned over to Franki. "I didn't even know they were holding two swords. Did you?"

"Not a clue."

She glanced at her sister. Franki looked as enthralled with Gianni as she felt watching Vinnie. That couldn't be good.

She tried to swallow, but her mouth was too dry.

Fine. She knew she liked him. She'd admitted as much to herself and to him. But what Franki and Gianni had. Uh-uh. No way. No. Not ready for that.

Vinnie ended his form with a complicated jumping kick, stabbing motion, and stance. He looked right at her, one of the swords pointing directly at her.

He was nowhere near her, but it felt like he'd impaled her heart.

Nope. Definitely not ready.

Swords were the only weapons they practiced on their own. Kali sticks and bo staffs, after doing forms, required partner work because they actually practiced attacks with them. The forms went smoothly enough, other than Jo struggling to camouflage her intense interest in one particular Brother.

Then the sparring began. Unlike the last time, Vinnie and Gianni paired up. They were the usual pairing, but an argument the last time prevented it. Coz and Nico moved together easily. The same couldn't be said for Vinnie and Gianni, as they had constant breaks in their movements and several near misses with the sticks. When Vinnie hit Gianni across the side of his head, Gianni stopped their session. He pulled Vinnie aside and had a private talk with him for a few minutes. Coz and Nico didn't stop their training, but they did drift toward their brothers.

Jo saw Vinnie's grip growing tighter and tighter on his kali sticks. Finally, he hurled them across the lawn.

"Five-minute break," Gianni called. "Get a drink. Then we're on to daggers."

Jo wanted to talk to Vinnie, wanted to know what Gianni said, but Vinnie stormed off into the garden area. Franki rushed over to Gianni, comfortable discussing anything with him. So Jo sat and waited for Vinnie to come back or her sister to return with information. It drove her nuts not knowing what was going on, but it was also proof to her that she was not at the same stage in her relationship with Vinnie as Franki was in hers with Gianni.

Nor did she want to be.

Which is why she refused to ask Franki anything about it when she got back.

During the five-minute break, the clear and sunny sky started to get thick with clouds. "Anyone check the weather?" Nico asked. When Vinnie emerged from the gardens, Nico said, "Do you know if it's supposed to rain?"

"What am I? The Weather Channel?"

"Just thought you might have seen an alert or something. I didn't think it was supposed to rain, but it looks like a storm's rolling in."

"Who cares?" Vinnie said. "It's water, not fire and brimstone."

"He's right," Coz said. "Let's get started. If it is going to rain, maybe we can beat the storm."

"All right," Gianni said. "We don't have any targets set up, so we just have each other."

Jo swallowed. She remembered what happened when Vinnie was supposed to be taking it easy on her in the gym. What was it going to be like when they used powers they couldn't control on each other?

"Let's start with shield defenses," Nico said. "No one's throwing any offensive powers until we're sure we can shield."

Jo couldn't tell if anything was happening or not. Maybe there was a certain ripple or shimmer around them, kind of like heat rolling off the asphalt in the summer. But she wasn't sure. Gianni didn't look like he was having any problems, but that wasn't surprising. Mike said his powers had fully manifested. In fact, while the other three struggled, Gianni started walking around and giving them pointers. When he got to Vinnie, it seemed to make things worse. Vinnie finally just dropped his hands. A few scattered raindrops fell.

"It's starting to rain," Gianni said. "Maybe we should just go on in."

Vinnie closed his eyes. "We'll be fine. Let's keep going."

"Is that you or your power talking?" Gianni asked.

"They're one in the same."

"No," Gianni said. "One is you proving a point because you want to get your ass kicked for some dumb reason. And one is legitimate power. Power that, if this shield is any indication, isn't even working right now. So which is it?"

Jo got hit with a few more drops and glanced up. Dark clouds rolled in from every direction, seeming to gather above the compound.

"Look, I'm strategy, and I say we'll be fine. And my powers are fine."

"And I say bullshit."

Vinnie squared off on him. "Then test me, dammit. My shield will hold just as well as yours."

"I don't even *need* my dagger and I can call a better shield than you."

"Let's go then. And keep your damn dagger." He tapped his temple. "Something tells me you're going to need it."

Coz and Nico looked back and forth between them, but the guys waved them off.

"Don't even think about it, Nico," Vinnie said.

"No manipulating mood," Gianni said. "Drop it. Now."

Nico sighed and dropped his dagger.

"Uh, what are they doing?" Jo asked no one in particular.

"Gianni," Franki said and stood.

But he waved her off, already facing Vinnie down.

They stood several paces apart, like duelers from centuries past. But instead of both 'firing' at once, for this contest they had to take turns. Assuming the first person survived the attack.

"You go first," Vinnie said. "I'll defend."

"That's all it's going to take."

"We'll see."

Franki grabbed Jo's hand. "At least if Vinnie gets hurt, Gianni can heal him."

"And if Gianni gets hurt? What do we do then?"

Franki blinked a few times. "Hope I'm enough to help. Like before. But it won't come to that. Gianni said. Right?"

Jo shrugged as Franki squeezed her hand tighter. She didn't want Gianni hurt, but she didn't know what it would do to Vinnie to lose. And given the determined look on his face, she didn't think he would.

"Ready?" Gianni said. When Vinnie nodded, Gianni flicked his dagger at him. There was a flash of light, and Vinnie rocked back, but his defense held.

"That all you got?"

"That's all I thought you could take."

"My turn." Vinnie didn't wait for Gianni to signal he was ready. He just aimed and released. Again there was a flash of light. Jo couldn't tell where the light came from, but she knew a focused burst of energy had been released. She also knew if Franki didn't let go of her hand, she was likely to have some broken bones. She pried her hand out of her sister's clutches and looked to the field. Gianni still stood.

Vinnie looked surprised. And winded.

"Okay," Gianni said. "You proved your point. Your shield works. Let's work on powers before the storm really hits."

"I didn't prove anything yet. And I told you. The storm's going to miss us."

"V, come on."

Vinnie held his dagger up. Jo saw a shimmer and assumed his shield was in place. "Again."

"V—"

"And don't hold back this time."

Gianni shook his head. This time he raised both hands and fired. Another flash of light illuminated the field. When Jo could see again, Vinnie was on one knee. Nico and Coz rushed toward him, but he waved them off.

"Better." He stood up. "How about this?" He pointed his dagger at Gianni without warning. Gianni barely threw his shield up in time and was knocked to his back.

Vinnie flung his dagger on the ground. "Don't ever talk to *me* about weak powers again."

Gianni scrambled back to his feet. "You took me off guard, V, and I'm still not winded like you. Pick it up." He gestured to Vinnie's dagger.

"Hey, man," Nico said.

"No. He wanted a lesson? Time for school. Pick the damn thing up, V."

"No problem." He grabbed his dagger.

"Ready?"

But Jo thought it was a problem. Vinnie was shaking. The clouds were roiling on top of themselves. And the scattered drops that had fallen had multiplied into an official drizzle. The next to last thing she wanted to do was call his manhood into question by stopping the fight. But the last thing she wanted to do? Put pieces of him back together. Hating herself, she stood. "Gianni."

But she was too late. Gianni put his full force behind the energy blast. The clearing was enveloped in blinding light for a moment, there was a loud 'boom' that shook the ground, and when Jo's vision cleared, Vinnie lay motionless on his back.

And the clouds poured rain down on them.

23

VINNIE WOKE UP to the sound of rain hitting his window. A second later, he realized it wasn't his window and he bolted up in the bed. He was in the room he and Jo had agreed he'd occupy while they were in Florence. And Jo sat in a chair in the corner of the room, cloaked in shadow.

"Vinnie," she whispered.

"Hi." His voice sounded hoarse, raspy.

She got up and walked to a table by the window, where a pitcher and glasses sat, and poured him a glass of water. "Listen—"

"I know. I've been a total ass." He swung his feet over the edge of the bed and started to stand, but sat back down, light-headed. "I'll apologize to the guys. To everyone. I'll make it right."

"It's not that." She turned and offered him his glass. Her eyes were red and puffy. Tear-trails lined her cheeks.

He reached his hand out to her and pulled her to sit beside him. Setting the glass aside he held her, rocking slightly. "Shhh. I promise. I'll fix everything."

She sobbed and shook her head. "That's not it."

"Then what?" He held her at arm's length and looked at her.

"Something's happened."

His blood chilled and slowed, felt like it retreated from his extremities to constrict his heart. "What did I do?"

More head shaking and a quivering breath. "It wasn't you. While you were unconscious, actually, right when Gianni blasted, or whatever, at you, there was this loud boom. At first, we thought it was him, that he hit you too hard. And maybe he did. We can argue over that later, given how you ended up. But—"

"What?"

"It's the orphanage. The orphanage exploded."

He jumped to his feet and the room lurched. Grabbing her to steady himself, he waited until his head cleared then he headed for his bag. "My—who was there? Was anyone hurt?"

"I don't know yet. No one's checked in, and no one's answering when I call. I tried to see, but Gianni made me promise to stay inside."

"Wait. What?" He stilled his movements. "Where is everyone?"

"They're all there."

"Everyone?"

"Yes."

"You're here alone?"

"I'm with you."

"I was out cold! What if someone—*merda!* What were you thinking?"

"We discussed it before they left. Someone needed to stay with you, but I said I could do it. The security here is tight, and—"

"I'm sorry. Did you say to look after me?"

"Well, like you said, you were unconscious, and—"

"Where are my damn pants?" He kept grabbing and throwing t-shirts out of his bag until he found a pair of jeans. He stripped his gym shorts off and stepped into the denim, nearly falling over in his haste.

"Vinnie, I don't think you're in any condition to—"

His look stopped her. "You don't want to finish that sentence. I can't leave you here alone. You're coming with me." He shoved his feet into boots and grabbed her hand.

"But—"

"Glad you agree. Let's go."

He dragged her down the stairs, through the foyer, then out the front door. She ran into his back when he stopped short. A plume of black smoke rose from the valley, right where his first home stood. Or used to stand. Between the olive groves and the smoldering cloud billowing beneath him, he had no idea what remained. Or who.

"Get in the car."

He didn't cross to open her door for her, barely waited until she was seated before he took off. Because of the hazardous conditions of the road, made even worse by the steady rain, and the winding path it took down the hill, the trip should have taken between fifteen and twenty minutes. He was at the orphanage in eight.

It looked like a war zone.

The back half of the orphanage, where the kitchen once stood, was blown away. Small fires still burned in places. Rubble lay everywhere. Smoke still lingered above them, not drifting away, but turning into black droplets pelting the people working to clear the debris.

"G! G!"

Gianni, soaked to the skin and streaked with soot, stopped moving stone from a pile and looked up. "You should be resting."

"Did you find… anyone?"

"Just Mother Superior. She's already gone to the hospital. She was under some rubble and burned pretty badly on her left side, but they think she's going to make it. Her biggest detriment is her age, but she's tough. I doubt that'll stop her from fighting back."

"What about—?" He couldn't say it.

"Teresa wasn't here, V." He tossed another block aside. "She walked into town for groceries. Probably would have been here, but we had her van."

Panic finally started to release its icy claws from Vinnie's heart. She wasn't there. She was safe.

Apparently he did care. And he still had time to talk to her.

Vinnie looked around and wiped the rain off his face. "Is she back yet?"

Gianni looked around. "I haven't seen her."

"When'd she go to town?" Dread's clutches began to tighten their grip again. "Shouldn't she have been back?"

"If you're worried, go look for her. We're working here."

Vinnie hesitated. Maybe he was overreacting. "I can help."

Gianni tossed another rock into a pile then stretched his back. "Shut up and listen, 'cause I'm only saying this once, and I don't want to be interrupted. We have too much to do here to carry your ass. You're in no condition to work here. You're almost out on your feet as it is. We'll watch Jo. Go find your mom, and for God's sake, make peace with her. Because as much as I need your body healed and back with us, I need your head right and back in the game. Right now, I'm pissed as hell at you for the shit you pulled today. I know why it happened. I get it, I do. But how do you think I felt knocking your ass out like that? It's not fair to me. What you're doing, punishing us because you're mad at your parents? It's juvenile. You need to get over it. We have a job to do."

Vinnie opened his mouth to say something, but Gianni raised his hand.

"Not done. I told you all that as leader of the Brotherhood. Now, as your brother, I'm telling you I'm sorry about the shitstorm that just landed on you. We're all here for you if you need us. But you need to get it together, man. Soon. Because not only does the Brotherhood need you, your *brothers* need you. *Capisci?* And so does Jo."

"I thought you didn't think me and Jo were a good idea?"

"I thought you were just screwing around. And that was going to complicate things. But that's not what's going on."

"Is that you talking or your powers?"

"What matters more to you right now?" He wiped his forehead with his arm. "Advice from your brother or knowledge from my dagger power?"

"So you're just telling me something you think I want to hear?"

"I'm telling you I *know*, man. I know with every part of me, supernatural and human, that you need Jo. So get your head out of your ass and get your shit together."

Vinnie tossed his wet hair back out of his face. "You sure you don't want my help here?"

"You look like you'll fall on your face if you bend over, let alone lift anything."

Vinnie narrowed his eyes and glared at him.

"Seriously, you haven't recovered enough to be out here, and we're almost done, anyway. Mike called in a ton of workers. This rubble will be gone in probably an hour, and then he has crews coming in to board the place up. Looks like Jo can meet the construction crew today or tomorrow. The investigator has already ruled it an accident. Said there was a gas leak. He's letting repairs start immediately."

"Accident. Right."

"We're lucky Mike greased some palms and moved things along. He also said what insurance won't pay for in upgrades, he'll cover. He wants only the best for the boys. And Teresa. He's talking about putting in an elevator, an intercom system, all new professional grade appliances in the kitchen. He's going to have the whole place rewired—"

"What about the boys? Where will they stay?"

"Before Mother Superior left, she said they can convert some space in the convent for them to sleep in. There aren't that many boys here right now, so it shouldn't be an issue. Go find your mom. We'll be okay here. I'll personally keep an eye on Jo for you."

Vinnie dashed back to his car. He saw Jo headed for Gianni. He probably should have told her where he was going, but he was worried about his mother. She shouldn't have been gone so long.

He continued driving at breakneck speeds. Everyone did in Italy. He might have been going a little faster than the average, particularly given the weather. He was going so fast, he almost didn't see the woman huddled under the tree with bundles in her arms. Slamming on his breaks, he fishtailed and came to a stop twenty meters past her. Then he turned and went back.

It was his mother.

Vinnie got out of the car and went to her. "What are you doing?"

"I was on my way back from the market when the strap of my bag broke and the oranges rolled down the hill. I came to retrieve them, but I stepped in this hole and fell and now, well…" She looked up at him. "I must have twisted it or something. It's stuck and swollen. I can't get it out."

He bent down and looked at her ankle and foot. It was really wedged in between tree roots and some kind of animal burrow. "How long have you been here?"

"A couple of hours."

He looked up at her. "Why didn't you call for help?"

"I forgot my phone at the orphanage."

He closed his eyes. She didn't know. He'd have to tell her. Then he looked up at her again. "Why didn't you put the bags down?"

"The ground is all muddy, and there is some expensive food in here."

He shook his head. "You realize I almost didn't see you because you didn't have your hands free to wave me down."

She shrugged. "God provides."

"Is he going to provide you with a new foot? Do you even have circulation to your toes?"

She didn't answer him.

He sighed. "This is probably going to hurt." He prayed it hurt. If her circulation was severely compromised, she wasn't going to feel much, and then he'd be concerned. Taking out his dagger, he cut at the roots. He swore her foot just swelled more as he removed the roots holding it in place. She didn't say anything. Just stood there, clutching her parcels against her slight frame.

He kept slicing at the roots until he finally had free access to the hole. Then he dug at the earth, which was really more mud and twig than anything else. When it looked like he'd made a big enough opening, he took careful hold of her calf and ankle.

Even though he tried to be gentle, she winced.

"Sorry."

"No, no. It's fine. Just a little sore."

He could feel her pulling, but she still wasn't strong enough to get her leg out. "Ready for me to pull?"

She nodded.

"On three."

"Okay." She took a deep breath and bit her lip.

He pulled without counting. Her foot slipped free and she fell back against the tree trunk, howling and shaking her foot. Stubborn woman never dropped her bags, though.

"You said on three!"

He shrugged.

She tried to walk away from the tree, but almost collapsed when she put her weight on her injured foot. He wrapped his arms around her and scooped her up. "I got you."

She looked up at him and smiled through tears. "It's not so bad. A little pins and needles."

"Yeah. And a lot of pain. Your ankle's the size of one of the oranges you were chasing." He set her down by the passenger side of the car, then put her bags inside. The rain slowed to a drizzle, then stopped. He wiped the rain and tears off her face.

She reached up and slicked his rain-soaked hair out of his face, then slid her hand along his cheek. "Thank you."

Closing his eyes, he leaned into her hand for the briefest moment, then pulled back. "I was worried about you."

"That's the nicest thing you've ever said to me."

The clouds parted and began drifting away, leaving the sun to shine down once again on the Italian countryside. He opened the door for her and helped her inside. As he walked around to the driver's side, he sincerely hoped he could do better in the future. But telling her about the orphanage was about the worst way he could think of to start a dialogue with his mother.

JO ALMOST DIDN'T miss Vinnie. Almost. About five minutes after he left, Gianni introduced her to Ottavio, the foreman of the crew Mike hired to board up the orphanage and then start the repairs. She liked him immediately, first because he looked a lot like her father. He wasn't tall and was smallish in stature, with salt-and-pepper hair, glasses covering dark and wise eyes, and sun-darkened olive skin. But second, and oh-so-importantly, he knew his stuff. He spoke broken English, but they both spoke the language of construction, and she bonded with him immediately over building codes, R-values, and construction materials. He even let her use his tools to help put up temporary walls. Contractors didn't share tools with anyone. She was honored.

When Vinnie returned with Teresa, the sun was shining, the rubble was hauled away, and the hole in the building was gone, replaced by a temporary structure of timber walls and waterproof wrap, much like she was used to at home. Ottavio laughed when she asked if this was the base for the permanent structure. He said in Italy, they must comply with the historical zoning requirements, and he would need to search for suitable materials to blend with the existing architecture. He promised to contact her before they started the repairs so she could see how they worked. He was leaving just as Vinnie returned.

She had been too busy and too enthralled to miss him—too much, anyway—but she had felt his absence and was relieved he'd returned. Especially with his mother, although when she saw Teresa limping, she grew concerned.

"Teresa. What happened?"

She hobbled over to Jo. "Are you okay? And the boys? Are they back yet?"

"The sisters returned a little while ago. They're settling the boys in the convent per Mother Superior's orders. She's been taken to the hospital. Mike went with her. He hasn't called with an update yet. No one else was hurt. What happened to you?"

"Me?" She looked past Jo, concern evident on her face. "It's nothing. I need to check on the boys. And on Mother Superior."

Jo took her by the shoulders and led her to a low wall, where she gently helped her to sit. "Here's my phone. Call Mike. See if he knows anything. Then I'll help you over to the convent so you can see what the boys are doing, although I'm sure the sisters have everything under control."

Teresa smiled up at her and squeezed her hand. "Thank you, Jo."

She placed her call, and Jo walked over to Vinnie.

"I'm sorry I ran off. Gianni said he'd explain."

"He did. By the looks of your mom's ankle, she needed your help."

Sighing, he ran his hands through his damp locks. "My mom. That sounds so weird."

"You'll get used to it."

"Are you mad that I ran off?"

"No. I get it. I wish I could have come with you."

"The car only has two seats, or I would have asked."

She shook her head. "You two need to spend some time alone together, anyway. Besides, I got to meet Ottavio and his crew." She talked to him about the construction for a while, until she noticed the vacant look in his eyes. "Sorry. I sometimes forget that just because you were on my crew for a while doesn't mean you actually like construction."

He took her hand. "I like everything that has to do with you. I'm just—"

"Tired?"

"No."

"What?"

"I think relieved. Earlier I was so mad and confused, but when you told me about the bomb, I was scared. Now that I know everyone is safe, I'm relieved."

She rubbed her thumb over his knuckles. "Did you talk to her yet?"

"No. But now I know I can. I will."

"And Mike?"

He squeezed her hand. "I'll get to it."

She stepped next to him and wrapped her arms around him. His clothes were damp, cool against her cheek, but she felt the strength and heat of him beneath them. He held her tight to him and pressed his lips to the top of her head. "Jo, I have so much to say to you, too."

"Do you want to go talk?"

He nodded against her, and she shuddered. This was the conversation she wanted. And feared. It was time.

She took his hand and walked back to Teresa, who disconnected the call and returned the phone to Jo. "He said Mother Superior had a broken wrist, which they set, and second degree burns on her left side, which they treated. She was suffering from smoke inhalation, but they don't think she'll have any lasting issues. Her throat's raw right now, so she can't yell at anyone properly, but that'll change quickly, I'm sure. Mike said she should make a full recovery."

"That's great," Jo said.

"Are you going to be okay here?" Vinnie asked. "Jo and I have some things to discuss."

Nico drove down the road in the van they'd borrowed earlier, followed by Coz in a Maserati. They walked over to where Teresa sat.

"Sorry we had this for so long." Nico put the keys in her hand and bent to give her a kiss.

"Don't be sorry. The fact that it wasn't here probably saved my life."

"Glad you're okay," Coz said.

"Will you boys help me to the van and get my things from Vinnie's car?"

"Why do you need help?" Nico asked.

She rolled her eyes. "Go on now," she said to Vinnie. "We'll catch up later."

Nico and Coz started helping her to the van while he and Jo walked over to the car. "I'll just give the guys her bags and we can go."

She watched him take the bags to his mother and confer with his brothers. He took the time to be sure she was settled, then he squared things with Nico and Coz before returning to her. That was the man she fell in love with.

Ugh. The *L* word. Given the pain in her chest, it was quite possible her heart skipped a beat. Or she had an arrhythmia. Or quite possibly had suffered a mild heart attack.

She didn't think it was a good idea to say that word aloud.

It might kill her.

THEY DIDN'T TALK as they drove up the hill. And Vinnie drove at a somewhat respectable speed, so the drive lasted close to fifteen minutes. They also didn't speak when they got out of the car, or walked through the house, or up the stairs.

When they got to Jo's bedroom door, she turned to him. "Are you coming in?"

"We're both wet and grimy. I just assumed you'd want to clean up first."

She shrugged. "Are you…"

Her cheeks were pink, and she couldn't quite meet his gaze. He put his hand under her chin and tilted her face up. "I'd like nothing more than to join you. But I'm not going to. Not yet, anyway. Get cleaned up, then meet me in my room."

"Don't you want to shower?"

"There are about seventy-eight bathrooms here. I'll find one."

She stepped into her room and closed the door. When Vinnie entered his room, he could already hear the shower water running in the bathroom. It was tempting to join her, but that wasn't going to accomplish anything. Instead, he gathered the clothes he'd tossed on the floor earlier and threw them back in his bag. He grabbed the first clean pair of shorts he found, rummaged around for his toiletry kit, and headed down the hall for an unoccupied shower.

It was the fastest shower of his life.

He hardly bothered drying off, but slipped into his gym shorts and rushed back to his room. He got to his door right when Gianni and Franki got to theirs. He saw them take in his bare feet, damp skin, shirtless body… the arousal his gym shorts did nothing to hide. Franki's eyes widened and Gianni smirked.

Vinnie turned so his body faced his door and pointed his toiletry kit at Gianni. "Shut up." He opened his door, slipped inside, and slammed it shut behind him. He heard them both laughing before they entered their own room.

The shower wasn't running, but Jo still hadn't come into his room. He didn't know how much time he had, but it was enough to finish his plan. He threw his kit in his bag and rooted around in his electronics bag until he found what he was looking for. Then he jumped on his bed, tucking his surprise under his pillow right before she knocked on the bathroom door.

"Vin? You decent?"

He chuckled. "Come in."

She opened the door and stood there for a moment, backlit, the light behind her creating a fiery halo around her head, her body a gorgeous silhouette surrounded by a golden glow. Then she stepped toward him. She wore tiny boy shorts and a clingy tank in the softest shade of pink. His gaze traveled the length of her legs, over her flat stomach, and across the swells of her breasts. He could see the protrusion of her hipbones, the indentation of her navel, the tips of her nipples hardening under his stare. Her breasts rose and fell faster as her breathing quickened. He glanced at her face to see her cheeks turning pink, a far darker shade than her clothes, and she spun around. The shorts were snug and hugged her bottom as she darted back to her room. She returned, breathless, seconds later, wrapped in a robe.

"I wasn't sure how casual this meeting was, so I dressed for bed. But you're in shorts, so..."

He held out his hand to her. "Come here, Red."

She walked to the bed, holding the neck of the robe tightly closed, and took his hand.

He pulled her to lie beside him in the crook of his arm. As he settled her against him, he took a deep breath. Lavender. Jo's scent. She was in his arms and she was safe. He breathed her in again, smiled, and loosened her grip on her collar. "I loved how you looked a moment ago. You don't need the robe. You don't need any clothes at all."

She snorted.

"Well, maybe you should keep some on, or I won't be able to keep my hands to myself. And I do want to talk to you. At least, first."

She let go of the collar, but instead of untying the robe, she turned toward him. "What do you want to talk about?"

"Lots of things. But first, I have to give you something."

"What?"

He reached under his pillow and fumbled around until he found what he was looking for, then he pulled his hand back out. It was a brown paper bag.

"What is it?"

"Open it."

"Famous last words." She reached into the bag and pulled out a camera. Then she raised her eyebrows at him.

"I'm sorry I didn't have time to wrap it. But it's a really good camera. I have one just like it."

"Why are you giving me a camera?"

"Did you think I'd forget? It's your birthday, Jo. Don't you get presents on your birthday?"

She shook her head. "No. I told you. I don't celebrate my birthday."

"Well, we're going to start."

She shook her head. He saw the beginnings of panic setting in, and he started stroking her arm. "Jo. Jo, listen to me. Listen to my voice. Breathe. That's it. Slowly in and out. Breathe."

She was settling, and he continued to press her. "Come on, *bella*. We dealt with Enzo, we dealt with your scars. None of that matters. Now you're here covered up again hiding from your birthday. What's the problem?"

"You're right. I know what you're saying makes sense. It's just—how can I make you understand?" She dropped the camera, got up and started to pace. "I don't celebrate my birthday because I don't want to be the center of attention. I don't want people staring at me. I don't want them looking at me. I don't want anyone to notice me. Ever."

It was like the sun rose and burned off the fog clouding his brain. He suddenly saw it all clearly. It all made sense. He went to her, held her by the arms and looked into her eyes. "That's why you keep your hair short. And don't bother with makeup and the clothes and stuff that your sisters do. Why you skip the client meetings. It has nothing to do with disinterest in any of it."

She threw her hands up. "Of course not. Do you think any girl wakes up and wants to look like a man? Do you think I want to leave my sisters to deal with the business on their own? No. But I don't know what else to do. That's how I stay under the radar."

"I have news for you, *bella*. You could wear a flour sack and shave your head. It wouldn't matter. You'd still turn heads."

"Because I'd be the bald freak in a flour sack."

"Because you're gorgeous. I fell for you while you were wearing flannel shirts and short, spiky hair. That won't keep people away. Besides, it's not about how you look, it's about who you are. And you're amazing."

"I don't like to be the center of all the fuss."

"Well, I thought I lost my parents today. Before that, I didn't even know who my father was. I'm tired of not celebrating what I have. So I'm celebrating you." An idea dawned, and he went with it. "We all are. I'll get everyone together and we'll have a big dinner and cake. You'll have to wait on presents, since I don't think the guys know what today is, but," he shoved the camera back at her, "we're taking pictures to remember tonight."

"How about I take pictures of you, instead?"

He shrugged. "Sure. Take as many as you want. Nico said the card should hold thousands of photos or hours of video."

"You talked to him about it?"

"When I bought my camera. I didn't tell anyone I bought you one. The guys don't even know today's your day."

"My sisters know. But they know I don't like the attention, so they didn't make a big deal of it."

"Do you really not want a party?"

"Is it really important to you?"

"Don't you think, after everything we're going through, that we should be celebrating life, not hiding from it?"

"You're right. We should."

"Then let's have a party."

"But something small," she said.

"Okay. Small. We'll let Gianni and Donni handle the details." He grabbed his phone and sent a text.

"And you really don't care if I take your picture?" she asked.

He snorted. "Why would I care?"

"You didn't look really into the whole having-your-picture-taken thing in the pictures I saw of you at Marcus's."

"That was more about how I felt about family than how I felt about cameras. And I'm changing my opinion about that, too." He wrapped his arms around her. "I can get used to closeness." He bent his head to kiss her, but she pulled away.

"Get on the bed." She pulled the camera out of the box and put the memory card in. "Oh, shoot. The battery was never charged."

"I already charged it for you."

She grinned and installed it in the camera. "Okay. Smile."

He laughed at her excitement, and she snapped the picture. Turning the view screen so he could see, she said, "You're very photogenic. And you should smile more."

His hair was still damp and curling at the nape of his neck. He could use a shave. He looked rough and rumpled in the messed up covers. But he looked genuinely happy. She was right. He should smile more. And he knew just the girl to make him. He reached his hand out to her.

"Let me take another," she said.

"Okay."

"Pose."

He tried not to laugh at her. "How do you want me?"

"Lie back." She helped position him. "Put this arm here, behind your head, and this arm here, like you're waiting for—someone. And stretch this leg straight out, but bend this one." She bent his leg up and slid his shorts so that most of his thigh was showing.

He swallowed a chuckle, causing his abs to constrict.

"That. What was that?" she asked.

"What?"

"Whatever you just did to your stomach. It made your abs tighten. Do that again. That looks good."

He felt like a total idiot, but at least she was loosening up. She hadn't noticed, but her robe had slipped open. He would enjoy the view while she played Annie Leibovitz.

She ran to the foot of the bed and turned to face him. "Now. Tighten your abs for me."

He did as she demanded, feeling foolish the entire time, but smiled for her. She took another picture. He noticed her breathing quicken, and she bit her lip when she looked at the photo. When she aimed the camera again, he flexed his pecs. She paused, cleared her throat, then took the picture. Then he flexed all his muscles at once.

"Good Lord," she whispered. The camera took five pictures in rapid succession. Her arm kept getting tangled in the robe that had slipped off her shoulder, so she yanked it off and tossed it aside.

That small gesture sent Vinnie over the edge from amused and embarrassed to aroused. In nothing but his gym shorts, it was impossible to hide.

She lowered the camera. "How do you feel about—" But she didn't finish her thought.

"About what?"

She bit her lip. "About more intimate shots?"

How did he feel about that? Certainly wasn't the top of his list, but for her, he'd do anything. She began loosening up behind the camera, which was a stepping-stone to her being comfortable on the other side of the lens. So, for her—to help her—he'd do it. "This is your party. Whatever you want."

She walked over to him and slid both sides of his shorts high on his thigh. From her vantage point at the foot of the bed, she'd be able to see something up the pant leg of the leg she kept bent.

"Hmm," she said, "that's not right. I need more."

"More?" Wasn't that enough?

She made him grab the sheets with the hand that had been free and ball them up in his fist. Then she took his other hand. He looked at her, and she met his gaze. Without looking away, she moved his hand slowly and put on top of his erection. She wrapped her fingers around his until he gripped himself loosely. When she pulled her hand away, she trailed her fingers lightly over the tip, which had just started to grow wet. He hissed.

"Is this okay?" she asked.

"Oh, yeah."

"Tip your head back, like you're enjoying yourself."

"Do you think I'm not?"

She giggled and ran to the foot of the bed again.

"Can you move your hand? You know, actually—stroke yourself?"

She was so innocent, but she was making him so hot. Fuck yeah, he could stroke himself. He could also blow his load in about three seconds if she kept talking to him like that. He felt the heat of his hand, the friction of the cloth slide against his skin, but all he knew was the sound of her voice.

"Slower."

He gripped the base of his shaft and slid his hand slowly up to the ridged tip, imagining what it would feel like if she was the one touching him, if she had her soft fingers wrapped around him.

"Look at me."

He angled his head and looked at her. The camera continued to click as he continued to follow her instructions, his breath growing ragged as he fought for control.

"Will you strip for me?"

It was the break he needed to gain his composure. He stopped what he was doing and sat up.

She turned around and put the camera down. "I'm sorry. That was really inappropriate of me."

"Jo, it's okay."

She shook her head. "No. No, it's not. I was out of line. That was way overboard. It's just that you looked so—"

"So what?"

"Beautiful."

He didn't expect that.

He stood and crossed to her, wrapped his arms around her. "That's you. I wish you could see yourself the way I see you."

She walked away from him, shaking her head. "I don't know what you could possibly see in me. Why you're even interested in me. All I do is bring you danger and pain."

His heart broke at the anguish in her voice, the tears in her eyes.

He walked up behind her and pulled her into his arms. "You're everything I could possibly want, Jo. I love you."

It just slipped out. He hadn't planned it. But it was out there. He couldn't take it back. And he couldn't stand waiting for her response.

So he turned her around and kissed her. When they broke apart, her eyes were wide, her breathing rapid and shallow. Good sign, right?

He took her hand and led her to the bed. "Let me show you."

24

SHE WOKE UP after the best sex ever to a pounding on Vinnie's door.

"Are you guys ever coming out?" Gianni called in. "You can't have sex all day and night."

"Well," Franki said, "you can, except for food and sleep breaks. But then you'll have family pounding on your door."

Bang, bang, bang!

"You know, like this," she called in.

Vinnie stumbled over to the door with his towel wrapped around his waist. "What do you want?"

"You said don't bother you till eight. It's eight."

Vinnie squinted at the clock. "Fine. We'll be right down. Stop banging on the damn door."

"Stop banging my sister," Franki said.

"Nice language," Jo called from inside the room.

Vinnie slammed the door shut. Jo could hear Franki and Gianni laughing in the hall. "What's this about eight?"

"We missed lunch. I told them to get us for dinner."

"Can't we just skip it? I'd rather go back to bed."

"Sorry, Red."

She hated when people called her that. Well, when anyone else called her that. He made it work, though. She tossed a pillow at his head. "Dinner isn't formal here, is it? I didn't bring formal clothes."

"Formal? No. But I wouldn't go in your robe."

She stuck her tongue out at him. He already was dressed. She envied guys their simplicity. Jeans and a dress shirt and he was ready. That didn't help her. What level of casualness was that for women? Jeans? Business casual? Ugh.

She grabbed his hand. "Come with me."

"Where are we going?"

She dragged him through the bathroom they shared to her room, where her luggage was. It wasn't in much better shape than his. Instead of being balled up in her bag, it was all thrown on the bench at the foot of her bed. "What should I wear?"

"I hate this game."

She glared at him.

Ten minutes later, they headed to the dining room. She had on a dress she'd borrowed from Franki—a dark green strapless sundress with a matching three-quarter length sleeve sweater.

"You look stunning."

"I feel over-dressed."

"Not for tonight."

"Why? What's tonight?"

They rounded the corner and entered the dining room.

"Surprise!" everyone shouted.

Jo wavered on her feet, but Vinnie supported her with his hand around her waist. He leaned down and whispered, *"Tanti auguri, bella,"* while everyone wished her happy birthday.

"Tanti auguri?"

"'Happy Birthday' would literally be said *'Buon Compleanno,'* but that's not what we say here. We say 'Many Good Wishes.'"

"Then there's cake?"

"Then, technically, you're supposed to take everyone out and buy them a round of drinks. And provide your own cake. We're doing the American version. Dinner and cake on us."

"And you pulled all this off with that text earlier?"

"Well, not exactly."

She raised an eyebrow.

"I had everyone planning this since we found out when your birthday was. The text was to be certain we could pull it off, after—" He didn't finish.

"Well, thanks." She heard the insincerity in her tone and vowed to be a better sport.

She allowed him to lead her to the seat of honor at the head of the table. Vinnie took the seat to her right, Franki her left. All her sisters and the Brothers were there. And Mike and Teresa were at the far end of the table.

She leaned over to Vinnie and put her lips to his ear. "Are you okay with them being here?"

"As okay as you are at celebrating your birthday," he whispered back.

Mike stood and raised his glass. "I have never had a celebration such as this in my home. In fact, I never thought I would have the honor. *Tanti auguri,* Josephina."

They all raised their glasses. The wine was heady, bold, and Jo gulped more of it than was probably proper. She felt ridiculous sitting at the head of the table instead of blending in at the side. But Vinnie squeezed her leg and she looked at him.

"You're doing great," he murmured. "I already told them, no speeches. Just dinner. Donni made your favorite."

Jo glanced at the expensive place settings and rubbed her hand around the edge of the plate. She wondered briefly if that was real gold before looking back at Vinnie. "I don't think she did. I mean, not my very favorite. Maybe Mama's osso buco recipe, or…." Her voice trailed off as Donni carried out a steaming pot and set it on the table. Gianni followed behind her with an enormous tray piled high with sandwiches. "Oh, for Pete's sake. You even wrapped them in paper." She laughed.

"What are they?" Teresa asked, squinting at them.

"There's a restaurant near where we work," Donni said. "They're famous for putting coleslaw and fries on their sandwiches. The pastrami is Jo's absolute favorite."

"I've never seen anything like that. I've never tried coleslaw."

"Well, it's not the traditional creamy one Americans are known for. It's vinegar-based," Gianni said. "Here. Try one." He started passing them out.

Teresa looked through the sandwich. "What all is on here?"

"It's meat, cheese, fries, slaw, and a tomato on warmed Italian bread," Donni said.

"Jo, would you like to say the blessing?" Teresa asked.

Everyone looked at her. Just what she didn't want. She felt her pulse quicken, her hands grow clammy.

"I'll do it," Vinnie said.

All eyes turned to Vinnie while he gave thanks for the meal they were sharing. Jo tried to listen to him, but she was torn between relief and shock. Vinnie didn't pray. He didn't believe in it. He only attended Mass because they did, and he had to protect them. Was he protecting her again, or had the explosion really changed his outlook?

When everyone started eating, she met his gaze. He smiled at her. "Eat."

"Thank you," she whispered.

He smiled and nodded at her sandwich. *"Mangi."*

Jo bit into her sandwich and closed her eyes. "Oh, this is just like home. Maybe better."

"How can it be better than the original?" Donni asked.

"I don't know, but you did it."

"It wasn't just me. And there's chili, too."

"You didn't?"

"Don't you always order a bowl of chili to go with your sandwich?"

Gianni ladled bowls of chili and passed them around. Jo took a spoonful and sighed. "Don't even think about leaving NBD and opening a restaurant. You'll put half the places at home out of business. I'll go broke buying all your food."

"Like I'd charge you. Besides, I love my job, and I feed you for free now."

"That's true." She dipped her sandwich in chili. Pure heaven.

"Anyway, this was Gianni's recipe."

"Franki, don't let him go. The way you cook, you need someone like him in your life."

"That's not why I keep him around. That's just a perk."

The banter continued easily throughout dinner. Jo was stuffed when they brought out the cake—almond cake with raspberry custard filling, whipped cream frosting, and toasted almond slivers on the sides. It was as beautiful as any wedding cake she'd ever seen. She thought she'd hate it when they sang and waited for her to blow out the candles, but by the time that happened, she was plied with wine, stuffed with her favorite meal, and completely comfortable with everyone in the room. Even Mike and Teresa seemed to enjoy the food, despite how casual and foreign it was to them. The only things missing, other than complete invisibility, were her mother and Chuck. She knew she'd see Mama soon. Chuck? That was another matter entirely.

She stood to make her wish and wobbled on her feet. Vinnie wrapped his arm around her waist so she didn't fall, and she clutched him with one hand and the table with the other. "Wow. I guess I had more wine than I thought."

"You've been enjoying the evening. I'm glad. I was worried you'd hate it."

She touched his cheek. "No. I'm glad we did this. I loved it."

"Not too horrible?"

"Not too horrible at all."

"Make a wish, then, and blow out your candles."

She closed her eyes and remembered Chuck's bloody and battered body on the video file. She hadn't had a chance to check for any other communications about him. Nico was probably intercepting any NBD communications, anyway. But she was responsible for Chuck. If she couldn't help him in any other way, he at least deserved her first birthday wish in years.

I wish Chuck returned to us safely and soon.

Pursing her lips, she made damn sure she got every candle with one breath.

The cake was exquisite, at once delicate and rich, sweet and tart, creamy and crunchy. After the filling meal she'd had, she could only manage a tiny piece and a little coffee. Her stomach churned and her head positively reeled when she was through.

"I think I've had about enough," she said. "I need to go to bed."

"But you didn't open your presents," Toni said.

"Presents, too?" She looked at Vinnie. He'd said no presents.

"Of course," Nico said. "You can't have a birthday without gifts."

"Thank you all so much. For everything," she said. "But I'm really not feeling well. Can we do it tomorrow?"

Franki hugged her. "I can't handle my wine, either. Happy birthday, sis."

"I'll help you upstairs," Vinnie said.

"That's okay. You should stay here and talk to your parents."

He frowned and pulled her aside. "I invited them. They were a part of this. It was nice having them here. Isn't that enough for right now?"

"You made me do something I wasn't ready for, and it was a success. You can do this."

"It wasn't a total success. You didn't open your gifts."

"I opened yours." That elicited a wolfish grin. As much as she appreciated the memory, and his reaction, it wasn't the time or the place to dwell on it. "Go talk to them. I'm heading off to bed."

He kissed her softly on the lips. "Good night, *bella*. Happy birthday."

He walked away, and she glanced around the room. Talk about being the center of attention. She knew they all knew about her and Vinnie being together, but they'd never witnessed him just kiss her like it was no big deal.

It was a very big deal.

Except no one acted like it was a big deal. Well, other than her. Everyone else lingered over coffee and cake. Teresa smiled at her. Panicked, she tried to smile back, but it felt a lot more like a grimace. She spun away, knocked over a chair, and ran to her room.

Maybe they'd think she was going to be sick.

There was a good chance of that now, anyway.

She stripped out of the dress and flung herself on the bed. She was hopeless.

Her scars were invisible in the darkness, but she knew they were there. Running her fingers over her arms, she could feel the slight change in texture where the blade had dug into her tender flesh. She remembered every cut, every drop of blood. Numb. She had been so numb, and she carved deeper and deeper, just hoping to feel something, anything. She'd been so cold, and the only warmth she'd gotten were the trails of blood trickling down her arm. The only way she felt alive was to see the flow of life leaving her. But never, never enough to matter.

She'd been so conflicted. It was her beauty that got her in trouble. So she'd made herself ugly. Undesirable. And she cut. And she cut.

And still she felt anesthetized, deadened.

So she cut. And cut.

And still she felt too noticeable.

Cut. And cut.

She was glad it was all behind her. Glad it was only faint scars that remained. But somewhere inside her, there was still a cold girl who felt exposed to the world, who felt the only way she could feel anything real was to feel pain.

That's why she hadn't relied on the Brotherhood. Why she kept running away.

She ran her fingers along the ridge of her deepest scar. Unlike the others, it was pink and puckered, not smooth and white. It was the one that pushed her family to take action. The one that made all the difference in her life.

Some scars fade. Others remain. But they don't need to define a person.

They can motivate, however.

She grabbed her phone. If the guys weren't going to let her in the loop, she'd just have to force her way in. She quickly logged into her Cloud drive. She was certain Nico had deleted the video from the NBD servers, but she hoped he'd forgotten about their backups. A quick search showed he hadn't forgotten about the Cloud. So she logged into their offsite storage account. Either he didn't know about that one, or he had forgotten it. She quickly located the video Dante had sent, pressed play, and fast forwarded it through the gruesome details until she got to the phone number. That's all she wanted. Nico had deleted it from her last phone, and she'd had two new phones since.

A quick Hail Mary, then she dialed.

"Dante? It's Jo."

"Huh. I have to admit, I was expecting a call. But I definitely didn't expect it from you."

"You obviously know I got your message about Chuck. Where is he?"

"I thought you'd be more concerned with how he is than where he is."

"Fine. How is he?"

"Why don't you meet us and see for yourself?"

"How stupid do you think I am? The last time I had the misfortune of meeting you, you tried to kill me."

"Then I guess Mr. Tyson isn't going to see the sun rise tomorrow. Goodbye, Jo."

"Wait!"

"What? I don't have all day. I told you, I'm expecting a call."

"I'll meet you."

"Alone. Unarmed."

"Fine. Alone and unarmed. When and where?"

"San Crisogono. Now."

Icy fingers of dread skittered up her spine. How long had he been in Italy? Was he behind the explosion? She had to stall, to dig for information. "Isn't that in Italy? How do you expect me to just—"

"Save it. We know you're already there. If you aren't at the orphanage in less than an hour, he dies."

"But the orphanage is barely there. There was an accident. A gas leak in the kitchen. Half the building exploded."

Dante laughed. *"Is that what they're calling it? It was us, babe. Just bad timing on our part. We thought you'd all be there."*

The hairs rose on the nape of her neck, her blood ran cold and settled into a frigid mass in the pit of her stomach.

"Clock's ticking. Less than an hour." He disconnected the call.

She sat there for a moment, staring at the dark screen. Then she stood. She had to get going.

GOD BLESS MANUAL transmissions. She took the keys to the Ferrari but didn't turn the ignition on. Instead, after unlocking the car, she put it in neutral and coasted well out of hearing range before finally turning the key. Chances were, with the fortress-like construction of the house and the commotion of the party, no one would have heard her, anyway. But she didn't want to chance it.

The ramifications of her decision weighed heavily on her as she drove slowly down the hill. She knew Nico would be angry that she'd called the number. But she had her phone with her, so they couldn't ping the compound location. At least, that's how she thought it worked.

Vinnie would be furious with her plan. He'd say it wasn't a plan at all. It was suicide. He was wrong, though. She had faith it would work out. She just hated to upset them so much. Again. She'd carefully considered all her options, all the angles. This was the best plan. This was the only strategy with a chance of working.

She parked in front of the orphanage. There were no other vehicles around, but that didn't mean anything. They could be anywhere. Or maybe they hadn't arrived yet. She stepped into the olive grove, but it disturbed her in the night. Shadows stretched long across the dark ground. Leaves rustled in the wind, their shadows like demon fingers creeping along the rutted path. She spun and returned to the courtyard. Pausing at the well, she made a silent wish that her plan worked as she hoped, then she headed into the orphanage.

Construction sites never bothered her, day or night. But this one had a different feel. There were no tools lying about, no overturned buckets to sit on, no stacks of wood or drywall, no bags of concrete. There wasn't a single stray nail, staple, or screw. It was like the ghost of a construction site, an unholy specter called into being to trick her into staying somewhere she knew she should be running from. But she ignored the niggling warning churning in her gut and instead, pressed on, picking her way through the uncleared debris. Not seeing anyone or anything on the ground floor, she climbed the stairs to the second story.

The upstairs was gone. What had been bedrooms was now an opening to floor joists and some subflooring. She was about to turn around when movement near the edge caught her eye.

"We didn't think you'd show."

VINNIE MADE SMALL talk with his brothers for about fifteen minutes, but his attention wasn't on anything they were saying. He was trying to figure out what to say to his—no, he couldn't do it. Calling them his "parents" still just sounded ridiculous.

He was relieved neither of them was hurt in the explosion. Glad he'd have the chance to talk to them again. About his childhood, about his heritage, about where they went from here.

And with the opportunity staring him in the face—literally, they were both sitting there staring at him—he couldn't do it. All the old insecurities flooded back to him. Feeling unwanted, unimportant, unnecessary.

Unloved.

He needed Jo. He needed to feel her warmth, her compassion. Needed to feel her embrace, her body pressed against his so he knew he mattered to someone. Knew he came first.

Excusing himself, he left the table and headed to her room.

And found it empty.

He checked the bathroom, thinking she was maybe sicker than he'd thought. Also empty.

A grin crept over his features. Maybe he was getting a present. He opened the door to his bedroom, expecting to see her in his bed.

Again, empty.

Anger rolled through him, quickly replaced with panic. She'd left again. She was alone, unprotected, in a country unfamiliar to her. The day a bombing could have killed them all. He turned on his light so he could gather his things.

In the middle of his bed was the camera he'd given her. It was acting as a paperweight for a note. Snatching it, he scanned what she'd written.

Vinnie,

Please don't be angry. I need your help, which means I need you thinking clearly.

I called the number at the end of Dante's video. He wants me to come immediately to the orphanage, alone and unarmed. I knew you'd never let me do it, which is why I didn't tell you, but I also know I'll never get through this without your help. So please help me. I don't know if they'll have Chuck or not, but I have to try. Best case, we get him back and take out Dante and maybe some of his crew. Worst case? Well, I know you won't let that happen.

I'm trusting you.

Love,

Jo

Clutching the letter, he arched back, releasing his frustration and anger in a wordless roar that shook the windows. Then he started strapping on weapons.

His brothers were at his door in seconds.

"What the hell was that?" Gianni asked.

Vinnie tossed him the letter. He didn't speak. He was in battle mode.

The guys skimmed the letter as Vinnie finished getting ready.

"Wait," Coz said. "We need a plan. You need to give us the plan. You're the strategy guy."

He forced his way past them and strode down the hall. "Figure it out on your own. I need to go get her."

"V, your powers aren't even—"

"Don't, G." Vinnie didn't even turn around. He snatched a set of keys off the console table and ran out the front door.

SHE LOOKED AROUND. This was her vision. She recognized the surroundings, the landscape. But it wasn't right. All the details were wrong. The building had an elevator shaft, and this one didn't. The second story had walls. This one didn't. And in her vision it was Dante who confronted her. This definitely wasn't Dante.

"Who's we? I only see you. Where's Dante? And who the hell are you?"

"Dante fooled you. He's stuck in the States, still trying to coordinate his travel plans. I'm Pasquale. Perhaps you've heard of me?"

"Dante never mentioned you. Sorry." She glanced around for any kind of weapon, biding her time. There was nothing.

"Not Dante. Vinnie."

"The only Pasquale Vinnie's mentioned is the one who—Oh, you've got to be kidding me."

"There you go."

"But why?"

"Why do you think? It all comes down to power, and I'll have a hell of a lot more of it when you're all gone and we take over."

"But Vinnie's been so good to you."

He scoffed. "Vinnie's an idiot."

"Don't you have any loyalty toward him? Toward the company?"

"If you want to be loyal to someone, be loyal to yourself. Vinnie never took care of me. So I'm looking out for number one. Now, move over there." He gestured toward the corner of the building to her left. The one she'd been standing by in her vision.

"Why? How're you going to make me?"

He pulled out a gun and waved it toward the corner.

Stupid question on her part. Of course he came armed. She picked her way over to the corner and looked out over the landscape. The moonlight was bright, casting a glow on the ground below. In the distance, she could see the lights at the compound, twinkling like stars set into the hillside. The olive grove looked like a bushy battalion in column formation, marching toward combat. The well stood sentinel below her.

Pasquale pulled what looked like a detonator out of his pocket. "What do you know about explosives?"

"I know they're dangerous. And illegal."

He laughed. "Before I went to work for MDH, I was in the military. Can you guess what my specialty was?"

"Linguistics? Your English is almost flawless."

"Explosions can be made big or small. They can do a lot of damage, or minimal." He stood in the opposite corner of the building from her, but stepped toward the middle. "Do you realize I could stand five meters from you and blow you off this roof while not getting a scratch on me?"

"I'll take your word for it. You don't have anything to prove to me."

He laughed again and stepped back toward the corner. "You're right. I don't. That's why I'll stand back here."

She wasn't sure what parts of her vision would stay the same and what parts would be different, but if Vinnie was going to rescue her, it was now or never. "You know, if it's money you want, I'm sure—"

"It's not about the money!" His eyes widened, glazed with the same insane rapture she'd seen on Dante's face before he cut her throat. "Do you know what it feels like to have someone's life in your hands? To know their breaths are numbered and you control how many more they take? You can't give me that. Vinnie can't. MDH can't. I'm not looking for money or glory. I'm looking to be a god!"

Jo swallowed. His hand moved to the button. Vinnie hadn't seen the note in time. Or hadn't had the strategic power to save her. She'd never get to tell him she loved him. The note would have to be enough.

How do you cringe from an explosion coming from beneath you? She hunched her shoulders and winced, waiting for the heat and the agony. Her mouth was dry, her pulse hammered in her ears. Pasquale's thumb moved in the slowest motion she'd ever seen. Minutes, hours, days passed in the second it took him to push the button. That time was all filled with images of her parents, her sisters, Chuck. Vinnie.

Vinnie.

Vinnie's head and torso emerged from the opening in the floor. He had his dagger in one hand and his Sig Sauer in the other. He fired at Pasquale and hit him in the gut. As Pasquale fell, shock slackened his features. Then he smiled and moved his thumb.

Jo saw Vinnie glow right before a wall of water slammed into her.

And everything went dark.

VINNIE LOOKED AT Jo's still body lying in her bed. It had been hours, but she still hadn't stirred. Her sisters had come and gone, all the guys had checked in. Mike stood in the doorway once.

Vinnie hadn't left her side.

Teresa hadn't left his. She handed him a glass of water. "It's hard, watching someone you love suffer."

"I'm afraid I was too late." He took the cup but didn't drink.

"Vinnie, look at me."

He stared into the water.

"Vincenzo." Her voice was sharp. She never used that tone with him. With the other boys, but never with him.

He never thought she cared enough to bother.

"You got her out of there. That's all you could have done. Now are you going to use your power to see if there's anything else that can be done, or are you going to sit there and wallow?"

"What do you know about our powers?"

"I'm your mother. Do you think I would have consented to you going with your father without a full explanation as to what you were getting involved with?"

"And he told you? Because he sure as hell didn't tell me."

"Everything has a time and place. You were fourteen. I understand you feel wronged by our decisions, but maybe you should consider that we did what we thought was best at the time. If we were wrong, we're sorry. But we can't undo it. We can only move forward. If you let us."

"I'm working on it."

"I know." She kissed his forehead.

He took his mother's advice and used his power. His head snapped up. "Can you get Gianni and Nico for me?"

"Sure." She left the room. A minute later, she reappeared with all his Brothers.

"She has a cracked skull. And some cranial bleeding. I never thought to check for injuries like that. I just thought I almost drowned her."

JO BLINKED. HER mouth felt like fiberglass insulation. Her muscles were a little sore. But other than that, she felt good. She ran her hands over her body. Damn good. She had all her fingers, all her toes. All her limbs were intact and apparently burn-free. And she hadn't drowned, either, so that was a plus. Vinnie had made it.

She bolted up in bed. Vinnie.

"Hey, Red."

"Don't call me that." She smiled, not minding at all. What a sight to wake to. He looked gorgeous. Mussed hair, five o'clock shadow, rumpled clothes. Her face fell. Shadows under his bloodshot eyes. Tension setting his features tight. Oh-oh. Something about her plan must not have gone as expected.

"What happened?" she croaked.

He handed her a glass of water. It soothed her parched throat.

"What do you remember?"

"My vision. It came true. But the details were wrong."

He ran his hand through his hair and stood. Turning his back to her, he paced the length of the room once, twice. He stopped and faced her, spun away, then faced her again.

"Vinnie, come sit with me."

He muttered something under his breath, but he joined her on the bed. She grabbed his hand, and he stroked her knuckles with his thumb. "Jo, let me ask you something. Everything we've shared. The secrets, the intimacy. What did that mean to you?"

She squeezed his hand. "I told you before. You know me better than anyone."

"But what does it mean to you?"

"Everything," she whispered.

"Then why did you run away again?"

She put her hand on his cheek. "The other times I left, I told myself I was running to protect the people I loved. And part of that was true. I didn't want anyone getting hurt because of me. But this time, I didn't run away. I tried to explain in my letter. I thought it all out carefully. I knew you had my back. I trusted you. And I don't trust easily."

"We should have planned it together."

"You wouldn't have let me go."

"Damn right."

"And if Chuck was there, they would have killed him."

"There was no way Chuck was there."

"You didn't know that."

He waved his dagger at her. "I knew that."

"Your powers weren't working. Well, you didn't think they were. I had faith. And you came through in the end."

He scrubbed his face with his hands. "You're infuriating."

She pulled his hands down. "So what happened?"

"After I shot him, Pasquale detonated the bomb."

"I saw him push the button. I'm confused about after."

He turned his head away and scratched at his neck. She swore he was flushed, but the light was dim in the room and she couldn't be certain.

"I, ah, I called up water from the well and knocked you away from the blast."

"I'm sorry. You did what?"

"It all clicked when I saw you on the roof. I was working on a plan to get you out of trouble from the moment I read your note, and something was picking away at me, kind of scratching in my mind. Like when a word is on the tip of your tongue, but you can't figure out what it is?"

"Yeah. Go on."

"It was like that. There was something I was missing. It was right on the periphery, and it was important, but I just couldn't grab it. When I passed the well on my way through the grounds, the feeling got stronger. It almost hurt. And when I saw you, I just knew."

"Knew what?"

"The water leak in chamber? That was me. Gianni saying it was my tears that healed you?" He stood and walked to the window. "Water. The waves on the beach. The rain when I was upset. Anyway, I saw the well, I remembered your vision, and I had this feeling. I knew I had to get you out of the way, and I knew I could use the water to do it."

"And you just wished it out of the ground?"

He turned to face her and sat on the sill. "Pretty much. Yeah."

"Why can't I remember any of it?"

"I was a little overzealous. I crashed you into the stairs, and you hit your head. You've been out for the better part of a day. My mom suggested I use my power to figure out what was wrong with you. You had a brain hemorrhage and a cracked skull. The guys patched you up."

"You called her your mom."

"Huh? Oh."

She held out her hand to him.

He crossed to her and sat with her again.

"I told myself if I got out of there alive, there was—" She stopped and took a breath. "Was something I had to say to you."

"Yeah?" he asked. "What's that?"

"Are you really going to make me go first?"

"Haven't I taken the first step in everything else with us?"

She sighed. "Fine. You're right. I should go first with something. But I'm not really first with this one. I mean, right now I am, but you beat me to it before, although—"

He put his finger over her lips. "Stop babbling. I love you, Jo. I'm so very much in love with you."

She bit her lip and giggled. "I'm so in love with you, too. I didn't think I'd ever say that to anyone."

"I didn't, either."

"This is really happening." She wrapped her hands around his neck and pulled him to her, resting her forehead against his.

"Oh, yeah. We're really happening."

There was a knock at her door.

She sighed. "We'll have to happen in a minute."

VINNIE GROWLED AT the interruption.

"Come in," she called.

"Ah, Josephina. I was just checking on your condition. I am glad to see the healing has worked, and you are awake."

"Thanks, Mike."

"Might I have a moment of your time?"

"I'll be in my room." Vinnie stood.

"Actually, this concerns the both of you. If you would not mind remaining?"

"Do I have a choice?"

Mike raised an eyebrow.

Vinnie sat back down beside Jo.

Closing the door behind him, Mike walked into the room then sat in the chair Vinnie had pulled from the corner. He adjusted it so he wasn't quite so close to the bed and sighed. Then he stared at Vinnie.

After a few moments, Vinnie said, "What?"

"I did not ever foresee sitting with you as anything other than an adopted son and an employee. It is a refreshing change. Although I believe it is not one you are yet ready to embrace."

"It was all kind of sprung on me suddenly. I'm going to need a little adjustment time."

"Very well. You will forgive me if I bask in my joy, even if you cannot join me in it."

"Okay." Vinnie adjusted his position on the bed until he sat with his arms crossed in front of him. "What do you want to talk about?"

"What has your brother told you about coming fully into his powers?"

"Not a lot, actually. He said he didn't want to affect or impact how we learn our powers by telling us how he learned his."

"I see."

"Why? What's this got to do with me?"

"Based on Josephina's safe return, I believe it is likely that you have come into your full powers."

"How do I know?"

Mike nodded to the pitcher of water on the table. "Put your dagger down and call the water forth."

Vinnie sighed. He'd play along, just to get Mike to leave. He put his dagger on the nightstand and no sooner did he think about the water rising out of the pitcher than it was in the air. He spun it in a circle, a fluid carousel, and with a flick of his finger sent it spiraling toward the ceiling in a slow, shimmering vortex. With a tip of his head, he sent it back into the pitcher. Not a drop spilled.

"As I suspected. You two have declared your love for one another, yes?"

"Excuse me?" Vinnie said.

"The daggers. At first, I believed Giovanni required Francesca as his anchor because his red dagger was a passion-based weapon. But now I believe it is more than that. You were unable to control your power successfully until you controlled your love. The dagger has light and dark properties. The love is the light property. You embraced it, therefore you were able to master it."

"Are you saying that if I didn't love Jo, I wouldn't have been able to save her?"

"No. I believe you only need to be open to love for your dagger to work. Who you love is immaterial, I think. Had you succumbed to the dark, however, it would have been quite different. Just as Giovanni almost gave in to his dark urges, you also had to walk that line."

"My dagger is white. Purity. Clarity. Beginnings. What possible darkness could I have faced?"

Mike stood. "Look at your history, my son. Look at your beginnings. If you were not ready to face them, accept them, and move past them, this endeavor could have had a far different outcome."

Vinnie's mouth dropped open.

"Think of your powers like a baptism, a cleansing, a rebirth. That is why you manifest water. Had you not come to terms with your own origins, well, then your powers would not have been sanctified. At least, not in the pure and righteous manner in which they were."

"Mike," Jo said, "you said you didn't foresee a reunion with Vinnie."

He inclined his head.

"Don't you have the power of foresight?"

"Not in the way you mean."

"Well, in what way, then?"

"That is a complicated matter best left to discuss another time. And judging by Vincenzo's expression, I have already overstayed my welcome." He started to rise.

"I'm just asking about foretelling the future because, well, because the mirror was wrong."

He sat back down. "I am sorry?"

"My vision. The big picture was close enough, but the details were all wrong. Does that mean that it didn't really happen yet and we still have to be wary of it? Or was the vision wrong?"

"Ah. I see." He nodded. "I do not believe either is the case."

"Then what happened?"

"It seems to me you changed the future."

"The future can't be changed."

"No? You go to Mass every Sunday, yet you believe that?"

"God already knows everything we're going to do. The Bible says He knows the numbers of hairs on our heads, the exact day the world will end. It's all preordained."

"It also says that we have free will. That He has stepped in more than once to alter events. And that you should not believe in fortune-tellers."

She opened her mouth, then closed it again.

Vinnie grabbed her hand. He had learned long ago not to argue with Mike. It only resulted in a headache. Besides, he wasn't sure Mike was wrong. Jo's vision wasn't accurate. So either she saw the wrong thing or they had changed the future. That could be good or bad. They'd just lost their best predictor of future events. But that also meant anything bad they saw wasn't set in stone.

Mike stood. "Rest, my dear. You still have not opened your birthday gifts, and tomorrow we must begin our work in earnest toward battling our enemy. We have not yet reached out to Paolo, and I think it might be time to go on the offensive."

Jo managed only an unintelligible garbled reply.

"Vincenzo, do you wish to talk?"

"About what?"

God, not about their relationship. He was *so* not ready for that.

"About Pasquale."

"Pasquale? Why?"

"I realize death in war is not a criminal offense, being a necessary evil. But that does not mean the person pulling the trigger accepts his role so easily."

Vinnie had been so worried about Jo, he hadn't let himself think about Pasquale. Didn't want to think about him now, either.

"I'm tight. I did what I had to."

"Yes, you did. And I would thank you to remember that."

Vinnie had so many feelings churning inside him, so many questions burning for answers, but he didn't know where to begin.

It was pointless, anyway. As usual, Mike didn't even bother with the door. He was just gone.

"*Che cazzo.*"

"That about sums it up, doesn't it?" she said.

"I hate it when he does that."

"I'm beginning to hate it, too."

He sighed.

"So, full powers now, huh?"

"I guess." Too bad it had taken him so long to get them. Maybe he could have rescued Chuck before they ever left Pennsylvania. Or saved the orphanage. Or redeemed Pasquale. Guilt squeezed his heart, stole his breath. He'd taken a life. Not a nameless, faceless life like in war, but the life of someone he'd worked with. Someone he'd hired and trained. Mentored. Befriended. Trusted.

Purity. Clarity. Beginnings.

No amount of purity could ever cleanse him of that.

He swallowed past the lump in his throat, ignored the tears that threatened to consume him. More water he would master. And tamping down the well of emotion, he turned his attention back on Jo.

"But you needed me to get those powers."

"I'll always need you." And he did. She already eased his burden.

"I'd love to see what you can do in the shower."

He raised his eyebrows, happy to put his doubts and fears aside for the moment. "I'm up to that challenge. Are you?"

She nodded. "Hell, yeah."

Vinnie jumped from the bed, grabbed her hand, then pulled her to him, claiming her mouth in a searing kiss. God, she tasted good. And she felt perfect against him. He never wanted to let her go. Instead of walking to the bathroom, he swept her into his arms.

"Whoa!"

"What?"

She giggled and nestled into him as he walked.

God, he loved her. They had so many uncertainties facing them in the coming weeks. He was damn sure he was going to take the good times where he could find them. And at the moment, he found one of them waiting for him with open arms.

HI! I HOPE you enjoyed *Mind Control*. This story is near and dear to my heart, and it's not done yet. You can now read the entire Medici Protectorate Series in print or online anytime you want. Just look for the other books, *Bleeding Heart, Body Armor,* and *Tortured Soul* at any bookseller or online retailer.

If you wouldn't mind investing a few more minutes in this work, I'd really appreciate it. Please let me know what you thought of this story by leaving a review online (Amazon, Barnes and Noble, Goodreads—wherever you got the book and wherever you share your opinions with other readers). It doesn't take long, but it really helps me craft stories you enjoy, as well as reach other readers. I value your comments and am grateful for whatever your share.

The other way we can connect is through social media. You can find my contact information with my bio. I'm really looking forward to hearing from you.

After you leave a review, please check out my other published titles and my soon-to-be-released works. You can read more about them on my website or my Amazon author page.

Until next time…

Staci Troilo

STACI TROILO grew up knowing family is paramount. She spent time with extended family daily, not just on holidays or weekends. Because of those close knit familial bonds, every day was full of love and laughter, food and fun. Life has taken her a thousand miles away from that extended family, but those ties remain. And so do the traditions, which she now shares with her husband, son, and daughter... even her two dogs. And through her fiction, she shares the importance of relationships with you. Mystery or suspense, romance or mainstream—in her stories, family is paramount.

Facebook: Author Staci Troilo
Twitter: @stacitroilo
Amazon: http://amazon.com/author/stacitroilo

www.stacitroilo.com